Printed in the United States of America

First Printing, 2013

ISBN 978-0-578-12453-7

Lulu Enterprises Inc.

3101 Hillsborough St.

Raleigh, NC 27607-5463

http://www.lulu.com

http://www.galacticdatabank.wikia.com

Ever since I've met her it's been so unreal
I thought love was something that I'd never feel
Our love is so grand, but all is not right
A terrible feeling lingers in the night
This feeling, it haunts every one of my dreams
A feeling that's not as nice as it seems
Since I've met her I've feared the day
That someone would come... and take her away
If I lost my muse, I'd be so alone
My heart would break, or return to stone
Last night I dreamed I saw how she died
The feeling I had... well... I died inside
We weren't as simple as love at first sight
But now, in my life, she's a guiding light
I'd be foolish and stupid to just let that go
It's my duty to love her, this I now know
So the woman I'll one day make my wife
I now swear to protect with my life
Through all our days, for her I will fight
Always by her side; always her knight.

That is not dead which can eternal lie,
And with strange aeons even death may die.

-H.P. Lovecraft

So long as life remains, so too does hope
So long as hope remains, an ending has yet to be written.

-Unknown

Twice-Shadowed Saint

Part I: The Soldier

Prologue

The Mindbank's throne room was dark. The only light in the room came from two and a half moons in the sky. Byzacis and Anicum, the two furthest moons, cast pale golden light down on the forested planet while the dome of Rhoditrand was visible rising above the Kevordala mountains. The Mindbank's tower, situated at the heart of the sprawling Amara District, was deserted. It was the middle of the night. Beyond its walls, not a Scain could be found in the shining streets of the capital city, and the only motion came from above, there four-winged birds flew through the darkened skies, or from below; gurgling rivers and rippling ponds filled with fish.

But within the tower, Mindbank Sovakadris sat on his throne, a single guard to his left and right, as the Scion awaited the one he had sent for. He was withered and frail, like the Scain he commanded, but his eyes burned with an inner light that made him almost seem mad. He was resting his heavy head on the fingers of his left arm—a mechanical skeleton of unknown origin. He'd acquired it after disappearing several dozen years ago, and had simply returned with it and offered no explanation... nor had he allowed its removal.

The doors at the far end of the room opened and a solitary Scain strode in. His black polyform flightsuit was covered in the markings of the Black Fleet, the Mindbank's personal special-ops team. He moved up to the steps that led to the throne and went down on one knee. "Mindbank," he said, the reverence obvious in his voice. "You summoned me?"

Mindbank Sovakadris leaned forward slightly. _"Yes, Turukaishal,"_ he said, the words not coming from his lipless mouth, which never moved, but instead echoing in Turukaishal's mind. Not words, per se, but a reflection of thoughts he was capable of comprehending. _"I appreciate your coming all the way here at such a late hour, but I have a mission for you. Please, follow me."_

Sovakadris stepped off his throne, his feet never touching the ground as he hovered on a cushion of Psionics. A show of power. Scions were a genetic mutation infinitely more powerful than Scain... and also fertile, whereas the Scain had inherited the near-sterility of the Erythians they had descended from. With Psionics to burn, Sovakadris drifted down the hallway like some kind of archangel, the blue glow surrounding him as Turukaishal rose and followed. The two guards took up position by the door, their gilded robes and adamantine weapons glinting in the dim light.

"You have performed admirably in the past," Sovakadris said as he drifted with Turukaishal at his side. His golden robes, inlaid with precious stones and gold plates which formed the Mindbank's crest – a shining star surrounded by outstretched wings –

reflected his Psionic light and kept Turukaishal from looking directly at him. *"Your military history is one many hope to emulate. It would not be erroneous to say that your race has every reason to be proud of you."*

"Thank you, Mindbank," Turukaishal said with a formal bow of his head, his eyes turning slightly pink in embarrassment at the praise. "But it is only due to your kind schooling and tutelage that I am where I am today."

"As true as it is that I trained you," Sovakadris said, *"and groomed to you to be one of the contenders to take my place as Mindbank when I pass, your successes are your own. I gave you the tools, Turukaishal, but it is you who have used them to build your accomplishments. You have every right to be proud of your achievements. However, I did not call you here to sing your praises. I could have done that during the daylight hours."* He said the last part with a small curve of his lips, glancing to his right at Turukaishal. He was fond of him, having taken him under his wing and training him personally to become a High Guard. However, Turukaishal's unwavering loyalty and military perfect led him to become Wing Commander of the Black Fleet instead of a stationary guard – a position much better suited to his talents, which the Mindbank was hesitant to squander.

The arches overhead reflected only silence as they spiraled away into the darkness. Small blue lights, the same color as Sovakadris' Psionics, dangled from chains on either side of the hall; staggered to bathe the pathway in cool blue light which was only intensified as the Scion drifted past. Turukaishal followed closely, keeping his eyes black as he suppressed any emotion. He did not know why he was here, and his eyes could very easily betray nervousness or hesitance. Not emotions that would inspire confidence in the Mindbank.

"You are familiar with the Vahran, are you not?" Sovakadris asked suddenly, waving his mechanical arm casually as if he was swatting a particularly nugatory insect.

"Naturally," Turukaishal said calmly. "They are a scourge upon the Galaxy, and have been the bane of it for at least five billion years."

"Quite," Sovakadris said, his eyes turning blue for a moment. Turukaishal was about to ponder on the significance of his leader being sad about Vahran before he spoke again. *"And do you know why this scourge still exists? Why we have not wiped it from the Galaxy as we should have done?"*

"Because the umbrella laws of the Senate, particularly those governing contact with underdeveloped species and those pertaining to the destruction of sentient life, have helped shield them from us," Turukaishal answered.

Sovakadris' lips quirked in a sardonic smile. *"Ah yes... we can thank the Alinteans for that, hm? However, from your words, I can tell that you—like me—believe something must be done about them. They are currently attempting to expand into the stellar void which surrounds their world... and if they get much farther, they may become a threat like they did before."*

"I understand this, but we can do nothing." Turukaishal said solemnly. What was Sovakadris playing at? The Galactic Code—the two hundred and twenty-two laws laid down by the Senate over four billion years ago—forbade them to act against the Vahran. Was the Mindbank merely venting? Turukaishal felt his eyes flicker to gray; a color denoting confusion or indecision.

"I believe I have found a way we can cure the Galaxy of this pestilence once and for all," the Mindbank said as he reached a pair of enormous double doors. He waved his metal arm, the fingertips glowing blue, and the doors slid downward into the floor without a sound to reveal the rear meeting chamber.

"A loophole?" Turukaishal asked, stepping inside. A ring-shaped table dominated the center of the room and a map of the Galaxy rotated impressively above it. Several parts had been blown up and set off to the side, labeled with the quick, spindly glyphs of the Scain.

"Exactly," the Mindbank said, his eyes turning yellow. Happiness. He was pleased, which was good. *"The Alinteans once said that if a race is proven to be TOO destructive, in the interest of the Galaxy's well-being, that species is to be eradicated as if they had committed one of the Five Unforgivable Crimes. In other words, they are to be wiped out entirely. This is why there are 'Kill on Sight' orders out for the Anu'bai."*

"Sir?" Turukaishal asked, confused.

"If we can prove that these Vahran are so destructive that they will never change, we may be able to convince the Senate to allow us to attack. And if they do not..."

"If they do not, sir?" Turukaishal asked, studying the Galaxy and keeping his eyes carefully black.

"The Heil and the Visoth are both willing to aid us in an all-out assault. The Visoth have been brought around to our way of thinking by our best diplomats and ambassadors, and the Heil are always willing to enter a battle. You know how they are. Going against the race that all but destroyed the Alinteans is too good of a war to pass up. Before the Senate could react, the Vahran would be gone. Even if they tried us in front of the Senate High Courts, we would be acquitted. Our assault unit will be made up of blacklisted members from all three races."

"An unauthorized assault?!" Turukaishal asked, his eyes flashing to orange to betray his shock. "That is treason against the Senate!!" It wasn't his place, but he couldn't believe the Mindbank was considering this. It was a huge risk, and certain species would be outraged. The Scain could be plunged into a Galaxy-wide war!

"I prefer a 'preemptive' assault," the Mindbank said with a small smirk. *"But that is where I need your help. I need you to go to their planet… Tergaia, now called Earth… and infiltrate them. Study their defenses. Their weapons. But most of all, I want you to study the Vahran themselves. Prove their guilt, Turukaishal, so that we may destroy them once and for all and bring peace to the Galaxy!"*

Turukaishal's eyes were back to black as he considered the Mindbank's orders. Refusal would result, likely, in being expelled from the military and from being able to ascend to the Mindbank's throne when Sovakadris died. The only other contender was that gasbag politician Demnechi, and Turukaishal was the favorite at the moment. He nodded, his choice made.

"I accept."

Sovakadris' eyes lit up with gold and yellow – admiration and happiness. He floated over to Turukaishal, placing the cold metallic arm on his shoulder. *"Turukaishal, you have the blessings of your race and the strength of the Mindbank's orders behind you. Go now and prove your worth and help us rid this universe of the cancer that plagues it."*

Turukaishal bowed low; a subtle motion to get that unnatural hand off his shoulder. "Thank you, Mindbank," he said. "I will leave at dawn." He turned and quickly left the meeting chamber, heading to his dwelling to pack. It would be a long trip and he wanted to be well prepared.

Chapter 01

BEGIN MESSAGE

LOCATION: Orbit of Teraneus

TIME: 17/40 Rotation, Local Time

MESSAGE: Turukaishal. I certainly hope that this message reaches you in good health. We all wish you luck on your upcoming assignment, and await your reports with baited breath. All of us are gravely concerned should the Vahran reach the stars. They have already built an orbital station, as I am certain you know. No good can come of this. Please continue your research for an additional 180 local rotations. After this time, please notify us if you require further time to study their defenses.

Some of us here are worried that Sovakadris is sending you on a farcical mission, though. The Vahran may be reaching for the stars, but how long until they realistically reach them? I admit that it will be to our interest to study them, but Sovakadris is bracing to attack as soon as your final report reaches him. Is such haste really necessary? Please, forget that I voiced this doubt. This comes not from any high-ranking officer, but from your friend, and I suppose it is born out of a concern for your health. Forgive me.

The war is not going well. I am sending this message from the Vermillion Comet, as most of our other technical ships have been destroyed. We have all but lost Teraneus, and we know that Edomai and Gelmore have both fallen to the Anu'bai. Containment is pointless once they get a foothold – we have no choice but to Cleanse the planets. You know what that entails, and how many lives are lost in the process.

Once your mission is at an end, please return to Chindrus – we could use a soldier like you. I hope we meet after this is over – it would be my pleasure to treat you to a huff of methane upon our reunion, if we both survive our respective assignments. Sovakadris has almost managed to completely ally our race with the Heil and Visoth and it will not be long before we move as one against the Vahran.

-Bandrumano

The room was dark; the only lighting coming from a blue-white screen projected into the air from a six-inch flat device which sat innocuously on a weathered old desk. An antique blue armchair was pushed up against it, the wings obscuring the individual in it when the darkness could not. Apart from the armchair and desk, the room was sparsely populated with a few tall bookcases, showcasing a variety of texts ranging from medical journals to astronomy magazines, the gaps filled with bric-a-brac such as bowls of polished stones, a music box and a replica of a human skull. A wide oriental rug covered the hardwood floor. The air was filled with the smell of paper, dust and a lingering scent of matches and cardboard.

All in all, despite the silvery-white rectangular object on the desk, the room could have belonged to any mid- to upper-class individual with a dislike for brightness. The ebony curtains had been drawn tightly across the sole window, but even they could not block out every ounce of light, and the motion of swaying branches was still visible between them.

The figure in the chair let out a thin, reedy sigh, standing up and reaching out. A four-fingered hand was briefly visible in the light, the ring finger missing and the little finger replaced by another thumb, all of the digits came to thin, hairlike points. Just prior to the luminous device being extinguished, any onlooker could have seen the silhouette of an impossibly tall figure—easily nine feet tall had it bothered to stand upright.

In the complete blackness, the only visible light (apart from the window's paltry offering) came from a pair of ovals that seemed to glow with an eerie gray hue, visible only because they were a hair lighter than the surrounding shadow. Footsteps echoed in the room as the figure began to walk, the two ovals moving with him as he walked over to the window, standing in the sliver of light for a moment and revealing himself.

He was blade-thin, his body looking like the furthest limbs of an aging willow tree. Long arms hung almost all the way down to strangely bent legs, each one ending in a three-toed hoof. A long, serpentine neck—easily ten inches long—somehow supported an egg-shaped head. The two grayish ovals were cast into sharp relief, standing out as enormous blackish-gray eyes embedded in the flat, ovoid head. Below them, barely visible in the mottled gray skin, two diagonal slits formed what could pass for a nose. A horizontal, lipless mouth was compressed into a thin line as the creature stared out from between the curtains, surveying the woods outside.

Turukaishal sighed, closing his eyes as he thought of home. Chindrus. Far away now, and it would be for the next six months as he lived among these vile, disloyal creatures. Creatures which his shorter, cousin race—the Erythians—used as genetic stock to avoid extinction. Creatures which believed his kind, and all like him, to be a myth or joke. He reached up, massaging his eyes as he felt them change from gray to vermillion, betraying his anger. Every nerve in his body screamed to attack; to slaughter these *things* where they stood, but he had to maintain control. He was a Scain. Scain didn't botch missions.

He reached up to his scrawny chest, clad in a black, form-fitting suit which covered everything but his head, hands and feet, and touched where his heart should be. Blue fire erupted from his chest, swirling around his fingers in a frenetic, energized dance. He continued drawing this energy—his Psionics, as they were called—out and guiding them around his fist. Slowly, the twisting coils of light began to seep up his arm, covering it. It was time. Time to go out into this world he despised so much and begin his mission. Time to learn how to think, act, look and speak like the creatures he would spend the next six months affiliating with. These Vahran.

The light covered his body entirely now, and he descended to one knee, touching his palm to the ground. The blue light expanded around him, forming a dome which shielded him completely from sight before hardening, forming fibers which crisscrossed like spiderwebs until he had been totally obfuscated by the translucent shell.

Nothing moved in the room for several moments as he gestated within this dome. It was as if even Mother Nature held her breath, for even the trees outside had ceased to sway. Turukaishal remained within the cocoon for a moment longer before a single crack appeared. A moment later, it was joined by another. Cracks began to form across the surface, breaking the dome slowly apart until it collapsed like a shattered window; shards cascading across the ground in a glittering storm.

In the center lay a Vahran, his arms wrapped around his nude body. The only thing to mark him as an impostor was his gaze: the lemon-shaped eyes which lacked a pupil, iris or sclera. Instead, the bulbous eyes of the Scain he had once been were embedded in his face; a mockery of the species he was emulating. Slowly, adjusting to his new body, he pushed himself to his knees and then to his feet, flexing his hands.

He was seven feet tall—the shortest he could possibly make himself—with black hair and white skin through which, with careful observation, veins and arteries were faintly visible. Turukaishal examined his hands for a moment. Five fingers. He allowed his lips to pull back, exposing a row of perfectly straight teeth—too straight—as he scowled at the appendages at the end of his forearms. So inefficient. What kind of cruel joke was Nature trying to perpetrate on the universe by creating such creatures?

This was not his first day on this planet and, as a result, he knew immediately that he couldn't just go walking around in the nude. A careful examination of the digital medium used on this planet had yielded a goldmine of information pertaining to clothing, and he had been able to synthesize a good portion of what he needed in his ship, the *Callsign 282*, which lay beneath this building. He pulled on a pair of denim pants, their color matching the black flightsuit he'd been wearing before, and a gray top which hugged his arms and neck. He ran his fingers absently through the black hair atop his head. He wasn't used to having it.

Turukaishal picked up a pair of mirrored sunglasses—his first and last line of defense against anyone who wished to see his eyes—and slipped them onto his face. He missed his ship already. It was a Nalsofto-class light frigate; spacious enough for him to live comfortably in but not so much that it required a large crew. Instead, it could be comfortably crewed by one, or improved by the addition of up to six crewmates. He sighed, looking around. He didn't like this kind of building. He'd averaged the data from 1,200 local dwellings and created this one where no one would stumble upon it—in a deserted section of forest sandwiched between a residential area and a golf course. (If there was ever a sport more pointless than golf, Turukaishal had yet to find it.)

Worse yet, these buildings defied all efficiency. Rectangular buildings? Round buildings were much more efficient for dwellings. And these were anchored to the ground instead of hovering like his home back in the Amara District of Chindrus. How in the name of the Hiin was he supposed to remain safe and secure in a building which shared the same ground as predators (and, of course, those blasted Vahran).

He picked up a small syringe, the bulb barely larger than the tip of his index finger but with the needle being six inches long. His protite dose was set to run out in a few hours, and he didn't want to be caught without it. It would spell death for him. Scain didn't breathe the same atmosphere as Vahran. These beasts were accustomed to primarily nitrogen and oxygen, whereas he normally breathed the argon, xenon and hydrogen of Chindrus.

Within the syringe was a blue mixture of tiny, medical robots. Protites. Once injected into his lung, they would break down all of the elements he breathed and convert them into a semblance of his own atmosphere. Any gas he inhaled would immediately be reduced to its component protons, neutrons and electrons before being recombined by the tiny robots. Turukaishal uncapped the syringe and pressed it into his chest, feeling the cold needle penetrate his single lung. He slowly squeezed the bulb at the far end, channeling the protites into his chest.

He opened his desk, making sure the other syringe was in place. This one would inject an emitter into his lung which would shut down all of the protites. Once deactivated, they would decay into their base elements within a few days, at which point they would be breathed out. Completely efficient and harmless to his body, protites were the best choice for anyone who had to engage in extravehicular or planetside activity.

Turukaishal sighed, closing the desk. Now he had to play the part he was selected for: a Vahran. He trekked through his house to the front door, opening it slowly and breathing in the earthy smells of the forest; so similar and yet alien to the woods surrounding the Amara District in every direction. Above him, the planet's sun burned brightly down on him. He winced slightly. A G2V yellow star, if he remembered the briefing. Chindrus was the second planet in orbit around an orange K6VI star, Mordakrelai, which was currently a kiloparsec and a half from this world.

How could these blasted Vahran live under this harsh, unforgiving glare? This blazing light? His skin bristled with uncertainty. Although his reptilian skin was no longer in danger of being burned, he wasn't a huge fan of walking out into such harsh light. He squared his shoulders, though, and walked toward the door that would lead him outside. He had a job to do, and he was a Scain. Nothing was going to stop him without killing him first.

Turukaishal used his hand to pull the door closed behind him. Vahran were frightened of things like his Psionics. He would need to adjust to doing things manually. He grimaced. Stupid, backward, unevolved creatures… He would suffer on their planet for his kind, but that didn't mean he had to like it. He looked around and inhaled, glad that his protites were working properly. So far so good. He tapped the side of his head, trying to remember everything he'd learned about this new environment.

After all, he couldn't keep calling it *"G77220-P3"* forever.

To the Vahran, this world was called *"Earth"*.

Chapter 02

BEGIN MESSAGE

LOCATION: Chindrus, Mindbank's Tower

TIME: 10/22 Rotation, Local Time

MESSAGE: It is good to hear you have made it to Earth. Please progress with the plan as outlined prior to your departure. In addition, if you can secure a sample Vahran, or at least their genetic information, it would aid us tremendously. The Erythians are convinced that Vahran DNA is able to help cure the genetic sterility, so perhaps we can study it in a similar fashion. Also, capturing a live specimen will aid us in learning how best to destroy these...beasts.

-Sovakadris

Turukaishal had become rather used to his daily routine. The data matrices they had on this planet were laughable—not even crystal wireframe—and he was able to remotely hack them from his lodgings. Every day, he would awake to see if anyone from Chindrus had contacted him. It worried him that his old post at Diathua Base had gone dark – had the Anu'bai infection spread that far already? Or was there some kind of interference from Earth itself?

Following his daily check, he would find nourishment. This was easy, if not truly nourishing. The Vahran had erected several nutrient dispensing plants. Unfortunately, the "nutrients" were so badly clogged with preservatives and chemical agents that they were barely of any use other than to abate the hunger pangs he felt. Even though the nutrient paste he was accustomed to generally tasted like a citrus bile, he began to miss it when confronted with the tasteless filth that the Vahran gorged themselves on.

He had finally adjusted to Earth's unusual time, learning that there were twenty-four "hours" in a day. Each hour was broken up into sixty "minutes" and these were further broken up into sixty "seconds". It usually only took him twenty of these minutes to reach a nutrient dispensing plant, and another twenty to walk back. He always ate at home.

Of course, he hadn't expected Vahran to be as evolved as Scain. They still forced one another to pay for food, which made him sick. Thankfully, their monetary system was digital and therefore could be hacked. After using his ship's laboratory to synthesize a piece of plastic common to these Vahran, he found that he could use it to purchase his food. Vahran currency depositories were also pitifully weak to his hacking attempts and it was easy for him to set up a program which deposited one-hundred thousand "dollars" into his supposed "account" every Earth "month".

Turukaishal shook his head. It was so much to take in. Even though he'd been briefed about these creatures, adjusting to using their terms was confusing. "Day" instead of "rotation" and "year" instead of "cycle". It was a lot to adjust to.

After he purchased his nutrition, he would return to his lodgings and nibble vacantly on it while he surfed the data matrix (apparently referred to as an "internet" – more of their strange terms) while hunting for traces of defense systems. This became his routine for a month, and Turukaishal learned a lot about Vahran weapons. Those records were the easiest to find, most of them were free knowledge anyway and those what weren't were easily hacked. Chemical or combustion-based firearms were still widely used on Earth. The only DEWs that existed widely were defoliant projectors, although other types were being researched. They had grenades, which didn't surprise him, but they were ancient. The Scain hadn't used basic fragmentation-style devices in centuries, having given them up in favor of EMP and laser-based varieties.

Orbital technology was laughable. Apart from Global Positioning System satellites, research probes, orbital telescopes and communications satellites, there was nothing of interest. Well, there was that one hideous looking space station that seemed to be their crown jewel, but it lacked defenses entirely, unless being ugly was meant to be its sole defense against attack. The only surface-to-space missiles Vahran had were ASATS, and they were only developed by three of the major political powers on the planet. More amusing still was that they were primarily used for destroying old or outdated satellites, although there *were* a few records of them being used to damage or destroy enemy units. Turukaishal scoffed when he reviewed the plans for them: plain ballistic missiles. A Scain dropship could withstand those indefinitely. These creatures were all but defenseless.

Turukaishal leaned back in the chair, studying the screen before him as he sipped on a plastic cup full of water. He could taste the fluorine. He'd managed to acquire a timetable of the Space Program that was set out for the United States of America. He wanted to laugh. The bureaucratic process had created a web of red tape an Ene'tami would be proud of. At best, the Vahran would be able to colonize their own moon in... he checked the date on the computer... 2050. He laughed openly. If Sovakadris wanted to burn this ball of dirt off the map, who was he to stop him? It would be laughably easy.

Turukaishal dutifully began to fill out his report regardless of the technology (or lack thereof) he had found. Ballistic ASAT missiles were still missiles, and a handgun could still kill a Scain if it got past his Psionic barriers. For a moment, he wondered if any other races that used the Vahran or communicated with them would object to their destruction. Surely the Erythians would bemoan the loss of their organic test tubes, but apart from them no one really had an interest in these beasts. The Alinteans would certainly be glad of their extinction, as the Vahran had slighted them before and couldn't even remember it.

He set down his Data Pad, leaning back and staring at the ceiling. Something was gnawing at him, and he wanted to resolve it. He closed his eyes, fielding his Psionics and lifting several of the crystal meditation spheres he kept nearby. They began to slowly orbit him like a miniature solar system, revolving around him on different orbits, some of them orbiting one another. He cleared his mind, isolating the issue as he made the spheres dance among themselves in a parody of cosmic order.

Sovakadris had lied to him.

He frowned, the spheres hesitating in their orbits before resuming. His thoughts of heresy, despite how much they made him feel as if he was betraying the Mindbank, spoke the truth. According to Sovakadris, Earth was a desolate cesspool of a planet inhabited by apelike lifeforms. These creatures—the Vahran—warred with one another over everything from mates to territory. The history of Vahran was the history of war; a nocturne of bloodshed over differences in rulership, ownership and afterlife. A dirge which had been sung in eons past and would be sung until the stars ceased to glow. Sovakadris had told him that Earth was a burned out wasteland; a husk of what it once was. It had been depleted by the greed and violence of the Vahran. Destroyed.

But from what he had seen, Earth was green and fertile. It rained more than he liked – a clear liquid composed of two atoms of hydrogen and one of oxygen – but the blazing sun and liquid had combined to create a beauteous atmosphere. Vahran, or at least those he saw, mostly kept to themselves or carried on conversations in small groups. From what he understood of their language (which was a considerable amount, although their slang escaped him) they discussed everything from politics to entertainment to a recent performance by a music group.

The topics of discussion varied based on age group and gender as well. Young males seemed to veer into physical topics, such as athletics, whereas middle-aged females were more focused on emotions. This fluctuation caused him no end of strife as he tried to catalog it and convey it clearly to the Mindbank. He sighed, allowing the meditation spheres to change their orbits, now having them mimic a system all to themselves; all ten spheres orbiting the central eleventh, spinning like multicolored planets as the 'system' moved around his head.

Vahran were not what Sovakadris had made them out to be. He had watched enough of their inane television programs to realize that. The media reported nothing but violence and hatred, as well as cultural aggression over everything from place of birth to color of skin, or even religious beliefs. He found himself glad that the Scain only ever believed in one faith, and that they never hunted down those who chose not to believe. The discrimination shown on their programs fit Sovakadris' image to the letter, but there were other things as well.

Vahran in the streets didn't always conform to the logic, for one. He saw dark skinned Vahran communicating peaceably with their pale skinned counterparts, and saw couples comprised of multiple ethnic backgrounds. Furthermore, their television also had a myriad of programs which portrayed Vahran as either stupid, weak, ineffectual or a combination of the three. He had sat through an entire hour of some program that showcased the most amusing home footage from around the country. Most of it pertained to genital blows (which he was thankfully immune to), scare tactics or amusing slip-and-fall situations. Could a race as erroneous as this actually be a threat? He leaned forward, the spheres calmly returning to their holders around the room, as he made a small footnote in his report.

Vahran threat level appears very low. Weaponry is insufficient to cause damage to our armored infantry, vehicles, or even structures. Technology level is barely cresting the wireless point, and they are still a disjointed race divided by cultural notions. It is my firm belief that attacking them would be of no benefit to the Scain other than to secure a Type-I planet for terraforming and habitation.

He sent the message and relaxed, massaging his temples. He was going to go out there and "mingle" for a little while. He still had five of their 'months' before he could pack up and leave anyway, and it wasn't like they could harm him. As long as he didn't blow his cover, there was very little danger involved. And if anyone actually tried anything, his Psionics could overpower the individual easily as a last resort.

He slid the Data Pad into a desk drawer and locked it. He was getting better at using his hands – something he wasn't wholly proud of. Soon, he was going to need to revert back to his Scain form. He ached to feel that sensation of being "Turukaishal the Scain" instead of "Turu Kaishal the Vahran". Perhaps he could last the entire five months, but he certainly wanted to be him again. It just wasn't the same in a Vahran body.

He chuckled, smirking lightly. Or the equivalent to it. Scain didn't move their faces that much, although they could. Their primary mode of nonverbal communication was their eyes. Their moods were easily discernible based on the color of the bulbous ocular devices. It made things far simpler than trying to read the myriad of varying Vahran facial expressions... and Vahran could lie so *easily*! That shocked Turukaishal to no end when he'd realized it. If a Scain lied, it took an incredible amount of power to keep their eyes from giving them away. Masking their eyes was so great a chore that the Scain race, as a whole, could be taken at their word without question. If a Scain said the sky was falling, then just about everyone in the room would get to cover. Not Vahran. Apparently, lying was easy for them. He'd had to use his Psionics to uncover more than a few untruths.

There was a unique structure a short distance away, and Turukaishal was intrigued by it. He had no idea what it was, to be honest, but it looked as if it served nutrition. But his nutrition was served s liquid. Correction: mostly liquid. They served a variety of pastries as well. He couldn't stand pastries. He had tried one or two at another location and they had made him violently ill. The Scain system wasn't equipped to handle yeast in high concentrations. He'd made a special note asking for he be given additional compensation for his suffering.

Naturally, that had been denied. It fell under the 'occupational hazards' heading.

Turukaishal was still intrigued by the liquid they served there. It was black and hot, and he could smell the caffeine from a distance – a compound that would effectively block his Psionics. He had taken caffeine tablets at first to help him get used to the concept of not using his abilities, but now he was bound only by his self control. Still, he was more than a little curious. Vahran flocked to the establishment in small knots, seating themselves and downing the pastries and thick black liquid while talking with each other. Apparently it was some kind of cultural meeting place.

Turukaishal decided that it would be a good idea to visit such a place – even if it was as an informational excursion. He didn't have to eat the blasted pastries. He'd probably just order a cup of cold water and sit in a corner pretending to read the Vahran newspapers. He stood up and stretched. Tomorrow, he would handle that particular hurdle. Not today. He had been sitting at this cursed desk for twelve hours, and he wanted to go down to his ship and sleep.

Scratch that, he couldn't. He had to adjust to living like a Vahran. Instead of heading to the airlock, he marched up a flight of stairs and lay down gingerly on the pale white mattress. How Vahran slept on those things was beyond him. The springs poked his back and the lumps kept him awake. Still, he felt that tonight he'd be able to get a good night's sleep. He was exceptionally tired. And the prospect of tomorrow's excursion left him needing his rest to operate at full capacity.

He did *not* want to be out among Vahran if he wasn't ready for anything.

Chapter 03

BEGIN MESSAGE

LOCATION: Chindrus, Mindbank's Tower

TIME: 12/22 Local Time

MESSAGE: *Your reports have been excellent. Please attempt to learn more about Vahran mentality while you are there, if possible. Vahran had such great potential – but somewhere they went wrong. I want to know where. If we can learn from them, we can prevent such errors in our own kind. I know that destroying them, as per your last message, would do very little for us, but if left to fester this wound will become cancerous.*

You still have a considerable length of time left on their world, Turukaishal. Please attempt to make the most of it and learn all that you can. Perhaps they even have one or two pieces of information that can advance us, although that is unlikely.

-Sovakadris

END MESSAGE

Turukaishal strode along the streets, his gait filled with purpose and grace. He was a Scain, despite how his form made him appear, and he would never stoop to the awkward shamble of these primitive beasts. He snorted inwardly. "Learn about Vahran mentality"? What mentality? Most of them were too preoccupied with a mixture of their daily grinds and whatever athletic activities appeared on that appalling television of theirs to have any mentality left. The younger Vahran only cared about sex, drugs, smoking or altering their appearances to fit the general norm. There *was* no mentality!

Something collided with him from the front, striking him hard enough to knock him back a pace. He hissed, feeling heat spread across his new white shirt. He bit his lip in pain, looking down at the large, dark stain that was spreading across his breastbones. Coffee. He could smell the caffeine and the temperature scalded his skin. He took deep breaths and looked up at his assailant. A tall, extremely obese Vahran stood there, talking on a cellular device. Rather than take any notice of the plight Turukaishal was in, he merely pushed him aside and continued down the sidewalk, tossing his now-empty cup on the side of the road.

Turukaishal closed his fists, taking a deep breath to keep from Psionically hurling the man down the road, when something equally hot splashed against the side of his face. He jumped, turning to see an equally large woman standing there, wearing clothing that looked more like it had begun life as a shower curtain before having the rings removed. A woman who was not so much 'dressed' as she was 'upholstered'. "That's for pushing my husband around, you stupid prick!" she seethed, pushing past him and waddling after her husband. This time, it took all of Turukaishal's strength not to attack, and he could feel his eyes glowing red with anger. Pushing her husband? The fat beast had run into *him*!

He let his anger out with a sigh, looking down and examining his shirt. It was ruined. Brown-black stains had soaked all the way to the lining of his new black jeans and it looked as if he'd need to wash his clothes several times to get the stench of caffeine out of them. He thanked the Hiin that it hadn't taken him more than a week (and a few ruined shirts) to learn how to use a Vahran washing machine. Of course, he was still hanging his clothes up in the garage because he couldn't figure out the dryer. His proudest achievement, though, was mastering the iron.

Turukaishal hung his head, clenching his fists in frustration before opening his eyes. He knew exactly what he was going to tell the esteemed Mindbank when he got back to his base of operations. That he should send an entire fleet in and Cleanse the planet, Anu'bai or not, and get rid of these stupid, insignificant—

He was suddenly aware of someone standing behind him. He turned, his head lowered slightly in case another barrage of hot coffee was heading his way, and found someone standing on the sidewalk offering him a damp paper towel. "It won't help much," the female said sheepishly, "but it's better than nothing."

He appraised her for a moment, studying her from behind his glasses. She was shorter than he was (then again, so was everyone) and looked like she was just shy of six feet tall. Her reddish-brown hair hung down to her lower back and was looped together in a loose braid. Her face was pale, almost looking like porcelain, and her nose was slender and tapered. A pair of emerald-green eyes looked up at him as if asking why he wasn't taking the towel yet. They stared at one another, Turukaishal wondering exactly what she was doing, before he slowly reached out and took the towel, wiping at his face.

"I owe you thanks," he muttered as he wiped his face and glasses clean, taking as much of the coffee out of his hair as he could. Thankfully, the shirt he'd been wearing was pure white. Some of that foul-smelling Vahran 'bleach' would clean it up. He hoped. He looked up, finding the girl still standing there, and blinked in surprise. "So I thank you." There. He'd said it. Now she could be on her merry way and—

"Are you alright, though?" she asked curiously, leaning forward a bit. He leaned away from her and her inquisitive gaze. "I've never seen you around before. If you're new, that was a pretty crappy welcome."

"I have been here for thirty-six days now," Turukaishal said mechanically. What was it with Vahran women, he wondered? Almost every time he dared show his face in public, they would talk. And talk. And then, just for a change of pace, they would talk some more. Or yell, if they realized he wasn't listening. The men glared at him from a distance, although he could never figure out why. It was almost as if they were aware that he was an anomaly, but were unable to pinpoint exactly *why*.

"Wow! You are a newcomer," she said, smiling. "Want me to treat you to a cup of coff—" she paused, looking down at his shirt. "Um… never mind."

Turukaishal resisted the urge to laugh. At least she'd had the good sense to stop before asking if he wanted *more* of the foul backwater that was currently adorning his chest. He winced. It felt as though the liquid had given him some minor burns, or at least sensitivity. If he ever saw those two Vahran again, he was going to kill them. Period. "No thank you," he said. "I have had enough coffee for one day."

"Alright. Hey, I forgot to ask, what's your name?" She looked up at him with those bright, almost childlike eyes, and Turukaishal found himself set on edge. He stared back, hoping his mirrored eyes would unsettle her. They didn't. She continued to stare, her vivid eyes seeming to penetrate his glasses as if they weren't even there. He cast his gaze away, making sure his head didn't move so she wouldn't be able to tell.

"Turu. Turu Kaishal."

She opened her mouth to respond, but a second voice yelled something at her. Turukaishal looked up as she turned around, spotting a male Vahran standing by the nutrient station that *had* been his original objective. He was wearing a white shirt—not unlike Turukaishal's—but hid it beneath a black vest. He also wore black dress slacks, the creases sharp enough to cut a man, and black boots. A blue greatcoat was draped around his shoulders, the bottom brushing his calves, and he carried a walking stick which rose as high as his waist. This struck Turukaishal as unusual – the only Vahran he'd seen carrying such an accessory had been the old or feeble, and this Vahran seemed to be neither. In fact, from what Turukaishal could see (considering the distance between them) he looked to be no older than thirty years old, with blond hair swept neatly up over the top of his head and a face radiating vitality, if not also suspicion. His free hand played with a wide-brimmed black hat, massaging the brim with narrow fingers.

"Richard, come here!" the female yelled, waving to him. "Meet Turu!"

As Turukaishal expected, the male walked with no sign of a limp. Was the stick ornamental? The male, Richard, reached them in a few seconds and looked up at Turukaishal with a guarded expression, his gray eyes the same color and hue of a thundercloud. Those eyes looked old—far older than his body or face suggested—and his clothing did the same thing. From what Turukaishal had gathered, his attire had gone out of casual style at least two hundred years ago. Was this Vahran that old? COULD Vahran live to be that old? He'd only seen records of them living, at maximum, to just over a hundred. Higher than that was rare indeed. Besides, if this male was that old, he would LOOK old. He wouldn't look twenty-something.

"Greetings," Turukaishal said, overriding his suspicions with an attempt to be genial. There was no danger at the moment. "My name is Turu Kaishal."

"Richard Sinclair," the male said. "Vicky, we should go. You have studying to do and I have work tomorrow. We cannot be out late."

Turukaishal looked up at the sky. The sun was almost directly overhead. Noon, or thereabouts. What did this Vahran mean by 'late'? His eyes changed to reflect his amusement, glinting yellow behind his glasses, as he realized the meaning behind Richard's words. He wasn't being trusted. This Vahran was clever with his words.

"I apologize for delaying you," Turukaishal said calmly. "Your young accomplice here was aiding me after an unfortunate incident with a large couple and their drinks."

"Yeah, I saw that," Richard said dismissively. "Jerks. Not like it's uncommon. If you're new, you picked a crappy place to move to."

"Richard!" the female Vahran, 'Vicky', chastised. "He's been here just over a month!"

Richard snorted, shrugging his shoulders. Turukaishal could tell by his motions that the man was built solidly. "Well, welcome to Oakbrook," he said. "Where are you staying?"

Turukaishal had no end of hesitations about revealing his location, but Vicky spoke first. "We live down by the water in Steilacoom," she said excitedly, her eyes bright and cheerful. "It's beautiful! You have to come down and see it sometime!"

"Victoria," Richard said sternly, his cane tapping against the ground.

Ah. Apparently 'Vicky' was the diminutive for 'Victoria'. Interesting. These Vahran were so lazy they shortened each others' names. Turukaishal's eyes remained yellow. "I reside in those woods," he said, gesturing vaguely with a wave of his hand. "I inherited some property from a relative a while back and needed an alteration of scenery."

"Really?" Victoria asked, her face scrunching up into an unreadable expression. Turukaishal was about to question her about it when she continued. "Well, if you wanted peace and quiet, you got it."

Richard chuckled mirthlessly. "Yeah, no kidding. No one goes back in there anymore."

"Really?" Turukaishal asked, raising an eyebrow in an unnatural but practiced motion. "Please, do share the reason for this."

"Well, there were some weird—" Victoria started, but Richard cut her off.

"Some folks kept seeing weird lights, but when they went into the woods they couldn't find anything. It started creeping out a bunch of the superstitious idiots to the point where they've got explanations ranging from devil worshippers to the Second Coming of Christ. Most won't go into the woods to play Frisbee golf anymore."

"Not to sound stupid," Turukaishal said, "but what is Frisbee golf?"

"It's a sport," Victoria said as she brushed a stray lock of russet hair behind her ear. "You throw this disc and try to get it into a basket in fewer throws than your opponent. It's really fun!"

"I see… and this is a recreational sport?" Turukaishal asked, his eyebrow climbing higher.

"Geez, where did you come from? Mars?" Richard asked, leaning on his walking stick. *Cane!* Turukaishal had to remember that it was called a cane.

"No," he said, "not Mars." He chuckled at how absurdly close Richard had come without realizing it. "As for where I came from, I prefer not to say." There was no sense in just making something up. Telling the truth would have produced an interesting reaction, but it would have led nowhere. Besides, providing any Vahran believed him, it would lead to disaster.

"Suit yourself. C'mon Vicky, we gotta go. Nice meeting you, Turu." Richard took his sister by the hand and led her away down the sidewalk. Victoria called out a cheerful goodbye, her good spirits evidently irrepressible, as they departed. Turukaishal watched them go before sighing, shaking his head and turning around. He'd turn back and cut through the forest to reach his base, at which point he'd go change his clothing.

Still, he couldn't deny that he was strangely intrigued by those two. They hadn't shown animosity, contempt or fear in his presence, and had been unusually polite. Most of the Vahran he had run across were nothing if not downright rude. They had also been able to understand him, whereas most of the locals had been unable to properly interpret his use of their words. He'd gone back to their books dozens of times to be certain, but no: he was saying the words properly. In the end, he had just decided that those he spoke to were stupid and illiterate and if anyone understood him, they weren't. Not completely, anyway.

Turu looked back over his shoulder. The Vahran were out of sight. He continued walking, cutting across the road and into the woods. Now he could go home and get some clothes that didn't positively reek of that blasted, Hiin-cursed coffee.

Thank the Mindbank for small favors…

Chapter 04

Turukaishal visibly flinched as he read the message in his inbox. Of all the people he'd forgotten to tell he would be away from the Amara District, why and how had he forgotten Kridoria. He was *only* supposed to marry the girl in two years time so that she could cinch her position as the political figurehead for the cross-district trade line… and, of course, the routine fathering of a child. It wasn't really something he wanted; as far as he was concerned, relationships were just too complicated. It was always the same story: the Eccemeria District (or "Gene Central" as it was often called) would name locate the Scain with the highest gene compatibility. The pair would be wed and would attempt to sire a child. If they could not do so naturally, the Eccemeria District would once more intervene and utilize gene samples, which were acquired prior to the marriage ceremony, to attempt to create a gene fusion child.

Two things were wrong with this system. Firstly, the Scain had descended from the Erythians over four hundred thousand years ago, long after the genetic sterility had afflicted their race. As a result, the child race – the Scain – was almost more sterile than their predecessors. Only one in ten thousand children made it to term. Even with the gene fusions, the odds were still one in four thousand. Secondly, the gene matchups usually seemed to pick the one Scain you were most incompatible with. Kridoria was a politician's daughter and, interestingly enough, a childhood acquaintance of his.

That didn't mean that he wanted to marry her!

In his case, he'd been relatively lucky compared to most Scain. His father, Ferthoroyia, had raised him for most of his youth. His mother had passed away in a training accident on the Alintean planet of Vormaga. Ordinarily, as Scain didn't exactly choose one another, families with both parents were warzones with both adults trying to tear one another apart and traumatizing the child in the process.

Turukaishal had, under his father's suggestion, tried out to become one of the Mindbank's Vanguard; his personal guard. However, Lady Vinyaiah, the Commandant of the Vanguard, had seen something else in him besides his unwavering loyalty. According to her, he had the valuable gift of thinking in unorthodox ways, which meant that his enemies would always have a difficult time defeating him. Rather than have him waste away standing at attention in the Mindbank's throne room, she had spoken to Sovakadris and had him placed in the Black Fleet while he underwent specialized training. That had been two hundred years ago.

Now he was Wing Commander Turukaishal of the Black Fleet, proud leader of a small detachment within the Fleet, and he had been selected as one of the two possible candidates to replace Sovakadris upon his death, the other being the Minister of Defense, Demnechi. A Scain he absolutely couldn't stand and was convinced that most of Chindrus felt the same way.

But if he married Kridoria, he would be setting all that aside with the *possible* exception of the Mindbank candidacy. And even if he did win the position, he'd never see his mate or their child, provided they had any. He shook his head. No, he was definitely meant to be a soldier and nothing else. He wasn't a father figure, to be sure, and he had no desire to get wrapped up in trade politics with Kridoria. If he did wed her, he'd probably lose the candidacy because of his attachment to her and the time lost during the bonding ceremony, attempted conceptions and gene therapy. Demnechi would outstrip him, and Turukaishal, as much as he didn't think of himself as perfect Mindbank material, would rather shoot himself than see that serpent upon the throne while he ended up playing nanny for Kridoria's child. He was perfectly content risking his neck as one of Sovakadris' elite soldiers, performing the riskier missions (or boring and stale, like this one) no one else wanted and building up a reputation as a result of it.

Turukaishal powered down the only piece of alien technology—his Data Pad—as he rose. He slid it into a hollowed out copy of *The New Webster's Dictionary 2009* and folded it shut, replacing it on the shelf. Even if a Vahran ever breached his sanctum, a dictionary was the last book they would be interested in. They'd probably be more interested in some of the other books he'd gone through the trouble of finding to decorate his lodgings; titles such as *The Iliad and the Odyssey* or *The Complete Works of Sir Arthur Conan Doyle*, both volumes being far more interesting than a dictionary. He left the bedroom, striding down the flight of stairs and out his front door.

The Vahran he'd spoken to—Richard—had set him slightly on alert. So some Vahran had seen flashing lights in the woods. Interesting. They'd probably seen his ship as it descended into the hidden bay in which it would remain concealed for the next five months. By the time anyone got there to investigate, they would have found only chain link fences and an ordinary, if not slightly mossy house. Nothing suspicious.

He checked himself in the full length mirror in the hallway. He hated mirrors. Scratch that – he hated mirrors when he looked like a Vahran. Every time he saw himself he wanted to retch. This form was so inefficient—so *barbaric!*—that it was a marvel Vahran had ever left the Stone Age. The five-fingers issue was no longer a real issue for him, as he'd gotten used to it by now, but he hated the loss of his second knee joints and his feet felt huge compared to the three-toed hooves he was used to. He shook his head, turning away from the polished surface.

He wouldn't lie; he'd been oddly touched by the gesture he'd been shown earlier that day: the female Vahran offering him a paper towel. *Victoria!* He had to remember names or he'd never get anywhere. 'That Female Vahran' wasn't a title anyone here would understand, nor was it a good habit to fall into. And if he started speaking Galaxian in human form, it would cause problems. He knew that some Alinteans were here on Earth already, using certain human vessels for their consciousnesses, and it wouldn't be wise to tip them off that other races were here.

Galactic Law dictated that interference with an underdeveloped race was forbidden except in certain scenarios and only by certain races. In this case, Erythians flew all the way from Besodaari to study them to cure the sterility that plagued them, the Zyzyts and the Scain. The Alinteans did it to keep tabs on a species responsible for beating them in a war before recorded history. The Taeski would occasionally slip in to ascertain their intellect and mental strength, although many races saw this as a waste of time. But the Scain? The Scain had no reason to be here. This was why his mission was a Black Fleet mission: he couldn't be caught. If he was, he'd be disowned by his race and left to the mercy of the Senate, which would most likely condemn him to death... not something he liked the sound of.

He felt a twinge of homesickness as he thought about other races. The Amara District of Chindrus was a melting pot of various races, many of whom were there to appreciate the Scain for their deep, rich culture which spanned everything from the metalwork to music, sculpture to architecture. When he was home, he had two different races living on either side of him. To his right was one of his closest friends, a taciturn Taeski by the name of Klakshan. On the other lived Nohtaep, an Alintean who was studying the Scain architecture on an academic trip.

Alinteans had always intrigued Turukaishal, mostly because they were somewhat similar to the Scain. They were the fourth tallest race, shorter than him by a foot (on average) and usually rising to eight feet at maximum (the maximum height for a Scain at rest being nine). They had jet black skin which was covered by light, barely-there fuzz.

Turukaishal had run across a unique fruit on Earth called a 'peach' which had a similar texture. Their heads had a curious shape, sweeping up in the back to a gently curving point, and their mouths and noses did not exist, replaced instead by a proboscis similar to that of a butterfly or moth.

Turukaishal supposed that his fascination began with their eyes which intrigued him the most. Like his, they were bulbous and prominent. However, unlike the Scain, no two Alinteans shared the same eyes. This one might have red, waxy-looking eyes while his brother could have metallic blue-and-gold. It was bizarre. Even the Alinteans couldn't predict the color of their eyes prior to birth. It wasn't like a yellow-eyed male and a blue-eyed female would have a green-eyed son.

Lastly, the Alinteans had a pair of flaps which hung down from their arms. After extensive study of Earth and its flora and fauna, Turukaishal had discovered that 'flying squirrels' (which didn't actually fly, you idiot Vahran) had a pair of flaps which fulfilled the same function: the ability to glide. Alinteans also had three toes – two in the rear and a third in the front – and five long fingers.

Taeski, like Klakshan, frightened him somewhat. They looked like scaly Vahran with clear, fibrous hair... which he knew from experience were actually nematocysts which could pack a nasty punch. Taeski also possessed far too many joints, all made from cartilage instead of bone, which made them extremely difficult to fight. Most Taeski had soft, shimmering scales because their original homeworld of Fezon had been a jungle world. However, that planet had long ago met its end. The Taeski now lived wherever they could, but preferred to colonize desert worlds where no one dared to tread; like their current homeworld of Altar. As a result, an Altar-native like Klakshan had scales which were weathered and worn, making them look scuffed and textured.

Apart from that, he had learned that their eyes were considerably better than even his, particularly at seeing in the dark. They had vertical pupils commonly associated to felines or serpents, and Turukaishal had noticed that their irises, which usually had any number of breaks in them, rotated around the center of the eye. Their scales were not comprised of skin cells, but their bodies produced a thin carbon-silicon layer which created interlocking plates. These not only made the Taeski more resilient than a species like the Vahran, but also helped them trap heat beneath their skin for the long, cold nights... cold-blooded reptiles did not fare well when the temperatures fell.

Quite possibly, though, the most fearsome parts of a Taeski were their eyes. Whereas their right eye saw the world normally, if they closed their left eye they could gain a short burst of "insight" (referred to as the Dryhulei) which allowed them to see four seconds into the future. They also possessed a third, normally closed eye on their foreheads referred to as the Cyulei, which allowed them to sync all four types of brainwaves with anyone who gazed into it. The ultimate cobra's gaze. They could make you see, feel, hear or even experience anything they wanted you to. And if they convinced you that you had died while under the influence of a Cyulei, you died in reality as well. Klakshan, after being prodded by Turukaishal for quite some time, eventually showed him the ability. Turukaishal had never been able to look at the thin vertical line on his forehead again without shivering.

Turukaishal shook the homesickness and daydreams out of his head. He hadn't been sent here to ruminate about Alinteans and Taeski. He'd been sent here to prepare the Vahran for their destruction. He had work to do and today, fat Vahran or not, he was going to examine that structure and see what it was like. Perhaps he'd run into Victoria and Richard again...

He promptly slapped himself several times in the face. He didn't really WANT to see them again, did he? No, he was probably still faintly touched with them for being polite and offering him a wet rag when he was covered in scalding caffeine. But today he had an agenda. He was going to go to that place, whatever it was, examine it and then leave. Nothing else. He stomped over to the front door, growling at himself under his breath. One act of Vahran kindness and he's enamored. Joy.

He threw open his front door and stomped out, slamming it behind him. In the woods, it didn't really matter much and it helped alleviate some of his anger. Or it did until he realized he'd forgotten his glasses. Swearing under his breath, cursing the entirety of the planet, he went back inside and snatched them off the table. Something was wrong with him. Something had to be wrong with him. Perhaps he'd caught some deplorable Vahran virus. Yes, that was it. He sighed, shaking his head. Just a virus. He'd get home after his little investigation and go to bed. Sleep for a few days. When he woke up he'd be as good as new and ready to face this world again. With that thought in mind, he pushed his way through the bushes blocking his front pathway from the main walk and began to leave the woods.

Chapter 05

BEGIN MESSAGE

LOCATION: Chindrus, Denuval District

TIME: 08/22 Local Time

MESSAGE: Uh, you might want to consider asking the Mindbank to shorten your little mission. I just returned to Chindrus, and your betrothed is raising the largest ruckus I have ever seen. She is demanding that he bring you home so that the two of you can begin courting. She doesn't want your union to end up like so many Scain betrothals, I guess. Things have gotten a little hectic in and around Amara, so I am staying with a friend in the Denuval District for the time being.

Also, remember Melokridai, that nice lady who owned the restaurant near the Academy where we used to visit after classes? Apparently she was almost killed in an explosion. She is still in the hospital, and no one is allowed to visit. I think it happened a rotation or two before I returned, but I don't know all the details. They're not saying anything at the hospital and I was evicted rather harshly. Anyway, I will keep you posted. I hope she is okay – her daughter is distraught. This was even enough to tear her away from pining for that Alintean flintskin she loves so much. I can never remember his name – the guy who won all those awards in the Academy. The one with the light blue eyes; Dar-something.

Sorry to take up so much of your time, and I apologize for the formality of the last transmission. The higher-ups were lurking around, so I had to type a ton of official-looking words to make it look like I was still being professional. Hope you come back soon – it has been too long since we huffed methane together.

-Bandrumano

Turukaishal flicked off the communicator and stowed it in his briefcase, locking it. It stood out from the rest of the things in the container; all of them benign items like pencils, pens, pads and a calculator. The Data Pad slid easily into one of the compartments in the lid, vanishing from sight and mind. Apart from it, the briefcase looked like that of a legitimate businessman: innocuous, non-threatening and professional. Sighing, he stepped out of his house and began to walk. The sole reason he was carrying the communicator with him today was that he had a vague sense of unease. He didn't quite know why, but it felt like a good idea.

As he reached the coffee shop, he began to doubt his judgment in coming here. He didn't really just want to mingle with Vahran with no purpose. He'd wander amongst them if he *absolutely had to*, but he didn't feel like electing to mix in with them. He looked down at his long, bony fingers. Was it just him, or did his hand look a little grayer than usual? Perhaps he really *couldn't* maintain his Vahran form for all six months. It looked like he'd have to disappear for a week or two and recuperate. He sighed. As much as he wanted to be a Scain again, he was finally adjusting to being a Vahran. The re-transitioning would be a pain in the rear. Before he could doubt himself further, he gave the door a push and stepped inside.

The interior of the establishment was dim; something Turukaishal was automatically thrilled by. The harsh G2V star this planet orbited was a vast change from the K6VI he was used to. And without the sheer volume of foliage and overhead cover found on his world, even the overcast skies were excruciatingly painful. Turukaishal found his hand inching up to remove his sunglasses and quickly snapped it back down to his side. Stupid! He couldn't let his guard down like that.

A single, tiled pathway led up to a dark wood counter, a glass cabinet displaying a variety of pastries. Turukaishal shivered. There was no Hiin-cursed way he was going to try another one of those revolting things no matter how nicely they dressed it up. A bookshelf covered the wall opposite the window which gazed out onto the street, and several round tables were scattered across the carpeted area. To his left, there was a pair of armchairs nestled around a small, cozy fireplace. To his right, a quintet of similar chairs formed a small nook near the door. Potted plants stood like sentinels in the corners and strange, contemporary artwork hung on the walls. Aside from the windows, light was produced by some amber-colored lamps hanging from the roof. Turukaishal looked around, blinking behind his glasses. As quaint and comfortable as this establishment was, it was almost totally empty. It was already noon, so where was everybody?

"Yo!" called a Vahran from behind the counter, startling Turukaishal from his reverie. He was slim and short, possessing a jovial face framed by shoulder-length blond hair. He wore a black apron with the coffee house's logo on the chest over a white dress shirt and black slacks. "What can I get started for ya?"

Turukaishal approached the counter, peering up at the chalkboard menu which hung above the back counter. What indeed? This facility had a selection that made his mind reel. What in the name of the Mindbank was an 'italian soda'? More perplexing still was the pronunciation of the word 'frappe' or the particulars of a 'Macchiato' versus an 'Americano'. He was lost. He stroked his chin for a moment. "What is 'tea'?" he asked, looking at the image. The picture showed an inviting mug of a translucent, steaming liquid. Obviously drawn by hand, the vapors of the mug were curling pleasantly above the cup, forming images of curved, red-and-white objects or little brown Vahran effigies.

"Uh…" the man behind the counter, his nametag identifying him as "Dave", looked slightly uncertain as he scratched at a small amount of stubble on his chin. "Well, it's a drink that combines hot water with ground plant leaves," he said at length. "It's really good; want me to fix you up a sample?"

"Is there caffeine?" Turukaishal asked hesitantly.

"Yeah, but less than coffee. Why, are you allergic?"

"Very mildly," Turukaishal said, pushing his glasses higher up his nose. That would have been a wonderful way to blow his cover. *"Not allergic, no, but it suppresses my Psionic abilities. You see, I'm really an alien from Chindrus. Watch…"* he chuckled quietly to himself as Dave turned around and gestured to a wide selection of small tan boxes.

"Alright then, what kind do you want?" Dave asked. "Pick one."

Turukaishal scanned the labels on the boxes, scrutinizing them carefully. By the Hiin there were a lot of them. Did these Vahran have nothing better to do than think of different ways to flavor this 'tea' of theirs? Chamomile, peppermint, cinnamon, chai (what the heck was 'chai' anyway?), lemon… was there no end to them? He honed in on a collection of red boxes. Why not; red was his favorite color. "Red Vanilla," he said at last, nodding towards his selection. "May I see the box?"

Dave handed it to him, taking a small bag from it and moving around behind the counter. Turukaishal made a thorough examination of the back, scanning it for hazards. He sighed in relief. It looked like this 'tea' was safe to drink. One-hundred milligrams of caffeine or more would shut down his Psionics. According to this, tea had forty-seven ounces in an eight-ounce cup. "May I have eight ounces?" he asked, looking up at the back of Dave's blond head.

"Sure. That'll be a buck twenty. I'll be there in a second…" he dropped the teabag into a cup of steaming water before walking back to the register. "Okay then…"

Turukaishal tossed two bills on the counter, watching as Dave dropped them in the register and gave him four coins back. These were quickly dropped into Turukaishal's pocket as he reached for his tea. He took a slow sip, gauging it, before almost spitting it back into the cup. "Yii!" he hissed, withdrawing from the cup quickly. "What temperature is that?" He glared at Dave through his glasses and could feel his eyes unnecessarily shifting to red.

"That's one-ninety," Dave said, "which is what most folks like their tea at. Did you want it cooler?" he wrung his hands apologetically in his apron.

"Yes please," Turukaishal said with a small inclination of his head. "One-twenty in future, if possible." He reigned in his momentary burst of anger, breathing deeply as his eyes returned to their normal black color. He carried the cup over to a table, taking off the lid to let it cool faster as he sat down and mumbled to himself about Vahran and their overheated teas.

Just as he was about to lift the tea to his lips and taste it, the steam having mostly dissipated, he heard the bell on the door jingle brightly as someone opened it. He looked over and paused, setting his tea down as the two figures entered the shop. The first one immediately turned to him, smiling brightly. "Hey Turu! Fancy seeing you here!"

Richard and Victoria stood in the entrance, the latter waving happily at him while the former looked as if he had just ingested a brick. Turukaishal let out a gentle Psionic thread, weaving it through the air and brushing it through Richard's aura. Sure enough, the Vahran was distrustful and, in some ways, mean. It didn't feel like a focused hate, though; it was more generalized. As if it was just common practice for him not to trust people he just met. At a guess, Turukaishal interpreted his aura to mean Richard was a misanthrope and that Turukaishal's anomalous nature had set him on edge.

Victoria's aura was considerably different from her brother's. It was bright and warm, with an almost upbeat musical quality to it. It carried none of his distrust, but it had... he searched for a way to convey it before settling on 'fractures'. It was as if pieces of her aura had been bitten out, leaving pieces. This was a phenomena usually brought on by yearning or loneliness, at least among the Scain, but he really wasn't sure if it held true for Vahran.

There were pitifully few articles on Vahran auras, even on Earth, and the Scain hadn't done an in-depth study. Most of their information was limited to secondhand sources, which Turukaishal was loath to trust, or from the painfully few encounters the Scain had with Vahran. Something like Richard's trust was easy to discern – Turukaishal himself was distrustful by nature, something he blamed on his father, Ferthoroyia. Partially devastated auras, like Victoria's, were uncommon and altogether rare. And Vahran psychology was different; whereas Scain generally yearned for unity with their surroundings, both with nature and one another, he had no idea what a Vahran would yearn for. It wasn't like he could just waltz up and ask her, either... and most of the Vahran-based information on auras was garbage, the authors of such texts being the greatest of charlatans and lunatics.

An aura, in essence, was an energeic expression of emotion. Everything living had an aura, right down to rodents, plants or insects and all the way up to sentient creatures like Vahran or Scain. The more evolved a creature was, the easier its aura was to read. However, if the creature was *too* evolved, like the mysterious Kelthos or the enigmatic Rhurni, their auras became complex and difficult to read. Scain were highly evolved despite how young their race was, and could read all but a handful of auras.

Auras were tricky to read, as they were just a thin layer of energy 'seeping' out of a being. Turukaishal had to brush the aura itself with his Psionics, and not touch the being itself. Had he touched Richard directly, the Vahran would have likely felt as if someone had just touched him. It may have alerted him to something unusual or even triggered a fight-or-flight response. Or maybe something totally different; he'd never brushed a Vahran before.

To Turukaishal, auras felt like glass. Or ice – ice was a far better example. Cool, crisp and clear, and often varying in density and thickness. Based on differences in the sensations, he could read moods and emotions. Right now, Richard's aura felt like rubbing coarse yellow sand – he was distrustful – and had a heated feel to it: anger. Victoria's, on the other hand, felt like blades of grass. They were soft and green and verdant, cool in temperature and flexible. The missing portions felt like voids; empty and cold, truly vacuous.

He shook his head, snapping himself out of his split-second rumination and nodded. "Greetings," he said, focusing on what he knew of Vahran 'social graces'. "How have you been?"

"Oh, you know, the usual," Victoria said as she approached his table. Turukaishal noticed that she wore much the same thing as she had on their first meeting – a maroon sweater and blue denim pants. Richard, too, was dressed in the outdated greatcoat and formal wear. While Victoria had no problems approaching his table directly, Richard let out a dissatisfied snort and marched up to the bar to order their drinks, his spine as stiff as if he'd swallowed an iron bar. Dave looked as if he was already making them; apparently the siblings were already regulars here. "How about you? No run-ins with the Whale Brigade this time, I see."

"Vicky," Richard admonished without turning around. Turukaishal snorted, recalling his Psionic tendril and focusing his abilities into his eyes. He could see her aura this way and it would be easier to watch from a distance. He focused in on her – still the same verdant, green aura. Good, she suspected nothing of him. Yet.

"No, not this time," he agreed as he finally took a painless sip of his tea. It was pleasant and sweet, with herbal notes and a smooth, palatable feel. He resisted the urge to sigh in contentment. All Vahran drinks should taste this good, he decided. Just hot water and those teabags, hm? Perhaps he'd have to take a small amount back to Chindrus with him and figure out how to make it there.

"So, do you always wear your sunglasses indoors?" Richard asked, walking up to the table as Victoria pulled out a chair and sat down. "I mean, it's kind of dim in here as it is."

"Yeah," Victoria said, leaning on her elbows. "How can you even see what you're drinking?"

The tea he'd been drinking almost went back into the cup as Turukaishal's mind went into a panicked overdrive. He'd never thought about it being strange that he wore his sunglasses indoors. He had no excuse for it! He looked up at them from over the rim of his cup, thinking furiously for an answer that would appease not just the curious Victoria, but her already distrustful brother.

Chapter 06

BEGIN MESSAGE

LOCATION: Chindrus, Amara District

TIME: 01/22 Local Time

MESSAGE: I have heard, millions of times in fact, that you are on a mission. Your dearly beloved has told everyone countless times about you, and how proud she is. I would deeply appreciate your swift return; her incessant need for some kind of companionship is beginning to irk me. She has convinced herself that my reclusive ways are the byproduct of maladjusted social tendencies. Hence, she had made her presence widely known in this area. She has also apparently become fond of pounding on my door at any given hour, attempting to pull me from my seclusion in an attempt to 'cure' me of my solitary nature. If this persists, I may need to hide in the Denuval District like poor Bandrumano.

In any case, please return as quickly as possible: my sanity is certain to suffer otherwise.

-Klakshan

Turukaishal was aware of the communicator buzzing in his pocket—sounding like an ordinary cellular device—but at the moment he was beset by a pair of curious Vahran. Richard stood behind his sister, his arms folded over one another as he stared down the bridge of his nose at Turukaishal; an unnerving sensation for an individual used to being taller than everyone else. Victoria, in the meantime, was leaning across the table and staring at him with those emerald-green eyes. He felt his palms begin to sweat and, cursing the Vahran body he was stuck with, began to think of an excuse. "I recently had eye surgery," he lied. "My eyes are quite sensitive, and they recommended I wear protection for a few weeks. And I am not certain when the light in here may brighten, so I decided to wear the glasses. Is there a problem with it?"

"No," Victoria said before Richard could answer. "I'm sorry; we didn't realize you were on the mend."

"It is fine," Turukaishal said, attempting to appear genial. "I don't usually discuss my medical state with people, so how could you have known?" he forced a polite smile, trying to show that there had been no offense taken. In reality, he wanted to strangle them both for almost catching him out. Eye surgery? He hoped that was a convincing enough cover. Of course, eventually he'd need to come up with another excuse. He could only use eye surgery as a reason for his glasses for a few weeks."

Victoria politely excused herself and departed for a pair of rooms at the back: restrooms. Turukaishal, after a particularly horrifying experience at a nutrient plant, resolved never to use the restroom outside of his home again. They looked like breeding grounds for diseases unnameable. Victoria was certainly braver than he was. Richard took the seat next to hers as Dave walked over, placing a pair of light yellow plates in front of their spots. Golden-brown croissants were resting on the plates, as well as a few squares of butter and some dull metal knives. Turukaishal resisted the urge to shy away from the plates; if he stared at the croissants long enough, he could almost see the yeast in them.

Richard removed his blue coat, revealing the frame of a man who was both thin and wiry, but likely as dense as a brick. His hat, the glasses resting on the brim, was neatly hung on the back of his chair. His brownish-blond hair, once more, was neatly combed up over the back of his head, exposing his forehead and a small scar above his right eye. His stormy eyes turned to Turukaishal, the pupils seeming to glow with inner fire. "I don't trust you," he said immediately. He had retained the cane, his long fingers wrapped around it as if prepared to swing it at Turukaishal's head at a moment's notice. "I don't know why, but there's something about you I don't like. I just can't put my finger on it. Yet."

Turukaishal had to fight down the urge to scowl. "Oh?" he responded dryly. Was his cover really being blown by intuition? By nothing more than gut instinct? He resisted the urge to attack Richard in self-preservation; attacking him in the middle of a coffee shop wouldn't be the best choice. Instead, he opted for a more tactical option. A Psionic thread crept out, curling through the air. This one was thinner and far less obtrusive than the one he'd used to read their auras and could not be seen or felt. This one was designed to actually connect with the Vahran.

Richard looked at him sharply, his eyes narrowed. His aura changed from the gritty orange of irritated to a series of vermillion barbs. Aggression. "Who are you?" he asked.

"Turu Kaishal," the Scain responded. "I am on vacation and decided—"

"And I'm the King of England," Richard said sarcastically. "No one takes a vacation in Washington, and I mean *no one*. There's too much rain and it's far too cold. That and Washingtonians are notoriously unfriendly. You're here for another reason." Richard seemed to ease slightly, his barbs shortening somewhat as if calling Turukaishal out had calmed him somewhat. He wasn't relaxed, but he didn't look ready to attack anymore, although his gray eyes bored holes in Turukaishal's glasses.

Who *was* this Vahran? The Psionic thread came into contact with Richard's leg and Turukaishal saw him stiffen slightly. Was he that sensitive? Gooseflesh erupted across his body: visible on his hands and neck as he rested his elbows on the table. The cane remained firmly gripped in his fingers. Turukaishal sighed as he saw the thread take. It wasn't designed to attack, merely to lower inhibitions. He could ply the Vahran for information like this. "Why don't you put the cane down and talk with me a moment," he suggested. "You look as if you're ready to cave in my skull."

"I am if necessary," Richard said, his voice having retained its steely edge.

Turukaishal shrugged. "I mean no harm. I am an innocent patron of a coffee shop, and you and Victoria came to join me. I have done nothing to you. However, you are filled with mistrust, which is obvious, and I seem to have earned a medal of some kind. Why?"

Richard looked as if he had relaxed, but his eyes hadn't. "I'm not so naïve as to believe you're here solely after Victoria, but I bet she's already caught your eye. And the answer is: no. You'll take her over my dead body." He picked at his croissant with a fingertip. "I'm her brother, do you understand me. You lay a finger on her and you'll be mourning the loss of your arm."

Turukaishal had the vague sense that he was intruding on something private, but he quickly shook it off. This was a Vahran – they were heartless beasts who only performed actions based on the rewards they could reap in the future. Still, he could understand the compassion for a sibling. Although he had no brothers or sisters of his own, he and Bandrumano were as close as blood relations.

"And what makes you think I have an interest in her?" Turukaishal asked. "Is she of particular value?" he was honestly curious, but more for future reference. If she *did* have value, she could be used as a bargaining chip against Richard if he decided to assault him. He scoffed to himself: what was the value of one Vahran? What was the value of their entire species? Six billion multiplied by zero was still zero.

"Why wouldn't you?" Richard asked. "Just about everyone who even *looks* at her wants something from her. I guess it's just human nature, but after last time—" he shook his head, his eyes clearing immediately and hardening further. "Why the heck am I telling you this?" he growled, looking at Turukaishal as if he *knew* the Scain had violated his mind.

So, he'd shaken off the thread? That wasn't unheard of. It was uncommon, but certainly possible. Scain shook off each others' threads all the time. A Vahran doing it was new, yes, but Turukaishal had no way of knowing if it was unique. Turukaishal snapped the Psionic tendril back to himself, pondering on what he'd just learned. So Victoria had some kind of connection to others, did she? What was it? "What do others attempt to gain from her?" he asked.

Richard almost exploded in his seat. "Her body, idiot!" he spat, his fist coming down on the table hard enough to rattle the plates and give Turukaishal a start. "You've apparently spent your entire life under a stone in a cave somewhere, so I'll clue you in: Victoria's an attractive girl. There're plenty of guys out there who have their eyes on her, and none of them are good. Heck, I have yet to meet a 'good' human being! I'm not going to let you make her into another notch on your belt as long as I'm alive, do I make myself clear?!"

Turukaishal was momentarily stunned by the vehemence which poured out of Richard, both from his mouth and his aura. The glow around him had shifted to be a venomous green, bubbling like acid and shot through with the crimson streaks of aggression. Richard had more volatility to him than a half-built fusion reactor and he was containing it through sheer force of will. It didn't surprise Turukaishal to discover that Richard was a misanthrope. It was interesting, of course, but obvious in the way he spoke to and looked at others. He was also protective—almost overprotective—of his sister. This made sense to Turukaishal, as Richard seemed to have been exposed to some things that others hadn't and he'd been hardened. Interesting. This could work in his favor.

"I, too, have found very little good in humanity. A shining example would be the pair that almost scalded me to death with their beverages. It is incredibly difficult for me to relate to them on any level and, truth be told, there are times I wish I could leave Earth entirely." It wasn't even all a lie. Turukaishal congratulated himself on using his true nature to his advantage.

"Yeah, that makes two of us," Richard growled, pausing as he looked up at Victoria. She had returned from the restroom and was chatting with Dave at the counter, smiling and laughing with him. "Unfortunately, Vicky doesn't see things like I do. She'd rather open and trusting, which'll probably be the death of her one day. All it takes is one wrong step, or one idiot, and she's gone. I'd rather die than see that happen."

Richard's aura, as he spoke, flashed a single time. Just once. But it was enough to stun Turukaishal into silence. For one moment, the vehemence and mistrust that seemed to saturate his aura lifted like a shell and Turukaishal saw blinding gold and white beneath it. Before he could even stop to read it fully, the miasma of misanthropy had descended over it again, hiding the brilliant light from view. Turukaishal had to resist the urge to stare, openmouthed, at Richard. Gold. Purity. This Vahran, for all the thorns on his tongue and for all the vicious, vitriolic beliefs in his heart... was good?

Turukaishal recalled the second thread he'd extended; one meant for Victoria. There was no need for it. Things were starting to make sense to him. Scain, with their chromatic eyes, had only one layer to their auras. The other layer, the outer 'shell' which others viewed, *was* their eyes. The second layer was the aura they read within one another. Vahran, however, had *two* layers! There was the outer aura, which was what they showed the world, and then the inner aura: what they really were.

How many 'good' Vahran had Turukaishal passed up by only reading their outer aura? How many good Vahran were there in all? Mindbank Sovakadris had told him that there *were* no good Vahran. Did he not know about the second layer to their auras, or had he deliberately withheld this information? Suddenly, everything Turukaishal had ever believed about the Vahran was shifting; on unstable foundations.

According to the Mindbank, there were no 'good' Vahran. All they did was procreate, pollute, and squabble amongst one another. And yet here, sitting in front of him, was a good core in a harsh body: a Vahran who, if Turu was reading his aura and emotions correctly, would lay down his life for his sister at a moment's notice. He hadn't had a chance to read Victoria's aura, not this closely, but he was almost convinced that it was similar. Why else would she have offered him that towel?

He rose from his seat, picking up his tea. "I am afraid I must depart," he said as calmly as he could. He took a sip from his tea, noticing how much cooler it had become.

"What?" Victoria asked, turning away from Dave as Turukaishal nodded to her and her sibling. "Wher are you going? Richard, what did you say?!" her aura had shifted to pliable and violet; worry and concern.

"Your brother said nothing," Turukaishal assured her. "I am just a busy man and I have things to do. It has been a pleasure." He dipped his head again before turning and walking away.

"But I thought…" Richard began, but Turukaishal was already out the door and halfway down the sidewalk, his long legs propelling him gracefully along. "…on vacation?"

Victoria walked up to her brother, watching the back of Turukaishal's head recede as he walked away. "Is he alright? He seemed upset or bothered."

"I don't know," Richard said, looking as confused as she did. "We were just talking, and he asked about you. I told him that I didn't want to see any harm come to you—since you're so trusting and all—and he just got up and left!"

The pair stared after Turukaishal, his figure long since vanished from sight as he descended the hill which led up to the coffee shop. Silence reigned supreme for a moment before Richard sighed. "Well, no sense in letting the pastries get cold. Maybe he just remembered something he had to do." And even as he said the words, Richard couldn't shake the nagging feeling that something had, in fact, shaken the taller man. He gave one more glance at the door, half expecting Turukaishal to return, before breaking apart his pastry. He'd see Turukaishal again; Lakewood wasn't very big, so he was certain to run into him at some point. Victoria pulled out her seat, sitting down.

"Brrr; did it just get cold?" she asked, looking around and brushing her arms through her sweater. Richard eyed her curiously before returning to his pastry. "Seriously Richard, this seat is *freezing!*"

"Well duh," he said as he munched on the croissant. "You didn't sit down to warm it up." He shook his head, sighing... totally unaware of the remnants of a Psionic tendril lingering just above the seat his sister had just taken.

Chapter 07

BEGIN MESSAGE

LOCATION: Diathua Base

TIME: 1/10 Local Time

MESSAGE: You never write, you know that? I mean, you can pen a wonderful mission report – I use yours in front of the cadets all the time – but they're too professional. Too clean. Crisp. It's like reading something a machine spit out. When you bother to interject your opinions or thoughts, it's always swamped in logic as to WHY you feel that way. It's way too mechanical.

Other than reaming you for not writing, how are things going? I hear you've been stationed on Earth for a little while. Half of one of their cycles, huh? That's rough. No, I can't tell you how I know, and I know it was supposed to be a Black Mission. I don't know the details, and I don't <u>want</u> to know. Just take care of yourself. Those Vahran can be treacherous. If you need me, send a message. TF Kirel will be there in a heartbeat regardless of circumstance.

-Bordra, Task Force Kirel

Turukaishal was almost halfway home, and he couldn't wait to check his communicator. Two messages? Hearing from his old friends made him feel a little less isolated. Of course, he was supposed to have severed all contact, left his communicator at his base, blah blah blah, but he was never really one to follow the rules to the letter. It was one of the reasons he'd stayed alive as long as he had. Just as he reached the bottom of the hill and was preparing to turn left into the forest, he felt what could best be described as a disturbance in the latent energy around him. Someone was following him. He fielded his Psionics, what little he could spare after the stunts in the coffee shop, and scoped out the energy signature. Two distinct points, both behind him. Cowards. He'd show them how a Scain dealt with his pursuers. "Make your presence known," he said, turning around. "You're embarrassing yourselves hiding like that."

Much to Turukaishal's surprise, and a small amount of amusement, it was Richard and Victoria who squeezed themselves through a break in the fence. Richard looked thoroughly annoyed (but, then again, he usually did) and Victoria looked like she couldn't decide to be irritated or amazed. "How'd you know?" she pouted, crossing her arms and appraising him with her eyes. "Sheesh, and here I thought we were being quiet."

"*I* was being quiet," Richard muttered. "*You* left a trail a blind baby could follow."

Before Victoria could round on her brother, Turukaishal cut her off. "Why were you following me?" His head felt foggy: he'd used his Psionics too much. Not only was he maintaining a disguise, but he had also used his energies for long periods in the coffee shop – something he knew was unhealthy while concealed – and then fielding his Psionics just now had truly taxed him. He growled to himself. In his Scain body, he *never* had issues like this. He probably could have shielded himself from every bullet on the planet and then some, but no... he was stuck masquerading as one of these monkeys. He winced. These two weren't *quite* the barbarous apes he'd initially thought them to be, but it would be some time before he could stop referring to them as chimps.

"I wanted to make sure Richard didn't say something to tick you off," Victoria said with a gesture to her sulking brother. "He can be a bit prickly sometimes."

A bit? If that wasn't the understatement of the year, he would marry an Iharsh-Daraz. Turukaishal waved his hand distractedly, noticing that it definitely looked grayer than it had in the coffee shop. He coughed. "I have things to do," he explained, "and I am not feeling at one-hundred percent. I deemed it appropriate to disappear before I passed on some malicious pathogen."

Victoria scanned him from head to toe. "Yeah, you do look a little gray..."

Okay. That confirmed it. Turukaishal was going to go home and hide for several days. Maybe a week or two. What was an easily faked disease? Pneumonia? Too dramatic. Botulism? He hadn't eaten anything odd. Influenza? Possibly; it was late in the year anyway. He coughed again. "I am glad we are in accord. I will—"

"Go home and get some rest," Victoria finished, nodding. Turukaishal sighed in relief; at least they weren't going to pester him. "And here's our phone number in case you need anything. Being sick is a drag."

"Vicky..." Richard growled, palming his face in exasperation and leaning against a fencepost. From what Turukaishal could see, he looked as if he'd rather be drinking paint than dealing with the current situation. The Scain decided to be merciful and not help the girl drag this out any longer.

"I concur," Turukaishal said as she handed him a small slip of paper. "However, I doubt I will require your assistance. I have taken care of myself for a long time." Of course he had. Compared to her, he was ancient. The ratio between their ages was at least one to ten. How old was she? Twenty? Twenty-five? He was two-hundred and forty seven. He felt ancient just thinking about it. Scain lived about a thousand years, give or take, but most didn't pass eight-fifty. Scions, on the other hand, could live up to twelve hundred years.

"Still, I can drop by later to bring you some stuff," Victoria assured him, earning another exasperated moan from Richard. "You're in good hands. Mom was a nurse."

Was? Turukaishal didn't want to touch that subject. Instead, he decided on a more logical, well thought out option: he panicked. "NO!" he blurted, far quicker and louder than he'd intended. He cleared his throat as the two stared at him, covering his face with a hand. "I'll be alright. Really. I haven't even moved in all the way yet, and it would be mortifying to showcase my domicile in such an unkempt condition..." They were going to try to find his base? In the woods? Were they *insane*? Firstly, if they toppled down any of the hills, they could be badly injured. If they broke a limb, it could be days before anyone found them. Not to mention that he didn't want them seeing him in his Scain body: that went without saying.

"That's nothing," Victoria said with a light, airy laugh. "Richard's room looks like someone blew up a library."

There was a muffled growl behind her. "There's an order to it, I swear," her brother muttered into his hand, putting his hat on his head and pulling the brim down over his eyes. Based on his aura—jagged and yellow-orange—he had somewhere else he wanted to be. It felt like tiny electrical jolts were arcing off him: impatience. He wanted to be gone, and Turukaishal was more than willing to help. He decided to just capitulate, however temporarily, to close down the discussion.

"Very well," he said with a sigh. "If you insist on performing such a nugatory task, I will prepare most of the home for you. Please, may I ask you to drop by no later than six-o-clock?" If she was going to be *this* insistent, he might as well just let her. It would help Richard see that he wasn't some kind of boogeyman, and she'd stop pestering him. He'd just stay in his Vahran body for a few more hours; maybe take a Booster when he got home. After all, it was just after two-thirty now.

"Okay, sure. Where about are you?" she asked. "That forest is kind of a maze, you know."

That had been one of the reasons Turukaishal had picked it. "I reside through the second fence," he told them. "Off the path on the right and down the hill." Hopefully those direction were vague enough to get them lost for a while without them coming to any serious harm. He rolled his eyes. The only real reason he didn't want them getting hurt down there was that it would attract lots of search parties and inquiries into his whereabouts at such-and-such a time and whether or not he had an alibi. What a hassle. If he hadn't heard from them by six, he'd scan the area with a large-scale Psionic burst. Once they were safe, he would go to bed and rest for several days. Maybe he'd even use one of the pods down in his ship... he shuddered in ecstasy at the thought.

"Okay, sounds good," Victoria said, smiling. Turukaishal stared at her for a moment, remembering how Richard had referred to her as an 'attractive girl'. Turukaishal gave her a thorough comb-over with his eyes, committing her image to memory. Fine. He'd admit it. For a Vahran, she was an excellent example of the female of her species. Whoop-de-doo. If it was that big of a deal to look attractive, these beasts should invest in genetic cosmetics instead of... well... he didn't even know what all they invested their time and money in. Weapons, most likely. By the Hiin, this planet was so backwards and primitive it made him sick sometimes.

He turned his back to the pair. "Well, it has been a pleasure conversing with you both, but I must hurry to make my dwelling presentable for you. I bid you farewell for the time being." Without looking back, he quickly rounded the corner and cut through the woods. He didn't want to waste any time, he had plenty of things to check...

Like the lock to the door of his ship...

Chapter 08

BEGIN MESSAGE

LOCATION: Chindrus, Orbital Relay Station 42

TIME: 6/22 Local Time

MESSAGE: Turukaishal, I have been reading over your messages quite thoroughly. More than ever, I believe we have to stay strong on the path we are treading. The destruction of the Vahran will be a breath of fresh air for the Galaxy as a whole, and retribution for sins past. Furthermore, I am convinced that the Alinteans will forge a permanent treaty with us for this.

One thing bothers me, and that was the closing line of your last report. "Possibility that Vahran possess good: 2%"? Please, Turukaishal, do not tell me that there are good Vahran. I know better than that. One or two may act it, but you must not be fooled! Read their auras, or watch them closely: that will surely expose them for the monsters they are!

-Sovakadris

Turukaishal sighed, setting down the communicator on his desk. He wasn't surprised that Mindbank Sovakadris was chastising him. Two percent had been extremely generous. After dealing with so many Vahran and meeting only two, he'd had to sit down and give a lot of thought to how many could *possibly* be good. He'd given the estimate of two percent. There were a lot of Vahran on Earth... still, he'd only met two he wanted to deal with a second time.

Namely Richard and Victoria Sinclair.

Because of this, he'd included the small tagline when he'd written his report upon arriving back at base. The Mindbank's answer had been as swift as it had been chastising. Within the hour. For what reason he'd included it, he couldn't say. Perhaps it was nothing more than blunt honesty, but there was a small part of him which wouldn't allow him to doom an entire race unless every fact pointed there. This was the anomalous fact which made him start questioning his mission, and he didn't like it. But he had been ordered to report *all* facts, so he had. If the Mindbank wanted to get upset, oh well.

He sighed, leaning against the wall in his living room. Unlike his office upstairs, he had kept this area relatively bare. There was a couch, two plushy chairs, a coffee table and a television which he had unplugged a few days ago after realizing he had *no* idea of how to hook it up. There were a few pictures hanging on the walls; mostly nature shots, as he was as fond of foliage as the next Scain. Apart from that, the room was undecorated. He didn't really understand why he had synthesized most of it. It just sat around collecting dust from disuse: dust which he had recently 'vacuumed' off with his Psionics, draining him a bit further. He'd been resting to recuperate a bit. He sighed, slumping down in an armchair for the first time. He could probably have survived in a three-room complex instead of an entire house, but he had to blend in with the locals.

The clock chimed 5:45. Fifteen more minutes and he could crawl down into his ship and sleep in the blissful euphoria of his pod. Oh how he'd missed it... Maybe he'd drag out one of the methane tanks and huff a bit. Relax. He turned his head and looked out the window, sighing at the current weather conditions. It had started snowing on the way home, and the soft flakes fell down like white rain. In the woods, where he had built his house, they were broken up by the branches above. They lit the forest with their radiance, sticking to his windowpanes as if curious as to what lay within.

Turukaishal dragged himself over to the window and opened it, leaning on the sill and staring silently out into the forest. He could hear the motion of the snowflakes as they drifted down from on high, brushing against one another and down through the leaves. The air was almost unbearably cold and crisp, but felt refreshing as he breathed it in. Turukaishal took a deep breath, inhaling the icy smell of the snow. On Chindrus, the only place there was ever any snow was up near the Koratar District to the far north. To the south, there was barely any land. Although there were small amounts of ice on the islands there, nobody really dwelled there. Koratar, on the other hand, was a thriving city and the main source of weapons for the planet, just like the Mengaia Province was to the Alinteans.

Turukaishal's eyes fell on the path leading to his front door; a simple dirt walkway with plants growing wildly on either side, and watched as it slowly disappeared beneath the snow. The plants to the left and right had already received a liberal coating of the white flakes, and every now and then a clump fell off, sending the branch it had fallen from into a frenzy of movement. Somewhere in the distance, he could pick out the sound of cars as their drivers made the white-knuckled commute home in the snow, the occasional horn shattering the silence of the forest.

Where were those two Vahran? He rested his chin on the back of his hand, watching the snowy woods. Although he wasn't particularly fond of the cold—especially after Limkalan—something about watching the whitewashed woods was oddly peaceful. He sighed, shaking his head, hoping Richard and Victoria were alright. They were the only two confirmed *good* Vahran on this planet out of how many? Six billion? Seven? Too many.

He closed his eyes, focusing his Psionics and widening them as he prepared to search the forest. He got the limit of his 'bubble' to push out to the end of his walkway before a sharp pain tore through his skull. His hand involuntarily flew to his eyes, holding his face in a vise as if his head was about to come apart. Oh yes, he was drained. Running on fumes. If he wanted to do anything, he had two choices: revert to his Scain form, in which he would have a thousand times the Psionic strength he had now, or he could take a Booster.

Personally, Turukaishal hated Boosters. They were like a drug, which was why Scain were only issued four per military cycle, and he had seen more than one soldier ruined because of the addiction that could develop. He'd watched the madness set in as they attacked their comrades to steal their Boosters, pumping themselves so full of the innocuous-looking blue liquid that they either went insane or died... or the Vanguard stepped in to handle them, dragging them away in a screaming, frothing delirium. Turukaishal still had three of his four, and had no intentions of asking for more. He had held onto the same syringes as when he entered the Academy almost a century ago, not really wanting to use them up too quickly. He saved them for emergencies only. He'd only used one, back on Limkalan, when he and the remainder of his team had been too near death to consider other options. He remembered the way liquid thunderfire had flown through his veins, his eyes all but glowing as he wielded the power of a Scion for a short time in his life.

He walked back over to the closet, picking up a strongbox on the table next to it and unlocking it. Inside, nestled with the syringe that would allow him to return to his ship, were the three tiny blue syringes containing the Booster fluid: lmost 500 milligrams of Trichloroacetaldehyde monohydrate. "Boosters", of course, was less of a mouthful. He picked up one of the syringes, removing the cap and fingering the plunger thoughtfully. To Boost or not to Boost... he looked back to the window, his unmasked eyes flickering between hues of gray and brown: worry and indecision. If he was going to poison his system, he'd rather huff methane. To a Scain, it acted like an expensive tobacco habit, producing a pleasurable floating sensation and a lingering high which robbed him of his ability to think clearly.

It had been far too long since he'd last huffed, and he was beginning to crave the gas more and more with each passing day. He knew he was addicted: both he and Bandrumano were and neither of them really cared. Methane alone wouldn't kill them; not unless they went and did something stupid while under the influence of it. Huffing was a mind-altering activity, which was one of the reasons they only did it in their homes, rather than going to the local Huff Houses. He sighed, wistfully thinking of that pleasurable high and craving it.

Turukaishal slipped the protective cap back over the needle and slid it into his pocket. Vahran couldn't huff methane. As they breathed it, it began to replace the oxygen in their bodies, depleting it. At first, if they only inhaled small doses, they experienced dizziness and headaches, but if they continued breathing it they would eventually die of asphyxia. A Scain's body was different: their lungs were geared to absorb the methane instead of cycle it with their atmosphere. This introduced it to the bloodstream and carried it to the brain where it produced the reactions he was so fond of.

The Scain stepped out of his house, sliding the glasses onto his hawkish nose and pulling the door closed behind him. He still had a very limited range with his Psionics, but it would be painful. As a last resort, he'd use the Booster. But it would have to be a foul scenario before he'd consider it. He shook his head, walking away from his house. Who'd have thought he'd end up wading through ankle-deep snow looking for a pair of Vahran? Not him, that was certain. He focused his Psionics in front of him, rather than fielding them, which gave him a slightly longer range. Slowly, using the beam of energy like a scanner, he began to sweep it back and forth through the trees.

The snow was falling thickly now, and Turukaishal was grateful that the Psionics illuminated every tree, shrub and blade of grass that still protruded above the white carpet. They were illuminated with a curious 'black light' which ebbed from them, creating a world of contrasting ebony and ivory. It wasn't the prettiest sight, and it made him feel as if he'd lost his ability to see color, but it was functional and kept him from running into a tree. As he walked, he suddenly saw a flash of watery white light— brighter than the surrounding snow—glowing on the ground about a thousand feet away. Aural energy couldn't be masked, only dimmed, and this source was certainly dim.

Turukaishal began moving toward it, the snow blanketing his false black hair with a dusting of the light flakes. He brushed them off, glaring at the ones which clung stubbornly to his shoulders and hands, before giving up. He could knock the stuff away for days, but until the snow stopped it would just keep building up. He sidestepped a clump of snow which, having taken aim at him from the high boughs of a tree, splattered on the ground where he'd stood a moment before. He hung his head as his long legs propelled him over the snow-covered ground, each footstep stirring up a flurry of white powder.

He reached the aural signature in a few minutes, staring down at the source and cursing quietly. Richard. Of all the people to find lying in his forest, it had to be the one he'd already pegged as valuable to his cause. He knelt down next to him and swept his Psionics over his body. A brief stab of pain caused him to lift his hand to his head, and Richard stirred and looked over at him. "Turu?" he mumbled, his eyes unfocused.

The Vahran looked like he'd been through hell. His blue coat was fanned around him and his clothes were dirty, scuffed and torn. In a few places, Turukaishal could see his alabaster skin and the scrapes and cuts that now adorned it. One of the two chains on his vest was broken, the end dangling limply. Turukaishal scanned carefully around and located what looked like a small locket, picking it up as he pressed his fingers to Richard's shoulder, examining him. A cut on Richard's forehead had let blood trickle down his face and it was congealing in his eyebrows. Turukaishal felt an unusual feeling seep into his body: guilt.

"What transpired," he asked, running his pencil-thin fingers down Richard's leg, looking for breaks. He would have to find a solution and move him quickly; the snow was melting on his body and the Vahran already looked like he'd been here for a while. Hypothermia was a very real danger and Turukaishal felt compelled *not* to just leave this Vahran to die.

"Vicky and I tried to find you," he growled, his lucidity returning slowly. His gray eyes seemed clearer with someone to focus on. "She slipped, I ran to catch her and wiped out... fell down the blasted hill." He moaned, grinding his teeth together as his eyes flared. "I can't move my leg..."

"Which leg," Turukaishal asked as he finished examining Richard's right shin. The Psionic tendrils which were gently seeping through his skin had revealed a small fracture, but Turukaishal could fix that with his abilities. Psionics had many uses, and it would be a cleaner repair than the archaic medicine used by Vahran.

"Left."

Turukaishal shifted his fingers over and was immediately rewarded with an involuntary cry of pain. There was a massive break in Richard's upper thigh, about halfway up. The bone was completely separated from itself. Not a good sign. "Where is Victoria?" Turukaishal asked, abandoning any pretense of a manual check and resorted to hovering his fingers just above Richard's body, his Psionics scanning him. "You said she was with you." There were minor breaks in a few places in Richard's upper body as well. What all had he hit on the way down? Every tree, rock and stick?

"She went for help," Richard muttered softly, looking up at the top of the hill (or where it would be if the snow wasn't completely obscuring it) as if he hoped he could see his sister there. Of course, there was no sign of her through the white flakes. Turukaishal cursed them and the clouds that spawned them, growling as Richard continued. "But that was... I dunno... an hour ago? Maybe a bit more?"

Turukaishal sat back on his haunches, his hands dangling over his knees as he surveyed the Vahran. The dilemma, oh the dilemma... If he used that Booster, he'd not only be able to heal Richard, but to get him out of the woods as well. But that would blow his cover. What to do, what to do...?

A loud crashing behind him disturbed his thoughts and he turned, instinctively aiming his hands at the source of the sound, until he saw that it was Victoria. Her clothes were ripped and scuffed, her sweater coming apart and the jacket she wore over it was bleeding white stuffing from jagged, mortal-looking wounds. Richard's cane was tucked through the back of her belt like a sword, sticking out on either side of her narrow waist.

"Turu!" she yelled, vaulting over a barely-visible log and racing towards him. "Thank God! Richard—"

"I can see," Turukaishal said, standing up and looking down at Richard. He sighed. Now his problem was worse. If he'd blown his cover in front of Richard, any 'alien anomalies' could have been blamed on shock and trauma. Victoria wasn't subject to that. If he helped Richard here (or anywhere, come to think of it) there would be a witness. He sighed again. "Your brother is not beyond my help," he said slowly, "but he is not in good condition. He has fractured his femur badly and his tibia is cracked. That's in his legs. Those are the worst injuries. He also has cracked his pelvis and his scapula and broken two ribs and his ulna." He looked up at her, gauging her reaction.

Victoria looked ready to faint. "Richard…"

"Get a grip, Vicky," Richard growled from the ground. "I've had worse. I'll live."

Turukaishal ignored him. He couldn't really imagine the Vahran having broken more bones at once unless he'd been hit by a moving vehicle. "Please," he said sadly, "help me move him back to my dwelling. We are close, and I do not wish for him to die of hypothermia. Once we arrive, we can discuss his treatment in more detail. Did you find help?"

"No," Victoria said, her eyes looking panicked as she drank in the sight of her brother's bruised, broken and bleeding body. "The snow's getting worse, and I couldn't find the path back out… and I can't just climb this hill, it's too steep, and—"

Turukaishal put one of his hands on her shoulder, realizing for the first time how small and delicate she was compared to him, or at least his Vahran body. With his thumb on her clavicle, his fingers easily touched her shoulder blades. "Victoria," he said seriously, causing her gaze to jerk from her brother up to his glasses. "I know you are worried for your brother, but you need to focus. If you want to help him, you need to get a grip on yourself. You are shaking like a leaf and you are displaying all the signs of a panic attack. Take a few deep breaths and calm down."

Victoria took several shuddering breaths, nodding and blinking rapidly as if she was trying not to cry. Turukaishal could all but smell her fear and worry and could see the teeth marks in her lower lip. He had to take a deep breath of his own; her anxiety was bleeding into him. "Alright," she said, nodding again. "Thanks."

"Of course. It is just as well that you did not find help. Now, if you will kindly help me lift him, we can move him back to my domicile. Ordinarily, I would not advise moving a patient in his condition, but… well, this calls for extreme measures." He walked over to Richard, crouching down near his head. "I will pick him up from his armpits if you could kindly get his legs. I do not believe your brother would appreciate being dragged around like a bag of refuse."

"Is it that obvious?" Richard muttered tiredly as Turukaishal hoisted his shoulders up, Victoria grabbing him by his boots, nodding at Turukaishal to lead the way. The Scain sighed, looking back toward his home, visible only to him.

He couldn't believe he was about to do this...

Chapter 09

BEGIN MESSAGE

LOCATION: Chindrus, Amara District

TIME: 3/22 Local Time

MESSAGE: Are you serious? The Mindbank was NOT happy with your little footnote on that last report. I have no idea what all he has asked you to do there, but I know it has to be dangerous. Vahran? I think he has it in for you. All I know about your mission is that it is Intel-related and that you're on Earth, but that little footnote send him into a black mood for at least a full rotation.

Okay, Vice-Commandant Neromaniel just left, so I can type freely. I read your report, don't you _dare_ tell that to anyone. Did you really find some good Vahran? Or do you just THINK you've found them? Have you checked their auras thoroughly? Made certain that they aren't trying to trick you? Vahran are supposed to be evil, Turukaishal! You have to be careful.

Now that you've got the Mindbank in a foul mood you've gone and made our jobs harder, by the way, so thanks for that. He's over here growling about how if you fail him now you'll be risking more than just yourself. I don't know all the details—you know me, everyone likes to keep me out of the loop—but please, Turukaishal, for the love of the Hiin, come back intact. AND BE CAREFUL!

-Bandrumano

Richard groaned audibly as Turukaishal and Victoria set him on the couch. Snow flaked off their bodies in droves, splattering wetly on the Scain's hardwood floor. None of them noticed. Victoria flitted about her brother like an anxious hummingbird, examining him from every angle and talking to him, trying to tell him that everything was going to be alright. Richard had closed his eyes and draped his good arm over them, trying to blot out the waking world and the pains it brought.

After Turukaishal directed her to his kitchen, she began dabbing at the blood on his forehead with a wet paper towel, her face pinched into a mask of concern. Richard swatted irritably at her, although his motions weren't aggressive, and she easily dodged his arm and continued cleaning him up. "Turu, what are we going to do?" she asked, her body shaking slightly again now that they had brought Richard to the relative safety of

Turukaishal's abode. "No one will try to come this far out here, especially in this weather, and they're saying there'll be a blizzard day after tomorrow..."

"Settle down," Turukaishal said as he drew the Booster out of his pocket, grinding his teeth. He rolled up his sleeve, seeking out a vein before sliding the needle through his flesh. He could definitely tell that his skin was grayer and more transparent as his Psionic reserves began to run low. He took a deep breath and depressed the plunger, the drug flowing into him. He felt the coldness, like frozen mercury slithering through his veins before reaching his brain. His vision distorted, Victoria and Richard standing out in sharp relief against his home as their auras flared to life, his Psionics expanding to pick up every nuance and subtlety he couldn't see before. Their physical forms melted away beneath his gaze, revealing their energeic patterns and faint, glowing remnants of their bodies. He shuddered, closing his eyes to blot out the hellish sights. "I require one thing from you," he said to Victoria. "In exchange for this one favor, I can restore your sibling to health."

"What?" she asked, biting her lip in worry as Richard turned and glared at Turukaishal. "How?"

Richard was having none of it. "You sick freak! If you think she's going to sleep with you for my sake, I'd rather die! Vicky, give me my cane, I swear I'll—AGH!"

Turukaishal had pressed two fingers to Richard's chest, just above his solar plexus, pushing him back down on the couch, his lips pulled back as he fought not to snarl. "Listen," he said, his glasses glaring down at Richard. "I have no intentions of defiling your sister. She's not my type, as you may soon come to see. I am asking for a pact of silence before I proceed, not sexual favors. I am begging you both not to ever share what you see here with anyone. Promise me this and I will heal you as if you were never injured."

Richard scowled. Turukaishal could feel the helpless rage boiling off him. Victoria cleared her throat, moving closer. "Turu, we promise, right Richard? I don't care what it is, just please, help him."

Turukaishal removed his finger, still gazing down at Richard before turning back to Victoria. "Thank you. Now, I must ask that you do not touch me, and please back up." As he spoke, he backed away from the siblings and knelt down, his fingers splaying on the floor. White light stretched from the tips, expanding until he knelt in the center of a white circle. Slowly, the light itself rose from the ground until it formed a dome over him, hardening into crisscrossing, colorless fibers.

Victoria instinctively reached for the dome before snapping her hand back. The dome, made from what looked like wrinkled plastic wrap, looked utterly foreign and somewhat frightening in the half-light of the room. It crouched near the coffee table like some

58

unknowable predator. Her brother, likewise, was totally fascinated by the dome. "What is that? What's he doing?" he asked, straining to get a better look.

"No idea," Victoria said, backing up until she stood next to the end table near Turukaishal's closet door. Her eyes never left the dome, watching it intently. Richard reached for his cane with his good arm, just in case, and gripped it firmly just below the head. His eyes shone with a mixture of curiosity and fear. Victoria, on the other hand, looked more as if she was considering running for her life and risking the snow again.

A harsh cracking sound echoed through the room, like dry twigs being broken underfoot, as a crack spread from one side of the dome to the other. It fractured across the surface, a tiny shard falling to the ground. Inside, an indescribable color whirled and danced, blocking any view of Turukaishal completely. The shard struck the hardwood with delicate *clink* – like glass – before it dissolved into a cascade of glittering sparks.

The lights in Turukaishal's home flickered once. Twice. And then they went out. All of the shutters on the windows slammed shut with a series of bangs. Gunfire born from wood. Richard let out a shout and tried to sit up, but his broken body couldn't handle it. Without the light from outside, the interior of the building was almost totally dark. They could only see the sliver of light from inside the dome, illuminating a patch on the wall. Another crack appeared. And another. And more. They kept growing, splitting the dome until the whole room was lit with that alien color. And then as suddenly as it started, the light was gone. There were dozens of clinks and the hissing of the colorful sparks, but beyond that the room was quiet.

A pair of dark orbs opened, each the size of Richard's fist; only visible because they were a hue lighter than the surrounding darkness. Slowly, they rose up into the air as one until they reached head level. "Please do not discompose yourself," Turukaishal's voice said in the darkness. The orbs continued to rise, going higher and higher until they reached the ceiling nine feet above them. Richard made a strangled sound from the couch, as if he'd been punched in the throat, and Victoria screamed at the top of her lungs. Her hands found the only thing in range to protect herself from the ominous, barely-visible orbs: a simple wrought-iron lamp on the table, and snatched it up. The power cable popped out of the wall, clattering onto the hardwood.

"I am aiding your sibling and you move to do me harm?" Turukaishal's voice asked from the darkness as the two orbs glowed red, turning to face Victoria. "Just what do you imagine you will achieve by doing this?"

She froze, biting her lip. Turukaishal could see her easily in the darkness: her skin was illuminated by her aura and he could see the energy flowing through her veins. How easy it would be to kill her, he realized. Her nervous system wasn't shielded like his. His Psionics could interrupt her nervous system without even taxing him, and could probably completely disrupt or shut it down without much more effort. She was so... fragile. She looked up at him, her eyes glowing like two emerald suns. "Who are you?"

"Turukaishal," he said, looking back at her. Those green eyes unnerved him.

She looked up at him, not understanding the difference between "Turu Kaishal" and "Turukaishal". Richard, however, coughed several times and emitted what sounded like a half-delirious chuckle. "Vicky, you always ask the wrong questions, you know that?" he said. He rotated on the couch, Turukaishal's eyes returning to their darkened state as he looked over. Richard, like his sister, had an infinitely fragile nervous system. The nerves in his brain were lit up like the fusion nodes of his ship; the Vahran's brain was in overdrive. "So, *what* are you?"

"Very well phrased," Turukaishal said, his eyes flickering up to yellow—pleased with this Vahran's intelligence—before going back to their dark hues. "I am, indeed, not like you two. What I am could inspire fear, aggression, shock or perhaps all three. I begged for a pact of silence because of this."

"Well I'm not going to be attacking you," Richard said, slumping down on the couch. "And I don't think I'm going to be too scared. You said you were going to help me, right? Yeah, well, can we hurry up and get to that part? I'd really appreciate it. I hate lying here with broken bones. But can you please show yourself? You're scaring my sister."

The two orbs rotated to look at Victoria for a moment. "I already have her vow of silence, but I require yours as well. Do I have it?"

"Naturally," Richard sighed, leaning back on the couch.

The lights came on without preamble, bringing with them a moment of blindness. Victoria dropped the lamp, the heavy object striking the floor with a crash as she covered her eyes. Richard squeezed his eyes shut, slowly opening them as he adjusted to the light. When both siblings could see again, they looked over at Turukaishal.

He stood against the wall, his back pressed up against it and his arms dangling at his sides. His thin, threadlike fingers brushed his first set of knees and his eyes were glued to the pair as if curious about their reaction. His flat, noseless face was turned towards Richard, his bulbous eyes narrowed in apprehension. Richard spoke first.

"I'm dreaming…"

"Are you in pain?" Turukaishal asked mildly, tapping one of his long fingers against his thigh.

"Yeah… a whole lot of it…" Richard answered, looking down at himself.

"You cannot experience pain in a dream," Turukaishal said decisively. "Still, if I am a phantasm of your fevered imagination, I suppose those fractures are similar in nature, hm?" he quirked a nonexistent eyebrow, watching the male. For one with this much neural activity, he could certainly say the strangest things.

Richard looked up at Turukaishal, his eyes and aura betraying a mixture of surprise, disbelief and confusion. Turukaishal was about to continue when Victoria stepped forward. Her reaction, in juxtaposition to her brother's, caught both Richard and Turukaishal completely by surprise. She inched her way forward, her wide green eyes staring at him in awe. Turukaishal turned to face her, his eyes glittering black, as she approached. She was within arm's reach: her arms.

Turukaishal tensed up, preparing to Psionically throw her if she attacked him as she lifted her hand toward his face, but no aggression was forthcoming. Instead, her hand connected with his cheek, so high above her own. First her fingertips, shaking like leaves in a gale, as if she expected to lose them. She slowly pressed down, her fingers sliding out as her palm touched his skin. "Beautiful…" she whispered, gazing into his eyes. "You're an alien."

Turukaishal said nothing, but his eyes immediately flashed from black to a hot pink. Richard stared at his sister in shock, as if he wanted to throw something at her to bring her back to her senses. Victoria smiled, her eyes filled with childlike wonder. "I never believed I would see one in my lifetime, let alone talk with it."

"I have a gender," Turukaishal said stiffly, straightening his posture. At nine feet tall, this put his cheek out of reach of her hand. His eyes turned back to black as he fought down his embarrassment.

Victoria's hand fell to her side as she watched him. "Why are you here?" she asked as he slowly made his way over to Richard. Turukaishal was unsettled beyond the ability of words or auras to convey. Her initial reaction—grabbing the lamp—was wholly expected. This recent behavior had him confused. And if Turukaishal became confused, he also became irritated.

"Initially?" he asked. "I was sent here to gather intelligence to aid in an assault on your planet." His eyes turned red as he remembered his mission. Vahran. He was *helping* them! Was he out of his Hiin-cursed mind?!

The words hit both Vahran like a blow to the stomach. Victoria's mouth fell open as if, by opening it wide enough, she could swallow her disbelief. Richard sent the Scain a murderous glare, his gray eyes carrying the same spark as the thunderheads they resembled. Turukaishal had the vague sense that Richard would have attacked him if not for the incapacitation. More unsettling still was the sense that, from Richard's glare, that it would not have been an easy fight and that victory would not have been assured, Psionics or not.

"You… you said initially?" Victoria said, her voice coming in shaky gasps. "What happened? Has something changed?"

"Yes," Turukaishal said as he knelt down, bringing his face within a foot of her brother's. "I was told your planet was wasted. Destroyed. A barren wasteland where even your cacti had difficulties stubbornly eking out an existence in the harsh, lifeless soil. I was told that your species was corrupt and iniquitous; that you *needed* to be destroyed. I came here for the benefit of my species and for the benefit of others to purge a dangerous threat from the Galaxy…" the fingers of his right hand brushed over where his heart should have been. Blue fire exploded to life, weaving between his fingers and crackling across the left side of his chest. It cast an eerie cerulean light across Richard's glaring visage, making him look more and more like he was capable of actually killing the Scain. "But I found world much different from the one described to me."

Turukaishal pressed the tips of his hairlike fingers to Richard's thigh. The thin threads burrowed into his leg like worms, vanishing beneath the pant leg and, undoubtedly, his flesh. Richard grunted softly, his eyes widening momentarily. The blue flames raced down Turukaishal's arm, vanishing into Richard's body and vanishing as the Scain withdrew his arm. He moved down to the male's ankle, replacing his fingers and letting them burrow in there as well. "My leader—the Mindbank—has entrusted me with this operation," he told them. "But I am losing faith in it. You Vahran are far from the monsters he described. Stupid, selfish, inept and primitive, yes, but you are not the planet-killers he described. I admit that I am conflicted… I would feel no pleasure in destroying this world. Some of its occupants, perhaps, but not all of them."

Turukaishal's hands had been busy, moving across Richard's body like a pianist. The blue flames blazed across his fingertips as he sank them through the injured human's skin. He stepped back, flexing his fingers as the blue light danced among them, shifting to look more like an azure mist than a flame. "Please, enlighten me if anything still hurts."

Richard flexed his joints, his expression conveying surprise when nothing pained him. Turukaishal had stepped back, watching him with those incalculable eyes of his. They were a deep blue, like the color of the ocean depths. Victoria had never once taken her eyes off his, and it was beginning to spook him. She had moved closer, staring at him like a soul transfixed. Moonstruck.

"But you don't look like you're going to kill us?" Richard asked, sitting up and rolling his right shoulder, massaging it with his opposite hand.

"I…do not know…" Turukaishal said, his eyes flashing to red—angry with himself—before returning to blue. "There is so much iniquity here that I—"

"But there's so much *GOOD* here too!" Victoria blurted, startling the Scain. His eyes flashed orange as his head whipped to look at her, before cycling through a myriad of colors and settling on brown. "I mean, you can't just sit in one place and watch the same people! You have to go to *different* places! Meet *different* people!"

Richard stood up, his back popping as he stretched. "I agree. Look, I have no problem if you want to go kill two-thirds of the population—"

"*Richard!!*" Victoria shouted, her hands balling into fists.

"—but make sure it's the *right* two-thirds. I advise you to go do your homework a bit better. She's right; not everyone's a prick." He looked over at his sister. "Relax, I'm not giving him permission."

"You are a misanthrope," Turukaishal said, not surprised that he had read Richard's aura correctly. He'd had almost two centuries of practice.

"One of the worst," Richard said, shrugging as if it didn't bother him.

Victoria had turned her gaze back to Turukaishal. "Um… Turu… is that your name?"

"Turukaishal," he said. "But you can refer to me as Turu if it is easier."

"It really is," she said, blushing and running a hand through her hair. "Um… can we show you some of the good here?" she looked up at him with the most pleading expression she could muster.

"You know where to find good Vahran?" Turu asked, his eyes betraying his shock as they changed to orange. If this female knew where other good Vahran were, perhaps he could convince Sovakadris not to burn this world.

"Some," she said. "Please, just trust me. I know you were sent here to destroy us, but can we make a deal?"

Turu stared at her, which she took as a prompt to continue. "Give me thirty days, starting tomorrow. If, after thirty days, you're still convinced we're all evil… our fate is in your hands. Deal?"

He decided not to mention that he was technically stuck here for four and a half more months as it was, making a show of considering it for several minutes before sighing heavily. "Very well. Thirty days. Although I suggest we make it thirty one. The snow is worsening and you will not be able to make it out of these woods. You will be spending the nocturnal hours here."

Victoria and Richard shared worried glances. "Um… what about you?"

"I have accommodations," Turu said as he walked toward his closet door. "There are bedrooms upstairs if you wish to use them." He felt like a traitor. What was he thinking making deals like this? He should flee Earth right now, contact the Mindbank from the edge of the system and have the Golden Fleet come in and burn this ball of manure. He paused, his hand on the knob. But what if she was right? What if there *were* dozens of good Vahran and he had merely been focusing on an area saturated with their counterparts?

He released the doorknob and ventured into the kitchen. He would give this female her thirty days. After that time, he would make a show of vanishing and go hide out on the moon or in orbit while he pondered his situation and mulled over any information he had acquired. If, at that time, the Vahran had failed to prove her point, he would call in the Mindbank and have this planet dealt with.

And yet, he thought as he poured himself a glass of water, what if he *had* been wrong all along. What if the iniquitous was the minority? The glass shattered in his four-fingered fist, water cascading over his skin. It was impossible.

Wasn't it?

Chapter 10

BEGIN MESSAGE

LOCATION: Chindrus, Eccemeria District

TIME: 11/22 Local Time

MESSAGE: This is an automated message reminding you that you have yet to send us a complete sample of your genetic material. Your match [Subject K-22475] has supplied us with hers, and we are waiting for yours. In order to ensure that the Scain race continues, we request that you send us the sample within five to ten rotations. Exceptions will be made if you are on a legal extended mission, hospitalized, enlisted in a current military conflict and deployed or are dead. If none of the above exceptions apply to you, please respond.

-Eccemeria Laboratories

Turukaishal couldn't sleep. He lay at a forty-five degree angle in his pod, his eyes fixed on nothing in particular. He was disturbed. Bothered. Why had he consented to that Vahran's asinine game? What could he learn from them? Vahran were evil; the Mindbank said so.

The Mindbank had also said this planet was a desert wasteland and that humans lived in subterranean bunkers.

Turukaishal looked around the interior of his ship from the confines of his pod. Lights blinked softly on the few active terminals in the condensed living area. Above him, glossy monitors stared back like sightless eyes; dead until his ship flew again. The cool metal floors glistened in the few dim lights, reflecting fluorescent blues, greens and golds back at him. Even inside his pod, he could smell the permeating effluvium of his ship's automatic cleaning system; the strange concoction which kept his ship clean and disease-free on this hostile, alien world.

He sighed. Things were so much simpler *before* he came here. It had barely been two months and he was already questioning his lifelong loyalties. Part of him longed for the days when he was flying around with his old crew, working in the service of the Mindbank to ensure the safety of the Scain Empire. Better still, he found himself missing the days when his waking hours were occupied by nothing more exciting than patrolling the Mindbank's Tower, or standing at attention in the throne room, as one of the Vanguard.

Above him, he could sense the two Vahran. Victoria had taken the master bedroom, where he usually slept, while Richard had remained on the couch. Both of their auras were a flat gray, indicating that they were both fast asleep. Richard's was a constant gray, undulating like waves against a calm beach. Whatever he was dreaming of was calm and placid. Victoria's aura, on the other hand, alternated between smoother contours like her brother and momentary bouts of spastic, jagged grays. She was definitely dreaming, but of what?

Was she like other Vahran inside, like the Mindbank and Bandrumano cautioned? Did she dream of violence? Of hate and greed? Of destruction and malice? For some reason, Turukaishal didn't think so: he had a very hard time applying those labels to the young female. How old was she anyway? He'd have to ask her in the morning.

Richard, when juxtaposed with his sister, was another story entirely. Well, at least on the outside and in parts of his aura. He was dark and bitter, parts of him twisted by some event which had bred intense dislike for his fellow Vahran. He was far more formal, in both appearance and speech, than most of his race. His behaviors were different as well, seeming to be prepared to defend himself (or his sister) at any given moment. Turukaishal couldn't quite shake the image of the male's fingers grasping that cane in the coffee shop as if ready to strike him with it.

Turukaishal sighed heavily, keying in the numerical release on the pad beneath his fingers. The lid on his pod slowly hissed open, dividing neatly in the center and sliding into the sides. He clambered out, stretching his lean body as he moved over some of the tables. He couldn't sleep, and lying around in the pod was going to make him go crazy if he didn't find *something* to do.

But what could he do? Work? He couldn't continue researching ways to harm Vahran — not for thirty days, anyway. He tapped his fingers on his workbench in irritation before brushing his hands over his chest. Blue fire raced out, twisting beneath his fingers as he cast it around his body like a field. One part reached above him, drawing down several round disks from an overhead compartment and placing them into a tray. With a flick of his wrist, the first one lifted up and slid into a large, cubical machine along one wall.

The top half of the cube lifted up as two side 'wings' folded down. The center of the upper half parted, revealing a screen. Static washed across it, warbling unhealthily in the silence of his ship. Turukaishal dealt the machine a swift Psionic swat. Stupid secondhand equipment.

The image slowly cleared, revealing a series of blueprints. Sprawled across the black background were the various three-dimensional shapes he would need to produce an EMP grenade. He flicked his wrist, sighing. Not what he was looking for. He should probably start labeling the discs. The machine read the disturbance in the Psionic fields and shifted to the next disc in the tray. This one looked like a rifle. Again, Turukaishal shook his head and flicked his wrist, finally finding what he was looking for. A blocky tube, blasted apart to reveal the internal components, rotated majestically on the screen. A shield generator. A different flick of his wrist opened several drawers beneath his workbench.

Within lay a variety of parts, all composed of iskindite. He drew out several with his Psionics, letting them dangle around his head like oddly shaped planets as he examined the blueprints again. He slowly began to attach different pieces together as they dangled in the air between his hands. Wires wove together, slotting into their proper grooves with satisfying clicks. The small deuterium fusion batteries snapped into place as the various metal plates began to slide into place, rotating together like the gears of a clock before laying flat along the length of the tube. Once the entire construction was complete, held together by nothing more than his mind, he carried it over to a tray which rested beneath a dangling piece of machinery.

Turukaishal slid his partially-finished creation beneath what looked like a gun barrel. A few Psionic threads wove around various controls and the barrel itself, turning it and fine-tuning it until Turukaishal was satisfied. He gave an ignition lever a psychic tug, starting the machine up. A thin beam of white light spiked downward from the gun barrel. A high-density laser. He slid a pair of black goggles over his eyes, muting the blinding light, before he began to rotate the construction beneath the beam, welding the gaps shut and producing thin wisps of smoke as the iskindite fused together.

Once he had finished with the first tube, he set it in a tray and slid it to the side, going back to the blueprint reader and starting over again, dispensing and assembling the parts with his Psionics before returning to the welding station. It didn't take him as long, now that he knew more or less what he was doing, and soon the two tubes rested innocuously on the workbench. He removed his goggles and gazed proudly at the pair of shield generators. If he was going to go prancing around with Vahran, he might as well wear some protection.

He lifted one to his face, examining it for flaws. It was a tube approximately a foot long, hinged on one side and with five apertures along a perpendicular edge. A small screen was mounted across from them, and the side opposite the hinges contained a small pin lock which would seal the tube. Across one of the openings was an elastic band, comprised of rubber and carbon microfibers woven into a high-density material. Apart from being mirror images of one another, the two devices were identical.

Turukaishal affixed them to his forearms, testing their weight. They felt bulky and awkward to him, but in reality weren't much thicker than a shirt (except where things like the apertures and control screen were placed). Scain technology was renowned for being light, thin and delicate while still getting the job done. They were also notoriously difficult to break, ever since the Alinteans had provided them with the technology to shape and work iskindite. Turukaishal's eyes glittered yellow out of happiness.

He loved iskindite, personally. It was his favorite of the supermetals on the periodic wheel, and had many properties that were valued in space. It was lightweight and sturdy, but could be made flexible by an exposure to tritium. It could be used in starship hulls, weapons, vehicles... there wasn't much you *couldn't* use iskindite for. Still, it was expensive – the only metals more so were mythril and tritanium – and it was difficult to manufacture without the proper materials on hand. The Scain had natural deposits of iskindite on their worlds, and Chindrus had a massive vein near its northern pole that they had been tapping for the past thousand years with no sign of an end. Learning to tap the properties of the metal had become paramount, and now they were one of the few races who utilized starships made solely from iskindite.

The fact that Turukaishal had as much iskindite as he did was due only to the larger paychecks from some of his more dangerous missions. He growled at the disc reader, glaring at it from the corner of his eye. Unfortunately, *that* piece of junk had been a resale. He'd bought it from a Visoth salesman and it had begun acting up en route to Earth. He was going to butcher that slimy cheat if he ever saw him again. Runs like new... yeah right.

Turukaishal pulled on a leather jacket he'd brought down with him, checking to make sure the bracers were hidden. They were. His eyes turned yellow again. For once things didn't look like they were going to go wrong. Any Scain could attest to the fact that Turukaishal was to trouble what a magnet was to metal. One look at his military history could attest to that.

Above him, he felt Richard fall off the couch, his transition from furniture to floor heralded by a dull *whump* and a muffled curse. The man's aura changed from gray to a mixture of pink and red. He was both embarrassed and angry. Turukaishal snorted through his nonexistent nose as he sensed Richard climb back onto the couch and roll over, trying to go back to sleep. The Scain figured that he should probably follow suit. There were six hours of darkness remaining, and he would need his rest. Now that his only preparations for the morning were complete, he could sleep in peace. Work always helped soothe his mind.

He climbed back into his pod, closing the lid without bothering to remove the coat or bracers. As the lid hissed down, the Scain settling into the comfortable gel-lined interior, he decided that sleep sounded very good right now. He was normally a bit of a late riser, but wanted to be up before these Vahran. He wanted to make every second of sleep he got count. So as he drifted away, his vertical eyelids closing and masking his eyes, the last thoughts in his mind concerned the two Vahran asleep in his home. The two Vahran who had defied the Mindbank's predictions.

Chapter 11

CHECKING FOR NEW MESSAGES...

...CHECKING...

...CHECKING...

...CHECKING...

...CHECKING...

...CHECKING...

...NO NEW MESSAGES. ENTERING HIBERNATION MODE.

Flames licked at the sky, standing out in stark contrast to the thick charcoal clouds blocking the skies. Smoke billowed up into the air, creating an impenetrable miasma which hung over the Earth like a shroud, blotting out the sun completely. Silhouetted against the smoke, gleaming like silver beetles, ships flew overhead in swarms, breaking off in groups to shell the ground with volleys of energeic fire. Explosions rippled along the ground, buckling the pavement as if it was balsa wood and throwing dirt and debris into the air.

Victoria raced through the burning streets, her green eyes wide with fear as she frantically searched. She had to find him! She just had to! She ducked under the remains of a building, canted strangely on its side like a transplant from an M.C. Escher painting, as another cluster of the silvery ships flew overhead. Another round of fire struck the ground in the distance, and she saw the burst of fire and flames roar upwards against the blackened sky. Hellfire burned at her face as she ran, the buildings all around her alight with the hellish blaze as she sprinted down the cracked and warped sidewalk.

Victoria arrived in time to hear the snapping of metal as her brother was hurled backwards, slamming into the wall of what had once been a grocery store. She heard bones break as his body met the unyielding stone. He slid down slowly, leaving a trail of impossibly red blood behind him as he came to rest at the bottom of the wall. Turukaishal approached him, striding purposefully along, his body a diaphanous hybrid of alien and human, ever shifting between the two and glowing with that alien cyan light. In his hands he held a long, oval rifle with blue conduits running along the sides, glowing with the same light as his body.

"NO!" she screamed, tearing forward, but her words fell on deaf ears. With his eyes dancing between red and blue, Turukaishal wordlessly raised the gun and aimed it at her brother. Another explosion drowned out her scream as the Scain fired four rounds: three into Richard's chest and a fourth through his face. Richard slumped sideways, collapsing on the ground. Dead.

"No!" she screamed again, grabbing hold of the rifle in Turukaishal's hands, fighting with him for it. "Turu, WHY?!"

He looked down at her with those chimerical eyes, throwing her off with a burst of energy. She landed on her back, scrambling backwards on all fours as she sought purchase. Turukaishal was on her in two steps, his foot—or was it a hoof—came down on her sternum and pinned her to the ground as he pressed the barrel of the rifle to her face. His eyes were completely blue now as he looked down at her.

"I am sorry," the alien said. For some strange reason, Victoria believed him. He looked away, unable to meet her gaze. "But this was my mission." He closed his eyes and pulled the trigger. The blast of the gun was impossibly loud, and light filled her vision as—

Victoria sat up with a gasp, clutching the soaked sheets to her body as she frantically looked around. She was in Turu's bedroom, the sheets of his gargantuan bed tangled around her body like pythons and her hair was sticking to her face as if she'd been caught in a rainstorm. The clock on his nightstand read 3:44 AM in glowing green letters and she fell back on the mattress with a groan. A dream. Thank God it had been just a dream. She sighed in relief, closing her eyes again. In the darkness, the walls of Turu's bedroom seemed to close in on her.

Would he do it? Would he actually destroy the human race? He seemed almost... well... too human to do it. Almost too human to be an alien. He seemed to sympathize with them, which was making him doubt his convictions. But he was far from benign – no, he was the furthest thing from it. He was a force to be reckoned with on the order of a natural disaster, but she couldn't figure out if he was good or evil, or even if he could be equated with the traditional forms of right and wrong. He was a being completely outside of any human's grasp, and possibly outside of the grasp of human morals or ethics.

But that just made him more dangerous, not less. She had seen him: those chimerical eyes, which seemed to portray his emotions when his face could not. She had watched, spellbound, as that energy power of his had healed Richard's broken bones as easily as she got dressed in the morning. Turu was so full of enigmas and power that it made him the most dangerous thing she had ever encountered in her life. One wrong move and he could probably tear her limb from limb, if not cell from cell, with his mind alone. And any technology he possessed, she knew, would dwarf that of humans by a gulf larger than the space between stars.

70

She rolled over, staring out his window. The snow had slowed down; gentle flakes drifting out of the heavens as she watched. No more quasi-blizzards to hem them in and, come morning, they would probably be heading out. A part of her couldn't wait to get out of here, but another part wanted to stay. To figure out the mystery that was Turukaishal.

Victoria sighed, closing her eyes and blocking out the vision of the slowly falling flakes beyond the windowpane. She would have to do her best to convince Turu that her species deserved to live. That was all she *could* do. She couldn't fight, and even Richard, who had a natural proclivity for combat, wouldn't be able to win in a fight with the psychic alien. If this month didn't convince him that they didn't deserve destruction… if he chose to wipe them out anyway…

She didn't feel fear anymore, nor did she feel anger. She felt only a deep, deep sadness. Because if Turukaishal, as empathetic as he was, had to wipe them out, the guilt would haunt him for the rest of his life.

Chapter 12

BEGIN MESSAGE

LOCATION: Demon Nebula

TIME: UNAVAILABLE, IN TRANSIT

MESSAGE: *Turukaishal, I am beginning to think the Mindbank regrets sending you on this farcical mission. And rightfully so. Most of the Scain Empire is familiar with your penchant for failure. Need I bring up missions like Limkalan or Dayislia? I didn't think so. Furthermore, you have always been the nosy type; likely to jeopardize the mission with "independent investigations". Don't.*

Your last report indicated that you had established benign contact with a pair of local lifeforms – "Richard" and "Victoria". With such brutish, alien names it is hard to imagine them as anything other than monsters. Just saying the words aloud is enough to make my tongues burn. What kind of creatures are you digging up down there, Turukaishal? Anyway, your mission and your competence are not the focus of this message.

I wish for you to abandon the current mission immediately and head toward Belphan. It is a small ice planet orbiting the blue star Kuroma in the Demon Nebula. The coordinates are encoded into your ship's systems… or they should be, unless you are as competent with your computers are you are with military missions. Contact me immediately when you depart, and I expect to hear from you in no less than four local rotations.

And one more thing, Turukaishal: no matter what mission you undertake, we both know that Sovakadris is going to choose me to succeed him. I'm the logical choice with the experience, age and wisdom to succeed him. Do yourself a favor: save face and pull out now.

-Demnechi, Minister of Public Affairs

Oh sure. It wasn't enough that they shunted him way out here to the edge of nowhere to monitor some little ball of dirt, but now they wanted him back? So soon? He frowned. He'd made a pledge to Victoria and Richard, so he couldn't just up and leave, not that he wanted obey Demnechi anyway. He rested his hand on his forehead, sighing. He had awoken prior to the Vahran and successfully retrieved his communicator from the study without awakening either of them. And there, among the usual messages (such as unsolicited advice from his father and pleas to return from his betrothed) was this message from the Minister of Public Affairs.

Of all Scain, Turukaishal literally *hated* Demnechi. He was a politician to the core, and was often sadistic and cold in his serpentine, offhand manner. He would insult anyone lower than his station with the same casual air as one commenting on the color of the plants in the garden. He had clawed his way to the Mindbank's Cabinet and was the only Minister to carry a knife... probably so he'd be ready when he got his comeuppance and someone stabbed HIM in the back like he'd done to so many others.

The last time the two had met (outside of the political dance floor, anyway) had been five rotations before Turukaishal had left for Earth, on the landing pad outside the Mindbank's Tower. Turukaishal had disembarked and found himself staring face to face with that sickly smirk Demnechi was renowned for. He wanted nothing more than to wipe that conceited half-smile from the Minister's face, preferably with a high impact round. Demnechi had come out to congratulate Turukaishal on the successful repulsion of a Constellation attack on a mining rig in the asteroid belt of Horakameston. After praising him for defeating every assailant, he had promptly asked how many of his team Turukaishal had allowed to die *this* time.

Turukaishal had walked off without a word, although the temptation to Psionically throw him from the landing pad had been immense, to say the least. Demnechi had the uncanny ability to learn things about others and use them as ammunition, and Turukaishal had long ago grown sick of it. If it wasn't for the politician's stellar public reputation, he probably would have been ousted long ago. But the two-faced idiot had managed to become a public favorite while weaseling and knifing his way up the political ladder. It made Turukaishal sick.

"Trouble back home?" Turukaishal jumped a bit, having been so lost in his fantasies of feeding Demnechi to the Anu'bai piece by piece that he hadn't heard Richard sit up behind him. Turukaishal sighed, shaking his head. He hadn't bothered to revert back to his human body. Yet. These two Vahran knew very well what he was.

"A politician is being... a politician," he said at length. "He wants me to leave Earth in under four rotat—days."

"Oh? You're leaving?" Victoria asked from the doorway, combing her long brown hair with her fingertips. Turukaishal had a strange urge to reach out and touch it. Scain had no hair. What did it feel like? He bit back the impulse, shaking his head.

"No. Regardless of what he wants, I agreed to stay here for thirty. I am going to inform Demnechi of this development and tell him to retract his order."

"And if he doesn't?" Richard asked, stretching. Turukaishal could hear his vertebrae popping. The couch wasn't the most ergonomic place to sleep if you wanted proper spinal alignment; he knew from experience.

"He will have to be patient," Turukaishal said. "My species may not be the nicest in the Galaxy, but we honor our promises." He rose, leaving the communicator open on his desk. Victoria peered curiously at it from a distance for a moment before looking at him. He looked back, keeping his eyes carefully black. "What is the first item on your itinerary?" he asked her.

"Well," she said with a small smile, sitting down next to her brother, "I was thinking we could play a little 'game'." Richard clapped a hand over his face, mumbling something about being childish into his palm before slumping down on the couch. She elbowed him in the arm. Turukaishal seated himself in the seat opposite the coffee table, appraising them. He felt uncomfortable under their gazes, but surmised that they probably felt equally at ease under his. They were, after all, aliens to each other.

"What kind of game?" he asked, sighing hesitantly. Scain didn't really play games that much. There was usually too much to do.

"It's called 'Twenty Questions'," Victoria said happily. "You ask us each ten questions, since there are two of us, and we ask you twenty. This way, we learn a bit about each other. It wouldn't be fair if we started this month without knowing anything about the other, would it?"

Turukaishal mulled this over. If they became too inquisitive, he couldn't lie. Not without his eyes giving him away, although he doubted they could tell what each color meant. Yet. Still, she had a point, and he couldn't deny that he would probably learn something about these two. Although her request was childish, there was no harm in taking her request. "Very well," he said, "which of you would care to begin?"

"Me!" Victoria said, grinning even wider. Turukaishal wondered if it was possible for her face to split in two. Hers looked like it was getting close. "First me, then you, then Richard before we start over again. Sound good?"

"Why am I always last?" Richard muttered, folding his arms behind his head and staring up at the ceiling. He looked to be lost in thought, probably thinking up his question.

"Alright Turu," Victoria said, reclining next to her brother. "What planet are you from?"

"I am not from a planet, I was born on a moon," he said simply. Nice and vague, the way he wanted it to sound. Victoria opened her mouth to protest, but he was already speaking. "My turn: why are you not afraid of me?"

74

She swallowed her protest, looking at him strangely. "Should I be? I always believed there was other life out there, and now I get to sit and talk with it. I'm excited, not scared."

Richard sat forward with a grunt, his elbows on his knees and his chin resting on laced fingers. His gray eyes bored holes in Turukaishal more effectively than any laser his kind had. "My turn," he said. "Can you tell us about your birthplace?"

"I was born on Velis," he said. No way of getting out of Richard's question. "It is the fourth moon of seven orbiting the methane-ammonia gas giant of Alpidra. Of the seven moons, it is one of three to have a moon of its own, and is one of only four habitable worlds. Velis is the primary world, whereas Manaeus, Khlorae and Velis' moon, Chalis, are the secondary colonies. Velis is slightly smaller than this world, and is always covered with an orange haze, broken up only by greenish clouds. The atmosphere of argon, xenon and hydrogen make for a warm, lush planet while the trace ammonia and methane make for intriguing flora and fauna."

"So much for a visit," Victoria huffed. "I don't think we can breath—HEY! How can you breathe our air then?!" she jumped up. "We breathe nitrogen and oxygen."

"I believe you must save that for your turn," Turukaishal said calmly, smirking to himself at her outburst. "That can be your next question, but it's my turn now." She sat back down, fuming as he watched. Richard was watching her with a sidelong, amused look on his face. Turukaishal cleared his throat. "Richard," he said, attempting to pronounce the alien name. It unfortunately came out as Reech-ahrd. He winced. "Why do you carry a cane when you obviously do not need it as a locomotion aid?"

Richard smirked at him, his eyes glittering. "Very good. I'd expect no less from an alien." He picked up his cane and showed it to Turukaishal. "I'm not the most popular guy around here, as I've bailed out Vicky from a few sticky spots with a bit more force than was probably needed. Some folks feel like they have to get even or prove something, so I carry this." He gave one end a twist and a pull, and the cane slid apart. Turukaishal had to fight down the urge to lean away from the keen, two-foot blade which glittered in the morning light streaming through his windows. "Now I've never had to do more than threaten with the blade," Richard reassured him, "but the whole thing makes a pretty handy beating stick when some folks step out of line."

Turukaishal sat back, appraising him. He'd been right in his assumptions. Richard Sinclair was a dangerous individual if provoked. He would probably have either drawn the sword or laid about with the casing had the Scain made an aggressive motion toward Victoria. Turukaishal shuddered, remembering the look Richard had given him in the coffee shop.

"My turn," Victoria said. "Same question – about the atmospheres."

"I take an injection of protites—small medical robots—which reside in my lung," Turukaishal explained. "They convert incoming elements into argon, xenon or hydrogen by altering the positions of protons, neutrons or electrons. They do not produce methane or ammonia, as the trace amounts are very low. Upon exhaling, the elements are changed back." He stared evenly at her. "Why would you want to visit Velis?"

"Come on, *seriously?*" she asked. "Visiting another planet...er...moon? Getting off Earth? That would be so cool! Right Richard?" her brother made a noncommittal noise, shrugging. His eyes never left Turukaishal. "Are there protites which allow us to breathe your atmosphere?"

The Scain paused for a moment. "Yes," he said delicately, "I only keep enough of a dose up here for one organism, though, so I cannot permit you to have any. He reached over and turned off his communicator as it hummed on the table. This was painful. They had only asked three questions out of twenty? He'd only asked two of his? This could go on forever! Maybe he could convince them to postpone the game. Before he could even try, he realized that Victoria wouldn't let him. He sighed. "Victoria," he said, his tongue once more betraying him. Veek-torry-ah. "Why did you offer to aid me on our first meeting?"

"Because no one likes being covered in hot coffee," she said. "It's the right thing to do, you know. I saw that from the coffee shop and you looked like you needed a hand."

Richard sighed, massaging the bridge of his nose. It looked like he was having as much "fun" as Turukaishal himself. He leaned forward, resting his palms atop his cane. "You said you only keep enough protites 'up here'? What or where is 'down there', then?"

Turukaishal shook his head. "Smarter than I gave you credit for, Vahran, and definitely more observant. This structure is built atop my sole method of exit: my spacecraft."

The silence in the room was palpable as both Richard and Victoria looked at the floor in surprise. As one, as if their minds were liked by some kind of gestalt connection, they looked back up at him. Their eyes spoke volumes. Richard was alarmed, his aura having become orange and jagged. Victoria was excited, hers filled with yellows and whites, a few purples weaving through the lighter parts. Their auras had become so vastly different it was hard to consider them siblings. Turukaishal decided to speak before they passed out from shock. "Richard, you mentioned in the coffee shop that there were individuals who were after Victoria. Why?"

"I thought I told you," he said. "Apparently a lot of guys think she's cute or pretty or whatever. One of them already decided to push things a bit too far and I ended up thrashing him. Hasn't wholly given up yet, though... might need to do it again." Victoria slapped his bicep, blushing.

Turukaishal filed this away for future reference, although he wasn't exactly certain why. Richard stood up, walking around the couch and bracing his arms against it. He stretched in a very feline manner, his back popping again. Apparently he suffered from stiffness. Victoria, having gotten over her blush, was beaming from ear to ear. "Okay! This is going well. My turn, huh? Let's see... hmmmmm..."

Chapter 13

BEGIN MESSAGE

LOCATION: Velis, Departure Station 089

TIME: 19/30 Local Time

MESSAGE: *Son, I know we have never been on the best of terms, but I recently heard about your deployment to Earth, and wanted to at least tell you that I wish you the best.*

Demnechi came around here about a week ago... What happened on Dayislia was not your fault, Turukaishal. I just want you to know that. You were acquitted – everyone else knew what I knew from the beginning. No matter what anyone says, you were innocent. We both know that. I know you blame yourself – I cannot say I would be different – but I just wanted to let you know.

I will be departing for Sillothel come morning. They want me to assist the Heil in the reconfiguring of some of their shuttles. I cannot say I enjoy working with them, but if it is for the good of the alliance, I will do what they ask. It is the Visoth that I do not trust. That tribal lifestyle of theirs bothers me, I suppose.

Are Vahran all that we've believed them to be? The Mindbank certainly does not seem pleased with some of your reports. At first, he was as pleasant as can be. But as soon as you established viable contact, he began to sour. Is something going on that I do not know? Please, if something troubles you, share it with me. I know I may not be the best one to offer guidance, but I can try.

I wish you well, son.

-Ferthoroyia

"So," Richard said after what felt like hours of this grueling interrogation, "what is your race like politically?" his fingers drummed on his thigh as he watched Turukaishal, waiting for an answer. The Scain sighed. When would this end?!

"The Mindbank," Turukaishal said, "rules the entire empire from his seat on the planet Chindrus. "He has a cabinet of ten Ministers, each one claiming dominion over certain portions of government. For example, one of the oldest Ministers is Castator, the Minister of Foreign Affairs, while one of the youngest is Aquon, the Minister of Public

Relations. Our political state could be considered a monarchy or a dictatorship, although neither really applies in our case. We elect the Mindbank in a democratic fashion, but it is from choices the previous Mindbank put in place, so it could resemble a dynasty. I am loath to call the Mindbank a dictator, though, as he has always had the empire's best interests at heart and such a title carries much negativity."

Richard sank back into the couch. "I agree. Dictators are generally considered tyrants."

"Quite. Now for something a bit mundane…" Turukaishal was running out of questions to ask these two, and had settled for picking them apart as individuals rather than as members of a species. "How did you get that scar above your eye?" He'd been meaning to find an opportunity to ask. The scar wasn't very noticeable, but fractured in every direction like spider webs as it arched above Richard's right eyebrow. The human reached up to touch it instinctively.

"I got in a fight," he said with a halfhearted smile. "Some punk started flailing punches and one of them caught Vicky in the side of the head. I told him he had five seconds to get out of my sight before I sterilized him, and he broke a beer bottle on my face. I had so many cuts I'm surprised I only have one scar."

Turukaishal snorted quietly. Evidently the Mindbank hadn't been *completely* wrong about these creatures. "Hmm… well, your defense of your sister is certainly admirable. Your turn, Victoria."

She watched him intently. "Are there lots of aliens?"

"Dozens of species," Turukaishal said. "We have confirmed sixty-eight. If you will give me a moment, I can show you."

Both Vahran jerked slightly as he stood up, towering over them. Victoria turned her emerald gaze to her brother, as if asking for permission. Richard nodded. "Alright," she said, "come back soon!"

Turukaishal walked over to the closet, scooping up the protites as he went. He would need them. He stepped inside, opening the small section of the wall paneling that revealed the keypad for his airlock and inputting his code. As the airlock began running the decompression protocols and descending, he injected himself with the protites so as not to suffocate when he reached the bottom. He felt the familiar tingle as he passed the electromagnetic grille that held the atmosphere inside his ship, before the elevator reached the bottom, the doors sliding open to reveal the short hallway to his lab.

His Psionics lifted every last knickknack from the shelves, drawing them into a slow spiral around his head. He could almost hear his father's voice in his head, reminding him that if he kept his ship cleaner he wouldn't have to expend his Psionics looking for things. Turukaishal sighed, selecting a small square device and letting it circle his head in a tight, retrograde orbit as he returned the other objects to various shelves, desktops and drawers.

One of his favorite acquisitions was an Alintean "Data Pad". It was an all-purpose information storage, retrieval and analysis tool with a multiform communications array. He took it from near his head and turned back to the door, levitating it around his hand as he walked. The only time the Scain paused in his stride was to snatch a handful of mixed protite tubes out of the tray near the door. If he was temporarily allying with these Vahran, he would probably be coming down here quite often. It would pay to have tubes for both entry and exit. Just in case.

"Here," he said as he reentered the room. The syringes floated spectrally over to the bowl on the table, lining themselves up in it as if by magic as Turukaishal swept across the room. He placed the Data Pad on the table in front of the two Vahran, the screen side facing up. "Let me show you a few of the other aliens that exist out there beyond your atmosphere." One of his long fingers tapped the screen. It lit up red for a moment, the machine coming to life after a month or more of inactivity. Turukaishal waited until it switched to an ochre gold before he ran his hand through the space above his chest. As before, blue light leapt from his heart and wove around his fingers. He cast it around the room, closing all the windows and turning off all the lights in one fluid motion.

He tapped a few more things on the Pad before sitting back. A hologram erupted from the screen, prompting both Vahran to jump back and take the couch with them. At first, the shape was formless – a random conglomerate of colors and mist – but it soon solidified into a cohesive shape: the Milky Way. Even in the darkness, Turukaishal's eyes seemed to glow *through* the projection – a pair of dark ovals which peered eerily at them out of the galaxy's center. "This, as I am certain you know, is the Galaxy our races share," he said.

Richard nodded. Victoria reached out and ran her fingers through one of the spiral arms of the hologram. As to be expected of Alintean cohesive light images, it swirled and danced around her fingers like smoke. As soon as she removed her fingers, though, the gas and stars returned to their positions. Turukaishal watched her for a moment, shaking his head at her silent wonder. If only all Vahran were like this.

"This," he said, "is Earth." A tiny blue dot lit up in the lower left portion of the Galaxy and some blue lettering appeared outside the perimeter of the Milky Way. Neither Vahran could read Galaxian, so Turukaishal translated. "The writing states that this star is "Oritseal Amiliurnus", which is the Galactic Standard name for your star. One of three-hundred and eighty-seven billion confirmed stars in this Galaxy. Over here, however, is Chindrus: my homeworld..."

About halfway between the blue dot of Earth and the Galactic Center and further along the curve of the Galaxy, a small golden dot appeared. It pulsed for a few seconds before a 'stain' of sorts leaked out of it, encompassing a tiny space around it. "And that area,"

Turukaishal explained, "is the extent of the Scain Empire. All of the planets we control form the border around that area, and we lay claim to the stars falling within it. All told, we own approximately one-hundred and seventy thousand systems."

"Fascinating," Richard said, leaning forward to examine the Galaxy in more detail. "You all are pretty close to us."

"Yes. Only one and a half kiloparsecs away, by human measurements," Turukaishal agreed. Richard watched intently as the golden stain of the Scain Empire passed him as the Galaxy rotated languidly.

"You said there were others?" Victoria asked, looking up at Turukaishal.

The entire Galaxy lit up with a myriad of different lights, each one denoting a race. A large gray ring encompassed the Milky Way, broken at only five points; three of them darker gray, one of them silver and another black. Patches of greens and browns, whites and yellows and every color imaginable dotted the wheel.

"The Galaxy's layout is as follows," Turukaishal explained. "The Senate, the Galactic ruling body to which we belong, owns one-hundred light years in the center of the Galaxy. It is here that their center of power lies. The outer ring of the Galaxy, on the other hand, is lawless territory belonging to the criminal organization known as the Constellation. The Senate has no power there. Now, the Alinteans..." a hologram of one of the bipedal black aliens appeared above the silver stain, "...are one place where the Constellation's territory is fractured. Over here..." he pointed to the silver break "...is the Kelacla Nebula, which sits at the center of an ocean of gravity wells and electromagnetic whirlpools, ion storms and neutrino vortexes. The other three areas are the Verges – areas where massive amounts of rock, debris, ice and metal accumulated after the Galaxy's formation. The Broken, Shattered and Desolate Verges are habitable, but it is extremely dangerous to do so, particularly the Broken Verge, as it lies partially within the Kelacla Nebula's hostile area."

"Wow," Victoria said, her eyes wide as she studied the map. If she reached out and touched any of the colors, there was a flash and an image of the corresponding extraterrestrial appeared above it. She had already gone through and called up images of several, from the trihydrogen-monoxide creatures known as the Arsu to the gold-based Kevilkamas, for which his uncle had been named. Looking at the half-avian creatures made his stomach do an unusual flop, but he pushed on.

"The largest empire," he said, "is the Alintean Empire, spanning just shy of ten million stars. Their homeworld is... here." A tiny silver speck appeared near the very edge of the Galaxy, three quarters of the way around the rim from Earth. "Over here is the Visoth," he continued as he called up an image of the barrel-bodied plants. The hologram walked awkwardly in place, its five legs alternating turns of three against the ground as the pair of wings flapped against its back. Five eyes protruded from around a mouth on top of the head and five more appendages—arms—extended from the leathery body.

Turukaishal did not like the Visoth. They had meddled with Vahran before, and had used them for a variety of experiments. Furthermore, they were far too in depth with psychological hang-ups and studies. Every time he spoke to them, it was as if they were trying to probe his brain. Plus, their knowledge of medicine was as good as that of the Zyzyts, which was the reason Sovakadris had forged an alliance with them. Still, their insect-hybrid nature bothered him extensively. "The Visoth homeworld of Mer is located here," he continued, indicating a red dot to the 'north' of Earth.

A large, four-limbed insect appeared as Victoria touched a tan splotch to the southeast of Earth, and to the south of Chindrus. Fifteen ropy tentacles hung from around the mouth of the four-eyed, chitinous creature as it lumbered in place above its empire. She squeaked in fright.

"So, how do you all keep track of who goes where?" Richard asked, resting his elbow on his knee as he studied the Galaxy. "I mean politically. You've explained your planet, and mentioned this Senate, but how do things actually WORK?"

Turukaishal waved his hand and the images of all the extraterrestrials vanished. The Galaxy stood upright on its end, retaining the colored blotches, before splitting into five parts. The center of the Galaxy remained as a circle while four wedges were carved from the outermost portions. The area consisting of Constellation Space, the Kelacla Nebula and the three Verges vanished.

"Each of these four sections," Turukaishal explained, "is governed by a Triumvirate of the three largest races in that sector. Each Triumvirate responds directly to the Senate, located here in the center of the Galaxy. All of the races have representatives in both the Triumvirates and the Senate, but are encouraged to attempt to solve issues on the Triumvirate level rather than the Senate level. There are two-hundred and twenty-two laws, but apart from them, 'law' is left open to the interpretation of the Triumvirate in which the crime or issue is occurring."

"So you're over here in this one with us?" Victoria asked, pointing to one of the Galaxy's slices.

"Yes. Our Triumvirate is formed from the Scain, Taeski and Heil, but we also oversee the Iharsh-Daraz, Visoth and Kevilkamas." He pointed to the corresponding colors: Scain were gold, Taeski were dark brown, Heil were white, the Iharsh-Daraz were the tan insects which had frightened Victoria, the Visoth were red and the Kevilkamas were yellow. "Our Mindbank is both the Triumvirate Seat and the Senate Seat, which worries me a bit, but that is the extent of Galactic Politics. Or enough to give you an inchoate understanding of it."

"Why are you worried?" Victoria asked.

"Well, the Senate controls almost everything," Turukaishal said. "If someone were to harm the Senate, the echoes would be great. The Scain would lose their Mindbank *and* their Senate-Triumvirate representative. But worse still, there are some races which are not at war only because the Senate prevents it. For example, the Iharsh-Daraz will attack almost anything, but have a special grudge for the Heil. If the Senate fell, war would break out in at least nine places throughout the Galaxy."

"And what would become of Earth?" Richard asked.

"Earth lies directly between the Heil and the Iharsh-Daraz," Turukaishal said gravely. "You would be caught in the middle of a battlefield between the two most violent races in the Galaxy."

Chapter 14

BEGIN MESSAGE: SECURE TRANSMISSION GRADE V: MINDBANK SECURE LINE

LOCATION: SOL3, NORTHERN HEMISPHERE

TIME: 2/24 Local Time

MESSAGE: Your eminence. I mean no disrespect by this message, but I am beginning to doubt the mission to which I have been assigned. I was instructed to study a race that had self-destructed beyond all hope, and had destroyed their planet. Instead, I found a world of lush greenery. Yes, there are deserts, but this world is far closer to Nihran than it is to Volomir.

Furthermore, after some remote study, I am beginning to theorize that Vahran are possessed by equal portions of darkness and light. Certainly there is an alarming number who choose the wrong path – at least forty percent, to be certain – but we cannot ignore the fact that a greater number remain neutral or choose their good side.

I am currently in contact with a pair of these "Good" Vahran, as you are aware. I have also received a message from Demnechi requesting that I abort this mission, but I have, unfortunately, not yet completed my assignment. To withdraw now would cause suspicion. I would need at least thirty-five days before a retreat would be possible. Please grant me this length of time with your blessing and I wish you well in all your duties.

-Turukaishal

Turukaishal couldn't deny that he was nervous as he trudged along behind the pair of Vahran the next day. The two had stayed another night, as the snow would make it difficult to leave, but the morning had only brought more of the accursed white fluff. Finally, in an act of desperation, Turukaishal had used his Psionics to free them from the lower reaches of the forest and set them on the path. Now, as he walked along behind them (obviously in his human disguise) he began to wonder about his decision.

It wasn't that they had done anything – quite the contrary. Richard had evidently expended some thought to thinking up a believable background story for him – namely that he was an astronomy professor coming to see where his father had grown up – while Victoria was happily prancing around as she regaled him with tales of the friends she and Richard were going to introduce him to. He chewed his lip – yet another portion of his anatomy he was unused to – as they walked.

The snow made the terrain beautiful in a haunting, dead sort of way. Every now and then, the silence would remind him of the Nazqiat Crystallands on Nihran, buried deep within the bowels of the Alintean continent of Mengaia, but Victoria's happy chatter usually broke him out of these thoughts. The Nazqiat Crystallands were a cold, whitish set of caverns in which aetherium crystals grew like weeds. Rainbow-hued fungi grew at the base of the colossal structures while underground streams and rivers burbled quietly through the empty halls. It was like having set foot into a place where life should not tread.

This, though, was a cool and crisp winter's day. The snow fell off and on as they walked, clouding his sunglasses and sticking to his face. Even amidst the calm, he could see groups of children playing in the fields to his left, building snow forts and crude, spherical representations of people before dolling them up with hats and scarves. Did they not know that dressing these bizarre sculptures in warm clothing would make them melt quicker? Evidently not. They also chose to waste vegetables and stones to simulate lopsided, grinning faces.

"Might I ask what those children are doing?" he asked at last, gesturing with one of his long fingers towards a cluster of the unusual effigies.

"They're building snowmen," Victoria said. "Come on, I'll show you!"

Turukaishal felt her grab his hand before he had time to process the information about 'snowmen'. Richard sighed, chuckling dryly. "I'll go tell the others you'll be a minute," he said, turning and walking away before Victoria could rope him into this inanity. Turukaishal, on the other hand, had already been ensnared. Her grip was surprisingly firm as she pulled him off the sidewalk and into the shin-deep (for her) snow.

The Scain stood there, watching her for a moment and feeling ridiculously out of place as he watched her pick up two fistfuls of snow and pack them together into a sphere. "Okay, watch closely," she said as she began to roll the ball of snow around on the ground, more and more accreting to it until it stood as high as her knees. Turukaishal reached down, one of his hands scooping up as much snow as had fit in both of hers, and packed it into a sphere as well, squeezing the soft, cold material between his fingers.

By the time he looked up again, Victoria's sphere was as high as her waist. He blinked. "Is that not a bit large?" he asked.

"No!" she said, grinning happily even though she was breathing hard. "Look, make another one with me, about half the size."

Turukaishal set his fistful of snow on the ground, squatting awkwardly down to begin pushing it around until it was about as big as his head. Victoria was already rolling another one and he shuffled awkwardly around as he tried to keep the large snowball in a "spherical" shape as opposed to a "wheel". Finally, he stood up and admired his handiwork. "Alright," he said. "Now what is this supposed to accomplish?"

Victoria grabbed his and grunted as she tried to lift it. Sighing, one finger massaging his nose, he gripped the sphere in his hands and subtly used his Psionics to lift it. She stuck her tongue out at him. "Cheater," she said, chuckling. "Put it on top of the first."

Turukaishal easily placed the sphere atop her first, the entire collection barely reaching his stomach. Victoria lifted hers, smaller even than his, and placed it on top before she pulled off her scarf and wrapped it around the top one. Turukaishal stood back and watched as she collected several sticks and stones, gifting her creation with them in a crude semblance of "arms" and "facial features" before stepping back and smiling proudly. "See? It looks like a person," she said happily.

"It looks no more like a person than a bird does a fish," he said flatly. "What is this supposed to accomplish, again, besides making me doubt your sanity?"

She stuck her tongue out at him again, and Turukaishal realized she only had one, as opposed to the two he kept hidden in his mouth and pressed together to enable him to speak her language. "It's just for fun," she told him. "Geez, you really don't know how to have a good time, do you?"

Turukaishal walked over to her 'snowman', examining it with a careful eye. He still couldn't see any resemblance between it and, say, her. He placed his hands on the sides of the construction's "waist", funneling his Psionics into it. The snow flaked off, splattering wetly against the ground as Victoria let out a dismayed moan... which quickly changed to a gasp as he removed his hands. The snow had dropped to the ground to reveal a solidified mass of near-ice which was an identical sculpture to her. He looked back at her, unable to keep a smirk off his face. "*This* is a snowman," he said, "or, as the case may be, a snow-woman."

Victoria examined it from all sides, gaping. "How... you big cheat! That's not fair!" she whined. Everything was perfect, down to the proportions of her nose and lips. "But it's really cool."

"I'll say," Richard said from his position leaning on the tree behind them. "Ambrose says take your time, and Turu... nice job."

Turukaishal's eyes turned pink behind his glasses as he absently scratched at his forehead. "Um... thank you," he said. He looked up at Richard in time to see the youth's eyes widen. He turned around to see what was causing the stoic man such consternation when something cold and wet splattered against the side of his head. He leapt in alarm, his hands coming up in preparation to defend himself. Victoria squealed with laughter and Richard chuckled, shaking his head.

A child, probably no older than nine, mumbled an apology before running away to join the throng of peers he'd been playing with before throwing the snowball. His cohorts were busy lobbing the spherical missiles at one another, and a stray projectile had chosen Turukaishal's face as its final resting place. The Scain stood there for a moment, as if trying to decide what to do, before he slowly lowered his hands. "Will someone explain to me exactly what THAT was?" he asked, reaching up to adjust his glasses while wiping the snow from his face.

Victoria covered her mouth with one of her hands. "It's a snowball fight. You've never had one?"

Turukaishal stared at her blankly. A snowball fight? What in the Hiin…?

"Basically," Richard said, "you scoop up some snow and pack it into a ball." he demonstrated as he spoke, his long-fingered hands moving over the slush as he sculpted it into a beautiful sphere, "Then you try to throw it at someone and hit them more times than they can hit you. It's one of the best winter games." He punctuated his statement by throwing his model snowball at the back of Victoria's head.

"Hey!" she yelled, scooping up a fistful of snow and throwing it back at her brother. He sidestepped, the snow barely dusting his black hat, as he looked at Turukaishal to see if the Scain understood. Turukaishal reached down, picking up a fistful of snow. Before he could even straighten up, one of the little demons from earlier threw another snowball their way. It sailed over his stooped form and collided solidly with the back of Victoria's neck. She shrieked as the snow made its way down her collar and whirled around to face Turukaishal. "YOU!"

Before he had time to do anything more than raise his hands to plead his innocence, her snowball (which had originally been meant for Richard) splattered in his face. He froze again before letting his hands lower to the snow-covered ground. This was a game, according to Richard, so why not bend their rules a bit…?

Richard and Victoria moaned and shrieked respectively as a multitude of snowballs apparently formed from nothing and launched themselves from out of the snow-covered ground. Turukaishal kept one hand on the ground, the other resting on his knee as he formed missile after missile, splattering the two Vahran as they raced back and forth, trying to dodge his Psionic snowballs. The little devils in the other field couldn't see him very well in his stooped position, and the hedge to his right shielded him from curious passers-by on the road. He was safe abusing his heritage.

"Just remember," he told the two as they ran around trying to dodge his attack. "Anything a Vahran can do, a Scain can do better."

Richard rolled under a snowball and launched a frosty missile straight into Turukaishal's chest. The Scain looked down, torn between amusement and irritation, before smirking. So they wanted to play hardball? Fine. He reached down with his other hand, manually forming a snowball as big as Richard's head. The Vahran took one look at it and backpedaled as Turukaishal stood up, holding the sphere between his hands. "You're right Richard," he said. "This *is* fun."

Chapter 15

CHECKING FOR NEW MESSAGES...

...CHECKING...

...CHECKING...

...CHECKING...

...CHECKING...

...CHECKING...

...NO NEW MESSAGES. ENTERING HIBERNATION MODE.

Their destination was a small library located about ten minutes from the site of frosty battle; an old brick building with sad looking trees standing out front and a few taller trees ones in back, their bases overgrown with thicker bushes. Plaques in front of the weak, snow-covered trees were completely hidden by the cold white slush, obfuscating any words they vainly tried to convey. As Richard and Victoria led him to the front door, he was surprised to see them slide open on their own. He inhaled, the smell wafting out filling his nostrils. It was an old, papery smell – something that reminded him of age or death.

Strangely enough, it evoked images of the Archival Halls on Chindrus. The large, domed structure dominated the southern part of the Amara District, the interiors containing preserved copies of ancient manuscripts dating all the way back to the Fourth Era, when the Scain met their Erythian ancestors, and even further back to when the Scain still carved on stones or burned their lettering on the flat leaves of the Engarava trees. Large, cylindrical file depositories contained more recent data, leading all the way up to the Nineteenth Era. The Twentieth Era was just beginning, starting with Mindbank Escandul, the predecessor of Sovakadris.

Turukaishal shifted restlessly as he passed through the doors, feeling an unusual pang of longing for his homeworld. He was on EARTH and he was thinking about Chindrus. He had to focus despite his urge to race back to his ship and take off... immediately, if possible. It was like planetary claustrophobia or interstellar wanderlust. He shook his head, squaring his shoulders. He was a *Scain*... and a Wing Commander of the Mindbank's Black Fleet. He could handle almost anything.

Emphasis on the 'almost'...

"Turu?" Victoria asked, turning and giving him a concerned look. "Are you alright?" Richard, too, had paused and was looking back at him. Turukaishal shook off his thoughts and any reservations that remained, burying them in the deepest recesses of his brain and stepping inside, following them into the library. He looked around at all the shelves, his eyes widening slightly behind his glasses. Books... despite having one or two in his apartment as decoration, he'd never bothered picking one up. All he had was a collection of reference books. These were fiction – stories that were untrue, told for the sole purpose of entertainment. Only a few other races wrote fictional stories: the Alinteans and the Taeski being the major two. With the information matrix on this planet, he had almost expected fictional novels in hard copy format to be extinct.

A small group of adolescents was waiting in the back of the building in a little sitting area comprised of a pair of plushy armchairs and a long blue couch. Turukaishal followed Victoria towards them, admiring the different titles on the spines around him. The shelves were at least eight feet high, so he was at least able to remain below their highest point, but if he reverted to his Scain form he'd be able to lean over the top of the highest shelves easily.

"Hey Richard!" one of the teens said, waving as their group approached. She spared Turukaishal a brief look before turning her glance back to Richard, blinking, and then doing a double take to look back at Turukaishal. The Scain suddenly felt the two other Vahran staring at him as well, as if he was an intruder. He panicked, although he refused to show it. Had he broken some social rule?

"Hello," Richard said as he breezed past the group without even looking at t hem, straightening a book on the shelf before drawing one out and sitting down in the sole vacant armchair, opening it in his long fingers and removing his hat. Victoria walked up a moment later, greeting her friends. Turukaishal quickly scanned the group: two females, one with brown hair and one with black, and a freakishly pale male. Nothing he couldn't handle if he had to.

"Guys, this is Turu," Victoria said, gesturing towards him. "Turu, this is Ashley Day, Jolene Buckley and Ambrose Spire; three of my best friends."

The first girl, Ashley, looked at Turukaishal from behind a pair of reading glasses. Her black hair hung to her shoulders, perfectly straight, and she had a relatively pretty heart-shaped face with a pert little nose. There was a smattering of freckles across the bridge of her nose, and her green eyes looked inquisitive. "Wow... you're tall..." she said, staring at him. She gave him a quick once-over before sitting back in the other armchair. Turukaishal rolled his eyes. A regular genius, this one... Jolene, the brown haired girl, shot her a quick glare before speaking.

"Hi, I'm Jolene. How are you? Did you just move here?" she asked, standing up to extend a hand to him. Turukaishal took it, shaking it as he'd often seen other Vahran do.

"You could say that," he said politely. "I just decided to spend a month or two in the area where my father was born." Thank the Mindbank for Richard and his airtight backstory.

"Oh? And where are you from?" she asked, smiling.

"I prefer not to say," Turukaishal said. "I—" he paused, a peculiar tingling rippling up his spine. He looked around, curious, before ignoring it. Usually he wouldn't just pass off such a feeling – a spike in the surrounding energy – but the only alternative would have been to revert to his Scain body to track it down. As a Vahran, he only knew that the surge had, indeed, occurred... but not from where. It was maddening. He occupied himself by shaking the hands of the other two Vahran – Ashley and the white-haired, pale youth by the name of Ambrose.

Victoria and Ashley immediately sank into a deep conversation. Apparently the latter had been unable to take a test due to an illness and had been offered a chance to retake it. The former was helping her study, but hadn't been able to really set a date. Their current conversation hinged on finding a date when they could get together. Julian and Richard were both reading, the former engaged in *The Complete Book of Origami: Step by Step Instructions for over 1000 Diagrams* (Turukaishal had absolutely NO idea what Origami was, but it looked complicated) while Richard had his nose buried in *The Art and Science of Fencing*. The question now was whether "fencing" referred to erecting barriers to keep neighbors or pests out or whether it pertained to selling stolen goods. Stranger still was the image of a dome-handled, bladeless sword on the cover. Jolene, however, was staring intently at the side of his head. He slowly turned to face her. "Is something the matter?" he asked.

"I've just never seen someone, as Ash said, as tall as you," she admitted. "Do you play basketball?"

Turukaishal had never heard of it. Instead, he answered with candid honesty. "No, I'm an amateur astronomer and part-time astronomy professor," he said as he leaned back. Okay, maybe it wasn't complete honesty – that would have been messy – but with as much honesty as his cover would allow.

"Cool!" she said, her eyes lighting up. "You're a teacher? You're only what, twenty?"

"Twenty-five," he said, rounding his Earth age.

"Please do not forget that Ms. Albertson at the middle school is only twenty-two," Richard muttered as he put his book back on the shelf. He picked up a display model on the table – a thick volume entitled *Foucault's Pendulum* – and sat back down. "And if I recall correctly, Miss Albright is a year younger."

"Okay, so there're younger. It's not that common!" Jolene said with a frown. "Most teachers are in their thirties or forties, and that creep Mr. Reeves is eighty-six!"

Richard shrugged, not looking up from the book. Jolene watched him for a moment longer, her eyes searching his face as if waiting for a response before turning back to Turukaishal. "Well at least *someone* around here knows something," she said. "The Astronomy professor at the college is a blithering idiot…"

"According to my dossiers, many people are," Turukaishal said mildly, looking at the various signs hanging from the ceiling. Curiosity tunneled its way upwards from the depths of his mind. Science Fiction? He remembered reading about this particular genre, and it usually garnered skepticism and mockery… but what DID Vahran believe to be out there? He resisted the urge to jump up and go grab a book.

Jolene laughed. "Trust me, if you think the teachers around here are bad, you should see some of the students," she said. "This one kid was bet twenty bucks he wouldn't snort hot sauce and they ended up taking him away in an ambulance."

Turukaishal stared at her in mute shock. Were some Vahran actually that stupid? Before he could answer her, he felt the energy spike again. Closer. This time, he looked around as casually as possible for anyone who might be causing it. There were very few things that could cause such a surge; a few other races and some machinery – usually on the order of fusion plants or antimatter reactors. The only machinery he could see was a quartet of computers… and those were incapable of triggering his Psionic reflexes. Therefore…

Turukaishal rested the bridge of his nose against his fingertips, slowly expanding his Psionics in the same manner as he'd used to locate Richard and Victoria. He had to be careful – in his human form he couldn't abuse his power, and he was still recovering from the use of the Booster. The last thing he wanted was a stroke in the middle of the library… a stroke which would undoubtedly shatter his disguise. He allowed the dome to continue expanding, engulfing the group of people he was sitting with. All of them showed normal human vital signs – no abnormalities which could be responsible for the energy surge.

He expanded the dome further, swallowing up a few of the nearby aisles. He was almost at his limit when he felt the unusual signature enter his field of awareness. It felt as if someone had just plunged a stone through the fragile wall of the Psionic dome, creating a resonating heaviness in part of his mind, as if there was a pebble lodged in his brain. He chewed his cheek, focusing on it.

The energy was dense and heterochromic, one part of it feeling smooth and calming while the other was a frenzy of aggression. This bipolar energy could only belong to one species – one currently allied with the Scain Empire. Turukaishal excused himself momentarily from the group, standing up and casually browsing the aisles as if studying the tomes contained between the simple metal bookends.

As he walked around the endcap of one of the shelves, he chanced a glance down where he knew the signature was coming from. A woman stood there, her brown hair hanging to her mid-back and her gray eyes staring at him with an unfathomable depth. Her hand was on the bookshelf as if she had paused midway through selecting a book. As he watched, she smirked at him… and then the energy pulse stabbed through his brain again. No doubt about it.

He strolled down the aisle, pausing when he drew near her and facing the opposite shelf, his back to her. Turukaishal knew it was rather risky, turning his back on her, but at the same time it would look a bit too suspicious (especially to Richard and Victoria) if they saw him chatting with this woman as if he knew her. Neither one spoke for several moment, both too absorbed in their respective ruses as they selected and returned books. Finally, Turukaishal broke the silence.

"I know you are a Heil," he said quietly, thumbing through an illustrated novel with images of "little green men" in saucers. Zyzyts. How quaint. He put the book back on the shelf, mentally readying himself in case his quarry attacked.

"And I know you're a Scain," the woman answered, casually thumbing through a book before putting it back on the shelf. "Your point?"

He said nothing, keeping his Psionics trained on her in case she made any move to attack him. As a result, they both turned around at the same time, the Scain finding himself staring into a pair of almost luminous gray eyes. She smirked up at him. "Why don't we step outside and talk?" she asked, smirking. As her lips moved, Turukaishal caught sight of a row of perfectly sharp teeth, each one as triangular and dangerous as those from the maw of a shark. "I'd just *hate* to make a mess of this library…"

"Very well," Turukaishal said, turning and walking back out to his group. He paused behind the sofa, clearing his mind. "Richard. Victoria. I am stepping outside for a moment. I need a breath of fresh air." He waited until Richard acknowledged him before striding out, focused on the Heil's energy signature as she walked out behind him. So focused, in fact, that he didn't detect the third signature at all.

Chapter 16

BEGIN MESSAGE

LOCATION: Chindrus, Amara District

TIME: 6/22 Local time

MESSAGE: *Turukaishal, you are not prone to doing rash things and making impulsive decisions. You are usually calm and rational. But telling the Mindbank that Vahran can change tops the list of idiotic decisions you have made in your life. He has been in a foul mood ever since your message and it has shown down here in the Mind's Quarter. We can see him stalking around the gardens looking as if he is contemplating the mysteries of the universe. That sneaky little runt Demnechi is usually lingering around him like a poisonous shroud as well. Be careful – who knows what he could put the Mindbank up to.*

I must depart for the time being. Your betrothed is driving me absolutely insane with her incessant rambling about you and her worry ever since your last message. Even from hundreds of light years away, you still know how to be something of an irritant, you know that? I am a humble blacksmith who seeks only to tend to his craft and grow old... not your beloved's babysitter and therapist. Please remind her of this when you next speak with her.

-Klakshan

Turukaishal stood in the small copse of trees behind the library, the snow crunching quietly under his boots as he faced the Heil, his arms folded. "I will not deny that I am mildly curious: how did you know I was a Scain?" he asked, drumming his fingers on his bicep as he stared down the shorter alien.

"You're taller than everyone else in the room, wear glasses and act like you've swallowed an iron bar," she said with a casual wave of her hand. "So either you're one heck of an awkward Vahran or you're a Scain in disguise. One pulse of my White Art made you stiffen. You're a Scain."

She, of course, had an easier time disguising herself than he did, Turukaishal supposed as he stared at her. The only physical differences between her and a Vahran were her hair and facial ridges. Heil lacked hair on any part of their bodies—something which this individual had masked with a long brown wig – and the facial ridges and any other minor details (such as four smaller nostrils instead of a Vahran's two) had likely been fixed by cosmetic restructuring. Lastly, her luminescent, pupil-less eyes had been masked by contacts. The glow wasn't going to be visible unless they were in a dark room. She had obviously had prior experience with disguises, as most Heil didn't hide unless they had to.

"Well with that aside, what are you doing here?" Turukaishal had little patience for most Heil, seeing as they had carefully maintained an archaic, clan-based society for several tens of billions of years. Their constant infighting and lust for dominance made Turukaishal sick to his stomach.

"To be frank, I'm here to kill you," the Heil said. "Or I was, anyway. I was sent here to do away with you because you're starting to side with Vahran and that's dangerous. It can't be allowed to continue."

"So, someone thinks I'm siding with these Vahran?" Turukaishal asked, arching an eyebrow as he ground his teeth together. He was going to have a difficult time fending off this Heil if she attacked, especially if he was in his human guise. Heil were fierce warriors and those hailing from Clan Mitragan were the worst of the bunch, easily capable of fighting even when mortally wounded. While unsure of her clan, he suspected that this Heil was of their ilk. "Two of these Vahran," he continued, "claimed that they could prove that their species deserved to live if I gave them thirty days. As an amusement, I agreed to see what they could show me. How is that treason? Heil play far more dangerous games with their prey than that."

"That alone is not treason," the Heil said as she leaned against the wall. Turukaishal's eyes narrowed, sensing a withheld sentence. After several seconds, she sighed and continued. "Look, it's nothing personal, okay? But a girl's got to eat. I take missions when I get them. We both work for a living, it's just that my work happens to entail killing you, get it?"

"So you are a bounty hunter?" Turukaishal asked, mildly surprised. Most of the Heil that left their homeworld of Sovereign were either bounty hunters or mercenaries, especially if they originated in the Mitragan Province. Things were beginning to fall into some sort of order for him. Although he lacked proof, it would make sense for certain people or parties to send a bounty hunter after him.

The Mindbank had recommended two Scain for the throne upon his passing, as was tradition. Of these two nominees, the public would cast a vote to determine which one was fit to rule the Empire. Turukaishal, to his surprise, had been selected as one of them. Demnechi was the other. If Demnechi or his supporters wanted him out of the picture, hiring a bounty hunter to kill him on this mission would be an easy way to do it, especially considering the nature of his objective.

"Well, 'bounty hunter' is kind of generic," the Heil said with a smirk. "I'm one of the best."

Turukaishal snorted, unfolding his arms and glaring at the Heil. "That remains to be seen. Now, are you going to talk me to death, or are we going to engage in combat. If possible, I would prefer not to do it here."

The Heil grinned at him before folding her arms, leaning back on her heels. "I'm not going to kill you just yet. Relax. I was sent here to find a Scain reveling in the world's filth... Unfortunately, I see very little filth and even less of a traitor. This place isn't quite the hellhole I envisioned."

"I had noticed that as well," the Scain answered, his response somewhat guarded. He didn't want to divulge too much information to this Heil, but perhaps the bounty hunter could help him glean some information. He wondered briefly if this was backlash for the message he'd sent the MIndbank. If so, they had already determined that he was guilty and deemed him worthy of execution. Even wanted criminals got a fair trial, so what was going on here? "Furthermore," Turukaishal continued, "only forty percent of Vahran are actually evil, by my estimate. The remainder are either neutral or-"

"Yeah yeah, your report said that," the Heil said with a careless wave of her hand, as if his statement was nothing more than some nugatory pest to be waved away. "Forty percent is still pretty high, though. Either way, if you find any of this supposed 'proof' that these apes deserve to live, let me know. I haven't seen any immediate atrocities, other than how much they charge for grub in this dump, but I don't think it'll be long before I do. Anyway, I'm leaving now. You can consider yourself warned. Go ahead and have fun toadying about with your pet monkeys, but remember: I'm watching you." She narrowed her white-gray eyes at him. "One sign that you're planning on turning traitor and I'm going to cut you down. There's quite a price on your head and like I said: a girl's gotta eat."

Turukaishal lowered his glasses, peering directly at her with his black eyes. His stare booked very little argument. So, she had read his report. That meant that Demnechi or the Mindbank were involved in this... that or there was a mole on Chindrus with a vested interest in seeing him dead. Something was going on here – something deep. He Heil stared at him for a few moments longer before tossing her hair over her shoulder and turning to go. "A pity," she said, "that I was hired to kill you. Your files make you sound like you'd have been a great partner."

He snorted again. "I am not a bounty hunter," he said flatly. "But at least give me the honor of your name, Heil."

"That'll be reserved for later, if we fight," she said, smirking over her shoulder at him. "Until such a time comes, I won't use yours."

"I do not particularly care for your Heil pleasantries," he said. "Use it if you wish. I am certain you know it."

"That I do, Turukaishal," she said, turning and walking away down the sidewalk. He stared after her sighing. Why did things always have to get complicated? He felt his heart begin to return to a more normal tempo. He was still alive, and his innards weren't smeared up the side of the library. That was good. Now he had to consider who would want him dead. Was it the Mindbank? Demnechi? Someone else? And was his report the cause or had this been in the works for a while? A moment later, he was jerked from his reverie by the sound of metal sliding on metal. He whirled around, finding himself staring into the accusing gray eyes of Richard Sinclair.

"So, who was your friend?"

Turukaishal scratched at the back of his head as Richard twirled his cane, stepping forward. "Sorry, but your 'breath of fresh air' excuse didn't cut it. I didn't catch everything, but it sounds like she wasn't a human either, was she?"

Turukaishal relaxed a bit. "No. She was not. She was a Heil."

Richard's eyebrow vanished beneath the brim of his hat as he cocked it at the Scain. "A Heil came all the way across the Galaxy to what? Chat with you? What does she want?"

Turukaishal bit back the majority of the truth. These Vahran couldn't know. Not yet. It was hard enough to show himself to them. To tell them that he was being hunted on suspicions of treason? That was too much. "I am not really certain," he said slowly, glad for his glasses to hide his half-lie. He wasn't really sure of her motives or intentions, but her initial objective – killing him – could be hidden by sin of omission. It wasn't really *lying*, per se, but... "She was merely alerting me to her presence." Turukaishal couldn't help but feel relieved that his faceless enemy hadn't sent a Taeski like his friend Klakshan. Had that been the case, Richard would be looking at a corpse.

"Huh," Richard said, leaning on his cane. "The tone you two were taking sounded hostile. I thought it was something nasty." He gave the Scain a long, pointed look. "You alright? Victoria'll be torn up if you give yourself a heart attack or the alien equivalent of one. She's taken a bit of a shine to you."

"Scain *can* suffer cardiac arrest, but it is uncommon," Turukaishal informed him. "Please, rest assured that I am fine. For now, anyway. Knowing that there is another member of the Senate prowling around does make me nervous, but it is far from an immediate threat. Facing down a Heil is difficult, but not impossible."

"I hope not. Come on – Victoria wanted to ask you something, but you wandered off before she could. It was part of the reason I followed you."

Turukaishal blankly followed Richard back into the library where he reseated himself. Victoria looked at him in mild amusement. "And here I thought you'd run off on me," she said, batting her eyelashes coquettishly at him. Turukaishal forced his gaze elsewhere, his eyes turning pink beneath the glasses.

"Never," he said. "I merely needed to speak with an acquaintance of mine." He placed a barely-there emphasis on the last four words. Victoria paled slightly, her aura jolting to orange, but nodded nonetheless. They had to keep up this song-and-dance, at least while these other humans were present. "Anyway, Richard has informed me that you wished to ask me something?"

"Yeah! Ash wanted to know if you'd help her with her homework. Astronomy – isn't that lucky?"

Turukaishal wanted to hit Richard in the face, but would never have resorted to something so barbaric. He glared sideways at the youth, finding him smirking beneath his hat. The Scain focused his glare, sending some Psionic energy at him until Richard massaged his temples, the energy giving him a mild headache. Turukaishal turned his gaze back to Victoria. "Am I not entitled to my vacation?" he asked, a slight pleading edge to his tone. "I deliberately left home to distance myself from the woes of being a teacher, and-"

"C'mon, please?" Ashley begged, clasping her hands in front of her. "Please? Help me? I *need* to pass that class! Please?"

Turukaishal looked helplessly at Victoria but quickly realized he wasn't going to be finding any support there. Richard was chuckling quietly beneath his hat, his face obscured by a book. Turukaishal sighed, mumbling something about a lack of peace and quiet before nodding. "Fine."

Victoria pushed herself out of the chair, walking over and giving him a big hug. "See Ash? I told you he was awesome!"

Suddenly finding himself in very close proximity to Victoria, Turukaishal did the only logical thing: he stiffened like a board. His skin prickled and broke out in an ocean of gooseflesh at the unfamiliar contact, his eyes flushing pink beyond his glasses. Unfortunately, so did his cheeks. And he could see from their amused expressions that both Ashley and Jolene had noticed it. He hung his head slightly, sighing.

It was going to be a long month.

Chapter 17

BEGIN MESSAGE

LOCATION: Chindrus, Eccemeria District

TIME: 14/22 Local Time

MESSAGE: You do know that all the techs here at ECL are anxious to get their hands on a sample of your DNA right? You've seen more missions than most, and you've survived all of them. Your genes must have SOMETHING that gives you an incredible will to live. Please, get back here soon so we can pair your genes with Kridoria's as soon as possible.

Now that the professional stuff is out of the way, it's good to hear you're still intact. After your previous mission, I was beginning to wonder if the Mindbank had it in for your or something. Anu'bai in an asteroid mine? There are many missions better suited to you. Whatever he's got you doing now has him angered though. There's even talk of dissolving the union between you and Kridoria. I wouldn't want to see your genes go to waste. Be careful. My daughter would be distraught if anything happened to you.

-Chief Geneticist Chemleki

Victoria and Richard watched, amused, as Turukaishal paced back and forth in front of the library table, his hands clasped behind his back. Ashley drummed her pencil on her pad, waiting for his next words. Finally, they came. "Now that we have covered the early history of the solar system, what else is on the agenda for things your instructor wants you briefed on?"

"Ahhh…" she flipped through her notes hastily as Turukaishal stared down at her, his glasses glittering in the light of the overhead fluorescent bulbs. "The formation of gas giants from an accretion disc," she read. "What the heck is an accretion disc?!"

Turukaishal paused, a disparaging comment on his lips, before remembering that she was a Vahran. Space, as well as everything in it, was a vast and unknown frontier to them. "I believe that what your teacher wants you to study are 'circumstellar discs', he corrected. Accretion discs can form around active galactic nuclei. Protoplanetary or circumstellar discs, however, are slightly easier to understand."

"Argh!" Ashley said, clutching at her hair. "Okay, back up a bit. Start with circumstellar discs."

"A circumstellar disc is a ring-shaped accumulation of matter composed of a variety of dusts, gasses, rock, ice or collision fragments—basically anything considered naturally occurring 'space junk'—in orbit around a star. Around a young star, these are the collections of matter from which planets and moons will spring."

Ashley was furiously scribbling in her pad, copying down Turukaishal's lecture word-for-word. Richard had lowered his glasses and was listening intently, and Victoria was watching closely. Turukaishal shifted uncomfortably as their gaze burned into him. He cleared his throat and continued. "As the material falls towards the center," he explained, "gravitational energy is released and is transformed into heat and rotational movement. The energy released is in the form of electromagnetic radiation, the type of which is based on the central object. The accretion disc around a young star, for example, will be infrared. Neutron stars or black holes generally fall into the X-ray part of the spectrum."

Ashley cursed quietly as she wrote, frantically trying to capture all the information Turukaishal was giving her. "Okay, so this stuff spins around the star and gives off energy. Got it. Now how do we get to gas giants from here?"

"One of two ways," the Scain said as he resumed his pacing. He found it easier to talk in facts if he was in motion, something he'd learned back in the Academy. "One way is for a solid body in the accretion disc to capture gasses and begin rotating, creating a larger and larger mass. Like a snowball." He was grateful to Victoria for showing him the practical uses of a snowball earlier that day. The metaphor fit perfectly. Unfortunately, the wetness of her demonstration would remain on his collar for most of the day. "Otherwise, the gas itself begins to form small eddies, eventually expanding to create a gas giant with no solid core – a planet made solely from gas."

Ashley finished her sentence with a flourish. "Gotcha. Okay, thanks. Hm... next question: what is a white dwarf?"

Honestly, did these humans know *nothing* about the heavens? When he had been her age, or the equivalent of, he was already filing reports on freestanding aquatic clouds surrounding active quasars. A fascinating topic, but one humans wouldn't stumble across for a while. He sighed. Admittedly, this student was still young, but did her teacher really not help her understand this? On Velis, students did not leave the universities until they understood everything the teacher could impart. It was one of the reasons the Scain made such good pilots: their astronomy and astrophysics courses were second only to the Alinteans.

"A white dwarf," he said, resuming his pacing, "is the core of a collapsed star that is too small to form a supernova, and subsequently a black hole. A star, such as Sol, will leave behind a white dwarf after it novas at the end of its life, shedding its outer layers." He waited until she had finished writing before continuing. "Based on my analysis of the available data, there are still approximately five and a half billion years between now and that final destination."

"I think we'll be long gone by then," Richard muttered, having looked away from Turukaishal in favor of his books. He'd long since finished *Foucault's Pendulum* and moved on to an equally thick book: *Mystery*.

Ashley rolled her eyes, sticking her tongue out at Richard. "I know that!" she said, shooting him an unusual stare before returning to her notes. Turukaishal swept her aura for a moment before shrugging it off. It wasn't his business, and he wasn't going to be dealing with her on a daily basis (he hoped). Still, his brief sweep couldn't shake the malleable pink sensation he'd felt.

He could sense some kind of connection between Richard and Ashley – as if the two had known each other for a long time. Richard's aura was calm and placid, but Ashley's was jagged and irritated. Even through this little teaching session she had been like that, and had stolen several glances at the man. Finally, seeing her staring at him again, Turukaishal spoke up. "If there is some kind of tension between you two, may I suggest you resolve it?"

"It's nothing," Richard said as he turned a page. Ashely, though, narrowed her eyes dangerously and stood up, placing her hands on the table. Turukaishal instinctively took a step back as her aura whirled around her like a tempest.

"Nothing?" she asked, her voice low. "You left for four years, Rich. *Four years* without as much as a letter! Not even an email to let us know you were alive! And then two months ago you came waltzing back and now start acting like nothing ever happened?"

"Now is not the time," Richard said, staring over his book at her. "And I left because I had to." His voice descended beyond cold, bordering on frigid. "What happened back then ended, Ashely."

Ashley stared at him for a moment before sighing, her aura simmering down and returning to its usual jagged state. "Thanks for the help Turu," she said, gathering up her things. "I have to go now." She gave him a brief not before walking out of the library without another word.

Turukaishal stared after her for a moment before turning to look at Richard. Jolene and Julian had stepped out a while ago, so it was just the three of left. Richard looked back at him before sighing in resignation, putting down his book. "I left for four years, okay?" he said, glaring at Turukaishal as if daring the alien to question his motives. "Martin watched over Victoria while I was gone, but things had gotten so bad I had to escape for a while. For all our sakes."

"Martin?" Turukaishal inquired.

"He's our older brother," Victoria said. "He looks like a carbon copy of Richard, just older. When our parents passed away, he took over as our caretaker."

"He's creepy as heck," Richard continued. "No one goes near him and he doesn't go near other people. He's made enough money to just sit back on his laurels and rot away, and good for him. But his reputation made it perfect. Vicky needed protection, so Martin took her in. I left. But I got delayed while I was away and ended up coming back to find this place radically changed with almost no place for me in it. Vicky and I reunited seamlessly – we're siblings, after all – but everyone else had a hard time adjusting to my return. Especially Ashley."

"They used to date," Victoria said, eliciting a growl of protest from Richard. "Well, it wasn't really dating, but they were almost inseparable. Richard left without a word to anyone but me, and it took me a while to figure out that he hadn't told anyone. Four years causes a lot of damage. I don't think it was malicious, but he was just too focused on running away. And after Jennifer, and having to deal with Micah, and-"

"Enough!" Richard's voice, although quiet, was enough to send a shiver down Turukaishal's spine and to had enough authority to silence Victoria on the spot. Micah, hm? Interesting. Apparently, not only did the Sinclairs have another sibling, they had this Micah on the edge of their radars. Curious.

"If I may inquire, who is Micah?" Turukaishal asked, seating himself again. He was still shaken by his encounter with the Heil, and things like the astronomy lesson or this discussion were helping to take his mind off it. For now.

"Micah is one of the jerkwads who's constantly trying to get Vicky to go on a date with him," Richard said. His aura changed to a sickly shade of acidic, hissing green. "He's probably the nastiest specimen of a human being you'll ever meet." Then, in a much lower voice, "If you're ever looking for a test subject, you're welcome to take him."

Turukaishal almost laughed. "I will make a note of that," he said, looking out the window for a moment and doing a double take. Snow was coming down again, and this time it didn't look friendly. The flakes were large and frenetic, whirling down with a savage intensity. "We had better get moving if we want to make it somewhere dry before that projected blizzard hits."

Richard put *Mystery* back on the shelf, nodding. "Yeah. Probably a good idea. Vicky? Got the keys?"

"Yeah, I—oh no!" she grabbed for her purse, digging through it in a frenzy. Turukaishal watched as she tossed a small compact mirror in his general direction, likely without meaning to. He evaded it easily, watching her interestedly. "So, do Vahran have matter compression technology?" he asked Richard, gesturing to her purse as she excavated several pens and pencils, her cell phone, two mirrors and a coin purse from its depths.

Richard shrugged. "Beats me. It's one of the great mysteries of women. Don't worry about it."

"Richard, I think I left them!" she wailed, looking at him. "Probably back at Turu's..."

Richard folded his arms and said nothing, thinking. Turukaishal sighed, looking out the window at the falling snow and massaging his nose. "You are welcome to accompany back to my domicile," he offered. "As you know, there is more than enough space." His eyes whirled through a myriad of colors as he spoke, his conscience and memories helping him remember what it was like to sit in the cold for any length of time.

For the second time in as many hours, Turukaishal found himself on the receiving end of a bone-crushing embrace from Victoria. Richard, ever the calm one, graced him with a slight bow and thanked him for his hospitality. Turukaishal looked down at Victoria and hesitantly patted her shoulder. "Er... you are welcome?" he offered, hoping she would let him go. It was rather strange, and he was having a conflict of opinions. On the one hand, this was a Vahran. She was touching him. He should be killing her. On the other hand, she had proven that she wasn't as iniquitous as the rest, and he had escaped unscathed last time. And it didn't feel painful, so she remained alive. Plus, if he moved to do her harm, Richard would likely kill him.

He closed his eyes and inhaled deeply, thankful for the shades. It felt like only yesterday that he was at his own home on Chindrus, reclining in his pod without a care in the cosmos beyond what he was going to eat for his evening meal. And now he was standing in Vahran territory questioning his own motivations. He looked down and gently pried Victoria from around his waist. "We should go," he said before he could overthink the situation. "If we are caught in the blizzard, it will be a crisis even I may have trouble managing."

Chapter 18

BEGIN MESSAGE

LOCATION: Ganovai, Orbital Station 61

TIME: 14/29 Local Time

MESSAGE: *Turukaishal, I must say I am surprised by some of your more recent messages. You seem to be under the delusion that you have located a pair of Vahran that are not evil. Believe me, Turukaishal – they are ALL evil. There is not a single Vahran that will not hesitate to cut you down if you get between it and something that it wants.*

Demnechi tells me that you disobeyed an order to return immediately. While I cannot say I am displeased, as my mission takes precedence over any of his orders, I am surprised as to the logic you supplied him with. As he says, I am beginning to think sending you to that ball of rock was, in fact, an error. Please do not give me any further reasons to think so. I like to believe myself benevolent and understanding. Continue with the mission as planned. I will speak to Demnechi about attempting to override my orders. Please inform me immediately if there is anything I can supply you with.

-Sovakadris

The blizzard struck almost ten minutes after Turukaishal and company left the library. Whereas before it had just been a thick dusting of larger flakes whirling down from the heavens, the blizzard carried with it pellets of ice and howling winds that seemed to slice through Turukaishal's body like blades. He almost gawked at the ferocity of it, certain that this was some misguided Antarctic storm. This part of the globe was not known for its heavy snowfall, and definitely not for its blizzards. This freakish monstrosity was one of those rare flukes of weather, it seemed, that would forever defy explanation.

The snow seemed to come at him from all sides now, pelting him with stinging ice needles and the chill of the howling gale. Visibility plunged to just under six feet, if that, and Turukaishal found his rail-thin form was as ill-suited to the cold as it had been a hundred years ago. Even more of a concern to him, though, was the condition of the pair of Vahran he was escorting.

Richard, clad as he was in his thick coat, seemed to fare rather well in the blinding blizzard. Turukaishal would never understand how his hat never flew away, but Richard's sunglasses were an invaluable asset against the snow. Something that Turukaishal was learning about his pair. Despite all his safeguards, though, he was still limited by how far he could see. After a while, he had also given up his coat, bundling it around his baby sister. Victoria had been shivering almost uncontrollably ever since the wind had kicked up.

The gnawing feeling in Turukaishal's stomach increased. Vahran were not designed for such cold climates: far too little insulation in their bodies, not enough exothermal insulation and, in Victoria's case, almost a complete lack of fatty deposits to provide ancillary insulation. Richard had muscle, which was a partial insulator, as well as multiple layers of clothing. Turukaishal had Psionics, which wouldn't hold out forever. With their pace slowed down as a result of the inclement weather, it would be another two hours before they reached the woods, provided they didn't freeze to death first, and another hour after that just to reach his temporary home. In short, their position was not sustainable.

"We need to find a warmer position until the blizzard alleviates!" Turukaishal yelled over the wind. Nature, callous witch that she was, immediately filled his mouth with a pile of snow, causing him to choke unexpectedly.

Richard removed his hat, clutching it in white-knuckled, frozen hands. "There's nowhere warm nearby!" he shouted back, covering his face with the hat to prevent a similar fate. "The closest thing is an underpass beneath the road! I think it's somewhere up ahead on the left!" Without his hat, his brownish-blond hair was immediately coated in a fine dusting of snow. In a few moments, it had either melted and soaked into his scalp or piled up on top of his head, painting his hair white.

Turukaishal cursed his luck. On their way to the library, he had inquired about the impending blizzard. According to Richard, it hadn't been due until seven or eight. It was now only a little bit past six-o-clock. Apparently, most of the locals had bunkered down ahead of time – there were painfully few, if any, cars on the road or to be heard in any direction – and those that hadn't were likely holed up wherever they had been when the storm hit.

Richard tried using his phone, swearing vehemently when he was unable to get a signal. Not that it was unexpected. If he had been able to get a signal, Turukaishal would have praised Vahran technology as superior to his own. Victoria, huddled up beneath his arm and coat, looked up at him with all the sorrow of an abandoned puppy. "I'm sorry, Richard," she said through chattering teeth. "If I hadn't forgotten the keys-"

"Blaming yourself isn't going to do anyone any good," he said. "If the weatherman had been right about when this storm was coming, we would have been able to plan better."

He drew her closer to himself, tucking the coat more firmly around her. "Come on, we'll get to that underpass and see if it helps."

Turukaishal scanned around with his Psionics. Unfortunately, there wasn't much to see. He could sense the opening of the tunnel Richard had mentioned – it was only about a hundred feet ahead of them – but there were no aural signatures in the area for him to get a good bearing with. His best guess was that they would reach it in under ten minutes if they kept up their pace. "Come on!" he said, looking back at the two Vahran staggering along with him. He fell back a few paces, placing one of his skeletal hands on Victoria's shoulder in what he hoped was a comforting manner. "We are almost there. Shelter lies just ahead."

Victoria chose that moment to collapse to her knees, shaking profusely. Richard, who had been supporting her, was thrown on his face next to her. He scrambled upright, his eyes wide and bare. His glasses had been lost in the snow. "Vicky! Look at me!" the panic was barely evident in his voice, but it was there nonetheless. He patted her cheek with his palm. "*Victoria Lorelei Sinclair!*"

Turukaishal gave her a quick Psionic sweep. Her aural signature was dropping – at this rate, she would slip into unconsciousness. Not a good thing to do in the middle of a blizzard. Turukaishal grit his teeth as he tried to think of a solution. He couldn't carry her far with his Psionics – at most, he could move her twenty feet without a Booster, which he didn't have.

He snarled at himself. He had a plan, especially with those bracers he'd been lugging around all day, but they had to reach the underpass first. Finally, as Richard struggled to pick up his sister, Turukaishal made his decision. He grabbed Victoria's wrist, sliding beneath her body and staggering up as far as he could. Scain weren't designed for carrying heavy weight and, while Victoria was nowhere near as heavy as most Vahran, she definitely weighed more than Turukaishal. Almost twice as much. Even with the Psionics bolstering his body he could feel his bones protesting.

With strength born of desperation he lunged toward the opening he could sense. Richard scrambled up and chased after him, hurtling through the blinding snow. Turukaishal, weighed down as he was, wasn't in any danger of leaving Richard behind. They raced as fast as they could through the blizzard, aiming for the slight incline that led down to the underpass. He stumbled, Victoria sliding partway off his shoulders and dragging them both towards the snow. Richard raced up next to them, catching Victoria's other arm and looping it around his neck as Turukaishal regained his footing. They slipped and stumbled down the slope towards the opening, carrying Victoria between them. As soon as Turukaishal spotted the opening itself, he pushed his body forward, dragging the three of them in and falling flat on his stomach, his chest heaving. Victoria had fallen on top of him, now more than ever feeling like a dead weight. Richard caught himself on the wall, panting with exertion, his shirt and vest soaked with melted snow.

Turukaishal rolled out from beneath Victoria a moment later, forcing himself to stand and moving over to the opening of the underpass. He removed one of the bracers, placing it down in the opening and activating it. A blue-white shield sprang up, bursting from the ports along the side and spiraling outwards until it filled the aperture. Turukaishal repeated this with the other bracer, placing it in the tunnel at the midway point to create an oasis from the storm. The barriers would keep out the cold and snow… they were designed to keep out bullets and fire, after all. More importantly, they would keep their body heat *in*.

The Scain struck the wall, sliding down it and sitting on the floor of the underpass, staring at Richard and Victoria. "Why is it that whenever I am in your company I seem to end up snowed in?" he asked, his chest still rising and falling much more than felt healthy. His glasses had come off during his leap into the tunnel and his eyes were glowing yellow. Amusement. Richard stared at him for a moment before snorting, picking up his hat and swinging it around in an attempt to rid it of the snow clinging stubbornly to the brim.

After a few moments of respite, the pair of them checked on Victoria. She was conscious and grateful to be out of the snow, which was good. Richard was worried about her sweater, which had gotten soaked. He took it off and spread it out on the floor near one of the barriers. They were exuding a small amount of heat, which he hoped would dry the fabric. It wasn't enough heat to warm themselves by, but perhaps it was enough to dry the garment.

Richard pulled his sister into his lap, having removed his wet vest and tie, and embraced her in an attempt to use his body heat to warm her. Turukaishal watched them from across the tunnel, trying to think of a way to get them out of this mess. He leaned back, staring at the ceiling. There were several halogen bulbs; inactive due to apparent power loss. An idea struck him just then. "Richard. Do you have any garments you can do without? I may be able to establish a conflagration for heat."

Richard threw his vest and tie over, digging in his pockets for a handkerchief. Victoria's sweater was added to the pile. Turukaishal took off one of the layered shirts he was wearing and threw it onto the growing pile before sighing in resignation and throwing his coat onto the pile as well. With his Psionics crackling through the air like a blue serpent, Turukaishal reached up and tore the cover off of one of the halogen lights. After extricating the bulb, he felt around the socket with his Psionics. There was still a small amount of residual energy left in the cables. This was good.

Focusing on his task, lest he kill them all, he drew out a small amount of the electricity, coaxing it down the copper wires. He let the sparks hang in the air before him, encased in a field of Psionics. Lightning tamed. He slowly extended the electrical arc until it touched the pile of clothing and waited. At first, there was no immediate effect. The garments just smoked as the electricity was conducted into the remnants of the snow and ice. A few moments later, the smoke became a glowing ember which quickly spread into an open flame. Turukaishal leaned back, allowing the electricity to return to its coil. The exercise was exhausting. First running with Victoria and now this? He was going to need a Booster at this rate. As one last afterthought, he used his Psionics to punch a trio of holes in the roof of the overpass, none larger than a quarter, for the smoke to filter out through. No sense in suffocating them.

Richard sighed, nodding gratefully as he pushed Victoria over near the warmth. "There're a few trees just outside," he said. "I might be able to get a few branches to use as fuel for that fire. Can you watch Victoria for me?"

"How far out are these trees?" Turukaishal asked, his voice betraying his concern. "And wouldn't it be better for me-"

"The trees are about ten feet out," Richard said. "And no, you stay here. I'm the one who knows where the trees are and you burned your coat. I've got a pocketknife and I should be able to feel my way along the stone wall to where the trees are."

He walked over to the energy field Turukaishal had set up in the mouth of the tunnel. The snow was knee-deep outside. He cautiously nudged the bracer to the side, a blast of cold air rushing into the slowly warming tunnel. With one last backward glance, Richard vanished into the blizzard. Turukaishal closed the barrier, focusing on the man's aural signature. If it started diminishing too quickly, he was going out there and would drag him back by Psionic force if he had to.

He scoffed at himself, shaking his head. His eyes flickered to orange before returning to his usual, carefully-guarded black. Why was he so worried about these two Vahran? If Richard died, even Victoria had said there were other good Vahran. Surely he could find them. But as he looked down at Victoria, curled up in the fetal position near his makeshift fire, he sighed and shook his head. No. No other Vahran would do. For some reason, his gut instincts told him that these were the two Vahran he needed to show him whether or not to spare the planet.

He turned his eyes to the barrier, watching the snow whirl and dance outside. Richard's aural signature was still strong and steady, despite the weather. Turukaishal sighed, rubbing his head. Spare the planet? He had to first make sure the planet decided to spare them.

Chapter 19

BEGIN MESSAGE

LOCATION: Belphan, Division of Strategic Administration

TIME: 14/30 Local Time

MESSAGE: Even if the Mindbank condones your flagrant disregard for my orders, I still will only warn you once more. Do not allow these Vahran to bend your mind more than the Anu'bai did. I do not care what happened to you on Dayislia. I do not care what honors you have won. If you ally yourselves with the Vahran, I will personally come and hunt you down myself! We both know that the pretense of a fair vote between the pair of us is a formality. You are a whelp, still awash in amniotic fluid for all intents and purposes. I, who have been seasoned by the political battlefield for twice as long as you have been alive, am the logical choice to become the Mindbank. You? You are a spare body for the sake of tradition.

-Demnechi

The barrier was nudged aside ten minutes later as Richard staggered back in, dumping an armful of twigs and branches on the ground near the fire. "Here… it's not much, but it should help." The branches dripped with snow and melted ice, but hopefully they would dry out enough to burn and provide some warmth before the fire went out altogether. Turukaishal had no wish to die of the cold on this Vahran-infested backwater planet. There was absolutely no way he was going to allow that to happen.

Again, his concern spread to the two Vahran that were with him. How long could they last in this tunne? Four hours? Six? Two? He ground his teeth again. He could almost *feel* their vital energies slowing down from where he sat. Or was it an illusion? Was it his mind playing tricks on him? He shook his head. The cold was dangerous and could kill them all. He knew from experience. There had to be something he could do! Anything!

"Richard," he finally asked. "What gets a Vahran's heart pumping fastest?" He looked up from staring into the fire, turning his gaze on the Sinclair siblings.

Richard looked over at him, shrugging. "Probably adrenaline," he said, looking back down at his sister. "Running, jumping, fighting, that sort of thing. Why?"

Turukaishal took his right hand in his left, squeezing at the wrist and focusing the remainder of his Psionics into his flesh. He undid his Vahran disguise, starting at his forearm, to reveal his four gray fingers, each one tapering to a point thinner than a hair. He flexed the digits for a moment before kneeling down next to Victoria.

"Wait, what are you doing?" Richard asked, his hand snapping out and catching Turukaishal's wrist. Pain lanced up the Scain's arm from the pressure, his radius and ulna creaking in protest under the Vahran's firm grip. His hand quaked involuntarily in pain, the fingers twitching slightly and shaking the feathery ends. His bones were naturally fragile, his strength being mental and Psionic, not physical. He bit back a wince and glared over at Richard.

"I am going to directly stimulate the nerve centers of her brain to elicit an adrenaline rush," he explained. "My fingertips can interface directly with macrobiotic nerve systems. Hopefully, by accelerating her heart rate, we can delay hypothermia. Do you object to that?"

Richard stared at Turukaishal with a clinical, degage glare before releasing his arm. "Why are you helping her? I thought you were here to destroy us."

Turukaishal gently lifted Victoria's head, his fingers feeling along her pulse. It was weak but present, but her aural signature was weak as well, the girl having fallen asleep. She was in no danger of dying at the moment, but if the fire went out or the sticks didn't dry out soon enough, they were going to have a problem. "Your sister," Turukaishal said slowly, "claims there are good members of your race. If she is correct, I cannot allow your species to be annihilated without a reevaluation. If she is wrong, my mission will proceed as planned. Until such a time as either answer becomes apparent, it is in my best interest to keep her alive. And you."

He lifted Victoria's head into his lap, slowly turning it so that the back of her head was visible. In a Scain, the nerve center was at the base of the skull. He only hoped that it was the same, or at least similar, in a Vahran. If not, he could feasibly trigger any reaction from 'fight or flight' to a coma. Not that he intended to tell Richard this, seeing as the protective Vahran was lurking around behind him like an overprotective shadow, ready to kill or maim him if he harmed his sister. He gingerly placed his Scain hand on the back of Victoria's head and took a deep breath.

Richard was staring at him intently, still circling them both and the fire as he watched. His gray eyes had taken on an intensity which reminded Turukaishal of a bird of prey. The firelight playing over his face cast shadows into his hooded eyes, making them glitter eerily as he stared down at them, almost daring Turukaishal to harm her. Slowly, the Scain slipped his fingertips beneath Victoria's skin, slithering them around as he searched for a viable conduit for connection. Although her skin was filled with nerves, most of hers were too thin and delicate for such a tenuous procedure. Finally, the feathery ends of his fingers almost completely buried in the back of her neck, he found one.

"Alright," Turukaishal said as he looked up at Richard. "I need you to tell me if and when her adrenaline is rising. I know the textbook symptoms, but I may have attached my fingertips to the incorrect nerve through ignorance of the finer points of your biology."

Richard moved forward, taking Victoria's hand in his. The contrast was startling. Richard's fingers were long and thin, but they had a calloused appearance to them which suggested years of hard work. Victoria's fingers, despite having the similar tapered appearance and length as her brother's, were smooth and pale, devoid of any kind of roughness. Richard looked up at Turukaishal, his eyes narrowed. "And if you get it wrong? She's not going to die, is she?"

"No," Turukaishal told him, shaking his head. "She cannot die from this unless I am intentionally and maliciously tearing at her nervous system with my Psionics, which I am not planning on doing. The worst possible outcome is that she will lapse into unconsciousness. How long is based on the strength of my Psionics. For this, I am planning on using only a minimal amount until I am certain I have located the proper nerve." Richard nodded, sitting back on his haunches. Turukaishal smoothly injected a small dose of Psionic energy into Victoria's nerves, triggering her body's natural reaction as he prayed he was connected to the right nerve.

The result was immediate. Victoria's body bent like a bow, her back arching off the floor. A rosy flush spread across her face and neck, sweat breaking out on her brow. Turukaishal, surprised by this intense reaction, almost tore his hand from the back of her head. The only thing that kept him from doing so was the thought of the damage it could do to her. Richard's eyes widened, red and white warring for control over his face and making him look extremely unhealthy. He surged forward, pinning Victoria's midsection to the ground as her legs shot out to the sides, upsetting the fire and kicking the flaming pile across their tiny shelter. Richard narrowly avoided her foot as it shot past his leg, growling. "You idiot!" he hissed at Turukaishal. "Wrong nerve! Shut it down! Stop!!"

"What? What nerve is this?!" Turukaishal asked, panicked as he tried to disengage his hand from Victoria's head. Her constant writhing motion was making it difficult. "What is this reaction?" his eyes were gray – concern and confusion – as he wrestled with her. This was *not* what an adrenaline rush looked like.

"That was her pleasure center!" Richard growled, his eyes flashing dangerously. "Oh for the love of peace, of all the nerves you had to pick!"

"Well in a Scain that is where the adrenal response is!" Turukaishal defended, finally extricating his hand and shaking it out. Victoria's frenzied motion had wrenched his delicate fingers around, straining them to the breaking point. "How in the name of the

Hiin am I supposed to predict that in a Vahran that is where your sexual pleasure centers are located?!"

"Maybe you should do some research first!" Richard snarled back, drawing his sister into his lap as she began to calm down, her face returning to normal and her breathing soon following suit.

"I *did* do some research," Turukaishal returned crossly. "But I only understood the basics. Am I supposed to memorize where every blood vessel in your body leads as well, or perhaps the electromagnetic values of every synaptic cell?" he slumped back against the wall, tired out by his Psionic expenditure and thoroughly embarrassed. His eyes were not going to change back from being pink for quite some time. He sighed, shaking his head. "I apologize."

"Yeah... sorry I yelled at you," Richard said as he scratched at the back of his head. "It just... caught me off guard."

"Perhaps there is another, safer alternative... one that does not involve humiliation for all parties involved? What do Vahran usually do to ward off impending hypothermia?"

Richard draped his coat, which had mostly dried by the fire, over his sister as he gathered up the remains of the fire, blowing on it to rekindle the flames. "We usually try to warm up, obviously," he said. "I wasn't exactly a model Boy Scout. I never learned any of this crap – never thought I'd need it. Guess I was wrong, huh?"

Turukaishal leaned forward, tapping his Scain hand against his chin. He didn't have enough Psionics in reserve to hide it again and, to be frank, he didn't care. Surely he could remember something from his Academy days. Survival, perhaps? Vahran were mammals, like the Elorskra, Alinteans or Heil. Perhaps similar methods would work. Now if only he could remember them... he sighed, leaning back against the wall. Why was his mind drawing a blank now, of all times? He should be able to remember *something* useful from his courses in the Academy. He'd gone to one of the best, after all. Why couldn't he...

Turukaishal felt the familiar sensation of someone staring at him and looked up to see Richard watching him intently. "What?"

Richard held his gaze for a moment before looking away. "I'm just trying to process what just happened a minute or two ago," he growled, leaning back against the opposite wall. He looked much smaller (but no less intimidating) without his coat wrapped around him. "By proxy, I trust you more than I'd trust any Vahran, but that was still..." he waved a hand distractedly as he searched for the proper word.

"I believe the phrase is 'awkward'," Turukaishal supplied. Richard grunted in agreement but said nothing else. Turukaishal tried to return to his previous frame of thought, but found it impossible. For some reason, probably because Richard had mentioned it, the incident was now first and foremost in his mind. He ground his teeth together and tried to push it from his thoughts, but the image of how Victoria had looked was embedded firmly in his mind's eye. "Should we tell her about the incident?" Turukaishal asked after a few moments of silence, his eyes never leaving the dwindling fire and the pile of sticks next to it. They were still damp.

"What?!" Richard asked, his head snapping up with enough force to strike the white tiled wall behind him. He massaged it gingerly, trying to rub the pain away. "Are you out of your mind?!"

Turukaishal blinked in surprise. "Um… no. Why do you ask?"

"How would you feel if someone told you they'd just manually stimulated the part of your brain that controls sexual functions while you were unconscious?" Richard asked, giving up on rubbing his head. "I know that I'd feel like I'd been molested."

Turukaishal mulled it over, flexing the fingers on his exposed hand as he did so. "But not telling her is akin to lying, is it not?" he asked. His mind immediately supplied him with the proper response: no it wasn't. It was the sin of omission, something he had used several times solely because it *wasn't* lying. Not telling her about this was just wrong, though…

Richard spent several moments thinking it over, staring at the fire. He chewed at the end of his thumbnail before narrowing his eyes. "Look. You didn't mean it maliciously. I'm not even sure if your species is compatible with hers—*ours*—but that doesn't mean that telling her is the wisest course of action. Ordinarily, honesty is the best policy. But this was just a mistake. No harm was done. If you told her, it could forever change the way she views you. And what if she doesn't like you enough to help you find any more "good" Vahran? What then? I don't think she's that type of girl—no, I'm fairly certain she isn't—but do you want to just take my word for it? I could be lying. Do you want to risk it?"

Turukaishal had to concede that Richard had a point. The differences between their species went far beyond the physical. Whereas a Scain might appreciate the blunt honesty, a Vahran might be offended by it. In the same way, Scain were honored if one knew their name prior to a physical meeting, whereas Heil became incensed and offended if one used their name without permission… and it could be to the point of attacking. He relaxed slightly. "So we never speak of this again?"

"No. Never," Richard said, relaxing against the far wall. Turukaishal noticed that Richard looked relieved. Turukaishal resisted the urge to smirk. Richard's deception and manipulation were good—very good—and would probably have fooled any member of his own race. But for someone who could read auras, it was painfully obvious that he just wanted to avoid an awkward topic… especially since he had condoned it a moment

113

before it had occurred. Then again, as he thought about it, Turukaishal didn't exactly feel compelled to bring up such an awkward topic either. He nodded, leaning his head back on the wall and closing his eyes.

"Never." He agreed.

Chapter 20

BEGIN MESSAGE

LOCATION: Chindrus, Amara District

TIME: 14/22 Local Time

MESSAGE: Turukaishal, why won't you write to me? I know the Mindbank sent you on that ridiculous Black Mission somewhere in one of the Central Arms, but other than that you've completely kept silent. Why? Is something wrong? Are you hurt? Please respond!

-Kridoria

Turukaishal snapped awake, and that scared him. He couldn't remember falling asleep. He was still in the tunnel, Richard and Victoria nearby. Both of them were still alive, which was a relief. He would never have forgiven himself if he'd let them freeze to death. Slowly, his heart resumed a normal pace. "How long was I out?" he asked Richard.

The Vahran consulted his phone. It might not have been able to get a signal, but it had a clock on it. "You dozed off about an hour ago," he said. "It's almost 10:00 now... 9:43 to be exact. They said this storm should be completely gone by 11 tomorrow morning, but I never trust the weathermen."

Turukaishal grunted, forcing himself to stand up. His mind was clearer after his little nap, and he remembered a few more things about keeping mammals warm in subzero temperatures. Things that *didn't* involve him tripping the arousal centers of a Vahran's brain, that is. He felt his eyes turn pink at the memory. Of all the nerves to attach to... "How is she?"

"Asleep," Richard reported. "She's much drier and warmer due to the fire. I've gone out a few times to nab some sticks for it, but I'm not really too keen on going out again. It's pretty cold out there now that night's fallen."

Turukaishal suddenly felt a hundred cycles younger and back on the frozen wastelands of Limkalan. "Are you alright?" Richard asked, noticing the change in the Scain's demeanor. Turukaishal nodded, shaking his head and blinking as he forced the memories to the back of his mind.

"Remembering," Turukaishal said as he looked out into the snow. "Ninety-five cycles—I guess you'd call them 'years'—a go, I was on a mission to a world where weather like this was commonplace. Limkalan. My team and I were supposed to secure an abandoned structure that was being operated by a group of Erythian rebels – an old tower out on the Gretafe Deadlands and at the base of the Kriuru Mountains. We secured the structure and were on our way back when some Erythians turned up in a patrol cruiser and shot us down at the foot of the mountains. We ended up seeking cover in a cave halfway up the cliff face for five full rotations... days, I should say. It felt very similar to this."

Richard looked toward the opening of the underpass, sighing. "And how did you survive that?" he asked.

"One of us didn't," Turukaishal said as he looked up at the Vahran. "My father's brother—Kevilkamas—died in the cave of wounds he suffered when our craft went down. We buried him there. His monument still stands, and as far as I know even the wreckage of our ship is still there."

"My condolences," Richard said politely. "Here's to hoping that doesn't happen here. I have no desire to be interred in a covered walkway for the rest of eternity."

"It won't," Turukaishal said, his voice filled with an unfamiliar vehemence. There was no way he was going to allow either of these Vahran to die in this godforsaken tunnel. Not when shelter was an hour's walk from his home! If he had to call his shuttle—"

"I am a FOOL!" Turukaishal hissed, clambering over the sleeping Victoria and toward one of the shield generators he'd lodged in the door. He ripped it open and began examining its contents. "Richard, may I destroy your cellular device?"

Richard slid it across the ground to him. "Go ahead as long as you can get us out of here. What're you planning?"

"Turukaishal immediately ripped it apart, using the little bit of Psionic power he had left to separate the components, allowing them to drift around his body like minor satellites. "This barrier is going to die," Turukaishal said to Richard, talking more to himself than to anyone else. "But with any luck I can use the phone as an amplifier. There is a small shuttle on my ship – I'm going to try to call it."

"Can it fly in this?" Richard asked, standing up as the barrier dropped. The snow had piled up against it and was almost waist deep. "The wind out there is-"

"*Nothing* compared to Limkalan," Turukaishal said, moving the electronic components around and attaching them as best he could without the aid of a heat source to weld them. "Limkalan's winds could blow water out of lakes if the water wasn't frozen solid!"

The cell phone's screen winked to life, displaying an army of unfamiliar symbols. Turukaishal continued to work feverishly at it, trying to get the signal through to the shuttle. To salvation. Finally, he sat back and glared at the discombobulated phone in annoyance. "I need to send the signal," he said, "but this technology is unfamiliar."

"What do you need," Richard asked, scrambling over as the cold air cut into him like a blade. "Explain it to me – layman's terms, if you don't mind."

"I need the data to leave the device," Turu said. "A phone call should do it, but I have no idea how to send it."

Richard reached down and pressed his finger to a button with a green, curved icon on it. The device lit up like a fusion node, vibrating harshly on the tiled floor of the tunnel as sparks erupted from any available jacks. The buttons and keys popped off, skittering across the floor like bugs. Turukaishal jumped away in surprise, but pointed triumphantly at the device. "It worked!" he said, A set of alien symbols winked across the readout, repeating the same set over and over again. Turukaishal translated. "Coordinates Received: Shuttle Deployed."

Richard sat back, massaging his cheekbone where the A and S keys of his phone had left tiny red marks. "Great. How long until it gets here?"

"No more than five minutes," Turukaishal said as he ran back to Victoria, putting out the fire with his Psionics. He clenched his mismatched fists in excitement. He had done it! The answer had been right in front of him and he'd almost let two good Vahran freeze to death because he'd been too blind (or dense) to see it. There was a small risk that his shuttle could be seen, of course, but in this blizzard it wouldn't be recognizable. Or it could even be blamed on shifting shadows in the storm. He wanted to dance with glee as he doused the fire.

True to his word, as Scain aren't prone to lying, there was a roar of engines outside a few minutes later. Richard squinted through the driving snow, trying to make out the shuttle. Turukaishal could sense it – he knew where it was parked and where the awaiting entrance was. "Come on!" he said, motioning to the two Vahran as Richard helped Victoria to her feet, one of her thin arms around his neck.

"I can't see the shuttle," Richard said, stumbling forward with his sister. "You'll have to guide me!"

Turukaishal reached back, gripping Richard's shoulder and pushing the Vahran ahead of him, steering him through the snow and wind as the three of them forged ahead up the ramp. Soon, the silhouette of the shuttle came into view; a boxy thing almost twenty feet long and at least ten high, streamlined and gleaming in the driving snow like a beacon. A lifeboat to salvation. Richard and Victoria pushed toward the opening door, a ramp descending to plunge into the snow at their feet, and Turukaishal followed him inside, hitting the switch to close the door. He made a beeline for the pilot's seat, not wanting to be out and exposed longer than he had to, as Richard set about pushing Victoria into one of the seats.

"Wonderful!" Turukaishal said, taking control from the autopilot and wrapping his hand around the U-shaped steering wheel. He allowed his disguise to crumble away – it was eating up his Psionic reserves and there really wasn't a need for it now. "First things first: cabin temperature."

Warm, welcome heat flooded into the cabin as the ship lifted off. Turukaishal aimed the nose of the shuttle into the air, burning fuel as he took off into the whitewashed sky, meeting the ice and snow head on. The elements glanced off the craft, spraying in all directions as the short, blunt nose forced its way through them, somehow managing to slice through the sheet of freezing particles like a blade.

One of the speakers bleated loudly, startling Turukaishal as he looked down at the navigation panel, narrowing his eyes. Richard stuck his head into the cockpit, his eyes sweeping over the myriad of blinking lights. "Don't tell me. You forgot to fuel up?"

"Nothing like that," Turukaishal said as he overrode the alarm. "This says there's someone else in the air – someone who is moving quickly toward us."

"Impossible," Richard said. "All airplanes or choppers should be grounded until the storm blows over." He resumed buckling his sister into one of the seats. She was stirring and showing more signs of life than before, which as definitely a good sign. Richard's coat, still wrapped around her, was getting in the way of the straps.

"Then it is obviously not an airplane or chopper," Turukaishal said as he forced the craft higher. He had to get high enough to be able to navigate safely. Snowflakes and ice danced across the windshield, obscuring his vision. At this rate, he could plow into a tall building or even the tops of the large hills. That would be a fantastic way to die... not. His mind snapped back to Limkalan – their transport ship going down amidst the unforgiving ice and snow, his fellow crewmen screaming and praying as the ground, ever invisible through the storm, rushed up to meet them.

Richard stood up behind him, taking hold of one of the overhead straps. "Alright. Vicky's secured. Now-"

Something struck the shuttle from behind, sending it reeling end over end through the blizzard, disorienting both pilot and passenger. Richard's grip on the strap was the only thing which kept him from being launched straight into the back of Turukaishal's seat. As it was, his feet left the ground for a moment as they completed their nauseating flip. Turukaishal growled as his instrument panel lit up, showing a hull breach in the rear storage compartment. Nothing life-threatening... yet. "We are under fire," he informed Richard. "Get yourself secured! Now!"

"Under fire?!" Richard asked, throwing himself into the copilot's seat next to the Scain and dragging an X-shaped harness across his chest. "Who's crazy enough to fly around in this blizzard shooting at us?"

"A Heil, for one." Turukaishal grimaced as a small craft shot by their starboard side, one of the wings barely missing them. It was designed to look almost avian, or perhaps chiropteran. Four large wings seemed to grow from around a streamlined cockpit with a long, needle-like cannon protruding from the underside. Turukaishal banked to the side as it swooped around, the red light of the cockpit marking it even in the blizzard. Avian? It looked more like a giant mosquito. The craft dove straight at their shuttle from above, like a bird of prey, but Turukaishal had other plans. He jerked a lever forward, descending and rolling sideways, evading the streak of white light that lanced through the blizzard a moment later.

"Not bad, Turukaishal!" His radio buzzed near his head, the mocking voice of the female Heil drifting into the cockpit. She'd hacked his communication system. While his navigation and operating systems had tenth- or twelfth-level security protocols, his communication systems were old. Probably only fourth generation. "I saw you saving those two Vahran. You *are* turning on the Scain, aren't you? Helping them? You should have just left them to freeze! I would have."

Turukaishal growled, his hands gripping the steering wheel tightly. "This isn't the place for a dogfight," he muttered. "We have to lose her in the blizzard. Somehow." He set his mouth into a grim line, his eyes flashing red. He'd dragged the Vahran out of the freezing tunnel, albeit after almost letting them freeze to death because of his own stupidity. There was no way he was going to get them killed now, much less at the hands of that stupid Heil. If she wanted to kill them, she was going to get out of that ship and fight them face to face. And he was going to be there to fend her off with his Psionics. He had no plans to die encapsulated in his shuttle. He gripped the steering wheel tighter in his hands. "Hold on. This could get a little messy."

Chapter 21

BEGIN MESSAGE

LOCATION: Chindrus, Amara District

TIME: 4/22 Local Time

MESSAGE: Someone has employed a Heil to go after you. Watch your back.

-Klakshan

Turukaishal gripped the controls in his skeletal hands and jerked them to the side, evading a streak of white light that lit up the cockpit with its proximity. He angled the nose down into a steep dive, evening out the thrusters as he hurtled towards the ground. A quick glance at the radar told him that the Heil had followed. How was she tracking him? She certainly couldn't physically SEE him in this mess. She had probably locked on to his communication array when she'd hacked it. He swore under his breath in his native tongue.

The sensors blared in the cabin as Turukaishal jerked back on the controls. The shuttle angled upwards, missing the ground in one of the parks by a few yards as he leveled out and took off again, ascending slightly to remain safe. His old flight instructor would have killed him for flying in weather like this, even though his craft could withstand it. He set his jaw and gripped the wheel tighter. One hand strayed over to his locator, dialing in his ship's serial number as he tried to signal it for backup. Nothing.

So that meant the Heil was flying with a jammer. His signal couldn't get far enough, or probably out of the shuttle at all, to reach his main ship. He cursed. It wouldn't really matter, now that he thought about it: if he docked with his main ship, it would reinstate *his* atmosphere upon decompression. Richard and Victoria would both be killed by the pressure and chemical changes.

The Heil's mocking laughter filtered into the cockpit as he banked hard to the right, avoiding another streak of deadly light. A magnetohydrodynamic weapon, if he wasn't mistaken. A well-placed shot could boil away his hull or fry his engines, driving him down. It was a potent and deadly weapon, and proved that this Heil had contacts among either the Alinteans or, more likely, the Erythians.

"What's the matter?" she asked, her image flickering to life on the viewscreen. She had removed her disguise, revealing her patchwork black-and-white body. There was a fist-sized four-pointed star of black skin directly above her right eye, but there was no rhyme or reason to the rest of her appearance. Her thin lips were drawn back, revealing a mouthful of sharp teeth, closer to that of a shark than to a human, and her eyes were glowing with a frenzied light. She wore a band around her head from which several streamers of braided hair hung, each one interwoven with bits and pieces of gold or silver. "You knew what would happen if you betrayed your Mindbank – betrayed the *Senate!*"

Turukaishal snarled, his eyes flashing red. "I betrayed no one!" he spat. "These two are the Vahran we discussed! I am within my rights to-"

The Heil's next shot flew true, lancing through the air with a metallic screech and striking the rear of the shuttle. There was an obvious drop in temperature this time: the cabin had been breached. Richard unbuckled his belt, scrambling over the seat despite Turukaishal's protests, crawling into the back to check on his sister. A large crack had opened along the wall opposite her seat and the snow was swirling in. Turukaishal saw Richard's brow knit, his teeth baring as he staggered back to Victoria, clutching the overhead handles.

"Listen to me!" Turukaishal yelled, his voice a mixture of rage and fear. He was not going to let this bottom-feeding bounty hunter kill him. "I have not betrayed anyone! I am still loyal to the Scain. I-"

"And I don't believe you," the Heil returned. "You saved the lives of two of the Senate's enemies. That's treason."

Richard leaned over Turukaishal's shoulder, glaring directly at the Heil on the communicator. "No it's not," he said, his face a mask of thinly veiled anger. "Treason would be if he gave out coordinates for strategic outposts or planets. Or if he gave us plans for his ships or weapons. Saving two Vahran hardly counts as treason. What about war criminals? Sparing them for information? Is that treason?!"

The Heil laughed. "Well well, is that a *Vahran* I hear yelling at me? Let me tell you something: the rules that apply to a Scain or a Heil are warped where your species is concerned. I have my orders, the Scain has his. This isn't a personal vendetta or war, this is business. I have to eat. But between you and me, I really can't stand traitors, which is why I'm more than happy to do this."

"I can't stand traitors either," Richard said as he gripped Turukaishal's chair in a death grip, the Scain having angled the shuttle upwards into a tight ascending spiral. "And trust me; I've seen my fair share of them."

The Heil was quiet for a moment as Turukaishal continued to ascend, Richard clinging tightly to the back of the pilot's seat. "You are a Vahran," she said at last. "You cannot be trusted."

"I'll be the first to agree with you. A huge number of people on this planet deserve to be wiped out. But what about the rest? Are you really willing to destroy an entire species over them? They aren't worth it. Believe me. I hate these apes as much as you all apparently do – I wish you'd been here five years ago to see some of the crap they were doing. But don't you dare sit around and generalize and then tell me you're better than we are: if that's how you play, you belong down here with the rest of the idiots."

There was a longer spell during which Turukaishal gave Richard a warning glare. She wasn't shooting at them for the time being, but whether it was because Richard was yelling at her or because of his piloting remained to be seen. Turukaishal banked hard to the left, trying to lose her in the storm. Her voice stayed with them in the cockpit. "I find myself loath to admit that I almost *like* you, Vahran. Tell me: what is your name, that I may have the honor of knowing it before I kill you."

"You give me yours and I'll give you mine," Richard spat, his eyes narrow. Turukaishal moaned, covering his face with one hand. Richard's belligerence was going to get them all killed. Asking a Heil for their name was as rude as kicking a Vahran in the groin to say hello. Names, to the Heil, were given when earned. He waited, his hands clenched around the wheel as he prepared for the barrage of high-density lasers that would surely come. Instead, he heard the Heil start laughing.

"You have a lot more backbone than some aliens," she said, grinning widely. The sheer number of teeth that were visible in her smile was nothing short of unnerving, making her look like a psychotic Jack-O-Lantern. "Since you'll likely end up dead before all this is over, I guess there's no harm in it: my name is Klaara'Doran kan Mitragan – Klaara to you. Now what's yours?"

"Richard Hilbrand Sinclair," Richard said, still watching the viewscreen. "And behind me is my sister, Victoria Lorelei Sinclair. And I see you already know Turukaishal." He kept his voice even. Turukaishal, on the other hand, was on the verge of a panic. This wasn't just a Heil, this was a *Mitragan* Heil.

Based on a Heil's name, you could infer two things: their family and their clan. In this case, Klaara's family was the Doran family. Turukaishal had heard the name before somewhere, but couldn't exactly place where. The Mitragan Clan, however, was notorious for raising the most violent, uncontrollable, battle-hardened and deadly Heil in the Galaxy. Facing down Klaara just went from 'difficult' to 'nearly impossible'.

Turukaishal scanned his control board while Richard kept her preoccupied. He might have time to find out how she was tracking them. It was impossible that she had slipped a bug into his shuttle – she probably didn't even know where his base was. Instead, she had either figured out the frequency of his communication array or was tracking an emission. After giving it a bit of thought, it would be a far easier task to track the latter, which was probably what she was doing.

All of the main emission levels were normal. There was nothing out of the ordinary for her sensors, no matter how finely tuned, to pick up and he wasn't burning any kind of radioactive fuels, so she couldn't pick up his radiation levels. He glared at the instrument panel again, trying to find a solution. And then the answer hit him with the force of one of the Heil's lasers. He groaned quietly.

Richard and Klaara were yelling at one another now, so Turukaishal waved his hand at the Vahran to catch his eye before indicating a single bar on the control panel. Richard, not missing a beat, followed his finger and arched an eyebrow. Turukaishal mouthed the word "heat" at him. The Vahran stared at him in exasperation but shrugged, not faltering at all in his argument with Klaara. Turukaishal slowly began dialing down the heat, looking back at Victoria. None of them would last too long without the heat, but they would die immediately if Klaara scored a hit on their engines. It was a risk they would have to take.

As the shuttle cooled, Turukaishal aimed the shuttle forward, down and then killed the thrusters propelling it. As the coasted through the air, he spun the wheel around, twisting the shuttle to face backwards before reigniting the engines. They burst forward, diving beneath the tiny assault craft and into the blizzard. The temperature was dropping quickly, aided by the hole Klaara had torn in their hull. The Heil shrieked in aggravation, her sensors trying desperately to locate her prey. She cursed into the communicator, her voice getting fainter as the storm swallowed her. "*Aelau bakan keviru, Scain!*" she yelled. "Not bad! Next time I find you, we're going to finish this!"

Turukaishal smirked. "What is it the Vahran say? '*All is fair in love and war*'?" he chuckled, breathing a sigh of relief as he sped away into the darkening blizzard. As soon as Turukaishal was certain Klaara was out of range, he switched the heat back on, leaning back in his chair. "That was too close."

His paranoia running high, Turukaishal piloted his shuttle through the storm, back over and around a forest. His instruments functioned well enough to guide him back to his base – thank the Hiiin for transponders... without them, it would be impossible to fly in conditions like this. He chanced a cursory peek back at Victoria – she was asleep, or at least he hoped it was asleep, or Richard was going to have an aneurism.

Richard said nothing, staring out through the frost-covered windows of the shuttle. "You realize that anything with a radar can still tell we're here, right?" he asked finally as he shifted to look back at his sister. The cold had taken quite a number on her. Richard seemed perfectly content in the low temperatures, but Victoria didn't seem to like them.

"I have masked our signal," Turukaishal assured him.

"How?" Richard asked, facing forward again, looking down at all the switches and gauges on the instrument panel. Now that they weren't being shot at, he had more time to look around. The cabin was roughly rectangular with two seats and a door leading into the passenger bay where Victoria sat. All across the control board were thousands of blinking lights, levers, buttons, switches and strange devices. It was everything a piece of alien technology *should* be.

"You expect me to understand everything, don't you?" Turukaishal asked, bemused. "I know that this ship is capable of hiding its signal – one would have to be staring right at it to see it – but I could not give you the exact methods used to produce such a result. I am sorry."

"No apology necessary," Richard grunted. "I was just curious. What's this do?" he gestured towards a joystick-style control that rested in front of him.

Turukaishal followed Richard's finger with his eyes. "Defensive mechanism," he said as the shuttle began to descend into the clearing in front of his base, the snow swirling around them. "It can aim and fire a pair of MA Cannons. Not the high-powered variants, but they are enough to tear through most forms of shielding and some forms of armor."

"MA?" Richard asked, cocking an eyebrow.

"Matter Acceleration," Turukaishal said simply.

The two of them stepped out of the shuttle into the blizzard. The trees provided some cover, which made Turukaishal's base visible through the haze of white. The shuttle's autopilot was set to return to the hangar as Richard extricated his sister and carried her up to the door. Turukaishal let them both in as the shuttle lifted off again, watching it sail through the snow-choked skies. As soon as the door closed behind the Scain let out a long sigh and slid down the wall to sit on the floor. His multi-jointed legs stretched out in front of him. They popped quietly in the dim light of his house as he stared up at the ceiling, letting out his breath in one long whoosh. It had been a very stressful day.

Chapter 22

BEGIN MESSAGE: SECURE TRANSMISSION GRADE V: MINDBANK SECURE LINE

LOCATION: SOL3, NORTHERN HEMISPHERE

TIME: 20/24 Local Time

MESSAGE: Your eminence. I regret to inform you that there has been a complication to this mission. A Heil complication, to be precise. Klaara'Doran kan Mitragan has appeared, and I am fresh from escaping from her assault. She nearly shot down my private shuttle in the midst of a blizzard, heedless of the fact that it would easily be recoverable by Vahran once the storm passes. I do not know who hired this bounty hunter, but I feel it right to warn you that things are rapidly beginning to grow more and more dangerous.

-Turukaishal

"Oh for the love of peace would you relax?" Richard asked, looking over at Turukaishal. The Scain was pacing back and forth, his narrow, hoof-like stomping across the hardwood floor. Whereas Richard was seated on the couch with several blankets wrapped around his shoulders, Turukaishal had insisted on standing. Standing had given way to fidgeting and then to outright pacing. The single blanket which looked amusingly undersized on his nine-foot frame fluttered behind him like a diminutive cape as the Scain continued to pace. "Sheesh," Richard continued, leaning back on the couch. "What's got you so bothered?"

"Your sibling, to be blunt," Turukaishal said, pausing only for a moment to stoke the fire he'd started in the fireplace before resuming his pacing; this time in a circle around the couch and coffee table. "I am concerned for her well-being and health. I am surprised you are not."

"I am," Richard said, "but pacing back and forth isn't going to do her any good. If it would, I'd be up pacing next to you."

Turukaishal paused, his fingertips flexing as he fought to control himself. "You are right, of course," the alien said as he moved over and rested his hands on the kitchen counter. "But I am still concerned for her nonetheless. When I am concerned I become active."

"More like antsy," Richard said with a snort. "You haven't quit moving since we tucked her in for the night."

It wasn't an untrue statement. Within minutes, the pair had undressed Victoria (rather, Richard had done this while Turukaishal ended up waiting outside the door) and put her to bed in Turukaishal's master bedroom under a mountain of blankets. Richard had closed the door and then promptly forbidden Turukaishal, in no uncertain terms, from going inside. Turukaishal couldn't help but be chagrined at being ordered around in his own home, but he still understood. After Victoria was taken care of, he had come downstairs and sent a quick message to the Mindbank... and that's when the overpowering urge to just MOVE came over him.

Richard gave the Scain a long and pointed stare. "What's with you anyway? Ever since the snow started falling you've been hovering around Victoria like a hawk. Why?"

Turukaishal gave Richard a strange look. "I have not."

"Uh, yeah you have," Richard said, leaning forward. "Most of what you did out there for us was general – helping us survive, that is – but a few times I noticed you watching her. You tried to accelerate her adrenal response, albeit with disastrous results, and you started the fire closest to her. If I didn't know better, I'd say you liked my sister or something."

The last few words were spoken almost as an accusation. Turukaishal stared at Richard in surprise before laughing... or rather, he emitted a few short barks which could pass for laughter. "You mistake my intentions," he said. "Please, cease your humanization of my actions. Victoria, with her slim body and smaller size, was in the worst state of any of us. It is only natural that I make certain she is alright. If she perishes, what happens to my dream of finding good Vahran?"

Richard said nothing, merely nodding and turning away. "Can I ask you something?" he asked after a moment, turning his gaze (but not his head) back to Turukaishal.

"Of course."

"How are you able to look like a human? Is that part of your ability?"

Turukaishal drummed his fingers on the countertop before answering. "Yes and no," he said. "I use my Psionics to rearrange the outer layer of cells to look human. However, I have certain implants which allow my body to rearrange certain cells into other parts of the body. For example, as I rearrange my skin to become smaller, the extra cells are used to create a fifth finger, nose, feet, et-cetera."

"Can anyone use it to look like someone else?" Richard asked. "I noticed that Klaara looked human-ish."

"Heil naturally look closer to your race than I do," Turukaishal said. "As do the Taeski. It does not take much to alter their appearance. With the Heil, it is usually their hands that give them the most trouble. With Heil, they either keep them hidden or in their pockets. If this is not feasible, they wear a type of 'glove'."

"So she was actually in an alien body out there?" Richard asked, cocking an eyebrow at Turukaishal.

"With alterations. She had hair, which Heil do not possess naturally, and her facial ridges were missing. It is likely that she had cosmetic surgery or minor cellular alterations performed before appearing in public. Reversible, most likely, which is why you saw her in her pure form over the communicator in the shuttle."

Turukaishal felt a subtle shifting of Victoria's aura above him and had to keep himself from leaping to attention. He leisurely made his way over to the stairs leading up to the second floor before turning to Richard. "Your sister is stirring. Since you have forbidden me access to my own bedroom, perhaps you should accompany me so as to ascertain her state of health."

Richard stood up and followed the alien up the stairs, his gaze burning holes in the back of the Scain's head. Turukaishal could feel his stare and suppressed a shudder. Richard unnerved him to some degree, perhaps more than creatures like the Anu'bai. At least he knew roughly what to expect from one of the viral plants. As they reached the top of the stairs, Richard pushed past him and knocked on the bedroom door, opening it a moment later and leaving Turukaishal standing out on the landing. The Scain couldn't help but suddenly feel isolated – cut off from even his own kind. He was on Earth, of all places, and currently aiding and abetting a pair of Vahran, however temporarily. Worse, someone wanted him dead. But who? And WHY?

The door reopened and Richard's head materialized around the jamb. "She wants to talk to you." He did not sound happy. Indeed, he looked as if he'd ingested something particularly sour. Turukaishal hesitated at the bitter look on the Vahran's face before following him into the bedroom and closing the door.

Victoria was sitting up in the bed, one of Turukaishal's synthesized tee-shirts hanging on her shoulders. The Scain hesitated again before leaning on the wall near the doorframe. "Your sibling has informed me that you wished to see me?"

She nodded. "Richard, can we have a moment?" she asked, pointing to the door with one of her thin fingers.

Her brother's eyes widened. "But-"

"Out, Richard," she said with a little bit more force. "I need to talk to Turukaishal and I don't want you intimidating him."

Now that was an odd concept, Turukaishal though. The Vahran intimidating him? He would never admit, under pain of death, that it was true. Richard sighed, waving a hand and turning away. "Fine. I'll be downstairs. Turukaishal, mind yourself." He grouchily closed the door behind him, and Turukaishal could see his aura through the wall as he stomped downstairs.

He looked back to Victoria, swallowing nervously. For some reason, she suddenly made him more nervous than Richard. "Anyway…"

"Um… yeah… I just wanted to know something…" she said, looking anywhere but at him. "I-ah-well…" Turukaishal frowned as he stared at her. Her aura was pink and gelatinous and her face was flushed with color. She wouldn't meet his eyes either and was fidgeting nervously with her hair. These were all indicators of embarrassment or humiliation. What had precipitated this?

"Please feel free to speak candidly," Turukaishal said as he moved away from the door, sitting down in an amusingly small chair by his desk. One of his desks, anyway: he had several around the house.

"Um… did you do anything to me in the tunnel?" she asked, looking everywhere. She pulled nervously at the collar of her shirt and Turukaishal caught a glimpse of her collarbone – starkly well-defined against her skin. The light from the nearby table lamp threw the shadows of her bones into sharp relief against her neck, as well as the hollow of her throat.

Turukaishal's eyes immediately turned pink. Suddenly, he found himself unable to look her in the face. "Ah… why?"

"Um… I remember this feeling… not one you usually talk about, you see… and then hearing you and Richard talking…"

Turukaishal wanted to shoot himself in the face – the bigger the gun the better. She had over heard their conversation? And she remembered his accidental stimulation of her arousal centers? Wonderful. Now she was going to hate him and his chances of finding good Vahran were officially shot. On the bright side, maybe now he could go home… if that was a bright side, seeing as someone there wanted to kill him. "I attempted to stimulate your adrenal fight-or-flight response," Turukaishal admitted, "in an attempt to increase blood flow and heart rate to help avoid hypothermia."

Victoria looked at him with those green eyes of hers. Unsettlingly green. Turukaishal wished there was a name for that color. "And? Did it work?"

The Scain coughed nervously, staring away from her. "Ah, no… not really…" he suddenly felt as if the temperature in the room had risen, closer now to the Kavinau District out in the desert. Heat seemed to come at him from all sides and he almost wanted to leap back out into the blizzard to escape the sensation.

"Well, what happened?" Victoria pushed, staring at him. Turukaishal looked helplessly at her and then at the door, almost wishing Richard would interrupt. Or kill him so he didn't have to answer the question. Of course, the surly Vahran was probably exploring his house right now, and wasn't going to be of any help. He sighed.

"Due to my lack of expertise with the Vahran nervous system, I inadvertently triggered the pleasure centers of your brain, eliciting a reaction from the part that controls arousal and sexual stimulation." He closed his eyes in humiliation. There. He'd said it. Now she could try to kill him. He sat there with his hands in his lap and waited for the forthcoming explosion.

Chapter 23

BEGIN MESSAGE:

LOCATION: Chindrus, Mindbank's Tower

TIME: 16/22 Local Time

MESSAGE: Someone has taken out a contract on you? I suspect the Visoth. We may be allies, but during all of our meetings they have barely concealed their hostility. Klaara'Doran kan Mitragan has quite the reputation, and her lineage is as impressive as it gets. I am impressed that you evaded her. Please be cautious, Turukaishal. Vahran are dangerous enough, but adding a Heil with an urge to kill you makes this even worse.

And be wary of the two Vahran you keep in your company. Those beasts are never to be trusted.

-Sovakadris

"Thank you."

Turukaishal's head snapped up, staring at Victoria in confusion with eyes the color of slate. "What?"

"I said thank you," she said, looking at him. Her face was completely red, which contrasted with her eyes, but her gaze never wavered. "You were trying to help me, right? So what if you screwed up... you didn't kill me. Sure it was embarrassing, but you were trying to do what was right..." Turukaishal felt his face heating up as she spoke, his eyes remaining gray by the sole fact that he refused to allow them to pink again. He was a Scain, for the love of the Hiin... he had his pride to maintain.

"You are not... upset?" Turukaishal asked tentatively. Part of him wanted to sigh and slump down in his chair with relief. The other part of him felt like this was a trap. He couldn't be sure of which side of his psyche to listen to.

"Okay, so I'm embarrassed beyond words, yeah," she admitted, hiding her face in her hands to conceal her growing blush. "And what happened is kind of... well... but no. I'm not mad at you. Like I said, you were trying to help me." She fidgeted with her bangs as he spoke, her cheeks as red as a conflagration behind her hands.

Turukaishal relaxed. It somehow felt as if a great weight had been lifted from his shoulders and, surprisingly, it left him at a loss for words. "I was afraid I was going to have to leave," he admitted. "If you were no longer willing to show me the good in Vahran-"

"You know what?" she said, slowly lowering her hands. "I'll show you some good right now. Is there a computer nearby?"

Turukaishal unzipped a bag on the floor near his desk and pulled out a laptop. It wasn't anything fancy – a Lenovo Ideapad S12 that he'd purchased for 'realism' in case anyone ever entered his house – and handed it to her. She gave it a brief once-over before opening it and turning it o n. "You have internet, I assume?"

"A basic connection," he said. "I did not need anything fancy. My Data Pad connects via different signals than a human computer, so I really have no need for it."

Victoria nodded absently, pecking away at his computer. He blinked once or twice before shaking his head. He'd tried learning to use the accursed thing, but it just wasn't designed for his Scain hands, and even with human fingers it was too bulky and cumbersome for his tastes.

Curiosity swept over him like a living thin, permeating his brain like water into a sponge. What was she planning on showing him? Finally, she leaned back. "I'm just waiting for this to download," she explained, "so let me tell you a few things. Nowadays, good music has been lost. Richard and I both agree on that. There's—"

"Music?" Turukaishal asked, cocking his head. "You have music?"

Victoria stared at him for a moment. "You didn't know we had music?"

"No, I… er…" he fell silent, looking at the ground, unsure of what to say. Telling her that he'd assumed her race was a collection of murdering savages wasn't the best thing, he supposed.

"Alright," she said as the file downloaded. "I don't know what your music sounds like, but here it is a lost art. In the past, there were people who created the most wonderful melodies. Nowadays, though, the definition of music has become far more lax. Any old garbage can fit the criteria, and I won't show you that stuff. It might make you decide to wipe us out."

Turukaishal nodded, leaning forward slightly. Back on Chindrus, most music was derived from crystal flutes, glass bells or stringed instruments. What did human music sound like? His mind was drawing a blank as to what it could possibly be.

Without warning a soft, warm sound filled the room. Turukaishal looked around in surprise before it dawned on him that it was coming from the laptop. Victoria was watching him curiously, trying to read his reaction. He stared down at the electronic device, his eyes slightly unfocused (although it wasn't immediately apparent, his eyes being as alien as they were) as he listened to the melody dance through the air.

The song began to increase after a moment or two, adding sharper notes and picking up its pace. It was definitely not just one musician, as was common on Chindrus. Rather, it sounded like an entire crowd of Vahran had been involved in the production of this single piece. Turukaishal found himself drumming his fingers again, this time in tune to the music. "What is this?"

"Tchaikovsky's 'Waltz of the Flowers'," Victoria said as his eyes shifted to gold and yellow. Admiration and happiness. Whoever this Tchaikovsky was, he was a genius. This was... he couldn't think of a word for it. The song had returned to its previous slower notes, but now they seemed to carry more intensity. "IT's from the ballet 'The Nutcracker Suite'."

"Nutcracker what?"

"The Nutcracker Suite," she said, smiling. "It's a ballet, or a type of on-stage dance." The music reached another crescendo as she explained. "It's perhaps one of the best loved Christmas—oh! Oh god, it's six days until Christmas and you probably don't even know what it is!" her hands had flown up to her mouth as she stared at him, wide-eyed.

Turukaishal suddenly felt incredibly stupid. Judging by her reaction, he *should* know about this "Christmas". He felt his eyes turn pink against his will. "Um..." he scratched nervously at the back of his neck with his long fingers.

"It's the biggest holiday of the year!" she said excitedly. "It has two sides to it: religious and commercial." Turukaishal motioned for her to continue, grateful that they weren't on an awkward topic anymore. Victoria continued, still bubbling with energy. It was hard to believe she had been comatose until twenty minutes ago. "The religious side celebrates the birth of Jesus," she told him, smiling.

Turukaishal had read about Jesus. He was one of the pivotal figures of Christianity, which was one of the major monotheistic Vahran religions. The teachings of Jesus seemed to have been founded on compassion and tolerance, but judging from how the Vahran behaved not many of them actually abided by them. While it looked fascinating, Turukaishal really had no intentions of joining a Vahran church.

"The other side," she continued, "is what most people celebrate. The commercial side. People go out and get Christmas trees, decorate them (and their houses) with lights and ornaments. On Christmas day, everyone gives gifts to each other, all wrapped up in shiny paper. Children are told that Santa Claus brings them if they are good."

"Santa Claus?" Turukaishal asked, blinking.

"Santa Claus is a big fat guy in a red suit," Victoria told him, smiling broadly. "According to the children's stories, he lives at the North Pole with his elves, making toys in a workshop. On Christmas Eve, he gets in a sleigh pulled by reindeer and flies around the world to deliver all the toys to the good little boys and girls!"

"So," Turukaishal said, staring at her with a mixture of confusion and trepidation. "In a single night an obese Vahran climbs into a sleigh pulled by animals—which cannot normally fly—to visit every house on the planet and deliver toys? Firstly, it is impossible to transit the globe in a single night with merely a sleigh. Secondly, reindeer cannot fly. Thirdly, the North Pole is virtually devoid of life, if I remember correctly."

"I *know* it's impossible!" Victoria said. "This is just the story kids believe in. Later, they grow up. It's just something fun to do. When we get older, we still do the gift thing though. Come on! We have to get you a Christmas tree before all the..." she tapered off, looking at the Scain. Turukaishal was pointing out the window of the master bedroom. Outside, the snow was still falling. It was no longer a blizzard, but it was still falling heavily. "...right. Tomorrow then?" she suggested. "Oh, and we can bake the cookies too!"

"Must I participate in this?" Turukaishal asked. For some reason, the whole affair seemed complicated and ridiculous. In six days, he was going to have to decorate his house, procure and decorate a tree, purchase and wrap gifts, bake these mysterious cookies (whatever the heck they were)... he'd chosen the wrong time of year to come to Earth.

"Of course! You'll love it! Christmas is the one time of year where everyone is nice to each other. Not to mention you get to spend time with those you love!"

"Then you should be with your brother, Martin," Turukaishal pointed out.

"Martin isn't here," Richard said. He'd come in, watching their conversation with detached curiosity. It reminded Turukaishal of how Scain scientists acted. "He's away on business and won't be back until February."

Wonderful. This was likely the reason Victoria was insisting on his participation: as a replica for her older brother. He frowned. "Surely you have relatives somewhere!" he said, looking between the siblings. "Besides, I do not fit the category. I am not a loved one, I am a Scain."

Victoria looked away. Richard coughed, clearing his throat. "That may have been a bad choice of words on her part. Christmas can be spent with close friends or family as well. And after you basically saved Victoria's life, I would certainly not object to spending the holidays with you. However, the matter rests in your hands. I won't try to force you into anything. I'll leave that to my sister."

"Hey!" Victoria stuck her tongue out at her brother before turning back to the Scain. Turukaishal noticed that her tongue was a single pink muscle. His was dark gray and divided down the center, each half as thin as her little finger and pressed flat. He had to keep his tongues pressed together to be able to speak their language, which was a challenge. "Come on, Turu!" she said. "It'll be fun! You'll never see the good to humans if you don't try something new every now and then!"

She had a point there, Turukaishal would concede that much. But decorating trees didn't seem like it was going to help him see the good in Vahran... or would it? He felt himself waffling on the decision. Victoria jumped out from beneath the covers, kneeling on the bed with her hands clasped in front of her. "Please?!"

Turukaishal looked away. "Fine. But please, for the love of the Hiin, get some clothing on." He walked out of the room, keeping his eyes shielded as he passed Richard. Their pink hue was more humiliating than anything he'd ever experienced before. He sighed, leaning his head on the wall outside with a thud. Did humans have no decency? Or was it common to beg and plead in nothing more than a thin tee-shirt and panties? He sighed, shaking his head and working as best he could to delete the picture from his mind.

Chapter 24

BEGIN MESSAGE:

LOCATION: Sillothel, Kinbara Shipyard

TIME: 16/53 Local Time

MESSAGE: What is going on, Turukaishal? I spoke with Klakshan less than a rotation ago and he says that he overheard someone saying a Heil bounty hunter is after you. Why? Son, please, talk to me. What is going on?

I do not know why we drifted apart. Was it Dayislia? Everyone knows it was not your fault. That trial was bogus and you know it. And even in a bogus trial you were acquitted. Demnechi is an idiot, and we both know that. He arranged that trial as a publicity stunt, and it worked. He got the High Councilor's post. Wonderful. Do not let it tear at you, son. No matter what you think, Dayislia was a fluke. No one could have prevented it!

- Ferthoroyia

Turukaishal sighed, allowing his communicator to clatter down on the table. His father was right, of course: Dayislia had been a terrible, terrible fluke. Nothing could have prepared his team for it and there was no way the blame should have fallen to him. At first, the public had blamed him for the failure, but after what his father had referred to as the 'bogus trial', he was acquitted and allowed to resume duty. But the scars of that mission ran as deep as Limkalan – far deeper than the compensation of the Black Fleet could heal.

He looked out the window, leaning back on the couch. The snow was beginning to ease up – perhaps in a few hours he would be able to leave. Until then, he was effectively imprisoned within his own home... and while the two Vahran slept and he had nothing but the darkness for companionship, he became easy prey for thoughts and memories like these. He looked at the clock, sighing again. It was two in the morning – Richard and Victoria were probably both fast asleep. He should really try to get some sleep himself, but he just didn't feel like it. He was tired, of course, but his brain just didn't feel like allowing him any kind of relief or respite from his thoughts.

Dayislia. He snorted, remembering it in vivid detail. The whole mission had been ridiculous from the planning phase onwards. War had been going on for several years between the Scain and their neighbors, the Sov-Nikan, a group of advanced arboreal sentients. Turukaishal had been the commanding officer of a twenty-Scain team at the time, and they had informed him that he would be used to choke a Sov-Nikan supply line on the planet of Dayislia. In order to avoid detection, they would be hard-dropped to the planet's surface in refitted atmospheric pods; devices usually used to collect date from atmospherically dangerous planets.

According to the briefing, they would be dropped on the island of Mis-Niguac in the Iso'ysial Ocean. From there, they would hike for half a day to the west, eventually coming across a set of Old Race ruins that had been discovered a few years prior. He was to garrison the ruins and set up a forward command post, hunkering down and awaiting further orders. Dayislia was crawling with Sov-Nikan and several scouting parties could stumble across the ruins, so he was to expect a night of gunfire.

Instead of the mission proceeding as planned, Turukaishal and his team had gotten the royal shaft. When his team flew over the projected area in preparation for the drop, it wasn't the archipelago on the maps: it was nothing but ocean. The charts were wrong. It had taken them almost four hours (local time) of working with their navigation spotter to even *find* the ruins. They had to hard drop directly into the forest, which Turukaishal knew was going to attract attention, and quickly pack up and march to the site.

And of course, things couldn't just stop there. Upon arriving at the gleaming white ruins, they found that the main structure was infested with Gaphet – large, furred beetles that were common to many planets in the Galaxy due to their resilience and ability to adjust to extreme climates. They could be found in the frozen wastelands of Nihran or the sweltering deserts of Altar and everywhere in between. And Gaphet are a threat to larger creatures than themselves... including Scain.

After fighting through the night to clear out the Gaphet, his team had set up the command post and bunkered down as best they could. Their twenty man cell had dropped to seventeen, the Gaphet having claimed the lives of three of Turukaishal's squadmates before having succumbed to the Scain's weapons. The following day, as the planet's twin suns burned down between the dense, tropical foliage, his team was attacked by the Sov-Nikan. What was unexpected, however, was that the monsters had attacked in an army, not a scouting party. Turukaishal and his squad had been overwhelmed in minutes.

Attempting to salvage their command post, Turukaishal radioed his commander. He was told to maintain position until additional troops arrived. A dropship, laden with weapons and soldiers, was on its way. Emboldened by the thought of salvation, Turukaishal and his group managed to force the Sov-Nikan back to the edge of their camp as they cleared a drop zone, but the ship never came. Instead, Turukaishal and his team were forced into a sixteen-hour firefight which only ended when their communications officer called for emergency extraction. Seven hundred Sov-Nikan lay dead and only Turukaishal and the officer, his best friend Bandrumano, made it out alive. The mission was considered a failure and blame fell to the highest ranking officer on the ground: Turukaishal.

Turukaishal stood up from the table and began pacing back and forth. Outside, he could still hear the whisper of the wind in the trees and the occasional soft thump as a pile of snow dropped from the overhead branches. His mother had never failed any mission in all her years as a soldier. Turukaishal had blown two. First there had been Dayislia. After the farcical trial and his subsequent reinstatement, he was shipped off to aid in the Erythian Rebellion and after a handful of minor skirmishes was sent to Limkalan... where his father's brother died and his entire team almost froze to death in some ice caves. Dayislia was bad intel – not his fault – but Limkalan was. He had believed that nothing else could fly in the blizzard and had convinced their pilot to take off. He'd been wrong, and it had cost him the life of his father's brother.

He'd distanced himself from family and the few friends he had after that. The Mindbank offered him a position within the Black Fleet and he accepted it quickly, signing up and passing the entrance exams with flying colors. His record was outstanding: a ratio of ninety-one successful missions to two failed. Most Scain would have killed for a ratio like that. Turukaishal threw himself into the hardest, most dangerous missions the Mindbank could offer him. Diathua Base... the Anu'bai... and now Earth... it was all part of his recent string of missions that he had taken. He sighed, leaning on the windowsill. Some days he didn't even feel like the same Scain as a hundred years ago. He felt like a machine, programmed to act when the Mindbank ordered it.

He remembered when the Mindbank had vanished – almost seventy years ago. His ship had vanished without a trace and had apparently crashed—it wasn't Turukaishal's place to know where—and he'd fallen off the radar for five years. When he finally returned, it was in the middle of a debate to elect a new Mindbank, which made for quite the dramatic reentry. Everyone had been glad to have Sovakadris back among his own kind, but only those closest to him, like an ex-Vanguard like Turukaishal, could see that he had changed.

He had come back missing an arm, for one – a closely guarded secret that not many were aware of. He kept his robes hanging limply to conceal the left side of his body, where a mechanical monstrosity had replaced his limb. It had been sloppily constructed from ship parts—namely the black iskindite alloy used in reactor plating—and clicked hollowly whenever he flexed the four sharp fingers. The first time Turukaishal had seen it, Sovakadris had told him that his captors had made it for him. Strangely enough, even after the Mindbank's cabinet managed to enlist the aid of the Zyzyts to regrow the arm, the Scion refused to allow it. Why Sovakadris was so devoted to the cybernetic abomination was something Turukaishal would never understand.

Turukaishal opened his front door, stepping out onto his porch and resting his long-fingered hands on the railing. Beneath the slanted roof, he was not in any danger of being buried in the cold, white flakes. This planet, he decided, was truly beautiful. He found himself yearning to protect it. How would the Scain come in to take the planet, he wondered? Would it be clean and efficient – a plague that only targeted Vahran, perhaps – or would they take it with all guns blazing and burn the world to ash?

He felt himself torn between two extremes. On the one hand, he was a Scain: loyal to the Mindbank to the point of death and committed to supporting the Scain Empire and her interests. But for some reason, Earth was growing on him. He sighed for a third time that night, shaking his head. He was an alien to this world and if they ever saw him like this, they would likely shoot him. Klaara, the annoying bounty hunter, faced the same dilemma.

His hearts went out to the Heil. He could sympathize with her plight to some degree. The Heil were a race that not many species wanted to affiliate themselves with. They were a clan-based, dominance-centered society that kept mostly to itself, and there was more than enough infighting between the Heil Clans and the Guilds that hid out on the deserts of their homeworld, Sovereign, to drive away the 'civilized' races of the Galaxy. Due to their seclusion, rumors and suspicions ended up swirling around the Heil like a storm – other races occasionally refused Heil service out of fear, which merely perpetuated a cycle of distrust which kept the Heil close to their planets or to the "border worlds".

Those Heil that did want to escape the lifestyle of their people were often forced to take meager, demeaning jobs that barely paid enough. Bounty Hunting was probably their best bet, which was why so many Heil tried it. Mercenary work, or "bottom feeding", was another vein many Heil tried. And there were far worse fates that befell some Heil. Turukaishal remembered traveling with Bandrumano to one of the border worlds near Sillothel, where his father was now working. He had seen a facility that was literally selling female Heil for services Turukaishal was hesitant to recall.

 What most of the Heil needed to do, in his opinion, was start showing up outside of the Senate and Triumvirate meetings. Those were the only two instances in which the Heil were *required* to be present. Any other time they ignored formal summons. If more people became exposed to the Heil, it would help to penetrate the miasma of dislike. Turukaishal actually had no problem with the two-toned sentients (unless they were trying to kill him) – both he and Bandrumano had served together in a variety of Heil-centric missions.

Turukaishal sensed a presence behind him and turned around. Victoria. She was standing in the doorway watching him with those endless green eyes of hers. He said nothing, content to merely stare at her for a moment. She seemed embarrassed about being found, but stood her ground before speaking. "You shouldn't be out here this late," she said. "You might catch a cold."

The Scain turned around fully to face her, sitting against the railing. He could feel the snowflakes landing on his shoulders. Now that the driving wind had stopped trying to peel up the ground, it was actually rather pleasant. "The same could be said to you," he said, gesturing to her attire. She was barefoot, still dressed in her sleep attire but sporting one of his bathrobes. It was far too big for her.

"I'm alright," she said, stepping out onto the porch and looking at the snow. "Besides, you can always try to do the adrenaline thing again, right?"

He looked away, cursing in his mind. That was a low blow. She just *had* to bring that up again. And then he shrugged, sighing. If she wanted to play, he could play. He looked back, keeping his eyes as neutral as he could. "You sound as if you *want* me to try it again."

The result was exactly as he'd predicted. Her aura immediately became pink and gelatinous again, her face lighting up red and almost glowing in the early morning darkness. "I-no-I-it was a joke!" she stammered, looking up at him with wide eyes. The height difference was so much greater when he was in a Scain body.

His eyes turned yellow involuntarily. "I was merely jesting," he assured her. "I saw it as fair."

"Yeah, okay... fine..." she said, turning and looking back out at the snow. The pair of them stood in silence before Turukaishal spoke again.

"Are you not tired?" he asked, looking sideways at her. She looked so thin and frail in his oversized terry-cloth bathrobe; as if a strong gust of wind could snap her apart. He had a faint urge to usher her back into the house before it happened, but managed to remind himself that she was still a Vahran. That meant she was likely hardier than she looked and would be difficult to kill. Tenacious. She'd be alright for a few minutes.

"Nah," she said. "I think I slept enough while you and Rich stewed about my health," she said with a small smile. "Oh well. When the summer comes around, we'll see who'll be laughing. Richard can take the cold, but *I* can take the *heat*."

Turukaishal chuckled. Hot and cold. Night and day. Just like on Chindrus, siblings (when they occurred) seemed to be opposite poles. Bandrumano, for instance, was a lax and easygoing specimen of a Scain. Nothing really bothered him, and he somehow managed to find something to grin idiotically about at all hours of the day or night. His twin sister, Kelmandi, was completely different. She was a high-strung and micromanaging piece of work with no talent for diplomacy. Turukaishal had met her once and had been shaken by the sheer volume of frenetic energy the female exerted. He shook memories of home out of his head – they would only make him yearn for it – and looked back to the door. "We should head inside, though," he said. "It is still winter, and you are hardly dressed for the weather. And I suspect your brother is very capable of killing me if you contract influenza."

Chapter 25

BEGIN MESSAGE:

LOCATION: *Seygahn Veil, Borderline*

TIME: *UNAVAILABLE, IN TRANSIT*

MESSAGE: *You are acting quite unlike yourself, Turukaishal. You have a Heil trying to kill you and you haven't called me to come aid you? Relax. I have a squad prepped and ready to go if you need us. Just send the word, and the coordinates, and we will be on our way. Task Force Kirel was on leave anyway.*

Most of us would rather have you back in one piece rather than in a vial, especially me: you still owe me a thousand credits from that bet back on Virathanca.

- Bordra, Task Force Kirel

Turukaishal winced as he slid that piece of plastic (Victoria referred to it as his "debit card") through yet another machine. Three-hundred and twelve dollars and eighty one cents... it wasn't like he had a shortage of funds, but spending large quantities of it made him nervous. As if he might draw attention to himself or blow his cover. But Victoria insisted on copious amounts of miniscule glass bulbs on greenish cables, so here he stood.

As soon as the lights were bagged, Turukaishal was more than eager to leave the store. They'd already gone and purchased a series of round, coniferous rings. Victoria called them "wreaths". Turukaishal called them hoops of fake, plastic greenery with bright red bows. Prior to that, Richard had made the evil suggestion of 'ornaments', which had sent Victoria into a tempestuous fury of "Christmas Spirit". This whirlwind had ended in over two-hundred dollars of tiny round baubles that would go in his tree... whenever he got it.

"Okay. Now all that's left is the tree!" Victoria said, all but singing the words as she veritably skipped out behind Turukaishal. Richard followed behind them, his dark clothing seeming to dampen the cheer and warmth of the holiday as he trudged along, glowering at people who paused long enough to look at him. He gave the ornaments and lights no more than a passing glance as they purchased them, clearly only barely interested in the whole ordeal. Instead, he kept his mirrored eyes on groups of people and individuals in much the same way a predator took note of unwary prey for later.

"And where, pray tell, does one procure such a plant?" Turukaishal asked as he shouldered the lights. Richard's car was snowed under and Victoria didn't own one yet, her brother being her main mode of transportation. The Scain, for all his intellect, had neglected to purchase one. Firstly, he had no intentions of driving anywhere and secondly, he doubted he would fit into a compact human vehicle. This was the primary reason he was all but buried under the lights. The ornaments and wreaths were at his domicile, thanks to a local taxi.

"Tree lots," Richard grunted. He didn't sound particularly pleased, which prompted Turukaishal to turn and look at the surly youth. Not that he ever sounded pleasant, per se, but his tone of voice made it sound as if he was contemplating homicide for suggesting such a location. "They're places where lots of trees are kept for people to buy during Christmas. If you want a good tree, go to a U-Cut-It place. Sadly, there're none around here. Closest lot is down in Steilacoom."

"I have the vaguest of notions that you will not be joining us," Turukaishal said.

"I won't be," Richard affirmed. "I'll take all this crap back to the house for you, but I'm not showing my face in Steilacoom. Ever." He reached out, extending his hand motioning for the bag of lights. Turukaishal gratefully handed it over to him—the blasted things were heavy for a Scain—and looked at Victoria.

"You would trust me with your sister's well-being?" he asked, looking back at Richard in mild surprise. "The other night you were not above accusing me of-"

"I wasn't thinking," Richard interrupted, giving the Scain a sharp, predatory glare as if to say "not now". Turukaishal took it to mean that he didn't want to discuss it in front of Victoria. He understood.

"Very well," he said, "I shall see you back at my domicile, if that is your decision." He turned and began walking, but paused when realized that no one was following. He looked back to see the two Vahran whispering together. Richard's aura was sharp and orange—he was surprised and shocked—but Victoria's was muted and pink. Borderline embarrassed, but not quite the same as their discussion in the bedroom. Apart from that, he had no way of knowing what their discussion entailed... which was enough to cause his innate paranoia to spike a bit.

Victoria broke away as Richard made a quick grabbing motion for her arm. Weighed down as he was by the lights, all he ended up doing was falling in the snow with a muffled curse. His sister, either heedless of his plight or outright ignoring him, danced over to stand next to Turukaishal. "Ready to go, Turu?"

"Is everything alright?" Turukaishal asked as he nodded in Richard's direction. The Vahran was swearing under his breath as he picked up the lights, his blue coat almost wholly white with all the snow sticking to it. Turukaishal distinctly heard the words "I hate Christmas".

"Richard's just being Richard," she explained. "He's a bit worried about me."

Turukaishal sensed a little white lie, but decided to ignore it. There was likely a large amount of truth in her statement anyway. Richard was overbearing and protective, although likely with a good reason. Victoria had been stared at many times during their outings. As had Richard, although for different reasons. Turquoise-silver auras gave away the humans who stared at her: lust. An alien surge of protectiveness had prompted him to engage in a few subtle tricks – small-time Psionic tricks like hurling snowballs from random directions or dropping merchandise from shelves near them.

The two of them set off along the sidewalk. Turukaishal could see the ice on the ground, and he found himself oddly thankful for his ability to look like a Vahran. Scain had naturally small feet – cylindrical and hoof-like in structure. They would have been the death of him on these icy roads. Anything less than this body would have made him look like a fool, humiliating himself with fall after fall on the slick sidewalks.

"Hey Turu," Victoria asked after a few minutes. "Can I ask you something?"

Turukaishal looked at her in surprise. Her aura was pink and malleable again – this was going to be awkward, he could sense it. He felt his own eyes match her aura's color and was insanely grateful for the sunglasses. He heard himself say "Certainly" before he could stop himself.

"Do you like me?"

Turukaishal cocked his head slightly, his eyes returning to black. He wasn't quite certain of what to make of a question like that. "I am not certain. For a Vahran, you have defied all predicted standards. I cannot honestly say I am displeased by that. You have shown me nothing but kindness, and for that I am grateful. I honestly believe that you are, in fact, a good Vahran. No, I should say, a good human. Does that mean I like you?"

Victoria looked up at him. "Well, kind of. It means you tolerate me. Let's see..." she fell into a period of contemplation. Turukaishal remained quiet, a natural state for him, until she spoke again. "Let's say you had to choose to spend time with one person on this planet. Who would it be?"

"You," Turukaishal answered automatically. "And for all of the previously listed reasons... what does this have to do with anything?" Some instinctual warning sounded – something telling him he was walking right into a trap that he wasn't going to be able to get out of.

Victoria beamed from ear to ear and gave Turukaishal one of her special 'bone breaker' hugs around his waist. She didn't say anything: just stood there with her arms around him. Turukaishal stood there, surprised, as he looked down at her. What had he done to deserve this response? Tentatively, he placed his hands on her shoulders. "Um... why are you doing this?"

"Because I like you!" she said, pulling away and looking up at him. "You're different – you may have been sent here to destroy us, but you've got a good heart. I like that."

Turukaishal was touched. A good heart? Him? Wasn't he, like she had just said, sent here to wipe them out? Or at least assist with it? He looked at her in confusion for a moment before allowing his hands to drop to his sides. "I am... honored that you would say that..." he said, suddenly feeling very uncomfortable. It was probably below freezing, but he felt very warm... just like he had in the bedroom. He knew his eyes were pink behind his glasses.

"Come on!" she said, taking his hand and pulling him down the sidewalk. "We have to get that tree. You'll love it when it's all decorated!"

Turukaishal followed behind her—not like he had much choice, seeing as she was pulling him along by his hand—with a small smile on his lips. He was slowly starting to realize something. It wasn't Earth that was growing on him: it was Victoria and her brother... mostly Victoria. Somehow, despite the fact that she was a Vahran, he was warming up to her. He could feel it.

It was pure happenstance that saved both their lives. Turukaishal caught a glimpse of something metal and gleaming in his peripheral vision and, with reflexes born of almost two centuries of being a soldier, he tackled Victoria and pressed her against the ground. Something whizzed past them, flying above them, and landed in the snow a good distance away. It exploded a moment later, throwing dirt and ice in every direction. Turukaishal growled as he heard an all-too-familiar voice ring out over the blast. "Found you, Scain!"

Turukaishal rolled off Victoria, remaining low to the ground as he faced the Heil. She was walking towards him from the other side of the park, lowering her gun as she walked and plugging another round into it from behind, snapping it closed. Heil didn't commonly use guns, and this wasn't a Heil-manufactured weapon. It looked Iharsh-Daraz in make, which meant it couldn't fire more than four shots at a time. This one was a single round weapon. If she missed with her next shot, she wouldn't be able to load another before he was upon her. She'd either have to use her arts or escape.

Turukaishal stood up, positioning himself between Victoria and Klaara, his eyes red and unmasked by his dive. "We can settle this, Heil, but not here. Not now. If the Vahran see us, or if they see that gun of yours, our covers will be blown. You know that."

Klaara shouldered the long-barreled gun—a grenade launcher by all rights—and smirked. "Just as smart as your dossier said you were. Impressive. Fine, you can walk away this time – I'm feeling charitable—but just remember that I'm watching you. The minute you let your guard down and you don't have any pesky apes guarding you..." she gave a long, pointed look at Victoria "...I'll be there."

She turned to leave, but paused for a moment and looked back over her shoulder. "By the way, where's that other brat? Richard or whatever his name was? I was looking forward to blowing him up face-to-face."

"Richard isn't here," Turukaishal said, not moving from his position between the Heil and Victoria. "But it is likely that he will confront you about this the next time we meet."

"Maybe," Klaara said. "I think next time I'll fight you with my sword... it'll be more fun. You can probably deflect these rounds with your Psionics anyway. Either way, bye bye for now!"

It was only once she was out of sight that Turukaishal released the breath he hadn't been aware he was holding.

Chapter 26

BEGIN MESSAGE:

LOCATION: Chindrus, Amara District

TIME: 21/22 Local Time

MESSAGE: Something is wrong. I can feel it. The balance of power is beginning to shift. Watch yourself. I suspect Demnechi has it in for you. Either that or the Mindbank no longer cares what happens to you. Watch yourself.

- Klakshan

Turukaishal sighed, staring dejectedly at the rows upon rows of coniferous trees. Most of them looked, for lack of a better word, dead. Brownish needles pooled around them on the ground and the branches on the trees stuck out like grasping skeletal arms. Others had been cast into a corner where they slumped pitifully, their crowns having snapped off or their trunks having cracked. "And this is where we are going to find the 'perfect Christmas Tree'?" he asked skeptically.

"Uh huh!" Victoria said, brushing at a bit of snow that was stuck to her sweater. "Come on – we have to hurry. This close to Christmas, the good ones are getting rare."

The Scain wanted to point out that it looked like these "good ones" were not just rare, but likely extinct as well. With a cursory glance around, namely to make sure there were no psychotic Heil hiding in the artificial forest, he followed Victoria into the trees, his hands stuffed into the pockets of his coat to keep them warm.

It took almost two hours. Turukaishal was on the verge of abandoning the whole thing and dragging Victoria away from the lot when she let out an excited cry and raced over to one of the trees. "This is it! It's perfect!"

He sized up the tree, one eyebrow raised. It looked very much like the others, if not a shade or two healthier… not to mention it was huge, just under eight feet in height. Victoria was dancing all around it, pointing out how the branches were "just the right distance apart" while the base had just enough room for "a ton of loot". Turukaishal shook his head in bewilderment. This much thought went into selecting a *tree*?

"Fine," Turukaishal said after a while, walking up and fishing the price tag out of the branches. "How much is—*blast* these idiots and their overpriced trees!" he said, dropping the tag as if it would bite him. "*Pirates* would offer a better deal!" The garishly colored tag announced that an eight foot noble fir cost just over a hundred dollars. What was so noble about ruining someone's wallet?

Victoria looked at the tag. "Around here, that's pretty good though. It was probably discounted because we're so close to Christmas."

The Scain mumbled something in his own tongue as he sized up the offending piece of foliage. On Chindrus, plants held a special place in the hearts of the Scain, which meant he really had no choice in the matter. "Alright. Fine. I'll buy it," he said, sighing. Of course, on Chindrus it would have been a third of the price. "How do we get it home?"

Victoria could only give him a blank stare. The Scain massaged his forehead, sighing. "Back to the taxi service then," he mumbled, looking over at the tree. Was all this really worth it? He looked down at Victoria. She was staring at the tree in complete rapture, her face lit up by a brilliant smile. He sighed again. Yes, he supposed it was. Since when had he gone so soft? He stalked over to the salesman to make the purchase.

It took almost another hour to call a cab and get the blasted thing strapped to the top. The cab driver kept shooting sidelong glances at Victoria during the whole process, and Turukaishal eventually intervened by stepping in front of him and announcing their destination. Another bout of piracy, in Turukaishal's opinion, ended with him giving the driver almost twenty dollars upon their arrival. And, since the road didn't lead all the way to Turukaishal's front door, another twenty to have the man help them drag the thing onto the doorstep.

As he watched the turquoise automobile putter away, Turukaishal had an almost irrepressible urge to hurl something at it. Not only had the driver been curt and somewhat rude, he had been ogling Victoria the whole time. And Turukaishal knew that he'd been extorting money out of them – there was no way his transportation costs should have been sixty dollars. The Scain rubbed at his eyes. Since when was he the overprotective one? That was Richard's job.

Victoria and Richard helped shove the massive tree through the door into Turukaishal's living room. The ceiling there was highest, actually up on the second floor where a balconied landing ran from one side of the room to the other. Richard, having come in during their losing battle with the eight foot plant, helped Victoria find the "perfect side" to display and held it up while Turukaishal used his Psionics to screw it into the base.

With the arboreal menace finally in place, Turukaishal took several steps back, admired his handiwork, and then collapsed on the couch next to Richard with a sigh. "I am so glad that is over," he said with a quick wipe of his forehead. "What is the next item on our agenda?"

"Well, we should probably decorate the outside first. Make it look nice and Christmassy." Victoria said, tapping her chin thoughtfully as she stared down at them. Turukaishal wanted to know where this whelp of a human got so much energy from. It was unnatural.

Richard grunted, removing his arm from its resting place over his eyes. "I'll pass. I've been trying to figure out which strands will go where… and failing miserably. I hate Christmas."

Turukaishal got up and placidly followed Victoria back out into the front yard. On the porch next to the door was a stack of bags and boxes: the decorations they'd purchased earlier. Turukaishal thought the pile was larger than he remembered it, and wondered if Richard had purchased a few extra necessities… not that any of this was actually necessary. "You do realize that these will probably remain here on Earth longer than I will, correct?" he asked as Victoria surveyed the front of his house.

The result was instant. She said nothing, but her aura plunged to blue. Sadness. Was she actually upset about him leaving? He frowned. "Victoria?" This shift in her behavior was alarming – she was usually upbeat and happy. This blue color didn't suit her.

"It's nothing," she said, smiling widely up at him. "Come on – we need to start with the wreaths!" Despite the smile on her face, her aura gave her away. It remained blue. She was merely masking what she was feeling, which didn't work on Scain.

"Victoria," Turukaishal said seriously, "if there is something you need to speak about, it is infinitely better to communicate it than to bottle it up." He looked at her, trying to gauge her reaction. He knew it to be true, but for different reasons. Scain who bottled up their emotions ended up unable to use their Psionics. Usually, they developed a cathartic release. Turukaishal, for instance, either smoked the methane canisters that were so popular back home or took his ship out for a few days and just cruised around. As far as he knew, though, humans tended to encapsulate their feelings.

"It's just…" she said, chewing on her lip. "I like you. A lot. And I'll miss you when you go." Turukaishal felt his eyes shift to orange. He shook his head, removing his sunglasses and tossing them on the porch. His disguise vanished as well – he had become far more adept at switching between the two, which meant it wasn't costing him as much energy.

"Victoria, you knew it was going to happen," he reminded her. "I was supposed to leave days ago, but I made a promise to you. You still have twenty-six days before I make my final judgment."

147

"I know," she said, one of her fists clenching. "But I just feel so helpless. I know that there are good people out there, Turu. Just look at Richard. But trying to find ways to prove it is just... I can't..."

Turukaishal walked over to her—three strides of his long legs—and placed a hand on her shoulder. "You are doing very well, in any case," he told her. "I find myself beginning to wonder about what my leader has told me for many cycles: whether or not humans are actually evil. This is by no means a certainty, but I find myself questioning him... something I am not supposed to do."

Victoria smiled up at him, and Turukaishal felt his own mood improve. Were humans empaths, he wondered? Did they possess the ability to project their emotions like the Amarchites? No, something like that would have appeared in the Erythian reports cycles ago. He blinked and looked around, seeking anything to hold his attention for a moment; anywhere but her. This was getting ridiculous. He was going to need to spend a lot of time researching what was going on here. He should still have access to the Galactic Data Matrix servers... maybe he could find something out there.

"In any case," Victoria said, providing him a momentary distraction, "we need to get these lights up. And then Richard and I need to go find your presents."

"Presents?" Turukaishal blinked owlishly at her.

"Yeah. Presents. On Christmas day, you give someone something nice! It's tradition. You get someone a gift and then wrap it up in bright shiny foil..." Turukaishal watched as she spoke at length about these 'presents'. She seemed, for lack of a better word, ecstatic. This left him with another problem. If these presents were an irrevocable part of Christmas, he was going to have to get them something. But what to get for a human? What did they want? He couldn't very well just ask them – that would void the logic of disguising the gifts in garish wrapping... so what was he to do?

He turned and looked at the house. "So what am I supposed to do with the wreaths?" he asked, folding his arms across his chest and looking for an excuse to distract her from the discussion she was having (mostly with herself) about presents.

"You use the little suction cups to hold them to your windows and doors," she explained. "Do you have a ladder? I'll get the upper floor while—*that's not fair!!*"

Turukaishal had drawn a hand through his chest and was currently levitating dozens of wreaths around the house. They sailed through the air like green birds, striking the building with loud thumps and adhering to windows and doorways. The remainder hung on the posts near his front door and attached themselves to the thick trees near his house. He turned and looked down at her, smirking. "What's next?"

"Can you do that with the lights?" Victoria asked. "They go along the gutters, around the posts or along the insides of the windows. Any extras are up to you."

The insanely long garlands of colorful bulbs unwound themselves from their packaging and slithered out of bags like giant snakes, winding around the house. Some twisted around trees, pulled taut against the bark by Turukaishal's Psionics. They wove between the lattices of his porch as Turukaishal moved his hands like a conductor, each strand leaping to obey him. They lined the windows perfectly, their ends snapping together and joining until he plugged the last one into an outlet—wired to his ship's power source—with a flourish.

The house, surrounding trees, and yard lit up with a spectacular display of colorful lights. All along the trees, the lights blinked and skipped through the sparse branches or colored evergreen boughs. The wreaths, even, had received a liberal sprinkling of small colored lights. Victoria gaped at him for a few seconds before sticking her tongue out at him. "You won't be doing that to the tree – that's special. But still, good job. I wish it went this fast every year!"

Turukaishal swelled with pride, looking back at the house. It didn't solve his dilemma of what to get the two humans for Christmas, but it certainly staved off the issue for a while. He drank in the image of his home (however temporary) blanketed with snow and twinkling with the cheerful holiday lights and wreaths. It was a foregone conclusion that his eyes turned a happy shade of yellow as he took in the scene before him.

Chapter 27

BEGIN MESSAGE:

LOCATION: Chindrus, Denuval District

TIME: 12/22 Local Time

MESSAGE: I spoke with your father today. He called me and asked how you were doing. He's over on Sillothel and worried sick about you. We all are. Klakshan did a bit of digging and found out about your Heil problem, and we're all nervous. Whoever this Heil is, they have their work cut out for them. You're not exactly easy to kill – any Anu'bai or Sov-Nikan will tell them that. But your father is taking this especially hard – I'm not going to vote for his state of mind being sound right now.

- Bandrumano

Richard's long, pale fingers quickly opened another box of Christmas lights. Turukaishal, forbidden by Victoria to 'cheat' with his Psionics anymore, dutifully took the string and began winding it through the boughs. Victoria, in the meantime, had vanished into the kitchen and closed the door. When asked why, she would only answer that it was a surprise. Turukaishal glared at the door, shaking out his hands. Surprise? She just wanted to avoid the needles and sap in this blasted plant! He wiped his hands off on his legs, feeling his fingers sticking to the material of his polyform suit, and sighed.

"Watch the twig," Richard said as Turukaishal ducked beneath one of the longer limbs and continued to string the lights into the tree. By ducking the first twig, however, the Scain ended up smacked with a second one. He recoiled, a large glob of the plant's adhesive resin stuck directly between his eyes. He held perfectly still for a moment before growling a long string of alien curses. He tossed the last of the lights haphazardly in the tree and stood up, wiping the sap off his face with one clean motion. This, of course, only got it stuck to his hands as well. Richard looked up in amusement. "Oh yeah... and the sap too."

Turukaishal opened his mouth to respond but was immediately greeted by Victoria as she bounced between the Scain and her brother. She was wielding a tray of small, flat objects, each one decorated with some kind of colorful paste. Tiny, glistening sugar crystals adorned the top of each object and there was a sweet smell in the air wafting from the platter. Turukaishal blinked, forgetting about his issues with the sap for a moment. "What, pray tell, are those?" he asked, pointing at the plate with one of his bony fingers.

"Sugar cookies!" Victoria said brightly. "I baked them without yeast – you told me you were allergic, remember?"

Turukaishal had to think for a moment before he remembered that it was one of the questions he'd been asked during their initial game of "Twenty Questions" on their second day of acquaintance. He nodded, reaching down and taking one of the 'cookies' from the plate and holding it up to his eyes. It was a disgustingly cute snowman. One of her snowmen, with the three spheres (or in this case, discs) stacked atop each other. It also had cute little stovepipe top hat atop its head, and she had gone through all the trouble of decorating the cookie with black buttons and a happy, smiling face. The alien gave her a skeptical look. "You want me to eat this?"

Richard snatched a cookie from the plate, earning him a scolding cry from his sister, and took a bite from it. "Yeah. They're good. Vicky makes the best cookies." He returned to sorting through the ornaments on the floor as Victoria stuck her tongue out at his back.

Turukaishal looked down at his snowman once more before taking a small bite, removing the little caricature's hat. The first thing he noticed was that it was sweet. Very sweet. The other thing he noticed was that it did, in fact, appeal to his tastes. He munched thoughtfully on it for a few minutes until it was gone. Victoria, beaming from ear to ear, placed the tray down on the coffee table and returned to the kitchen. Curious, Turukaishal walked after her. As if she'd read his mind, he heard her yell to stay out – she had another surprise for him.

Properly chastened, Turukaishal returned to the Christmas tree and managed to get the last strand of lights hung without incident. He stepped back to admire his handiwork and heard a loud CRUNCH from beneath his foot. Richard snorted. "Way to go," he said as Turukaishal looked down at the crushed remnants of the glass ornament. "I liked that one." Turukaishal waved his hand, the shards levitating and reassembling into a sphere before he snapped them in place, using his Psionics to melt the edges seamlessly together before handing it back to Richard. The human shook his head, grinning. "Dang... I wish I could do that."

In contrast with the outer lights, Victoria and Richard had insisted upon white lights for the tree. Grateful for the change, Turukaishal had agreed. Now, as he stared at his tree filled with hundreds of twinkling white lights, he couldn't help but feel both proud and happy. It did, in fact, look very nice. Of course, according to Victoria, he still had to set the star on top and the ornaments in the branches.

"What do you think?" Richard asked, hanging the first ornament—the one Turukaishal had repaired—in the lower boughs before handing a delicate-looking red sphere to the Scain. Turukaishal took it in his cobwebby fingers, hanging it on a branch at chest-level.

"It certainly looks far better than I would have originally thought," Turukaishal admitted. "And I will not deny it: I am enjoying myself to a certain extent."

Richard chuckled, handing him every other ornament. "Christmas does that to people." The two of them hung several ornaments in silence before Richard spoke again. "Vicky really likes you."

Turukaishal fidgeted with a tiny lace angel. "I know," he said, focusing intently on the ornament as if it had suddenly become the most fascinating thing in the room.

Richard pulled a set of glass bells out of the box, hanging them in one of the central branches. They chimed pleasantly as they swayed back and forth. "You don't sound happy."

"I am confused," Turukaishal told him. "I do not understand why she likes me the way she does. I am an extraterrestrial being sent here to prepare her planet for destruction. I am also leaving in twenty-six days. For some reason, despite those facts, she seems to have grown fond of me." He looked down at Richard. The youth was toying with a golden ornament, looking into the tree as if deep in thought. "More unsettling to me is the fact that I have come to enjoy her company as well. And yours. I do not understand exactly why, but I do."

Richard hung the ornament. "Neither do I. My company? You seriously need to meet more people. I can understand liking Victoria—she has that effect on people—but me?"

"You have a good core," Turukaishal explained as he finally hung the little white angel near the top of the tree. "Despite your outward bitterness, your love for your sister is still apparent. Anyone capable of love is not a bad person."

"Interesting logic," Richard said, chuckling. "Do all Scain think like that?"

"Scain, as individuals, believe different things. Soldiers, for example, will believe differently than scientists... just as I am certain human soldiers and scientists differ on their beliefs. It would be irresponsible of me to answer that question."

Richard laughed – a deep, rich sound that filled the room. "Okay, good point. Got me there, I guess. But I'm curious: let's say you cook up a report saying that humans are good and you take it back with you. What will happen?"

"That really depends on who I give it to, I suppose," Turukaishal said as Richard handed him another golden sphere. It found its home in the center of the tree. "If I gave it to the Mindbank, my leader and the one who organized this mission, I do not know the result. If I gave it to my political rival, Demnechi, I would likely be killed. If I gave it to some of my friends, they would probably think I was insane. However, I know there are groups and races in the Galaxy who believe that humans can change for the better... it would just be a matter of finding them or convincing others of this fact."

"Hate to break up the discussion," Victoria said from behind them, "but I've got cider ready for you two."

Turukaishal turned and looked at her. "Cider?" he asked. "What is cider?"

"It's a drink made from apples," Victoria said happily. "It's a kind of hot, spiced apple juice. It's really good – come try some."

The Scain trailed behind the two humans into his kitchen and eyed the trio of mugs that were resting innocuously on the countertop. The liquid inside them steamed gently and was a suspicious murky color – a dark amber hue. A pleasant, tangy aroma filled the air. Turukaishal looked skeptically at the mugs before looking back at Victoria. "Is that a stick in the cider?" he asked, pointing at the mugs with one of his long, spidery fingers.

"No!" Victoria exclaimed before pausing. "Well, yes… no… it's a cinnamon stick, not the kind of stick you're thinking. Come on, it won't kill you. Just take a sip."

Victoria picked up a mug and pressed it into his hands before doing the same to Richard. She picked up the third mug and took a swig from it, smiling. Turukaishal nodded in thanks, noticing immediately that the mug was very warm. He had no want to repeat his performance at the coffee house a few days prior and end up scalding his tongues. He paused. Had that really only been a few days ago? Less than a week? By the Hiin, it seemed like it was another lifetime entirely.

Turukaishal blew gently on the 'cider', watching Victoria and Richard chat in low undertones on the other side of the kitchen. Richard said something and Victoria laughed, a light sound that reminded Turukaishal of the glass bells in his tree. It sent a strange ripple through his body and he looked away, focusing on something else: their presents.

This was stupid, really. He was a Scain. He was in no way obligated to get them anything. As a matter of fact, he wouldn't. They were Vahran –the scum of the Galaxy! They deserved to… Turukaishal looked back at them and felt something akin to guilt wash over him. These weren't Vahran… they were humans. They weren't unfeeling monsters. They had shown him kindness and compassion; things the Mindbank said the Vahran didn't possess.

He took at tentative sip from the mug. Victoria was right – it was very good. He stared into the bottom of the mug, trying to think. What would a Vahran… no, a human enjoy? He tried to cast aside the preconceptions and racism that had been instilled in him as a child. What could he get them?

A thought struck him. An insane, ridiculous thought, but a thought nonetheless. He almost dropped his mug at the absurdity of it. It would take time and preparation, and he'd be hard-pressed to complete it in time, but it was doable. He set down his mug and rested his chin on his fingertips. It would take careful planning, but it was definitely a gift they would remember. His eyes turned yellow. Oh yes, they would enjoy this one.

He resumed drinking his cider, content in the knowledge that he now had an idea for a present. His logical mind tried to tell him that a backup idea was in order, but he knew it wasn't necessary. The idea he'd come up with was certainly going to be a hit.

And then his mind ground to a complete and utter halt. They'd said they were going to get *him* presents. What on Earth could a pair of humans get him? He looked suspiciously back at the pair – still whispering together – and felt his curiosity mounting. What indeed...?

Chapter 28

BEGIN MESSAGE:

LOCATION: Sillothel, Kinbara Shipyard

TIME: 30/53 Local Time

MESSAGE: As the son of Ferthoroyia, I beseech you to keep your father under some kind of placating control. This morning, he abandoned his post at the shipyard and marched straight into the Mitragan Heirarch's office and demanded that they recall one of their bounty hunters. I am not certain of the details, but heated words were exchanged before Ferthoroyia left. It is Mitragan policy not to recall bounty hunters until their job is complete or unless a substantial tithe is paid. As neither occurred, your father left empty handed.

- Juurak'Metel kan Laqian

Turukaishal looked up from his workbench as his communicator binged quietly near his elbow. Down here, in his ship, the sound seemed awfully loud. All of the lights were off to conserve power, except for those that were absolutely necessary to his work. He leaned over, giving the screen a cursory glance before frowning. His father was trying to get them to recall Klaara? That wasn't going to work. Whoever paid her was likely able to put down more credits than Ferthoroyia could ever match. Klaara was an obstacle that Turukaishal would have to overcome on his own, unless the Mindbank intervened somehow. He flipped over his project in his hands, looking down at it. There was no longer any question of getting it ready by Christmas; it was just a matter of making sure it was up to his usual picky standards.

It looked something like a human oxygen mask connected to a pair of thin tubes. These tubes, subsequently, were connected to a pair of cylindrical containers about the size of a small water bottle. The first set was almost complete. He unscrewed the bottom of one of the bottles, picking up the next set of parts. A gravitic spinner was inserted into the center, attached to a central bore which ran along the length of the cylinder. Attached to the intake valve of the spinner was an ion converter. Together, the two could take in a liquid and convert it to a gaseous form. He welded the parts together with a thin, hairlike tool before running the necessary wiring to a switch on the side of the bottle. That done, he screwed the bottom of the bottle back in place: one finished, one to go.

Turukaishal cast a glance over at his Data Pad's clock. It read 23.5/24 LT – or 11:30 in standard numerals. It was late, both of his human contacts having retired for the evening. They seemed to have adjusted fairly well to staying with him – Richard took the couch every night while Victoria slept in the Master Bedroom, leaving Turukaishal to retreat down to his ship and sleep in his pod. It wasn't necessarily a bad thing, although he had become rather used to sleeping in the plushy bed.

He set the first breathing mask aside. What he was doing was probably not going to be viewed favorably by the Scain, Triumvirate or Senate if they found out... which was why he wasn't planning on them ever knowing. He didn't exactly want the Forward Fleet coming here looking for him over a little thing like a Christmas Present. Phrasing it like that caused him to chuckle.

Turukaishal briefly debated on the merits of sending Klaara a Christmas present: something along the lines of a disruptor bomb. Knowing his luck, though, she'd find a way to turn it on him. He decided against it in the long run, mostly due to the fact that he would have no clue where to send it. And leaving disruptor bombs lying around was generally a bad idea and went against a lot of regulations, specifically those concerning self-preservation.

He began assembling the second mask, forcing himself to focus on it. The face piece was made of a high-elasticity polymer which could reshape and conform to the outlines of a face. He'd salvaged it from an emergency atmospheric kit on one of the lower decks of his ship. The fact that it could adhere perfectly to the face made it clear that there would be no breach when breathable gasses were involved, either from outside the mask or within. He looked down at the tank, chuckling quietly. If anyone thought these were for continued use, they were a fool. The tank couldn't hold more than ten minutes of atmosphere: this was a temporary unit designed to circumvent a painful but standardized alternative.

As soon as the facemask and tubes were attached, he set to work on the second cylinder. Hopefully, should the Hiin bless him with good fortune for once in his life, no one but Richard and Victoria would ever see these constructions. He sighed, placing the finished product with the first and standing up. He languorously stretched before climbing into his pod, not bothering to switch his polyform or even remove the safety shields from the corners of his eyes. It was just after midnight and he wanted some sleep. He allowed the lid to slide closed, resting his hand on the keypad inside which would allow him to reopen it. Tomorrow, he'd find and secure a pair of boxes and wrap the masks up like Victoria had mentioned. When Christmas came around, he'd hand them out and see if this was actually a good idea. Or, he reflected, he could decide against it at the last moment and buy them something at the last moment. He chuckled as he drifted off to sleep.

***

"Turu, are you sure you're alright?" Victoria asked. "You look like you stayed up all night." She stared at him for several seconds after asking, waiting for his response. The Scain turned and stared at her for a moment before his sleep-deprived brain registered that she was, in fact, addressing him. He shook his head before resuming his task – staring stupidly at a wall of merchandise while trying to decide if he should get anything else for the pair of Vahran.

"I am fine," he said, blinking a few times. He hadn't slept well, mostly due to the fact that his communicator had binged every two hours. For some reason, he was also having nightmares – an issue he hadn't had to deal with since his therapy following Dayislia. They weren't the same nightmares, but different ones. Either way, they had inhibited his sleep and that was enough for him to be irritated. "Do you know what sorts of things Richard likes?"

"Books," Victoria said with a chuckle. "Books, books and more books. And just for a change of pace: books. That or you can always get him a new sword – he'll never turn one down."

Books were infinitely easier than blades, but Turukaishal immediately realized the issue with this. "Wonderful. How am I supposed to know which books he has?"

Victoria blinked before shrugging. "That's actually a good question – I don't even know how he keeps track of all of them."

The Scain sighed, returning to staring at a rack of disgustingly cute stuffed bears. The last time he checked, *ursus arctos horribilis* didn't hold a giant sequined wreath and smile happily, waiting to be squeezed so he could sing horribly off-key songs about the holidays. And grizzly bears weren't known for their festive caps and sweaters either. He sighed, looking around. Richard had wandered off somewhere and Victoria had established herself as Turukaishal's escort – just in case he got lost. It wasn't like he was going to lose his sense of direction in a medium-sized convenience store, though. "I do not think we are going to make any headway here," he said at last. "Where is Richard?"

"Present." As if on cue, Richard emerged from behind a rack of plush reindeer. His motion set off some kind of detector within the rows of toys, setting off a cacophony of high-pitched voices singing *"Rudolph the Red-Nosed Reindeer"*. He glared dourly at the head-bobbing objects as if wishing they would catch fire. He looked more irritated than Turukaishal had ever seen him, and the Scain was willing to conjecture that the holiday cheer was having the opposite effect on the man.

Victoria, heedless of her brother's steely glare at the reindeer, smiled happily. "Why don't we all go for ice cream?" she suggested.

"In the middle of winter?" Richard asked skeptically. "It's cold enough outside. Ice cream is meant to be eaten in the summer."

Victoria smiled and shook her head, grinning like she was privy to some divine secret that they, the poor, uneducated mortal fools, were clueless about. Turukaishal stared at her, curious, and waited for her explanation. Richard sighed, rubbing the bridge of his nose as the reindeer finally quieted themselves, the last few notes of the song trailing off into silence. Finally, she spoke. "Winter is the *best* time to eat ice cream," she said. "When it's summer, it's hot and the ice cream melts all over the place. When it's cold out, like now, you don't have to rush to eat it."

"Okay, fine," Richard said, throwing up his arms. The motion once more set off the reindeer, and Richard snarled in their direction before stalking away from the singing dolls. "Turu, you up for some ice cream? Milkshake maybe?" he looked up at the Scain before shooting a murderous glare back at the reindeer. Turukaishal waved a hand over his chest and pointed at them, the dolls falling silent. Richard breathed a sigh of relief, but before he could thank the Scain, Turukaishal spoke.

"What is ice cream?"

"Oh my God!" Victoria squealed, grinning from ear to ear and clapping her fingertips over her mouth. Turukaishal turned red and Richard winced at her volume. "You've never heard of ice cream? Geez, you must've led such a boring life before we came along, huh? Come on, we'll show you!" Turukaishal had no time to protest before she seized his hand and, almost dislocating his wrist, dragged him off. Richard followed behind at a brisk walk, easily keeping up with his sister.

The little shop Victoria dragged him to was small and well-lit. A long counter displayed several glass cases, each one filled with large tubs full of a variety of brightly colored malleable substances. Turukaishal walked up and down the row, analyzing them. The tubs apparently had to be kept cold, or at least cool, based on the thermometers on the inside... although with a name like "ice cream", this was pretty obvious.

"What's your favorite flavor?" Victoria asked him happily, looking into the cases next to him. Turukaishal looked at all the different labels before giving up. There were just too many. And how was he supposed to decide if he didn't even know what half of them were?! What the heck was "bubblegum"? And what in the name of the Hiin was a "praline"? It sounded like some kind of grenade!

"Vanilla?" he asked, blinking into the case. That had been the flavor of tea he'd enjoyed. Hopefully this would have a similar outcome. He really didn't want to waste his money on something that would end up tasting like Alintean nutrient paste. He shivered, remembering the taste. Other races said it was "tasteless", but there was no reason to be so nice. The substance tasted like rotting vegetables and pond water filtered through a sewage pipe.

Richard, surprisingly, footed the bill this time. "You've let us use your house for a few days," he said by way of an explanation. "It's the least I can do."

Turukaishal seated himself in a little plastic booth, resting his chin on his hand and gazing out the window. Five days. Five days until this infernal holiday hit and then what? Besides opening those presents Victoria kept going on about, what did Vahran do on Christmas?

Richard slid into the booth across from him, his hat and glasses still in place. "It'll be right over," he said.

Turukaishal said nothing, but nodded in acknowledgement. It was better than admitting he was currently feeling like a giddy little child about to try something new. Something that Victoria, during their walk/drag over here, had told him was a favorite treat of all Vahran.

He opened his mouth to address Richard, but Victoria slipped into the booth next to him and the Scain suddenly found it a lot harder to concentrate.

Chapter 29

BEGIN MESSAGE:

LOCATION: Chindrus, Eccemeria District

TIME: 13/22 Local Time

MESSAGE: Turukaishal, what's going on? I'm hearing talk about a bounty hunter now. Are you out of your Hiin-damned mind? What are you doing? I demand answers!

- Kridoria

They say First Contact is always frightening. Unsettling at best. Like something in you, when confronted with anything sufficiently alien, instinctively tries to rebel and run away; to hide and seek that which is comfortable because it is familiar. To forget that the contact had ever been made. To slip back into the endless normalcy that had made up your life before.

Turukaishal felt like that staring at the cup full of "milkshake" in front of him.

Richard and Victoria had gotten him the largest size imaginable: thirty six ounces. The massive plastic cup seemed to be bursting with the whitish semiliquid, the swirls of white foam and the suspicious red sphere only adding to the mystery surrounding the delicacy. Turukaishal cast a sidelong glance at Victoria. "There is no lip on the cup."

Victoria looked up from her ice cream, which was situated in a large cone of carbohydrates and sugar. She licked her lips, clearing them of the remainder of her treat – fudge brownie, whatever that was – and smiled. "You drink it with a straw," she explained, retrieving one from the dispenser on the table. She jerked the papery wrapping off and plunking it into his milkshake. The plastic cylinder plunged right through the whitish cloud of aerated dairy atop the drink, narrowly missing impaling the hapless red orb. "You put the straw in your mouth and then suck on it," she explained. "The milkshake moves up the straw and into your mouth. I think you can figure it out from there."

Turukaishal smirked, giving her another sidelong glance. He reached out and tentatively touched the side of the cup before recoiling. He'd been expecting it, for some reason, to be like the tea. Instead, in character with the name "ice cream", the drink was absolutely frigid to the touch. He gripped it firmly in his hands and lifted it to his eyes, examining it. "What is this?" he asked, carefully dipping a finger int eh whitish foam at the top of the drink and holding it up for inspection.

"Whipped cream," Richard grunted.

"And what do you do with it?"

What happened next almost knocked Turukaishal off the bench. Victoria leaned over and took his finger into her mouth, swirling her tongue around the digit and removing the cream quickly and effectively. "You eat it," she said as an afterthought.

Turukaishal sat there, his eyes an uncomfortable shade of pink as his mouth hung slightly open, stunned into silence. Richard, too, seemed shocked. His glasses had slipped down to the end of his nose as he stared at his sister in wide-eyed surprise, his hands gripping his cane as if he was planning on interceding should the Scain atomize her on the spot or something equally as horrible. Instead, attempting to retain his dignity, Turukaishal looked at his finger before lowering it to his side and looking back to his milkshake. "Um…"

"I'm sorry," Victoria said, her face matching Turukaishal's eyes. "I wasn't thinking."

Turukaishal looked anywhere but at her. "And this suspicious crimson thing?" he asked, pointing at it with one of his long fingers. "What is it?" he had to change the topic. Now. Anything and everything to save himself from the awkward incident which had just occurred.

"It's a cherry," Victoria said. It looked like she was grateful for the change in topics as well. Richard was still staring at her, which was causing her to squirm uncomfortably. "You can eat everything but the stem. It's fun to play games with those though."

"Games?" Turukaishal asked, lifting the cherry by the stem and eying it. Upon closer inspection, it seemed to be a seed-bearing fruit. It wasn't fresh – frozen, most likely – as there wasn't even the faint, residual aura usually found in plants and fruits. "What kind of games?"

"It depends," she said. "I remember a bunch of us sitting around last summer eating them at the park. Ashley said that if you could tie the stem in a knot with your tongue, it meant you were a good kisser. I could never do it…" she reached over the table, stealing the cherry from atop Richard's cup of caramel ice cream and popping it in her mouth, stem and all. A moment later, she removed the stem, kinked and bent, but in no way, shape or form resembling a knot. Richard rolled his eyes.

Turukaishal knew it was unfair, but he couldn't help himself. He separated his two tongues, smirking to himself as he imagined the reaction on Victoria's face. He gripped his cherry by the stem, tossing it into his mouth and guiding it in with a gentle push of

Psionics. He chewed carefully, minding the tiny pit he could sense at the center as he worked at the stem with his tongues and his Psionics. A moment later, he removed the stem, three knots tied in it, before placing it on the napkin next to Victoria's. He placed the pit next to it, looking back to his milkshake as Richard leaned on his hand to conceal his smirk. Victoria stared at the stem for a moment before folding her arms. "How the-that's not fair!" Turukaishal smirked before putting the straw into his mouth and sucking on it.

Nothing happened.

Incensed, Turukaishal sucked harder. The milkshake still made no effort to climb the straw. After sucking until his cheeks burned, he set the drink down and took a few deep breaths before turning to Victoria. "Is this your interpretation of humor?" he asked sweetly, trying to bite back a slew of alien curses he knew she wouldn't understand.

"What? No! It's probably just a bit thick. Give it a minute or two and it'll be drinkable," she said, lifting his milkshake and examining it. "Yeah, it's just thick."

Turukaishal took the drink back and gave it a light shake. The liquid inside, if it could be called that, didn't move. He turned it upside down. Still nothing. He gave it a little shake.

Victoria clapped her hands to her face to keep her ice cream from finding its way out her nose as the contents of Turukaishal's thirty-six ounce cup ended up in his lap. Turukaishal jumped up, banging his knees on the unyielding table and cursing in three languages. The icy temperature had quickly soaked through his pants and was chilling his legs and groin. Richard grabbed the table to keep it from crushing him as Turukaishal staggered out of the booth, easily stepping over the laughing Victoria, before vigorously attacking the napkin dispenser. Turukaishal noticed that Richard was making no attempt to hide his grin.

"Who makes food like this?!" Turukaishal hissed as he wiped the thick white globs off his pants. Victoria immediately jumped to his aid, bringing with her another stack of napkins. Despite the assistance, she was laughing openly as she began wiping off his legs.

The woman who had served them stuck her head out of the back room, her curiosity aroused by all the commotion. She watched as Turukaishal staggered around like a drunk while Victoria chased him with the napkins, trying vainly to scrub the milkshake off his pants. "Can you two lovebirds step outside and do that?" she yelled. "You're dripping all over the floor!"

Richard stuck up his middle finger beneath the table, but grabbed Turukaishal by the wrist and dragged him out the door and handed him a fistful of napkins. Turukaishal, having calmed down somewhat, resumed his quest for cleanliness. The smell of vanilla filled the air, and the Scain could feel his pants starting to stick to him. He sighed. This was what he got for testing the viscosity of a milkshake, apparently.

Victoria followed after them a few moments later. "I got a rag from the cashier," she said as she handed Turukaishal the piece of damp gray cloth. "Maybe it'll do a better job than flimsy recycled napkins."

Turukaishal gratefully took the rag and finished wiping the remnants of the milkshake from his clothes. Curse this planet! Curse it! Since when had food started fighting back? And by the *Hiin* that stuff was cold! Finished with his task, he tossed the rag down on the curb and glared daggers back at the ice cream parlor. He couldn't even blame them, though, as turning the cup upside down had been his own stupid idea. He sighed, looking down at Victoria as she burst into another round of laughter. "Was it really *that* funny?"

"Actually, yeah," Richard admitted with a smirk. "It wasn't something I would have ever expected."

Turukaishal gave him a withering look. "Are you sure this wasn't some scheme you cooked up to humiliate me?" he asked, looking down at his pants. The entire front was covered with a large dark spot where the moisture had soaked in. Wonderful: he looked like he'd wet himself. He growled a few more curses beneath his breath.

"That's actually not a bad look for you," said a familiar, mocking voice. Turukaishal groaned, turning around and glaring at Klaara. The Heil was leaning on the wall of the ice cream parlor, her smirk irritating the Scain beyond words. It wasn't bad enough that he'd just humiliated himself in public, so here came his not-so-friendly rival to make things worse. She pushed herself off the wall, sauntering forward. "Aww," she continued. "What's wrong? Where's your 'Christmas Spirit'? It looks like—" she stopped dead, her luminous eyes looking down towards her chin before following the path of the silver blade that traced back to Richard's hands. Her eyes, glowing with some insane inner light, locked with his.

"What do you want?" Richard asked, his grip on the sword tightening. Klaara grinned mischievously at him, continuing to stare into his lead-grey eyes. Turukaishal could see that Richard was unsettled, but he was doing a superb job of masking it.

"What does it matter to you?" she asked, her lips drawing back wider as her grin expanded. Richard could see that her teeth were all sharp: the jaws of a shark. With her head tipped slightly back, intensifying her arrogant posture, he could also see her quadruple nostrils. Gooseflesh broke out along Richard's skin, and not due to the cold, but he didn't waver. Instead, he continued to stare levelly at her until Turukaishal lifted a hand.

"Enough. This is neither the time nor the place for a conflict. Heil, why have you sought us out?"

Klaara's eyes snapped back to Turukaishal, their luster fading as she met his gaze. "The usual: I wanted to challenge you."

Chapter 30

BEGIN MESSAGE:

LOCATION: Chindrus, Mindbank's Tower

TIME: 3/22 Local Time

MESSAGE: I certainly hope you are doing well, Turukaishal. I just wanted to notify you that the preparations are going nicely. I cannot send anyone to aid you with your Heil problem without arousing suspicion, so do be careful. Hopefully this whole business will conclude before long. I am heading off to Nihran to meet with Crowned Star Omyuris. Use the secure line to contact me.

- Sovakadris

Klaara's grin widened further as she saw Turukaishal pause, looking over her. The wider her grin stretched, the more of her monstrous teeth were revealed. The Scain shook his head. "And if I decline?"

"Then I'll just jump you some other time," Klaara said with a noncommittal shrug. "I mean, it's not like your pet Vahran is going to kill me here in the middle of the parking lot, is he? And for the love of peace, quit poking me with that thing. Who the heck are you?" she slapped Richard's sword aside, heedless of the cut it opened beneath her chin. Her blood, red and metallic, appeared as a red line against her pale skin.

"Richard Sinclair. You're Klaara'Doran kan Mitragan."

Klaara's demeanor changed entirely the moment he spoke. She froze for a moment before staring at Richard again, taking in his face before looking over every inch, propping her fists on her hips as if appraising him. "You're Richard Sinclair, hm?" she asked, stroking her chin at length. "Hmmm... Interesting. I thought you'd be bigger."

Richard didn't respond. Klaara grinned at him again. As quick as a snake, she darted forward, ducking as the blade sailed overhead. She stood up in front of him, thumping both of her middle fingers into his eyes before gripping his shoulder. With all the grace of an acrobat, she pushed herself into a vertical handstand, causing Richard to stagger, before landing behind him and ducking a swing which passed far too close to her head. She spun away, rising and facing Richard as he aimed the blade at her, blinking rapidly as his eyes watered. She whistled. "Not bad. You could do some damage against that thing.

165

Probably would've killed me if I was human." She turned and looked at Victoria. Richard immediately stepped between the two, his blade held horizontally. "You," the Heil said. "You were Veronica, right?"

"Victoria," Turukaishal corrected crossly, checking Richard's aura. He was irritated and angry, but otherwise unharmed. Klaara couldn't have thumped his eyes very hard or he'd be blind.

"Eh, whatever. All the same to me. Anyway Stretch, are you ready? We've got a fight waiting for us."

"In full view of an ice cream parlor?" Turukaishal asked, gesturing around himself. "Why don't we take this somewhere more private? After all, if we fight here, both our covers will be blown. The woods near my base are secluded enough for a battle... would that suit your fancy?"

Klaara snorted, unable to hide her grin as she wiped the streak of blood from beneath her chin, licking the red liquid from her fingertip. Her tongue was far longer than a human's, probably at least twice as long, if Turukaishal had to guess. "Sounds good. Lead the way." She fell into step behind Turukaishal as he turned, leading them back towards the woods which sheltered his base.

Richard sheathed his sword and walked along behind Klaara, his eyes glaring at the back of her head. Victoria stayed near the front with Turukaishal, periodically looking back to make sure the Heil wasn't going to pounce on them from behind. They traveled in silence for several minutes before Klaara broke the silence. "So where'd you learn to use that thing?"

It took a moment for Richard to realize that she was referring to him. He looked at her out of the corner of his eye, his gaze distrustful. "My brother taught me the basics. I learned the rest. Why?" his grip tightened on the cane that hid his blade.

"Eh," Klaara said, lacing her fingers together behind her head, staring at the sky with a tranquil, if not bored, expression. "You look like you could be a threat. Maybe I'll have to take you—"

"*Enough!*" Turukaishal snarled, turning around. His eyes were blood red, and he was certain their color could be discerned through his shades. "Your quarrel is with *me*. Killing off these humans is not part of your contract and could very well void your contract. These two are my informants. You are not to touch them."

Klaara smirked. "That depends on what kind of a fight you put up. Informants, huh?"

Richard spoke up, cutting off Turukaishal's response. "If you are looking to fight me, you probably use a sword too." He picked up his pace, walking up next to the Heil. "Which probably means you have one either close by or in that backpack of yours."

Klaara reached over her shoulder and patted the black leather bag slung over her shoulder. "Yep. Smart kid. But trust me – it's nothing an amateur like you can face. Trust me – that little toy you have is as a toothpick to mine."

"So what? You've got a big sword. Big swords can be brought down. Or is it some of your alien tech?"

"Tech," she said, grinning down at him, her arrogance filling the air with an almost palpable wave. Richard frowned, but said nothing. Turukaishal could already tell what was going through the man's head. A larger sword, as he'd said, could be defeated if the opponents was unskilled with it. However, a blade designed around advanced technology would be far more problematic. For all he knew, he was going up against something with the same power as a gun.

The rest of their walk was spent in absolute silence, apart from the steady sound of their feet on the ground. Turukaishal and Victoria remained in the lead, the former using his long arms to move the branches in the woods aside when it became necessary. Finally, when it seemed that they had been walking forever, Turukaishal led them down a steep hill to a flat, wooded area, the tall pine trees rising to the sky like silent sentinels; quiet judges to the duel that was about to take place.

Klaara tossed her backpack against a tree, flexing her neck. Several sharp pops echoed through the clearing, echoing hollowly off the trees and fading quickly into nothing. Despite her stretching, which took several minutes (and which Turukaishal suspected she was doing to intimidate, unnerve or annoy him, possibly all three) her quasi-luminous eyes never left his. As soon as she had limbered up to her satisfaction, she opened the bag.

"Straight Duel, No Arts?" she said, more to herself than to Turukaishal as she drew out a pair of metallic clawed gauntlets, each one with a glowing spot on the back of the hand. She slipped the four-fingered devices over her hands, flexing them experimentally. Even across the thirty-something foot area, the sound of grinding hinges could be heard. Turukaishal suspected the claws had seen a lot more use than they had care. "Yeah, that sounds good. Let's make this fun, huh?" she pointed the claws on her right hand at Turukaishal for a moment before reaching back into her bag, rummaging around.

Richard looked at Turukaishal. "Straight Duel, No Arts?"

The Scain nodded. "A Straight Duel means that it is a standard match – no special rules. No Arts implies that she won't use her innate abilities against me this round." He narrowed his eyes at the Heil. "This actually improves my chances, but by no means guarantees a victory."

Klaara drew what looked like a pair of sturdy fencing foils out of her bag, giving it a quick swing before pointing one down at the ground. "I heard that, Stretch," she said nonchalantly as she sauntered toward him. Richard immediately began analyzing the swords, his stormy gray eyes narrowed. There were two buttons along the side of the D-shaped grip, both of them small and circular. Klaara raised one sword and pressed the upper button.

With a hum, a wide band of light formed around the 'blade' of the sword, almost a foot thick and ending in an angled point. Richard had to fight not to recoil. Whatever the golden light was, it didn't look like something he wanted biting into his arm or leg. Richard pushed Victoria behind himself and backed them both up to the edge of the clearing, his fingers tightening around his sword cane, his eyes never leaving Klaara's weapon.

The second sword activated as well, humming in concert with its sister. Klaara twirled the swords between her fingers, grinning. "No weapon, Stretch?" she asked, pointing one blade at him.

Richard took a step forward, lifting his sword cane towards Turukaishal, but the Scain held out a hand. "Those blades will shear through your weapon as if it was wood," he said. "I'll use my Psionics," he said to Klaara. "I'm confident that they'll be more than enough to handle you." The Scain narrowed his eyes, wishing that he felt as confident as he sounded.

"Now THAT'S what I like to hear," the Heil said as she spun the swords around again, grinning madly at him. "Who's staring this match?"

Turukaishal dispelled his disguise with a wave of his hand, his Scain form twisting and emerging from its human husk. Klaara laughed, her wig falling from her head as her disguise melted like cheap wax, exposing her narrow, patchwork face, her squaline teeth glittering as the Scain drew a hand over his chest, the blue flames leaping out and dancing between his fingers. "I'll start," he said.

Without warning, he thrust his palm out towards her. A burst of thick, bluish light extended, racing towards the Heil. Klaara rolled sideways, springing out of her roll and racing forward as the Psionic burst stuck a tree behind her hard enough to peel the bark from the trunk. Turukaishal was ready for her, the burst having latched onto the tree as well as stripping it, and he jerked himself out of the way as one of Klaara's swords bit into the ground where he'd stood a moment before. She turned, baring her teeth as he landed off to the side, turning and already drawing his hand through his chest again. She jumped forward, pulling a small trigger located beneath the guard.

Jets on the reverse of the sword sprang to life, sending the blades crashing down at an astonishing speed. Turukaishal, having already primed his Psionics, had barely enough time to raise a blue wall of light before the twin sabers crunched through him like a chainsaw through bread. The two aliens stood there, locked together for a moment, before Turukaishal drew his second hand through his chest and thrust it towards his adversary, blasting her away.

Klaara somersaulted end over end, tossing one of her swords into the trunk of a thick tree and using her claw to catch herself before she slammed into it. She hopped down, grabbing her sword on the way down, and landed in the loam, grinning and wiping her mouth with the back of her hand, smearing a faint trickle of deep red blood across her chin.

Both aliens sized each other up from the opposite ends of the clearing. Turukaishal's eyes swept over her, analyzing her. She had weapons which he could counter with his Psionics, yes, but his Psionics were drained from masquerading as a human. Although smaller, she was infinitely hardier than he was, and also far stronger. If he was going to walk away, he couldn't beat her head on.

Turukaishal waved one of his glowing hands and pointed at Klaara. The Heil's head snapped to the right as several stones, logs and branches came hurtling out of the foliage, each of them encased in that eerie bluish haze. She cut a log apart before rolling sideways away from a dense cluster of rocks. A branch smacked across her chest, tossing her backwards, and a rock collided with her thigh. She let out a bark of irritation and pain. Turukaishal waved his hand again, bringing the surviving projectiles around for another volley. Klaara was already on her feet, catching one of the branches in her clawed hands. Turukaishal's Psionics carried her several feet before she released, kicking off a second log and landing on the ground out, racing directly for him.

With a wave of his other hand, a thick root dug its way out of the ground, causing one of the fifty-foot evergreens to lean precariously. Klaara, unprepared, tripped over the root and was sent sprawling through the leaves. Richard and Victoria both gaped at the tree as it swayed unsteadily, leaning away from them. Turukaishal, his eyes blazing and his hands glowing, brought the rocks around and up into the air, aiming to bring them down on Klaara as a finishing blow. The Heil smirked, rolling forward and then kicking off the ground, springing backwards like a gymnast, arching over the root as the rocks collided with the ground like meteorites. Dirt and debris flew up like shrapnel from a grenade explosion, showering the area with filth.

Klaara, having remained balanced on her hands, compressed her arms and sprung forward, landing on her feet and rushing through the still-settling cloud of loam and earth as she raced straight for her Scain quarry. She lifted the swords, aiming for his head, with a savage gleam of triumph in her eyes. Turukaishal smirked at her, flicking the third finger on his left hand and ducking as low as he could.

The fragments of the log she had split came hurtling from his left, smashing into Klaara's torso and her forearm. One of her swords spun away, stabbing into the ground behind her. The impact knocked Klaara off her trajectory, hurling her to the side. She rolled over several times, digging her sword into the earth to stop her momentum. She pushed herself up, popping her neck as she glared at Turukaishal. "Think that's funny?" she growled, spinning her sword and racing forward, scooping up the other as she passed it. Turukaishal fired up his Psionics again, feeling the twinge in the back of his head that warned him of impending exhaustion. This time would be a worse assault. She was angered and upset, which meant careless as well as equal parts of ferocious. He braced himself, his hands blazing with blue fire, as the Heil leapt through the air towards him.

Chapter 31

BEGIN MESSAGE:

LOCATION: Chindrus, Denuval District

TIME: 7/22 Local Time

MESSAGE: *Your father sounds like he is on the verge of a nervous collapse, you know. You may want to drop him a line if you have not already, provided that it is allowed on your mission, that is. Kridoria is not much better. She found out about this bounty hunter chasing you and things just exploded to new heights of ridiculous. Bordra, your pal from ETF Kirel, called in the other rotation too. Been a while since the two of us caught up, so we figured we would hit some of the local spots and chat. He has been following this bounty hunter bit closely, and almost wants to head over there right now and help.*

- Bandrumano

Turukaishal hardened his Psionics, using one of his hands, wreathed in blue lightning, to physically counter Klaara's blade. With the other, he extended a field and gripped her other blade, wrestling with the Heil before managing to dislodge one of her sabers. He drew it into his palm, swinging it at the side of her head and pulling the trigger. The weapon accelerated like a runaway train, narrowly missing Klaara and leaving Turukaishal feeling extremely chagrined and irritated to find her already dancing back several paces, flipping backwards over the root he'd pulled up. His blow wasn't entirely fruitless, though: one of her facial ridges had been chipped, and badly. He'd been within a fraction of an inch of her face.

Klaara ran forward, her boots kicking up the loam as she lunged at Turukaishal, aiming to exploit his opening. Turukaishal's free hand reached out towards her, a blue line of light coiling around her ankle and causing her to stumble again. Before she could recover, Turukaishal had lifted her into the air and slammed her into the ground like al mace. He lifted her up again and hurled her as hard as he could into the bushes on the far side of the clearing. He swung his commandeered sword, watching the shrubs. A little damage wasn't going to keep a Mitragan Heil down for very long, especially not a bounty hunter.

True to his expectations, Klaara burst out of the bushes and raced directly towards him. Turukaishal lunged forward as well, swinging the blade downwards, aiming for her skull. She sidestepped, swinging the saber at his ribcage, but Turukaishal had anticipated her dodging his blow. He pulled the trigger on the sword, letting it pull him flat against the ground as his free hand waved once, summoning several more stones from the side of the clearing. He rolled away from a downward slash, blocking a savage kick aimed for his face by holding up a Psionic barrier, and then watched in satisfaction as the rocks slammed into Klaara like missiles, lifting her into the air.

She flipped over, catching herself on her hands and performing a handspring which would have put an Olympic gymnast to shame. She twisted her body around, embedding her claws in the trunk of one of the trees before kicking off, landing on one of Turukaishal's levitating rocks, grinning maniacally at him. The Scain swung the rock at full tilt against one of the trees, watching peevishly as she leapt off and clung to the trunk like a spider again. She smirked, leaping from her perch to a second, nearby tree and scrambling up it, perching on a branch forty feet above his head.

"Whew," she said, making a big show of running her gauntlet across her forehead, rubbing a line of dirt and mud across her face. "Not too shabby," she added, grinning. "You're a hard check to cash."

Turukaishal crouched on the far side of the clearing, breathing heavily. He was tired – exhausted, in fact – and this Heil was barely breaking a sweat? Not for the first time, the possibility of his death crossed his mind. His arm ached from where the afterburners in the sword had damaged his muscles: he wasn't designed for this kind of abuse. Not that he was going to let her know, though, and he'd happily pull that trigger a thousand times if it would defeat her.

Klaara jumped off the branch, her sword raised over her head. Turukaishal balked, taking a step back. A jump from that height was suicidal! He jumped away, one of his hands glowing with Psionics as he grabbed a tree from across the clearing and pulled himself out of danger. Klaara struck the ground like an orbital missile, throwing dirt and debris in every conceivable direction. Richard turned his back on her, throwing his coat around his sister as fragments of rocks and branches rained down on them. Turukaishal turned around, still breathing heavily, the base of his skull throbbing with exertion. Surely that had been lethal. *Please* let that have been lethal!

No dice. Klaara stepped out of the settling wreckage, falling leaves and pine needles drifting down around her as she aimed her remaining sword at Turukaishal. "Getting tired yet?" she taunted, swinging her sword at him. Turukaishal countered the horizontal swing, pushing her back and aiming a sideways swipe at her chest. Klaara blocked it with her gauntlet, pushing him back against one of the trees, her face split by a wide grin. It was then that Turukaishal realized her plan.

She closed the gauntlet around the blade of the ion saber, pinning it against her palm. The claws were likely made of the same material as the swords – the energy from his blade wouldn't be able to cut them. Her fingers physically latched onto the core of the

sword,   the part that resembled a fencing iron, and held it still to prevent a
counterattack as she lifted the other blade and swung it at his head.

Turukaishal released the saber, ducking to the side as her weapon bit deep into the
trunk of the tree he'd been pressed against a moment before. He didn't escape
unharmed, feeling his bluish blood seeping from the cut in his shoulder. He hissed in
pain, jumping backwards and forcing Klaara way. In a fortuitous stroke of luck, she left
the weapon embedded in the tree. Turukaishal quickly drew it into his hand, sighing
with relief. If she grabbed the blade again, he was done for.

Klaara knew it too and pushed her attack, lunging forward like a rabid beast. She
loosened her grip on her blade, pinning the trigger down with a single finger and letting
the blade spin like a saw at the end of her hand. Turukaishal danced backward at an
ever increasing speed, struggling to stay ahead of her onslaught. His back hit another
tree, and a momentary surge of panic shot through him. Moments later, Klaara's blade
bit through the trunk of the forty foot tree, sawing completely through it. Turukaishal
had stabbed his sword into the wood above him and jumped up, crouching on the hilt.
He kicked off the tree, landing behind Klaara and kicking Klaara in the face with one of
his three-toed feet, the end of his leg wrapped in blue fire to protect the weak bones.
She grunted and stumbled back, clutching her eye as the tree behind her crashed to the
ground with an earsplitting crunch, startling birds from the trees and shaking the
ground. Turukaishal rushed forward, pulling the trigger on the sword again and aiming
for Klaara's head while she was distracted. Instead, he swore in his native tongue as his
blade locked with hers.

Klaara pulled the trigger on her own sword, pushing back against the Scain. Although
both swords were accelerating the same amount, she was *far* stronger than he was.
Turukaishal felt himself being pushed backwards, step by step, until he was stumbling
over himself to remain upright. In a moment of desperation, he threw himself down on
his back, Klaara's blade passing over head. He swung his in her general direction and
heard her shriek in pain, a foot-long gash appearing in her torso. Sadly, it wasn't nearly
deep enough to be lethal – the Heil probably had at least an inch of muscle, not to
mention her skeleton, protecting any vital organs. He hadn't even pierced her flesh.

From his position on the ground, Turukaishal stuck out a Psionic tendril, tripping Klaara
by winding it through her shins. She didn't fall, but she stumbled for several paces,
turning and bringing up her saber instinctively in time to block a rock Turukaishal threw
her way. Another shot past her head, missing her by inches and embedding itself in the
trunk of a tree. She raced sideways, dodging several more stones before jumping
towards Turukaishal, narrowly evading a barrage of rocks falling from above with the
force of bullets. Their blades clashed together, both aliens pivoting around in the center
of the clearing before Klaara leapt back. They circled one another like sharks, each trying
to anticipate the others' next move. The tension in the area was palpable, filling the
forest like a thick, cloying mist.

Klaara jumped forward, an overhead strike poised to split the Scain from head to groin. Turukaishal blocked it and forced her back – another Psionic burst – and swung at her midsection. Klaara blocked it with the back of her gauntlet, swatting it aside. Turukaishal evaded a thrust, ducking beneath it and dancing backwards. He had to ration his Psionics – he hadn't brought a Booster with him, and even if he had one it would be tricky finding the time to use it. Klaara kept him more than busy. He frowned, his eyes glowing red and betraying his inner anger.

He closed in, thrusting toward her torso with the blade. Klaara brought hers up and around, knocking his out of the way and forcing him to evade backwards at an angle to avoid a strike to his midsection. She chuckled, spinning her blade on her fingers, jumping forward only to be parried aside again. "You don't make it easy for a girl to eat, do you?" she asked, ducking a swing at her head. "I mean, you don't get a great body like this by starving." She ducked another swing. "Geez. You are tenacious, aren't you?"

"One of my more charming attributes," Turukaishal said dryly, refusing to allow himself to grow complacent. Just because she was admitting he was hard to kill didn't mean he'd won. On the contrary – Mitragan Heil could take so much punishment it made his body ache at the thought. He'd seen them stand up after having limbs severed and try to fight. They were wonderful soldiers, fierce and powerful, but by the Hiin they scared the Psionics out of him. "it is obvious you are no amateur either – at least allow me the use of your name."

She laughed. *"Aelau bakan keviru,* why not? It's not like you don't know it anyway, and you've lasted respectably long... not that you'll get to use it."

Turukaishal blocked a slash to his neck, stepping back and using his Psionics to launch Klaara over his head and into a tree, upside-down. She grunted something in her native tongue, rolling over at the base of the tree and snarling. Turukaishal inclined his head towards her. "My thanks, Klaara'Doran kan Mitragan."

"Whatever," she said, racing forward. "It's time to finish this."

The two of them crashed together without prelude, their swords moving like streaks of lightning. Turukaishal ducked beneath a horizontal swing, attempting to bring his saber up and under only be met with her grasping gauntlet. He backpedaled, avoiding a disarming motion, and jumped away from a thrust aimed for his shoulder. Their eyes met for a moment, both burning with adrenaline, before they landed and came together again.

He saw it coming, but Turukaishal had no way of countering it. Their blades locked together, sparks flashing from where they met, and Klaara let go of her sword. Turukaishal's continued its downward motion, the blade landing right in her waiting gauntlet. She kicked out at him and Turukaishal barely had enough time to raise a Psionic barrier before he was launched away. His sword was left in Klaara's hand, a triumphant grin adorning her face. She picked up the other one, twirling them both in her hands before jumping after the Scain.

Cursing, Turukaishal forced out his Psionics and shoved her away before her blades could score a hit on him. She landed and was on him like a possessed monster, her blade aimed for his head. Turukaishal lifted his hands, burning with blue flames, and tried to catch the saber; to retrieve a weapon. Klaara, unwilling to lose her sword a second time, pulled the trigger. The force of the weapon colliding with him knocked Turukaishal to the ground. He rolled away, slamming into the loam again and again, before coming to a rest at the edge of the clearing.

"Turu!" he struggled to sit up, hearing Victoria's voice from across the clearing. Before he could rise further, he found the tip of a glowing saber at his throat. She planted her foot on his chest and forced him back against the ground, smirking.

"Turu!" He could hear Victoria's voice. He forced himself into a sitting position and found Klaara's sword pointed at his neck. She planted her foot on his chest and forced him back to the ground, smirking. Turukaishal glared back at her, his eyes burning a defiant red. Both of their chests rose and fell heavily; evidence of how hard they had fought. Blood was caked across Klaara's lower body, dripping from the gash on her midsection, as well as staining the side of her face. One of her eyes was almost completely swollen shut, courtesy of the kick he'd given her. She was also adorned with various scrapes, cuts and bruises. He was still the worse off – his right arm felt torn to shreds from the saber, and he was covered in deep cuts from his slide across the ground. The cut in his neck was still bleeding, and he'd taken a severe blow to his head during his final fall, which was bleeding heavily as well. The dirt in his wounds made them sting and burn.

Klaara grinned, lifting the sword over her head. Turukaishal tried to pull a rock over to aid him, but she cut it out of the air with her second blade, laughing as it fell apart around them. Now almost fully drained, Turukaishal could do nothing more than stare at her as her blade rose into the air, glowing like a star as she prepared to lower it and deliver him into the oblivion someone so desperately wanted him to experience.

Something moved rapidly behind Klaara and she barely had time to turn around. Richard, armed with his sword cane, had leapt through the air towards Klaara. She barely had time to raise her ion saber before he was upon her. She grinned, ready to laugh as his pitiful human weapon was torn apart. Richard, however, had other ideas.

Midway through his lunge, he hurled the sword cane like a spear, the point aimed directly at Klaara's chest. She moved to swat it aside, but Richard had already closed the distance. He barreled into her, pushing her away from Turukaishal and aiming a swift kick at her knee. There was a loud thud as the tip of his steel-toe boot impacted the shin guard of her boot, but it was enough to destabilize her. Enraged, Klaara thrust her sword toward him as she leapt forward, trying to use her weight to her advantage.

Richard wrapped his arm around hers, pinioning her forearm against his ribcage. Klaara's eyes widened as her lips pulled back from her teeth: Richard's ribcage felt like a solid wall of muscle; hard and immovable. His leg snapped out, coiling around her left shin as he pivoted on the spot, hurling her down on the ground as he braced his hand against her elbow.

Klaara could feel the strain on her skeleton as he fought to break the bones in her arm. She shrieked, kicking him hard in the thigh before aiming her saber at his head. Richard ducked the swing, growling. He shifted tactics, squeezing her arm until she felt the second saber drop from her fingers. He shoved her away, scooping it up and dancing back several paces, swinging it. It was far heavier than a normal saber, but it wasn't anything he couldn't use.

Klaara lunged up from the ground, snarling at Richard, but he was already prepared for her assault. He blocked her blow, kicking her in the midsection hard enough to make her cough blood, before swinging the stolen sword down at her head. She brought hers up, afterburners blazing, to block the attack. Richard, too, pulled the trigger. The two fought against each other but Klaara, weakened from her fight with Turukaishal, lost the battle. Richard hurled her backwards, the force of her own weapon working against her as she was launched into the bushes on the far side of the clearing. Richard turned, his dispassionate eyes looking down at Turukaishal.

"What are you *doing*?!" the Scain asked, forcing himself to his knees and spitting out a globule of his blue blood. "She'll kill you!"

Richard turned as Klaara burst from the bushes, shrieking with rage. "Vicky's gone to get you one of those syringes," he said coolly. "She should be back soon. I'm buying you time." Turukaishal pushed himself to his feet, swaying unsteadily before falling back on his rear, moaning. Richard snorted. "Stay there," he said, turning and meeting Klaara's lunge. Unlike Turukaishal, he didn't have to pace himself with the trigger. Quite the contrary – from what Turukaishal had just witnessed, he probably had more muscle mass than Klaara.

The two sabers clashed together again before Richard hurled his full weight sideways, firing the afterburners and swinging the sword like a bat. Klaara was launched through the air, this time latching on to a tree trunk like she had before. She took several deep breaths before grinning. "Heh, and here I was thinking it was over. Silly me. Looks like it just started getting interesting."

Chapter 32

BEGIN MESSAGE:

LOCATION: Chindrus, Amara District

TIME: 17/22 Local Time

MESSAGE: *Bandrumano came and sought me out. He wanted to know if I had heard from you. Please, Turukaishal, give us some signal. I know you are alive – your messages to the Mindbank are proof of that – but we need to know if you alright. This scare with the bounty hunter has put all of us on edge. If you need our assistance, I am certain Bordra and Bandrumano will be on their way in a heartbeat, as would I. My sons can manage the smelter while I am away, albeit not with the same talent I have, so if you need me, tell me. The* Pinnacle *is always ready to fly by your side.*

- Klakshan

Klaara launched herself off the tree, her sword carving a glittering arc downward toward Richard. He leapt forward, hitting the ground with his shoulder and rolling beneath her onslaught. She struck the ground like a bomb, spinning quickly and trying to catch Richard across the back. He stayed low, the blade passing over his head and ruffling his brownish tresses, before bringing his sword upwards toward Klaara's face. She was forced backwards, jumping away to avoid the blade. "I knew you used a sword," she said, landing and blocking a slash aimed for her torso, countering it and pushing him away. "But I never knew you knew how to use *my* swords!"

"It isn't the origin of the sword that matters," Richard said, evading a thrust by sidestepping, kicking Klaara in the thigh and slashing downward toward her collarbone. She threw herself out of the way, the blade nicking her shoulder, rolling away from him. "It's the skill of the wielder. I picked up any remaining nuances from watching you and Turu."

They came together again, their swords locking and forcing them face to face. Richard kept his face relaxed and blank, focusing instead on overpowering the Heil. Klaara, on the other hand, was grinning like a maniac, her eyes glowing with a ferocious intensity. "Such a pity you aren't a Heil!" she said, kicking him in the stomach and swinging her clawed gauntlet at him. There was a ripping sound as Richard's dress shirt was torn to taters near his bicep. Luckily for him, she had avoided actually cutting him – just maiming his clothes. He countered with a quick swing, pulling the trigger and letting the afterburners on the sword accelerate the blade toward her. Klaara caught the blade with her gauntlet, aiming to disarm him.

Richard reached beneath her arm with his free hand, gripping her other sword at the hilt, their fingers overlapping. They stood there, struggling with each other; locked together like yin and yang, wrestling with the blades. Eventually, Richard twisted her wrist far enough to where he felt her shaking and, with a final triumphant twist, wrenched the sword from her fingers. Klaara, not to be outdone, gripped the blade tightly and jumped into the air, kicking Richard solidly in the chest. He fell backwards with a grunt, catching himself on his hands and using the momentum to flip backwards, landing in a crouch with her commandeered sword. Klaara landed on the ground, holding his. They looked at each other for a moment before Richard snorted. "That went well."

"Indeed," Klaara chuckled. "Back to square one." They both tossed their blades into their dominant hands and rushed at one another again. Their blades locked for the briefest of moments, sparks flying from where they met. Klaara made to grab at Richard's again, her claws racing towards the blade. Richard gave ground, releasing the hilt of his sword with one hand and punching her solidly in her already-swollen eye. She staggered back; howling with rage and pain, and Richard took the initiative and rushed her. He once more tried grappling for her sword, throwing his full weight against her and carrying them both to the ground. They rolled over and over, snarling and cursing at one another, before Klaara kicked him off. This time, her sword went with him.

She looked at him in surprise as he threw her blade skyward, embedding it firmly in the trunk of a tree some seventy feet in the air. It quivered there for a moment like an arrow as Richard turned his gaze back to the Heil. "Give up yet?" he asked, aiming the second sword at her face.

Klaara stared down the length of the blade, her chest heaving again. Her eyes glowed brightly, almost blindingly so, against the black patches on her face. For the first time, Richard noticed that one of them, above her left eye, looked like a four pointed star. After a brief moment to catch her breath, she swallowed and laughed. "Not a chance!"

Both of her gauntlets lit up, the claws lengthening with the same golden energy as the blades. Richard, caught off guard, backpedaled quickly out of range, but not fast enough to avoid the clawed assault entirely. The tips raked across his chest, slicing through his vest and his dress shirt like butter and carving four shallow grooves in his chest. He hissed, crying out in irritation more than in pain, before his boots found purchase in the loam and he counterattacked. He swung for her legs, cursing as Klaara leapt back, evading it and landing in a crouch before barreling towards him again.

Victoria raced into the glade, one of the Boosters clenched in her fingers. She raced over to Turukaishal, collapsing next to him. "Oh God..." she whimpered, scooping his head and upper back into her lap, tears running down her face. "I hope I grabbed the right one. There were so many syringes and I…"

Turukaishal reached up, flinching as he heard the sound of Richard's saber sparking off Klaara's gauntlets. His four-fingered hand gently touched the side of Victoria's head, stroking her hair. "You are crying…" he said, perplexed. "Why?"

"Why? For the love of God, Turu, I wish you could see yourself! You look…" she fumbled with the syringe, pressing it into his other hand. "Please tell me this was the right one."

Behind them, Klaara kicked Richard in the chest hard enough to force the saber from his hand. He flew through the air, slamming into a tree trunk and grunting in pain and irritation. He fell to his knees for the briefest of moments, shaking his head and rising again. Unarmed, he raced straight for Klaara, scooping his sword cane out of the loam as he ran. Klaara jumped backwards, grabbing up the saber he'd dropped and racing for a tree, scrambling up it with her claws. She yanked the second one free, balancing on a thick branch and gazing down at Richard as he took up a position in front of Victoria and Turukaishal, his fingers holding his blade tightly.

"You think you can beat me with that thing?" Klaara asked, spinning the swords in her fingers. "I'll cut through that thing like paper!"

Turukaishal depressed the plunger on the syringe, injecting himself with the Booster. "Relax… Victoria…" he rasped, feeling the jolt as the Booster raced into his system. "It is the right… syringe."

She sighed in relief as Richard snorted. "I told you once: it isn't the sword as much as it is the skill of the wielder. And besides, if this sword isn't a threat to you, how come you're hiding in the tree to like a cat from a dog?"

Klaara leapt down from the tree, hissing with anger. She kicked off of two lower branches, landing almost on top of Richard. He ducked the first swing, evading the second, and then lashed out with his foot, kicking Klaara in the midsection. She stumbled backwards, gasping. Before she could recover, he flipped the sword around and drove the rounded pommel into her damaged eye, eliciting another shriek of pain. He spun the blade around, sinking it deep into her thigh. The tempered point of the weapon emerged from the back of her leg, and Klaara roared in anger and pain. Using the brief distraction, Richard grabbed her wrist, bringing it down hard onto a rising knee. The saber jumped from her fingers, landing in the loam.

With a savage grunt, Richard tore the blade from Klaara's leg, shoving her away and picking up the ion saber, facing her once again. Klaara snarled, lunging forward and slashing savagely at him. Richard backpedaled, on the defensive and having to abuse the trigger to keep up with the onslaught of blows Klaara was raining on him. Out of the corner of his eye, he saw Turukaishal stand up unsteadily, using Victoria's shoulder as a crutch.

Richard faltered for a moment, jerking his head backwards in time to avoid having it split in two. The tip of her saber sliced into his cheek, opening a three-inch gash that dripped blood down his face and into the collar of his dress shirt. His lips curled, exposing his teeth as his eyes glittered fiercely, his spirit unbroken. Victoria's face lost some color at the sight of her brother's blood and Turukaishal, now steady, brushed the fingers of both hands over his chest and thrust his palms off to one side of the arena.

Klaara heard the snapping of branches and turned in alarm, jumping away from Richard and watching as a twenty foot tree uprooted itself, the ball of earth still clinging stubbornly to its underside. It flew through the air, a blue glow surrounding every branch and leaf and stopped a moment before it reached her. Klaara dove through the air, trying to evade it, but to no avail. It pivoted on the root ball, spinning like a massive sword, and brushed her off her feet and sent her soaring into the foliage for the millionth time. A loud curse, clearly in English, resonated from the bush.

Klaara fought her way out of the shrubbery a moment later, her eyes blazing as she ran the back of her luminous gauntlet over her mouth and nose. "I have to fight two of you? Sheesh..." Blood was caked on the lower half of her face, making her look savage and frightening. Richard leveled the saber at her again, but Turukaishal stepped up next to him, his palms glowing blue and azure lightning arcing from around his eyes.

"I advise you to drop her weapon and back off," Turukaishal said. "I will take it from here."

Richard tightened his grip on Klaara's weapon, refusing to drop it, but took several steps backward. Turukaishal instinctively knew that Richard was prepared to come racing back in if things went south. Again.

Without further ado, the match between the two aliens resumed. Klaara leapt for Turukaishal's throat, aiming to slash at the thinnest part of his body and decapitate him. Instead, she impacted a Psionic wall, blue light emanating from her body for a moment before she was launched skyward into the treetops. She slammed into one of the upper trunks, her claws digging into the wood until she came to rest on a branch. She leapt away a moment later to avoid being smashed by the tree from earlier, catching a branch on an adjoining tree and swinging around it like a monkey, coming to rest on the top.

"Running on full again, eh Stretch?" she asked, grinning. She wiped some blood from her mouth – more having emerged from a cut on her lip; sustained when impacting Turukaishal's barrier – and spat on the ground. Turukaishal watched her, thinking. Trying to hit her from down here was almost impossible. She was almost seventy feet in the air and had more room to dodge if he threw anything her way. Instead, the Scain settled for biding his time. The Booster in his system was enough to keep him running for a while as he puzzled out how to end this fight.

Richard stepped forward, scooping something off the ground and hurling it straight up at her. Klaara, focused on Turukaishal, didn't react until the stone bounced off her shoulder, snarling. She glared down at him, chuckling. "You're a persistent one, aren't you?" she asked.

Victoria watched the three of them with wide eyes. Klaara, high up in the trees, looked battered and half-dead. Her posture and language, as well as her arrogance, bespoke of plenty of fighting spirit left. Richard, although cut and bruised in a few places and favoring his left side, looked as irritated as ever and filled with as much spirit as Klaara. Turukaishal, too, looked battered and worn down, as if his Psionics were all that kept him going. Even with the both of them fighting, Klaara wasn't going to be an easy victory.

Turukaishal looked at Richard. "I can throw you up there," he said quietly, hoping Klaara wouldn't hear him. It didn't' look like she even could. Richard looked at Turukaishal out of the corner of his eye before nodding almost imperceptibly.

With a wave of his hand, Turukaishal coated Richard in the glowing blue mist. Richard took several steps back, never taking his eyes off Klaara, before starting to run forward. He jumped into the air as Turukaishal made a second motion, sweeping his left hand upwards like a conductor signaling for the crescendo, and never landed. Instead, Richard sailed into the treetops, his jaw set in determination.

Klaara jumped off the branch as Richard approached, lifting the saber over his head. With a grunt, he fired the afterburners and cut through her perch, sending the bough crashing downwards through the trees. Turukaishal caught it with a Psionic tendril, turning and throwing the limb after the dodging Heil before moving Richard after her. Klaara, undeterred, caught another branch and spun around it, kicking the flying branch away from her. When it came back, she used her clawed gauntlet to shear through it, letting go of her perch and landing against the trunk of a thick tree.

Sheer luck was all that saved Klaara. The section of bark and wood her claws were in ripped free, sending her sliding several feet down the trunk. She caught herself with her other hand, shaking the bits of bark from her claws, as Richard's saber embedded itself in the tree where she'd been a moment before. Snarling, she lashed out with her claws again. Richard pulled himself up on the sword's handle, feeling the tips of her gauntlet raking his boot. He lowered himself sharply, kicking out with his heel, and felt something fleshy give way beneath him, followed by a cry of pain. Klaara slid a few more inches down the tree, screeching angrily.

Richard let go of the sword entirely, falling straight down onto the bounty huntress. Their combined weight was too much for the gauntlet to handle and they were both dragged away from the tree, plunging towards the ground. Turukaishal jerked Richard away just in time to avoid a vicious swing of Klaara's claws and guided him safely back to solid ground. Klaara wasn't so lucky. She impacted the ground like an anvil. This time, when the debris cloud settled, Klaara remained in the bottom of the crater.

Turukaishal walked to the edge of the ditch, staring down at her. Richard stood next to him, his bloodied sword cane in his hand. The Heil lay there, her luminous eyes open and staring up at the sky through the trees. "Not bad," she coughed, spitting up a globule of blood before looking at them. Klaara pushed herself up into a sitting position, wincing, before dragging herself to her feet. "Yeah… not bad at all."

She chuckled, turning and looking at Richard, brazenly ignoring the Scain. "And you," she said, grinning rakishly and exposing her sharpened teeth. Two of them were chipped, probably from when he'd kicked her. "That was one of the better matches I've had… you're a better swordsman than I gave you credit for." She coughed again, clutching at her chest. Blood trickled past her lips and she spat it derisively into the dirt, as if her own vital fluids were poison in her veins. "I'll let you have this match," she decided, shrugging. "After a fight like that, you deserve it."

She went low, her black hand touching the ground. A sable ring of light expanded rapidly, encompassing Turukaishal and Richard in seconds. Richard froze, growling as he realized his body had been rendered immobile by the constricting black aura. Rather than accosting him with it, however, Klaara allowed the aura to spread up into the treetops, retrieving the sword embedded there. It flew into her free hand, joining its sister, before she rose again. The light faded away as soon as her hand left the ground.

She looked upwards for a moment, studying the sky before grinning back at Richard. "Hope to see you around, kid," she said, winking at him before showing him a small cube. "Keep practicing. Next time, I don't plan on giving you an easy win." She tossed the cube towards him, the crooked grin never leaving her face. A moment later, it exploded in a blinding flash of light, heat and noise. Richard and Victoria threw their hands over their ears, looking away, and Turukaishal turned his body away from the light. When it faded away, Klaara was gone. Richard sighed, shaking his head and looking at Turukaishal.

"You okay?" he asked, wiping his sword cane on his thigh before sheathing it.

"Yes," the Scain said, relaxing now that the Heil had been driven off. "You?"

"I'll live. I've seen worse," he said, smirking with self-satisfaction as his body seemed to relax. The posture he'd kept while fighting seemed to withdraw inside him, making him look far more at ease. "I'm going to bill her for the shirt though."

Chapter 33

Turukaishal winced as he smeared protite paste over some of his cuts. The silvery ooze, dispensed from a rounded syringe, was filled with tiny machines that worked at knitting his skin back together, courtesy of the Zyzyt and their astounding medical technology. Even so, the little nanobots left a dull stinging sensation wherever the goop was applied. He looked down, his body a canvas of minor cuts and abrasions, each one filled with shimmering, metallic liquid. Across from him, he could see that Richard looked similar, the gashes on his chest having been filled already. The human grunted quietly as the robots did their work... work which they did remarkably quickly. Turukaishal could see the human's skin growing together.

"I apologize," Turukaishal said at length, waiting until he could speak without grinding his teeth. "I never intended for you to get involved in our duel."

Richard shrugged, discarding one of the bulbous syringes. "No big deal," he said. "It's what I do."

Turukaishal leaned back against the couch in his living room, his eyes turning upward to stare at the ceiling. Victoria sat nearby, anxiously fidgeting with her hair, and the Scain turned to look at her. "I suspect I have you to thank for the Booster, do I not?" he asked. When she nodded, he continued. "I owe you my thanks and my life," he said quietly. "My most heartfelt thanks. It was your quick thinking that enabled us to win the match. Without it, I doubt I would have lived."

Victoria turned a very unhealthy shade of red, looking away from his eyes. "It wasn't... it was no big deal," she said, tugging at her hair.

Turukaishal pushed himself away from the sofa. "I believe proper thanks are in order," he said. "Please wait here."

The Scain glided to his closet-conduit and descended into his ship, drumming his fingers on the wall of the elevator as he was conveyed through the cylindrical tube. He sighed as he stepped out, looking around his laboratory. He was going to have to power it up soon – for the first time in half a year. He chuckled to himself, looking around. There were a few things down here that needed to be powered up to be fully appreciated.

He didn't want to waste too much time, though. Instead, he strode across the room to the counter in his laboratory. There, gleaming on the counter, were two boxes. They had been carefully wrapped in gold foil – something which had taken the Scain forever to figure out – and they were each sporting a ribbon and a bow. That hadn't taken him as long to learn, but it had still been aggravating beyond words. He whisked them off the counter, returning to the elevator and ascending back to the top. Back to Richard and Victoria.

"I constructed these for you both as Christmas presents," Turukaishal admitted as he stepped out of the lift with the boxes in his hands. Turukaishal was silently hoping he wasn't forgetting anything. He handed the boxes to the two humans, stepping back to see their reactions. Part of him wondered when he had started seeking approval from these creatures. What was *wrong* with him?

Richard fiddled with the bow for a moment before shrugging, reaching down and opening his belt buckle. Turukaishal was unsurprised to see a small, serrated blade attached to it. With a few deft slices, he was through the wrapping paper and was replacing the knife in his belt. Turukaishal suppressed the first question that popped into his mind: how many other weapons did Richard carry?

Victoria was slightly more tenacious, tearing into the wrapping paper and managing to get through it a moment after Richard succeeded with the knife. They both stared into their boxes wearing expressions of mixed surprise, confusion and wonder. Victoria reached into the box, slowly withdrawing one of the masks he had made for them, holding it as though it might shatter into dust. "What are they?" she asked, looking over at her brother as he, too, drew out his gift. She gingerly held the canister at the end, filled with a metallic vapor the color of seafoam. She gave it a little shake, watching the mist move around.

"Those are protite rebreathers," Turukaishal explained. "As I understand you may have some reservations about stabbing yourselves in the lungs with nine-inch syringes, I devised these as a way for you to breathe my atmosphere. Place it on your face and activate the seal. Once it is in place, breathe deeply several times – until that mist is

184

gone. You will be capable of breathing the chemical mixture I normally inhale, but you will not be able to inhale your own atmosphere until you switch back."

"Fascinating," Richard said, "but what good does it do us?" he looked up at Turukaishal in confusion.

The Scain smiled, his eyes turning yellow. "Well, I hardly think you will be able to see my ship if you can't breathe my atmosphere…"

It was as if someone had lit a box of fireworks underneath the two humans. Victoria leapt to her feet, almost dropping the mask in excitement. "Ship?!" she asked, her voice quivering with barely-contained excitement. "As in… *spaceship?*" Richard, too, was on his feet, although he looked much more composed than his sister. His aura, though, was still frenetic enough to betray his enthusiasm. Turukaishal's eyes deepened in color. This was a good sign.

"Yes. My spaceship," he confirmed. "We can go down whenever you are ready."

Both humans grinned at each other before Victoria saluted at him, smiling. "Which way, boss?" she asked playfully.

"Wing Commander, actually," he said as he led them over to the closet door, focusing on it as he tried to figure out why her smiling face brought him so much discomfort. Was that even the word? It was more of a tightening of his ribcage; as if someone had wrapped a belt around it and was squeezing.

He opened the door of the hidden elevator and stepped inside, stepping all the way to the back. It wasn't a large space – he probably should've thought this through a bit better – but there was no time to back out now. The two humans crowded in with him, and Victoria pressed herself firmly against him. He looked at the ceiling of the elevator in disbelief. No matter what he tried, this girl ended up being plastered against him at every turn. Slowly—far too much so for Turukaishal's liking—the lift began to descend. "Please," he said, "begin breathing into the rebreathers now." He reached over her head and pressed a few buttons on a keypad.

Both Vahran immediately placed their tanks to their faces, breathing deeply and sucking the aquamarine gas into their lungs as if their lives depended on them. They did. The lift slowly continued its chelonian march down through the conduit, heading down into the bowls of the earth; deep beneath the forest floor. The three of them rode in silence until the elevator ceased moving with a quiet hum. Richard and Victoria were all but short-circuiting with nervous energy, their auras alive and awake with excitement. Turukaishal opened the opposing door, situated at his back, and stepped out into his lab.

The room was roughly rectangular, each corner smooth and rounded instead of flat and angular. Counters lined the walls, contoured to match the curved corners, and there were rows upon rows of machines. Cabinets and shelves cluttered the walls above and below these workbenches, tools and boxes lined up neatly. A single pod rested forlornly in one corner, the interior lit by a gentle blue light as it rested at an angle. Screens, all of them dormant, hung from the ceiling around the outside of the room. Victoria and Richard looked around in wonderment, stepping out onto the silvery floor as they took in all the sights of the darkened room. Light invaded from only two sources: the dim interior of the pod and a single terminal stationed over near a round door.

"If you will give me a moment," Turukaishal said as he walked by them, "I will power on the ship. There is much more beyond this room. You can also take those masks off now, if you want."

Richard and Victoria removed the rebreathers as Turukaishal walked over to the only active console. He placed his hand on a black screen, waiting for a moment. The screen flashed white for a moment before a hum filled the room. Two more panels, seemingly made from blue light, extended from either side of the now-white screen and one more, in gold, rose from the top. This one folded out to the sides as well with two more screens. Turukaishal began to type on the upper one, his fingers making soft, musical pings as they touched the hard light surface.

It didn't take long. Two elongated conduits, running from one side of the room to the other, lit up with a brilliant blue light. The screens all around the room winked on, immediately cycling through several programs before starting to display various charts, readouts and graphs. Turukaishal gave them a brief once-over before touching one of the two blue screens. All of the screens around the laboratory faded out, returning to their dormant states. He tapped another one of the glyphs on the luminous screen. The five holographic panels slid back into the main console with a quiet purr, the machine going silent again.

"This is the laboratory," Turukaishal explained as he gestured around him. "This is where I spend most of my time, up here on Deck Three. There is also a fourth deck, which is the storage and engineering compartments, at the bottom of the ship. Deck Two is the crew quarters, although it is technically possible to fly this ship by myself. Deck One is the bridge. We descended past two other decks to reach this one."

The two humans were fixated on him, hanging on his every word. Turukaishal walked over to the door near the console he'd operated and waved his hand. There was a soft sound, like chimes, before the door parted into five equal segments which withdrew into the walls in a single fluid motion. Soundless. As if they had never even been there. Turukaishal motioned them through and closed the door behind them. Once more, the five triangular wedges closed with a haunting, phantom silence.

"This is the access hall," the Scain said as he gestured up and down the corridor in which they now stood. "On this level, I also have access to the armory, life support and maintenance areas. Continue down to the end of the hallway and stand on the circular dais: it will take you up to Deck Two or down to Deck Four."

Turukaishal paused for a moment, peering into his armory through a rectangular window. Like the layout of the laboratory, the corners of the window were smooth and rounded. The glass was barely there, visible only due to the reflection of the domed lights in the hallway. Inside, weapons and battery packs were arranged all over the walls, hanging from hooks or laying on tables. He knew it was psychosomatic, but he could almost smell the telltale reek of galvornite through the glass as he looked at a disassembled rifle – something he'd been working on before he'd arrived: simply a standard maintenance check, but time consuming. He prayed he'd never have to use one on Earth, but with that aggravating Heil lurking around it might be beneficial to take one up to the surface with him. He'd think about it. For now, he was content to follow the two humans to the end of the hallway and ride the lift up to the second floor.

The tour progressed smoothly, the two humans watching in fascination as Turukaishal pointed out the different components of the crew quarters. There were six rooms, each one longer than it was wide. There was a long, horizontal pod along the wall, similar to the one in the lab, and a series of cabinets on the opposite wall for personal effects. He also pointed out the medical facility, which was equipped with no end of mechanical arms, vats of multicolored liquid and clean, sterile tables.

"My ship is a *Celestial*-class frigate designed to be able to comfortably fit a crew of twelve and keep them comfortably contained for up to one standard year, or roughly four hundred and fifty days, Earth time," he explained when asked about the medical facility. "We even have mildly inane ways of entertaining ourselves." He nodded over at a recessed area pockmarked with small holes.

They moved over to the area and Turukaishal watched for a moment in amusement as the two humans attempted to scour it for clues as to its purpose. When they gave up, Turukaishal stepped in front of it with a smile. "This is a game called Rachdarm," he explained. "It is designed to be played with two teams of two. Rather pointless when I am the only one here, hm? Anyway, the first player uses his Psionics to lift up one of the spheres of his color – gold or silver – and hold them in the air." As he spoke, a golden sphere the size of Richard's fist lifted out of a square hole in the floor, surrounded by bluish light.

"Another Scain," he continued, "would then attempt to use his Psionics to throw this sphere at the far wall." He indicated it with his free hand. The far wall, about twenty feet away, was covered in large square holes. Each one was illuminated by a holographic screen, divided into red, yellow or blue sections. Each section had a series of glyphs printed in it. "Based on which hole it goes through and what part of the hole, the team earns points. After thirty throws, whichever team has the most points wins. Harder settings can involve the holes cycling patterns or positions in the wall, moving continuously, or incorporate more or less throws."

"So, it's kind of like a team game of darts then, hm?" Richard asked with a grin. "Any way we can give it a try?"

Turukaishal tapped his chin with one of his spindly fingers. "I will try to think of a way. Perhaps the simulators, but I make no concrete promises. Instead, why don't I interest you in something a bit more interesting for the moment?"

"What's better than alien darts?" Victoria asked, looking up at him with a wide grin. Turukaishal felt as if he was falling into those green eyes of hers and forced himself to look away. He felt as if he was drowning in them: an unfamiliar sensation.

"How about the bridge?" he asked nonchalantly, trying to push the feeling down into the recesses of his mind.

There was no further objection... not that he expected any.

Chapter 34

CHECKING FOR NEW MESSAGES...

...CHECKING...

...CHECKING...

...CHECKING...

...CHECKING...

...CHECKING...

...NO NEW MESSAGES. ENTERING HIBERNATION MODE.

Klaara's Rover docked with her ship shortly after sunset, giving the Heil a spectacular view of Sol as it seemed to vanish behind Earth. From her position in geosynchronous orbit around the Moon, she could see the lights on the night side as they glowed brightly; highlighting major metropolitan areas... places she never wanted to go.

The Heil had no time for sightseeing, though. She angrily jumped out of her rover and stormed through the rusted, worn-down hallways of her ship. The clean lacquers on the walls had long ago begun to peel and bubble away, revealing the brownish metal beneath. Panels of metal had been removed or hastily welded on, exposing the wires and cables behind as she stormed down the cramped, narrow corridor.

It didn't take her long to reach the bridge, cursing profusely in her native tongue as she seated herself behind the communications relay. The ship immediately responded to her touch as she ran her hands over a holographic console: four large, rectangular screens seemed to grow out of the panel, each one scrolling with a myriad of glyphs and symbols and glowing with a soft golden light. She reached out and touched the third panel, dragging it down in front of her and orienting it horizontally before tapping one of her thin fingers against a particular line of code.

The four screens condensed into a single panel, large and square, and the center deepened to black; an oval of pitch-dark night in a panel of gold. A chime echoed through the bridge as she waited, drumming her fingers on the panel. "Answer, you—"

The panel morphed again, twisting and contorting until she was looking at the holographic of a Scain, his fingertips pressed together. Below the waist, he faded away into a cloud of particles. His magnificent, flowing robes were reproduced perfectly, showing off every swoop and whorl of the malkathite inlays of his clothing.
"Klaara'Doran kan Mitragan?" he asked, looking both pleased and surprised to see her. *"I trust you have good news?"*

"Not really," she said, standing up from her chair and pacing back and forth. The Scain's head followed her motions. "There was a complication."

"What kind of complication?" the Scain asked, lowering his fingers. *"What went wrong?"*

"Well, I found him and challenged him to a fight. He agreed, and we went somewhere private to beat the crap out of each other. We agreed on the fight, blah blah blah, I won't bore you with the details. Anyway, we started fighting, and everything was going well. This guy was tough, yeah, but nothing I haven't fought before."

The Scain was nodding his head. *"Which was why I hired you in the first place,"* his voice said, sounding all at once both honeyed and synthetic. *"Go on."*

"It took me a minute, but I beat him down to nothing. Had him on the ground and was ready for the killing blow. Next thing I know, one of his little human pals comes barreling out of nowhere like a stampeding jurash and tackles me. While he kept me busy, some girl went and fetched the Scain a Booster and now I'm fighting two of them."

"And, based on the fact that you are here, I take it you won?"

"Not really," she said, waving her hand disgustedly. "That human—he's tough. Wore me down. By the time Turukaishal came back into the fight, I didn't have much left in me. I ended up falling back."

The hologram was silent for several moments before nodding. *"I see. So you lost the duel. Either way, you have provided me with valuable information. Thank you."*

"Huh?" Klaara asked, looking at the Scain. This wasn't a reaction she'd expected.

The hologram leaned forward. *"You have proven to me that Turukaishal is, in fact, collaborating with the Vahran. Furthermore, he has revealed both his extraterrestrial nature and the location of his base to them, or the second Vahran could not have provided him with a Booster. These allegations of treason are most severe, you know."*

"I thought you already knew he was a traitor, hence the reason I'm here!" Klaara growled, turning to face him.

The Scain waved his hand dismissively. *"We suspected that he was a traitor, and lacked everything but concrete proof. You've provided that, for which I am extremely grateful.*

190

Continue your mission as usual and I will see to it that you are well rewarded for your service."

"Yeah, got it," Klaara said. "Not like I have a choice, having to eat and all. Anyway, I'll call you later. I have to prep for the next time I fight him."

"Of course, Klaara. Thank you for your report, you have been most helpful." The link went dead without another word from the Scain, leaving Klaara alone on the bridge. She snorted, striding out of the room, her heels echoing on the metal floor of the ship. The first thing she was going to do was take a radiation shower to get herself cleaned off, and then patch up her leg and chest. Damn that human for his swordplay. He was just so... so...

Klaara shivered involuntarily, running her hand over a blue sphere near a triangular door. It slid away into the walls and floor, dividing neatly into three segments, and she entered the living quarters. That Vahran had talent, which wasn't something she admitted easily. Part of her ached to fight him again, but her survival instincts cautioned her against it. Even though she'd been handicapped this time, she knew that the Vahran was exceptionally ruthless in a fight, as if he'd been doing it as long as she had. Whatever lay in his past, it had made him into a powerful fighter. She grinned as she crossed into the showers, closing the door behind her. Powerful fighters were what kept her sharp. Suppressing her survival instincts, she decided to fight him again someday.

***

Meanwhile, on Chindrus, the Scain from the hologram sat back in his black, curved chair and pressed his fingertips together again. This was a lot more problematic than he had initially expected it to be. Sending Klaara after Turukaishal was an unprecedented act of treason against the Mindbank, but it had paid off by proving that Turukaishal was, indeed, working *too* closely with these Vahran. If they were aware of his physiology enough to know he needed a Booster, he had told them a lot.

Now the only issue lay with presenting his findings without making it look like he'd taken out a hit on that witless Turukaishal. He swiveled his chair toward one of the windows, gazing out across the Amara District. He also had to think about how to get this Heil off his back. If he paid her, it would look suspicious if anyone ever looked at his financial records.

There was silence in the room as he pondered his dilemma. The only interruption in the stillness was the sound of the waterfalls cascading down along the sides of the room, interspersed with the calling of the vemorai birds flying in the gilded, decorative chutes crisscrossing the ceiling. The plants in his room were still, shifting slightly but silently in the breeze from an open window. Their brightly colored blooms contributed a rich, spicy aroma to the chamber, filling the air with their scent. He breathed it in deeply, smiling to himself. This job, despite the political grandstanding that went with it, was well worth the stress when he looked at the perks.

He looked down at the Data Pad in his lap, reaching down and picking it up and scrolling through the numerous messages there: all from Turukaishal. It wasn't hard to get them – he was part of the mission staff, after all. Things looked neat and orderly on Turukaishal's end, but this Heil told a different story.

His eyes alighted on a message Turukaishal had sent to a Taeski – Klakshan. A friend of his, if memory served. In it, they discussed the state of Ferthoroyia, Turukaishal's father. The Scain leaned forward as he read, drumming his long fingers on his chair as a plan began to form in his mind. He set down the Data Pad, looking across the room at one of the holographic displays on the wall. There was a gap two days from now – perfect. He'd have to be subtle about his actions – he didn't want to arouse suspicions – but it was definitely doable.

He smirked, his eyes turning yellow as he leaned back in his chair, tossing the Data Pad on his desk. With Turukaishal out of the picture, he wouldn't have any more impediments to his goals: something he had been looking forward to for thirty cycles at least. Before he could indulge in a laugh, a hologram of a Zyzyt emerged from a column next to his desk.

"Sir, your next appointment is here." The shorter alien held a Data Pad that looked far too large for him, and the device had multiple additional screens open. He was furiously tapping at them, undoubtedly keying in a message to the next appointment, informing them that they were next in the queue.

"Send them in," the Scain said, moving his Data Pad and hiding it inside his desk. "Thank you."

A rather irritated Alintean swept into the room, her brownish-gold eyes fixated on him as she approached. The Scain leaned forward, touching his fingertips together and smiling falsely at her... not that she could tell. "Ah, Flight Commander Alaniel. It is a pleasure to see you. Please, sit down... what can I do for you today?"

As the Alintean took her seat and began to speak, the Scain settled in to listen, the back of his mind still working its way through his plan. It was brutally simple, and left almost no room for error: just the way he liked his machinations. Shelving them for now, he devoted himself fully to his normal duties – babysitting every foreign official who came to his desk. With any luck, in another twenty cycles, he could delegate this task to some other, less important official.

After all, if he made it to Mindbank, he wouldn't have time to do such a menial chore.

Chapter 35

BEGIN MESSAGE:

LOCATION: Chindrus, High Councilor's Towers

TIME: 4/22 Local Time

MESSAGE: *It seems that even a Mitragan Heil cannot be more than interference to you. I had rather hoped that you would end up dead. It would certainly have taken care of a lot of problems for me. And for you – you would have at least had an honorable death and no one else would have to worry about dying under your command.*

-Demnechi

Turukaishal gestured grandly as the elevator reached the top level. "This," he said proudly, "is the nerve center of my ship: the bridge." All around him, lights winked on in response to the presence of his Psionics, the bridge coming alive. A single walkway ran from end to end, dividing the bridge in half, and at the far end was a bulbous cockpit. It was slightly recessed into the ground, and lit by a soft blue glow. To the left and right of the walkways were numerous other terminals, each one recessed like the bridge and lit by hundreds upon hundreds of lights. Charts, graphs and readouts scrolled across holographic displays, creating a lightshow of information and data.

Most impressive of all, though, was the hologram of the Sol System hanging in the air above them like the specter of an omnipresent God. Earth was selected, its bluish representation surrounded by a green ring. Information streamed off to one side, alien glyphs scrolling through various measurements. Turukaishal looked up at the icons, reading off the numbers to the two humans and translating the symbols: atmospheric composition, pressure, gravity, length of day, length of year... the list continued to trail on and on.

"These are cohesive light nodules," Turukaishal explained as he finished reading off the bracket of information next to Earth. "They can be touched and manipulated. For example..." he reached up and tapped the planet Mars with his long-fingered hand. Immediately, the green ring highlighted the new planet, Earth shrinking away to a tiny dot on the hologram while Mars expanded to show the terrain. The data bracket shifted as well, now reading off Mars's statistics. Up in the cockpit, a hologram of Earth also shifted to display the red planet. Victoria watched, spellbound.

Richard tore his gaze from the hologram, looking at the terminals in a moonstruck daze. "So what do all these do?" he asked, gesturing to the seats. "Are they for flying the ship, or what?"

"The four terminals towards the bow of the ship control secondary weapons fire," Turukaishal explained as he indicated the terminals in question. "The terminals toward the rear control communications, shielding and defensive parameters, including the cyberwarfare and stealth systems. The pilot," he pointed straight into the cockpit, "flies the ship itself and has control of the main gun."

Richard and Victoria followed Turukaishal up to the cockpit, taking in the vast number of cohesive holograms around them. It was effectively one big terminal, constructed around a large black chair which floated above the floor. The Scain seated himself, taking a deep breath and closing his eyes. Seated as he was, for once, he was shorter than the two humans. "Aaah," he said, smiling. "It feels good to sit here again."

He pointed to various parts of the control deck, naming them as he went. Surprisingly, as he explained it, the control and design were relatively simple for a starship. Despite the plethora of buttons and levers, the ship was primarily controlled by a pair of black joysticks. The left one controlled horizontal turning, or the yaw of the craft, while the other was responsible for vertical orientation: pitch. On the floor was a single round pedal that shifted control of the first joystick from yaw to roll, allowing him to bank off to avoid attacks or to perform sharp turns.

There were other pedals on the ground as well. One controlled speed, based on how it was pushed (tilting it forward increased speed while tilting it backward decreased it) and another was akin to an emergency brake. He pointed out what some of the buttons on his control board did as well, indicating the green glowing node which activated the 8th Dimensional Drive – an engine down on the Fourth Deck which allowed him to enter, for lack of a better moniker, a sort of hyperspace.

He'd explained the general dynamics of the drive many times during his courses at the Academy, as well as having given both humans a very brief overview of the device during their game of "Twenty Questions". The universe they were currently a part of was, for simplicity's sake, referred to as "Light Space". The Old Race, a now-extinct superspecies that had vanished some sixteen trillion years ago, had created the ability to link to a counterpart universe, called "Dark Space". Turukaishal explained that, regardless of what the speed of light was, solid matter could not move at one-hundred percent of that speed.

"This means," he said as he turned his chair to face them, "that no object can ever exceed 186,000 miles per second in Light Space. However, in Dark Space, the speed of light and the laws of physics are not the same. Over there, the speed of light is approximately sixty million miles per second. By using the drive to jump into Dark Space, I can accelerate up to ninety percent light speed and then decelerate before reemerging. This means we can cross the entire plane of the Galaxy in under an hour: a considerably quicker trip than trying to crawl across the Galaxy at light speed, which would take us over a hundred thousand years, plus or minus a century or two."

"So you could take off right now?" Victoria asked, gesturing to the controls in front of her. "I mean, like actually go into orbit?"

"I could," Turukaishal said. "But it would be tricky. Plus, returning my ship to this exact position would be impossible at best. I would probably attract attention trying." He cocked his head slightly, looking up at them. "Do you *want* to go into space?"

Before Victoria could answer, Richard chose that moment to interrupt. "You said the pilot controlled the main cannon? Where from? I don't see anything with a trigger."

It was true. The joysticks in front of the pilot's seat weren't equipped with any kind of triggers to signify an attack method. Instead, they were oddly blank, composed solely of that gleaming black metal that shimmered innocently at Richard from the control panel.

Turukaishal grinned, leaning forward and grasping the joysticks. A smooth motion of his thumbs caused the metal to shift and flow like a liquid, reshaping to reveal two greenish buttons atop each stick. "Each of these fires the chainguns," he said as he used his Psionics to reshape the joysticks. "Each chaingun is fusion-fed, firing electromagnetically-sealed energeic particles at supersonic speeds. Very devastating."

A different pulse of his Psionics caused the joysticks to flow again, this time revealing a pair of long purple lights along the edge which thrust forward. Turukaishal rested his fingers on them. "This fires the Piercer Unit," he continued. "A 5500 Energy Unit mass driver mounted on the underside of the ship. Good enough to tear through the shielding of any ship in the Galaxy save for maybe the Alintean Empire's."

Richard watched as the joystick flowed back into its original shape. Turukaishal turned back to Victoria. "As I was saying, Victoria, you sound like you would like to go into space. Do you?"

Victoria all but danced on the spot in eagerness. "Can we?"

Turukaishal rose, the seat swiveling softly and returning to its neutral position. "I may have a way."

The Scain led them back to the elevator and lowered them back down through the ship, passing Decks Three and Two and depositing them in the Storage Bay. All along the walls were crates, rows upon rows of them, stacked and strapped down for transport. Long, flat containers were stacked in the corners while odd, dome-shaped lockers hung from the walls. As opposed to the blue lighting in the rest of the ship, the Storage Bay was lit by a deep red light which made all the silvery crates shimmer. Richard moved over and scrutinized some of the labels before giving up. Turukaishal, noticing his activities, translated a few of them for him.

"Food," he said as he pointed to a row of small, cubical crates. "Medical equipment, drones, tools, weapons..." he looked around before continuing onwards through the bay. At the far back, he keyed in a nine-digit passcode to open a large pressure door. "And this is the Shuttle Bay", he said as he led them through. All along the walls were several small shuttles, similar or identical to the one that had rescued them during the blizzard. They hung along the walls in nearly-vertical slots, anchored in place by glowing bands of light.

Sitting in the middle of the chamber was a larger, more robust craft. It was a sleek, streamlined ship; oval, more or less, with a long tail which tapered to a rounded point. Two thrusters were mounted to the left and right of this stalk, cables sprouting from them and joining the main body of the craft. A wide, oval viewport in the front revealed a small (by comparison) interior while two rectangular windows on the sides showed a crew compartment. Like the other shuttles, this one swayed gently inside a vertical coil of glowing, golden light.

"This is the *Dirego*," Turukaishal said. "A Rover-class vehicle. It's designed for more remote scouting missions, quick reconnaissance and salvage runs." He watched as the two humans moved around it, examining it from all sides. Richard placed his palms against the smooth, silvery metal while Victoria was plastered up against one of the windows, looking inside. Turukaishal reached past her and placed his hand on the side of the Rover. Immediately, the metal shimmered and flowed into the sides of the craft, parting like a fissure and revealing the sleek, smooth interior. Within, there was enough room for a small group – perhaps five humans or three Scain – plus a pilot in the front. Turukaishal stepped back and allowed the two humans to examine it.

"Can we go?!" Victoria asked eagerly, turning to look at Turukaishal and dancing in place, excitement radiating from her features. "Oh wow! To go into space! *Space!!*"

It was at that precise moment that the Scain realized just how different these beings were from him. She was excited about going into space: something he did every day, sometimes more than once. Their kind hadn't even truly begun to explore their own moon yet, apart from a handful of manned landings, and he was sitting on a technological Holy Grail that could propel their species into the space age... no pun intended, of course.

"Unfortunately, you are ill-suited right now," Turukaishal said as he ran his hand over the *Dirego* again, the metal flowing back into place. "You lack hard vacuum suits, for one, and you have no rebreathing apparatus. I can manufacture these for you – quite easily, in fact, if you'll follow me to the Medical Bay – but you'll need to comply with some... ah... odd requests..." his eyes turned pink. Hiin take him, why hadn't he remembered that *before* he offered.

Richard narrowed his eyes, taking a step toward the Scain. "What kind of requests?"

"You will need to strip down to almost nothing so that the polyform suit can fit flush against your skin," Turukaishal explained, looking everywhere except the two Vahran. "Did it just get hot in here?"

Victoria laughed. "How much clothing is "almost nothing"?" she asked, playing with a lock of her hair. Despite her outward appearance, her aura was pink and soft; this was probably making her as uncomfortable as it was him. Turukaishal found his eyes drawn to the lock of hair she was playing with. Somehow, he was unable to look away from the distracting motion.

"Your undergarments should do," Turukaishal said, wishing his eyes didn't turn such an embarrassing shade of pink whenever he felt awkward. Hiin, what was he supposed to do? He palmed his face, humiliated. His pride and dignity had, hand in hand, just waltzed out the airlock.

"Alright. Fine." Richard acquiesced. Turukaishal noticed that he didn't look too pleased with the arrangement either, but was willing to go along with it; likely for his sister's sake. "We'll come along, but you have to wait outside while Victoria undresses."

"And you can operate Scain machinery?" Turukaishal asked, folding his arms. "I have to be there to operate the devices. I'm sorry."

He sighed, watching Richard frown for a moment before nodding. "Fine. Let's go," he said, turning away and massaging the bridge of his nose with two fingers. Turukaishal wordlessly swept past him, leading them out of the Shuttle Bay and towards the elevator. If all went well, they'd be departing inside of two hours.

That was if Richard didn't try to kill him first.

Chapter 36

BEGIN MESSAGE:

LOCATION: Chindrus, Eccemeria District

TIME: 14/22 Local Time

MESSAGE: *Well look at you: all grown up and fighting Mitragan Heil. You have most of the Erythians in Eccemeria on the razor's edge of a stroke, you know. They're panicked that they will lose the opportunity to pair you and Kridoria up. All I did was come try to visit a friend and now everyone wants to know if I've heard from you. I swear this mess would have been easier if you'd just called me to handle the Heil. At least that way she wouldn't have escaped, hm? Oh well – if she comes back again, you've got my number.*

-Bordra

The Medical Bay was a large and ovular room lit by a single blue-white light. There was a large, black table in the center of the back wall, large enough for one or two people to stretch out on; or perhaps one Scain. The square table didn't look like it was made from metal; rather, it looked as if it had been formed form some kind of sable gelatin. Folded up against the wall like the arms of a praying mantis were numerous robotic appendages, each one labeled with the strange, spidery glyphs of the Scain. There were shelves and cabinets along both walls, some of them with glass doors and others connected to large tanks which seemed to regulate the temperature inside.

With his eyes furiously pink, Turukaishal instructed the two humans to disrobe. Once they both stood in front of him in their undergarments, he directed Richard to the table. "Please lie back and spread your arms and legs," he instructed him. "I will initiate the procedure. Please remain as still as possible."

Turukaishal swept over to a command console against the wall and ran his fingers over one of the interfaces. Like in the lab, a series of holographic screens folded open around him as he began to peck at the keys with those long, alien fingers of his. A moment later, a large red beam of light began to sweep back and forth along Richard's prone form, prickling the hairs on his body as it passed. "This will determine the dimensions of your body," Turukaishal explained. "The light is completely benign."

"I figured," Richard said as he lay there. The light moved back and forth several times before blinking out. Turukaishal keyed in another series of commands before tapping a large turquoise button. Two robotic arms descended from the ceiling, carrying between them a large block of the same black gel that Richard was laying on. Richard's eyes widened slightly. "And *that*?"

"A block of the polyform sealant," Turukaishal said without looking. "It will press down against you and conform to your body. It will recede and then press down a second time. Do not be frightened – the substance is very malleable – but I still must ask you not to move. Polyform has to be skintight for it to work well, and if you move it will skew the dimensions. Once this is complete, we will begin phase three."

The black ooze descended and Richard couldn't help but close his eyes. As predicted, the block was extremely soft and pliable, easily shaping itself around his body. Only his hands, head and feet were left free as the polyform compressed slightly against his body, holding still for a moment before rising up into the air. It descended for a second time, pressing back down over Richard's body. This time, there was a faint hiss and a gray vapor hissed out between the upper and lower blocks.

This time, when the block lifted, Richard was encased in a skintight black suit. It covered him from the underside of his chin all the way to his wrists and ankles, the surface feeling slightly reptilian—like scales—but softer. Richard plucked at it, watching as the material moved away from his body before snapping back into place like rubber. "And this is my flight suit?" he asked. "How do I take it off?"

"That is phase three," Turukaishal said, as if chiding an impatient child. "Please do not discompose yourself."

Richard grunted, mildly irritated, as Turukaishal resumed his typing. "I see you've done this a lot, huh?" he asked, trying not to move his head to look at the Scain.

"Several dozen times," Turukaishal confirmed. "Crewmembers sometimes need their polyform suits repaired or replaced, although it isn't common. Still, it happens." The ceiling above Richard parted as a mechanical arm descended and pointed what looked like an elongated, bullet-shaped object at Richard. Protruding from the end was something that resembled a streamlined gun barrel. Richard instinctively flinched.

"And just what the heck is *THAT*?" he asked, his eyes nervously shifting to look at Turukaishal. "It's not going to reduce me to atoms, is it?"

Turukaishal laughed. "No. That's a protite dispenser. It will create the openings for your suit. I am just going to give you a standard configuration, as it will keep confusion to a minimum." The Scain keyed in several more lines before an image of Richard's body appeared on the screen to his left. He reached over, drawing a line from the throat to the waist. Another button lowered the gun until it was pressed against Richard's chin.

There was a gentle humming as the gun began to vibrate, the end lighting up. It choked for a moment before stalling, as if waiting for something. Turukaishal snorted. "Richard, choose a color. What's your favorite?"

"Uh… blue." Richard said. Turukaishal pressed a few more keys and the gun began to move, tracing its way down the human's torso, ending at his waistline. A vivid, electric blue stripe ran down the length of the black suit. The gun slowly moved back up to Richard's chin, humming as it traced back over the blue line, before drawing away from him and hovering overhead.

Turukaishal looked back at him, surveying his handiwork. "Would you like the accents to be the same color?" he asked.

"Accents? What accents?" Richard asked, lifting his head slightly to look down at himself.

"Each suit is given a different patterning of lines to aid in rapid field identification," Turukaishal said, sounding like he was quoting a textbook or file. "These can be left up to the individual to design, or can be generated at random."

"Yeah, let's stick with the same color, and just randomize it," Richard said. Turukaishal turned back to the controls, nodding. He had to give the human credit – he'd moved very little, if at all, during their little project. Victoria, with all energy and pep, would probably need to be strapped down. His eyes cycled through a myriad of colors before he fought down any aggravating feelings and returned them to their usual black color.

Several smaller arms descended from the same ceiling compartment as the main gun, each one tipped with what looked like a laser pointer. These turned on, emitting a series of blue beams which traced a myriad of random lines across Richard's suit. Turukaishal nodded as they finished. "Roll over," he instructed Richard. "Same position." Almost as soon as Richard was still again, the lines resumed drawing the meaningless patterns across his suit, picking up seamlessly from where they had left off. Turukaishal nodded, admiring his handiwork. "Alright. You can stand up, Richard. Your armor should be ready by now. Victoria, if you would be so good as to lie down on the table."

Turukaishal set the machine to run through the last scan command up through color selection before moving over to Richard, leading him over to a large dispenser along the wall. As if on cue, the machine produced what looked like a jumble of machine parts, dumping them into a curved chute where they tumbled out onto a waiting table. Turukaishal picked each one up and presented it to Richard, telling him where to put it.

Each piece, when held against the polyform, seamlessly adhered in place. "This is just a basic hard-vacuum suit," Turukaishal told him as he helped Richard put on the front and back of the torso armor. The greaves snapped into place around his thighs, protecting the front, back and sides. A pair of boots sealed in place around his calves, preventing his feet from being exposed. Each boot also had a knee guard attached, and was only loosely attached to the foot to provide maximum mobility.

The shoulder and upper arm guards functioned similarly to the greaves, protecting everything but the underarm. The gloves had an elbow cap which fulfilled the same function as the knee cap on the boots. Richard examined himself, flexing his arms and legs to see if the suit interfered with his mobility at all. It didn't. Rather, it seemed almost like the polyform moved his armor out of the way if it would have touched another piece. He straightened up and nodded. "Good stuff," he said, looking up at Turukaishal.

Behind them, Victoria was being scanned by the machine. She called over that she wanted her color to be gold, and Turukaishal broke away from Richard and keyed in the sequence before returning to the armor station. Hopefully this would finish up soon – he couldn't bear looking at her in her underwear for too much longer.

"Next is your helmet," Turukaishal said as he brought up one of the holograms. "What style would you like?"

"You're all concerned with aesthetics?" Richard asked curiously.

"More like… customization," Turukaishal corrected. "By making certain that the suits look different, or conform to the wearer's occupation, status, unit or individual tastes, we can identify one another quickly if necessary. It is far more functional than you might think. I now know that if I see a human wearing gold or red armor, it is you two. Now, if you will please step over here, we can begin the designing of your helmet."

The Scain could hear the protite dispenser behind him hum to life. Victoria was almost done. He indicated the screen, focusing on the task at hand. "There are two main types of helmets: open and closed," he explained. "Open helms allow you to see your opponent directly, but are more fragile. Closed helms are stronger, but rely on miniature cameras to provide you with a real-time integrated feed… which can be shut down by an electromagnetic pulse. It is up to you: which do you prefer?"

In the end, after a moment or two of thought during which Turukaishal checked on Victoria, Richard selected a closed-face helm. Turukaishal helped him bring up the helmet design, giving him control of the customization. Richard spent a few minutes drawing his design before nodding in satisfaction. A moment later, the helm rolled from the dispenser and Richard picked it up.

The design was relatively simple: a Y-shaped camera interface outlined with the glowing blue lines. Without preamble, Richard fitted the helmet onto his head. It sealed shut with a hiss, the lines flickering and the camera interface lighting up. There was a soft ping as the helmet integrated with the rest of the suit's electronic skeleton, signifying completion. "Woah," Richard said, looking around. "Now this is a spacesuit: far better than the marshmallow costumes NASA has. Now how do I take it off? Or the suit?" his voice had mechanical ring to it, as if he was speaking through a fan.

"Run your fingertip along the protite stripe on the front of your suit," Turukaishal explained. "It responds to your aura only, so you do not have to worry about someone else opening it... not without shredding through both it and you. As for the armor pieces, they can simply be pulled off, although once more they respond to your aura alone."

While Richard practiced removing the parts of his suit, Turukaishal turned to address Victoria, swallowing nervously. Staring down the female human in form-fitting polyform was not doing anything for his eye color. Indeed, they had returned to that unhealthy (and uncomfortable) shade of pink. He sighed, shrugging and resigning himself to it. Seeing as his eyes were going to be pink for quite some time, he might as well just get used to it.

"Like what you see?" Victoria teased, pirouetting slowly for him. Turukaishal turned his back on her, palming his face and swallowing nervously. What was she playing at? By the Hiin...

"Yes. Now can we get on with your armoring?" Hiin, had he really just said that? He wanted to slap himself. Hard. He sighed, presenting her with each of the armor pieces, watching and directing her as she put them on. When they were finally in place, he handed her the gloves and boots to finish up the set. She smiled, putting them on and admiring herself, watching the way the gold lines shone through the armor segments, their patterns reflected on the surface. Lastly, he moved her over to the panel to design a helmet.

Unlike her brother, Victoria chose an older model open helm, the visor bisecting her helmet horizontally and bulging slightly. Composed of protites and silicon-wireframe glass, it could withstand anything but a direct hit from a meteorite. Or, of course, bullets. Polyform wasn't designed for combat – it never had been, and it never would be. The helmet was streamlined and graceful, very much like her, and had the golden accents that matched her suit. Turukaishal stepped back and admired his work on the two humans.

"Not bad," he said with a small smile as he surveyed them. "Not bad at all." He'd have to find a few workarounds, of course. He'd used Scain-model suits (customized to fit their hands and feet, of course) but this left them bereft of shields. Shielding was normally provided by drawing off a small portion of Psionics and amplifying it. Humans, lacking the ability, would be unshielded. But just for a brief space jaunt, it wasn't really necessary. Not yet. "Alright," he said, closing down the consoles. "Let's head back to the *Dirego*."

Chapter 37

BEGIN MESSAGE:

LOCATION: Chindrus, Amara District

TIME: 1/22 Local Time

MESSAGE: Turukaishal, what is going on? Klakshan disappeared a while ago and Bandrumano is gathering up several of his closest friends from the Vanguard. Bordra showed up here this morning as well, carrying with him the full might of ETF Kirel and several additional Erythians. What is going on? I do not know if you are forbidden to talk about your mission or not, but please just tell me you are going to be alright? Please? Bandrumano won't tell me anything – he keeps saying that I don't have to worry about it, but I do... and Klakshan is about as useful as a sword with a bladed handle, so he won't tell me anything. And Bordra... he scares me way too much to talk to. So that leaves you, my betrothed: please tell me what is going on... I love you.

-Kridoria

The *Dirego* lifted smoothly off the ground and floated a foot or so above the floor of the hangar. It was almost totally silent, the only noise coming from the pair of lightly humming engines. The exhausts glowed with a faint violet light, like an amethyst held in front of a flame, and threw a soft illumination across the rear wall of the chamber. Turukaishal gestured to the rear compartment, watching quietly as Richard and Victoria sequestered themselves in the seats. The Scain barely filled the cockpit with his scant form, reclining into one of the seats and flipping a few switches on the dashboard. The rear area lit up with the same muted light as the thrusters.

"Is everyone set back there?" he asked, his voice sounding even more alien from within his blue-lined helmet. His, like Richard's, was a closed-face variant which completely obscured all of his features. Rather than going for the human's angular red accents, Turukaishal had three vertical blue stripes and one horizontally which bisected them.

"I'm game," Richard answered from the rear. "Everything looks fastened down back here."

Turukaishal nodded, flipping two more switches and reaching above him to pull a lever. He'd given the two a brief rundown of how to behave inside the Rover and what to do, but was still a bit concerned about taking them into space. However, he was too far along to back down now, so he planned to push ahead. He looked behind him, confirming that they were firmly strapped in with the X-shaped harnesses. Although there were overhead handles, even some within reach of their arms, Turukaishal didn't want to take any chances. Neither of them had undergone any formal Zero-G training and he wasn't going to be held responsible for one of them being hurled from the *Dirego* due to some unforeseen catastrophe.

The far end of the hangar hissed open, folding outward and downward until it struck the ground outside. Beyond the metal wall was a cavern, carved out of what looked like solid rock, with an almost perfectly circular tunnel cut into it. A metal hoop was mounted inside, four supports drilled into the rock face. Lining the interior of the ring was a series of blinking red lights and what looked like a disc of water or some other liquid; it shimmered and pulsed as though alive, reflecting the red light and refracting them across the nearby walls.

Turukaishal smoothly piloted the Rover out into the cavern, his hands moving rapidly across the controls as he worked to keep the craft steady. Underground, and in atmospheres in general, Rovers weren't an easy craft to handle. Their excellence lay in their zero-gravity capabilities and low-gravity maneuvers. He lined the Rover up with the ring, pressing a series of buttons. The lights inside the hoop turned blue. "I am going to ask you to brace yourselves," Turukaishal said. "Once we clear the barrier, things will be smoother and we will be using radios only. But until then, things may be a bit choppy."

"Barrier?" Victoria asked, her helmeted face glittering in the light of the passenger area.

"This cavern leads out into public, and therefore human, territory. I had to take certain precautions to avoid detection. You will see soon enough. For now, please grasp the handles above your seats and hold on firmly."

Their craft accelerated into the narrow tunnel, striking the liquid barrier. As soon as the nose of the *Dirego* impacted the silvery substance, they shot forward like a bullet from a gun. Ahead of them lay another ring, the lights switching from red to green as they approached. The Rover struck this one a few seconds later, flying down the tunnel toward another. This process repeated, accelerating them down the path at a breakneck pace, the rock walls flying past them. Each time they struck one of the hoops, the *Dirego* shook as if struck by a cannonball, jostling the occupants.

They struck an angled hoop that guided them downward before striking a horizontal one with yellow lights. This one broke apart into three thinner rings and began to revolve rapidly, spinning around the *Dirego* like a gyroscope. It lifted slightly before plunging downwards like a stone. Victoria yelped and Richard let out a surprised shout. Turukaishal closed his eyes, focusing on not losing his latest meal. These supports were invaluable when it came to guiding the Rover through this narrow tunnel, but they still made him sick.

The spinning rings reached the bottom of the vertical shaft, the largest locking into place vertically. The others quickly spun into place, thudding into place against the first before launching the *Dirego* down another tunnel. The passage evened out after four more hoops and the blinking lights had ceased to flash, instead burning with a steady red glow. Turukaishal sat up slightly. "Hitting the barrier in three…" he warned them.

The two humans leaned forward, looking up into the cockpit. Up ahead, beyond a few more of the semi-transparent rings, was a long metal tunnel. At the end was a wall of golden light that pulsed and throbbed with a greater intensity than the rings, although the technology was obviously related. The Scain hit a few more buttons in the cockpit. "Two," he said, his demeanor completely relaxed as they struck the last ring before the barrier. They shot forward like a dart, aimed straight for the wall of light. "One…"

The *Dirego* slammed into the barrier, bowing it outwards as if it was made of rubber. It pooled and splashed past them like liquid, resealing behind them as if they had never touched it. The entire craft shook to such a degree that Turukaishal was certain they would all be tossed around like a grain of rice in a salt shaker if it wasn't for the harnesses. The exterior lighting changed from the reddish-white color of the tunnel to a deep greenish-blue and an oppressive silence filled the cabin. Victoria spoke quietly, as if afraid her voice would trigger some catastrophic reaction. "What happened?"

"We are out of the base," Turukaishal said as he typed something in on a pad to his right. "And we are currently beneath what you call the "Puget Sound"."

Richard coughed. "Hold the phone… we're beneath the Sound?"

"Yes," Turukaishal said without looking back at them. "Why?" Both humans seemed to be at a loss for words. Turukaishal checked a few of his instruments before aiming the rover upwards and increasing the speed. They began to move through the water like a fish, accelerating as they approached the surface. "Reaching escape velocity phase one," Turukaishal told them.

The *Dirego* burst from the water like a breaching whale, shooting into the sky like a missile. A hum resonated throughout the craft and much to the two humans' surprise the exterior of the ship seemed to fade away. Turukaishal leveled out the craft as they rose above the clouds. It was sunset, the sky tinged with various hues of flaming oranges, and Victoria was all but plastered against the window in an attempt to take it all in; to see the skies with her own eyes.

"Increasing speed," Turukaishal recited automatically, "reaching escape velocity stage two."

The *Dirego* accelerated further, racing upwards through the clouds at a breakneck pace. The clouds whizzed past, smearing together like white paint. The orange skies flickered between gaps in the white, eventually smearing together as well until everything outside the window became a blur. "How fast are we going?" Victoria asked, her hands gripping the safety handles.

"We are approaching five hundred miles per second," Turukaishal said. "In another minute or so that should have doubled. I am approaching the standard speed for gravitational escape."

"That fast? It shouldn't be that much to get away from Earth's gravity," Richard called. The *Dirego* shook more and more with each passing second, although it was a more subdued shaking than the kind in the tunnel. This was more of a constant thrum – like a vibration.

"I am using a safe, established standard that I can control with a simpler set of protocols," Turukaishal told him. "Rather than try to calculate the escape velocity for each individual planet, we set up a system that uses the equivalent of 1000 miles per second as you can escape almost all planets at that speed. There is a more severe variant – ten thousand miles per second – but that is only used in and around brown dwarves. As a last resort, we use the 8th Dimensional Drive."

Richard sat back, nodding and staring placidly out the window. Unlike his sister, he didn't seem to feel compelled to glue himself to the viewports. Turukaishal resumed focusing on the controls, working them like a pianist. "Standard escape velocity achieved," he reported. "Exiting Earth's atmosphere."

Victoria released her hold on the grips and leaned forward into the cockpit, her head pressed alongside Turukaishal's. Their helmets clacked together in the confines of the small pilot's chamber. Turukaishal sighed, grateful that his helmet hid his gradually changing eyes. Why did they always turn pink? "Please make certain you are properly secured," he reminded her. "I do not wish for you to come to any harm."

"I am," she assured him, smiling at him through her helmet. He gave her a confirmatory nod before returning to his controls.

The *Dirego* angled upward sharply, shooting into the upper atmosphere. They began to climb ridiculously fast through the sky, the little Rover quivering and shaking as though it would come apart at any moment. And then silence filled the cabin – a type of silence that made the calm at the bottom of the Sound seem deafening. No more shaking, no more rattling. Just a deep, quiet, all-consuming silence.

"Welcome," Turukaishal said calmly, "to orbit."

The viewports on either side of the *Dirego* seemed to expand, moving like something organic as opposed to synthetic. Outside, Earth turned slowly beneath them as Turukaishal brought the Rover around so that it was in orbit around the blue marble. Off to the right, the moon slowly was rising from behind the planet, its gray form slowly swelling as it moved into view.

"It's beautiful!" Victoria said, her voice sounding breathless in her helmet. Turu looked over at her, watching as her eyes seemed to dart everywhere at once, trying to take in everything she was seeing. Richard, even, was up against the viewports and staring into space.

Turu eased back in his chair, folding his hands comfortably in his lap. He surveyed the pair of humans, both of them encapsulated in their suits. He'd taken the liberty of installing the software that allowed him to connect their suits to his monitoring systems, so he called up images of their vital signs. Heart rate and blood pressure were both elevated, but not dangerous. Richard was perspiring more than usual, but again it was nothing that couldn't be explained by excitement. He disabled the monitor and spoke. "Is it everything you thought it would be?"

"And then some," Victoria breathed excitedly. Again, her voice sounded as if she was on the verge of asphyxiating from exhilaration. Turukaishal quickly called up the charts again and checked her breathing. Apart from shallow breathing, she was fine. "I never thought I'd actually see it in person!"

Turukaishal aimed the Rover back down toward Earth, his fingers already dancing over the keys again. "I am going to bring us back down for now," he said. Victoria sighed but nodded and Richard merely grunted in assent. The *Dirego* began to descend, reentering the atmosphere at a much slower pace. "But the next time I take us up," he promised, "I will show you Saturn."

The smile on Victoria's face was evident even inside the helmet.

Chapter 38

BEGIN MESSAGE:

LOCATION: Chindrus, Amara District

TIME: 21/22 Local Time

MESSAGE: *Klakshan is starting to organize several groups. I do not know what he is up to, and I am usually leery of Taeski, but seeing as he has that unnerving tendency to be right, I have decided to go along with him for now. He has made some very convincing arguments, and in light of the mercenary threat, I think it would be best for us to work out a way to protect you. Busy as you are with your mission, and likely the Vahran, you need all the help you can get. Besides, if we weren't here to protect your dumb self, you'd probably have gotten yourself waxed decades ago. And remember: you still owe Bordra some cash, and I think you still owe me a drink. Watch yourself out there.*

-Bandrumano

Turukaishal sighed, checking his preferred weapon once more before setting it down with an irritated huff. Scain technology far outshone that of most other races (barring, perhaps, Alinteans and Erythians) but was a royal pain in the lower vertebrae to maintain or repair. He grumbled and glared at the offending assault rifle, muttering a string of expletives in his native tongue before drawing the gun across the table and leaning over it again. The weapon's inner workings were far too delicate for his Psionics to handle – the energy could short out any of the optical fibers or fry the motherboard that controlled the ammunition gauge, for instance – so he was stuck using the hair-thin tools from the repair kit. Heck, he had to use said tools to even open the darn thing before he could *look* at the wires inside.

This particular weapon had been hanging in his ship for at least a decade, the focusing lens having warped under the severe temperatures on Hyalmaz. The surface temperature there had melted the lens to the point where the rifle couldn't even shoot straight, and he figured now would be a good time to work on repairing the thing. If Klaara attacked again, it might be nice to be able to retreat somewhere with functional weaponry.

Unlike conventional weapons, which fired solid slugs, Scain technology used ammunition that was easily available and didn't need constant reloading, meaning they could walk into battle behind a wall of suppressing fire. The sight of a fully-armed

Vanguard soldier was something to behold – terrifying and awe-inspiring. Each rifle was built with a connection port along the top (or rear, in some cases) into which a long cable could be plugged. These cables ran back to a backpack power source.

Scain guns didn't need solid ammunition. Instead, three fully functional fusion nodes built up power in the backpacks. This energy was then transferred through the conduits to the guns where it did one of two things. The largest portion simply spilled into the main chamber where it was stored prior to ejection. The rest was sent to a miniature stabilization unit within the barrel. Each time he pulled the trigger, the stored energy was pumped through the stabilizer where the energy was wrapped in a magnetic pocket and fired at subsonic speeds. Each backpack could continue to run for several months – there was almost no reason to replenish ammunition the conventional way.

In fact, the larger backpacks could be plugged into *any* weapon with a conduit port, be it a pistol, rifle or anti-aircraft cannon, it didn't matter. He could plug in and start firing in seconds. The only drawback was if the gun overheated from repeated fire. If this happened, the conduit was forced out of the gun and ventilation ports opened along the body. Once the gun had cooled, the conduit could be reattached and combat could resume. Turukaishal scoffed at himself as he continued to work. To think that Vahran ran around shooting one another with chemically propelled metal slugs that were specific to different types of firearms. Solid-state ammunition had gone out of style thousands of cycles ago. It was as archaic to him as a stone spear was to a Vahran.

Turukaishal turned and looked behind him. In the rear of the laboratory was another chamber, designed for testing various antigravity components. Both humans were currently inside, the gravity set to zero, practicing their movements in an environment where direction meant nothing. Victoria was a surprisingly quick study, but Richard was having some problems, mostly with moving around.

The Scain slipped the backpack onto his back, tightening the straps to hold it in place. Two looped over his arms while another wound around his waist. A final strap encircled his neck like a collar, keeping the device firmly attached to him. Once it was firmly attached he reached behind him and jerked one of the three power conduits out of the bottom of the pack, bringing it around and plugging it into the top of his rifle, just above the grip. With that done, he released his rifle and gave the cord another jerk, allowing it to retract back into the backpack, a magnetic dock gripping the rifle to keep it from bouncing around.

That was the eighth gun he'd repaired. He was done. After three pistols, two rifles, a combat shotgun, a high-powered sniper rifle and an anti-aircraft cannon (which gave him no end of trouble), he was finished straining his eyes at the circuitry. Turukaishal removed the pack, hanging it up on a bar with fourteen others, before pushing the whole assembly back into a niche along the wall. It clicked into place, the metal of his ship liquefying and sliding shut over the packs, storing them safely away.

He walked over to the chamber containing the two humans, stepping in through the airlock. A few moments later, he drifted up next to Richard, floating between the two. "Would you like to see any other part of my ship?" he offered. "Play with any other toys?" the latter being said in a teasing manner.

"I saw you working on the guns out there – do you have a firing range where I could try one out?" Richard asked, windmilling his arms awkwardly as he drifted upside-down next to the Scain... relatively speaking, seeing as they were both horizontal when compared to the rest of the ship.

"I have a simulator," Turukaishal said. "It's on Deck Three. Victoria, would you care to try as well?"

Victoria, who had up until now been entertaining herself by kicking off the walls and flying in every direction, turned around and stuck both of her thumbs into the air. "Yeah! You bet!"

Turukaishal kicked off one of the crates that drifted around the room that the humans had been practicing with, floating over to the door and gripping the ladder, using it to orient himself properly with the keypad. "Please head down," he said, gesturing to the bottom of the area. Once the two Vahran were as low as they could get, he reinstated the gravity. The empty crates clattered down, as well as a pair of larger clanks that marked the two humans in their new suits. Turukaishal gestured to the ladder, "I will meet you by the elevator."

***

The simulator was effectively a large chamber, the walls patterned with laser scoring and large indentations. It had seen a lot of work. Turukaishal led Richard inside first, handing him a single large pack and connecting both a pistol and a rifle to it. The large packs could be connected with three weapons – usually referred to as the primary (rifle), backup (pistol) and special (third weapon). The special weapon was a category that encompassed anything other than standard rifles, shotguns, or pistol-based weapons. The sniper rifle and AA cannon were special weapons, for instance, while the pistol was a backup and the primaries could be a rifle or a shotgun.

"I am going to activate the simulator. Once it is active, you will be facing multiple simulacrums – little homunculi of mine that are relatively easy to defeat. They are holograms wrapped around kinetic barriers, so they are solid and "real". They will fire back, but their shots will not hurt you physically. I promise. The more you defeat, though, the more difficult it becomes. Please, make sure you are ready."

Richard drew the rifle as Turukaishal walked over to a panel to start the simulation. He could already tell it wasn't going to last too long – he hadn't found a viable workaround for the shielding. To compensate, he turned down the level of the AI controlling

Richard's "opponents" to keep the practice from ending too soon before starting up the projection arrays.

The simulator went dark, and suddenly he was standing in a sea of rolling fields. Blue-tinged clouds wafted through a navy-colored sky, and strange, multicolored trees grew nearby, their branches laden with seven-sided teal leaves. Richard looked around for a moment before his first target appeared. From the treeline, a featureless gray biped jumped out, aiming a rifle at him. Richard turned and pulled the trigger, the small energeic packets spraying out of his gun and blowing the hologram away in a shower of digital cubes.

Another appeared to his left and Richard turned, drawing the pistol as he did, and fired. The shot struck the hologram in the leg, causing it to stumble. The second shot pierced its head, finishing it. Richard stood his ground in the center of the visualization, switching between the rifle and the pistol for several moments until the AIs began returning his fire. After that, it wasn't too long before the simulation faded away to be replaced by the walls of the room. "What happened?" Richard asked, looking over his shoulder at the window where Turukaishal and Victoria stood.

        "You died," the Scain explained as he opened the door. "I have not yet figured out how to implement shielding on your suit. It is normally drawn from Psionics, but..." he looked away. "I'm fairly certain I could pull it from the pack, perhaps use a few augmentations to make it stronger, but it would lower your cooldown rate on your weapons, perhaps drop power routing by a substantial percentage..." he drummed his fingers on his forearm. "I haven't yet got any concrete solutions, but I'm working on it. I'm not an Erythian, you know."

Victoria laughed. She had taken off her helmet and had it tucked under her arm and her face was split into one of the widest smiles Turu had ever seen. "I never thought I'd be having this much fun on a spaceship," she admitted. "I mean, look at me! I've got a spacesuit! Don't I just look awesome?!"

Turukaishal had to refrain from telling her what was running through his mind. His helmet was off, of course, which meant his pink eyes were visible. The humiliation this caused him made his eyes deepen in color as well, and he briefly wondered if it was possible for his eyes to be caught in an endless cycle. He looked around before swallowing. "I am glad you are enjoying yourself," he said.

Richard leaned against the wall. "Hey Turu, can I ask you something? Honest answer?"

Fearful that Richard was puzzling out his pink eye problem, the Scain almost immediately began to perspire. "Hm?" he asked. "What is it?"

"What're the odds that you're going to call your leader to come kill us? Honestly. Don't sugarcoat it for us."

Turukaishal sighed with relief, perplexed that he'd rather discuss this topic over his eyes. "I estimate the survival of your race to be approximately seventy-five percent, provided my word carries any weight with the Mindbank."

"Wow! That high!?" Victoria squealed, leaping forward and hugging him around the waist. "Awesome! Thank you!!"

Turu placed his hand on Victoria's shoulder, patting it awkwardly and affectionately. "You're welcome?" He didn't want to tell her that it was primarily *her* that was influencing his decision. Was he really that weak? He'd have to hit up the Scain data storage banks before he made any final decisions. His actions might be suspect – some virus in the atmosphere, perhaps… but as he looked down at the girl wrapped around his waist (and doing his best to ignore the scathing glance from her brother) he knew, somewhere in his chest, that it was no virus.

Chapter 39

BEGIN MESSAGE:

LOCATION: Sovereign, Mitragan Province

TIME: 18/29 Local Time

MESSAGE: *Klaara'Doran kan Mitragan. You have hereby been terminated from the Mitragan bounty payroll for your crimes against the Clan. Your actions have reflected poorly on us all, and especially upon your father. You have one rotation to appear before the Hierarchs to plead your case before you are permanently disbarred from Clan Mitragan.*

Political niceties out of the way, I cannot say that you do not deserve this. You should know when the path to opportunity is open, and Araan was your best option. Instead, you spurned him and cast him aside. Whatever arises from this, you deserve every moment of it, breeder.

-*Kuurz'Megim kan Mitragan*

Klaara tossed the Data Pad down in disgust, a growl rumbling through her chest. What in the name of Aruned was going on? Termination? Crimes against the Clan? The growl intensifying as she kicked the underside of one of the communication terminals hard enough to dent the metal.

Two pings sounded on her radar and she turned towards it. There was a ship in the system heading straight for her. At first she thought it might be that idiot Turukaishal, but the signature on this ship didn't match the one in his dossier. She leaned over the terminal, calling up a detailed callout of the intruder.

It was the *Myriad* – a Scain ship hailing from one of the moons of Alpidra. She waited, hoping it would pass the dusty red planet she was using as a base and head for Earth. No such luck. The *Myriad* stopped in the shadow of one of the red planet's lumpy moons, scanning the surface before hailing her. She sighed, shrugging and accepting the hail, picking up her armor and putting it on. This didn't feel right, and her instincts weren't wrong often.

The Scain ship touched down a little ways away, the thrusters kicking up the fine regolith on the surface. She stared out of one of the windows at it, her luminous eyes narrowing. Assault derrick. That wasn't a good sign. She grabbed a Taeski C-01 "Haze" pistol and slammed a clip into it, holstering it behind her back. Most Heil hated guns, seeing them as weapons of cowardice, but she was a bounty huntress: she couldn't always afford to be choosy.

She watched the door open to reveal two figures. The first was a Scain in crimson armor, his rifle already drawn. An armed Vanguard – this was getting worse by the second. Her hand instinctively curled around the handle of her Ion Saber, tempted to turn it on and rush out there. Her Heil instincts were warning her to fight – *screaming* at her to do something. Her tactical instincts reminded her that as long as she was in her ship and they were out on the surface, she had an advantage.

The second figure was a nightmarish little thing that barely reached the Scain's thighs. Klaara was familiar with the Visoth by reputation, but seeing one was another matter entirely. It's barrel-shaped body rose four feet into the air, divided by ribbing and membranes which separated the torso into five equal parts. The top of the torso was open like a flower, five petals hanging downwards to reveal the reddish-pink insides. From the center of this flower emerged five flexible stalks, each one with a red eye at the end. Five solid stalks poked straight up from inside the body as well, moving up and down as the creature spoke to its Scain companion.

At the base of the purplish-black body, Klaara watched in morbid fascination as five suckered limbs propelled the stout alien along the ground, unaffected by the fine layer of regolith on the planet's surface. Along the torso itself, she could see two coiled arms; each ending in what looked like a serrated leaf, while above each leg was another limb of some kind – a tentacle ending in a small suckering mouth. Lastly, and possibly the most unusual part of the creature, was a pair of wings which curved upwards from behind the first and third leg.

She sheathed her weapon, reaching for the gun instead. Visoth were nasty and a pain to take out, although not particularly hardy. Their technology was based around altering their bodies, rather than external technology. This one, for instance, was wandering around without a polyform suit at all. She wasn't planning on getting too close.

The two aliens halted outside her airlock. Klaara waited in the corridor with bated breath, unsure of what the two were doing here. The Scain hesitated for a moment, looking at the Visoth. The squat alien turned three of its eyes toward the Vanguard soldier before touching one of its limbs to the airlock door. Klaara's eyes widened and she took three steps back as the tendril passed through the solid metal, writhing around inside her ship. She aimed her gun at it, almost pulling the trigger on instinct. Instead, she backed up further, waiting. It would be better to wait until the Visoth was all the way inside before shooting it.

It didn't take long for the Visoth to come through the door. Its five eyes swiveled around, searching for her. She ducked around a corner, watching it carefully. The tendrils waved around as the Visoth scanned for her before turning back to the door, placing one leaflike hand over the keypad. The airlock immediately hissed open, admitting the Vanguard Scain. Klaara stepped around the corner, her pistol in her hand but not aimed at the two. "Who are you? What do you want?" she growled. "And who gives you the rights to break into my—"

Klaara threw herself back around the corner as the Scain lifted his rifle, aiming it down the hall at her. She waited for a few seconds before leaning back out, this time aiming her gun at him. "Last chance, pal. Scram or I shoot."

The Scain opened fire, one hand moving over his chest as he drew out his Psionics. Klaara fired three shots, two of them striking his rifle and knocking it off target, before ducking back around the corner and out of sight. Curse them a thousand times. If they damaged her ship, she might be trapped here. She had to kill them. She jumped to her left, kicking off the wall and grabbing a series of pipes overhead, swinging herself up against the ceiling and rolling atop the metal girders. She held her pistol close, waiting.

The Visoth stumped around the corner, each sucker leaving a wet mark on her floor as the leathery alien walked beneath her. A moment later, the Scain followed, backing around the corner with his rifle held at the ready. Klaara smirked – too easy. As soon as her target walked beneath her, she dropped from above and landed on his shoulders. The Scain's slight body crumpled under her weight, striking the ground with a curse. Klaara quickly placed the pistol to the back of his head and emptied three slugs into his skull. The Scain stopped struggling, his body going limp.

Klaara jumped off him, ducking around the corner as a pocket of white energy slammed into the wall at the end of the hallway, denting the metal. She leaned around the corner, aiming at the Visoth. The stout creature was stalking down the hallway, its wings wide open. As soon as it saw her, it leaned forward like a cannon, the top of its head glowing.

"*Aelau bakan keviru*," she growled, throwing herself flat as a sphere of the same white light burst against the wall. She fired three shots at the Visoth, watching them impact its torso with a sick slapping sound. The holes bled for a moment, black liquid splattering to the deck, before sealing back up. Klaara growled at it, rolling behind the wall and sprinting away, hearing the Visoth coming after her.

She knew it wouldn't fall for the same trick the Scain had – she needed something new. She opened the door to her living quarters, rushing in and looking around. Weapons, most of them stolen from deceased targets ("donated", as she liked to say). Most of them were heavy weapons capable of blowing up her ship from the inside. She couldn't use those.

Instead, she grabbed a fistful of Alintean grenades out of a bowl near her bed and jumped back out into the hallway. The Visoth was already rounding the corner at the end of the corridor. It caught sight of her and immediately leaned forward, its head glowing again. Klaara ducked back into the alcove near the door as the light moved past her again, slamming into the far wall. Some mounted weapons that she'd put up for decoration came crashing down.

Klaara sprinted for the Visoth, priming one of the grenades. "Oh please," she snarled, jumping forward. "Have a snack."

Her shoulder struck the Visoth's torso, knocking it over. The two tentacles reached out, grabbing hold of her and pulling her down with it. Her flesh sizzled and burned where the leafy hands gripped her shoulders. She lifted one of the grenades and slammed it down into the top of the Visoth's head, shoving it down through the flowery appendage before releasing it. "No please," she ground out, her skin aching from the burns, "I insist!"

She tore free of the Visoth's embrace, one of its arms snapping off and clinging to her wounded shoulder as she scrambled away. The alien sat up for a moment, its body flexing like a slug's, before it erupted in a shower of black tar and bits of flesh. Klaara covered her face as the gory mess splattered across her, resisting the urge to vomit. Finally, after recomposing herself, she stood up.

Those two had been a nuisance, but she was alive. They weren't. Now came the fun part – finding out why they were after her. She stalked over to the Scain's body, picking up his Data Pad and narrowing her eyes, reading over the contents. When she'd finished, she sighed. It looked like she was going to have to tear their ship apart for answers... and when she was done, she knew an alleged traitor who was going to love what she had just read.

Chapter 40

BEGIN MESSAGE: SECURE TRANSMISSION GRADE V: MINDBANK SECURE LINE
ERROR CODE 331932184. REROUTE. TERMINAL #9193, AMARA DISTRICT, BUILDING 23

LOCATION: SOL 3, NORTHERN HEMISPHERE

TIME: 3/24 Local Time

MESSAGE: *Bandrumano, I need you to listen carefully. The Mindbank has lied to us. The Vahran, or at least all that I have found, are not the beasts we have been led to believe. I intend to report this to him – confront him with the facts. This may not end well. If things sour, I need to know that I have friends in my corner. Can I count on you? And on Borda and Klakshan? Possibly even Kridoria?*

I do not want things to end badly. I do not want to see a planet burned because of false information. I would never be able to sleep again, and I know you are the same way. Please, Bandrumano, help me. If you need, I can give you proof of what I say.

-Turukaishal

Turukaishal groaned as he tossed the communicator in the corner of his desk. Victoria and Richard were both out at the moment, giving him time to send this message. As far as he understood, the two were out doing some last-minute Christmas shopping. After all, this big "Christmas Eve" was tomorrow night, and Victoria was insisting on everything being perfect. Meanwhile, he had some very difficult choices to make.

Mindbank Sovakadris was lying to him. He knew it. There was a motive behind the lies, of course, but he couldn't for the life of him figure out what it was. The only thing even registering in his memory banks was the mission Sovakadris had returned from right before his inauguration: back when Turukaishal had been a mere child in the Academy.

He remembered Sovakadris returning, battered and bruised, from a Black Mission almost seventy Earth years ago. It hadn't taken long for the rumors to start circulating – especially some of the ones which came from the Vanguard themselves. Rumors of a Black Mission gone wrong which had stranded Sovakadris on the Vahran homeworld. Turukaishal had dismissed these – rumors had been whizzing around like flies over a carcass. However, looking at the grudge Sovakadris seemed to have, he had begun reconsidering. Perhaps that rumor had a grain of truth to it. Did it? Had the Mindbank stood here, on this very world, so long ago? And if so, what had happened to instill such a grudge in his heart?

Turukaishal intended to find out, one way or the other. He'd managed, with the time on his hands, to "repurpose" the Mindbank's secure channel and was attempting to hail Bandrumano. If the worst came to pass, he would need someone who could get him as far from Chindrus as possible – maybe into the Gray Belt or the pirate-infested territories around the edge of the Galaxy. No one went there. Ever.

He heard the door on the floor above him open and close. One or both of the Vahran must have returned. He sighed, shaking his head and resting it in his hands. What was a Scain to do? This whole mission had turned into the biggest mess he'd ever been involved in. He was questioning his loyalties, warring with himself over whether or not to just abort the mission and disappear. And then there were those pesky feelings he was having around Victoria, and—"

Turukaishal froze as the energy crackled along the left side of his neck. Little bolts of lightning arced from the ion saber held at his throat, jumping to his skin with tiny little snaps. His eyes turned, looking up into the grinning face of Klaara'Doran kan Mitragain. "How did you get in?" he asked, his eyes narrowing before he turned away, lowering his face back into his hands. "Whatever. Can't you try to kill me some other day?"

This was obviously NOT the reaction Klaara had anticipated. "What, not a good enough moment for you?" she asked sarcastically, drawing the saber away and flicking it off. "Seriously though, you look like hot garbage. It wouldn't even have been a fair fight. Heck, I was able to break into your house and get all the way here before you noticed me – don't you have some of that freaky mind-power of yours to alert you?"

"At the moment, no," Turukaishal said, his head still in his hands. "And I *feel* like garbage – glad you agree. I swear, if anyone had told me ahead of time how complicated this mission would get, I would never have taken it..." It dawned on him that he was actually having a more-or-less civil conversation with the Heil that had been sent to kill him, but at the moment he didn't really care. Heck, if she grabbed his pneumatic hammer and pulped his head with it, at least he'd be out of his misery.

Klaara yawned, leaning on one of the laboratory walls, twirling her ion saber in her four-fingered hand. "Yeah, I hear you. Some big-shot tells me that you're on Earth and he wants you gone. Now. Next thing I know I'm neck-deep in a ton of Vahran. Didn't mention them in the mission report, he didn't, but at least I knew beforehand... this isn't my first time here."

Turukaishal laughed humorlessly. "I wasn't a traitor back then," he said, "but I may be one here in the next few days."

"Yeah?" she asked. "Well, it doesn't look like it matters anymore. Honestly, I came here for other reasons today: take a look." A Data Pad, scuffed and worn from years of being tossed around, landed on the counter near his elbow. There were two files blinking on the interface. Turukaishal tapped the first and felt his stomach bottom out.

"Your father," Klaara said as the image resolved, showing an elderly Scain. "Apparently he shot and killed one of the Hierarchs of Clan Mitragan. The treaty between the Scain and the Heil has dissolved as a result... unfortunately, he was cut down soon after. I am sorry about that."

Turukaishal read through the article several times, just to be sure he wasn't hallucinating. His father, Ferthoroyia, had indeed walked into the Hierarch's Tower and emptied an entire clip from an Erythian LP-12 into a Mitragan Hierarch's skull. Shortly after, the High Guard mowed him down. Turukaishal slumped down in his chair, his mind and body numb. This wasn't happening. Not his father... the only parent he had left...

He shook his head and opened the second file, shelving his emotions for the time being. A picture of Klaara stared back at him – a facial reconstruction plastered all over a bounty memorandum. Klaara'Doran kan Mitragan – Dead or Alive – Forty Million Credits. He looked up at her in surprise, watching as her face twitched in a combination of amusement and annoyance. "Yeah," she said drily. "Check out what for. That's the doozy."

Turukaishal gave the hardlight image a swipe of his finger, scrolling the article to the bottom. *"Accomplice to the murder of Veeil'Mikran kan Mitragan?"* he read. "What?"

"Yep. Since you won't get it any other way, check this out. This'll blow your mind..." she leaned over his shoulder and tapped a section of the screen – the name of the person who had posted the bounty. "That's the idiot who hired me and who contrived this ridiculous story. Talk about a royal double-cross."

Turukaishal's eyes narrowed into red slits as he red the name, half of him not wanting to believe what he was seeing. "Demnechi!" he spat, the name coming off his tongues like a curse, glaring at the Data Pad so hard his Psionics actually started to boil the edges. "That idiotic, stupid self-absorbed serpent... he was the one who hired you?" He really shouldn't have been as surprised as he was, he reckoned, seeing as it was no big secret that Demnechi wanted him dead. However, wanting someone dead was a lot different than acting to get them killed. He was probably trying to bump off Turukaishal to claim the Mindbank's throne for himself, if Turukaishal wanted to guess. Curse him and his infernal machinations of—

Turukaishal looked over as the elevator reached the bottom level. Richard, standing in front of his sister, immediately unsheathed his sword cane and leapt straight for Klaara. Turukaishal snatched the man out of the air with a gentle Psionic tendril, lowering him to the ground. "Now is not the time, Richard," he said in response to the confused look. "We have... much larger problems."

As soon as Richard sheathed the sword, (and Victoria had crept from the elevator to stand behind him) Turukaishal explained the situation. He started with his intent to tell Mindbank Sovakadris to flush the mission, followed by the events surrounding his father's death and the framing of Klaara for the Hierarch's death. He finished by filling them in on Demnechi as well, growling out the Councilor's name each time he used it. By the time he was finished, both Vahran were shocked into absolute silence.

"I'm calling the Mindbank," Turukaishal said, standing up and kicking a piece of machinery out of his way, booting up one of the largest screens. "Right now. I don't care what he says anymore, this is getting out of hand. Either he keeps that idiot Councilor in check or so help me I am going to go to Chindrus and impeach him with bullets."

Turukaishal waited while the system connected, watching the display as his signal was bounced through two dozen Dark Space Communication Arrays before connecting with Chindrus. Klaara chose to remain out of sight, standing off to one side around the corner of the display. Richard and Victoria slunk over to stand next to her, the swordsman remaining between the Heil and his sister. A moment later, the screen blinked on. Instead of the Mindbank, however, Turukaishal was greeted with the grinning, yellow-eyed face of Bandrumano. "Turukaishal!" he said, speaking in perfect Scain. "You called! Geez, I thought you were dead or something."

"Almost," Turukaishal answered in his mother tongue. "I have a slight problem."

"So I'm hearing," the Scain said as he waved his Data Pad. "Looks like a storm's coming, huh? Thank the Hiin you turned the imager on. I've been trying to contact you forever!"

"You and everyone else on Chindrus," Turukaishal told him drily. "I was on a Black Mission. So, are you behind me or not? If so, my next call is to Sovakadris. This has got to stop."

"I'm behind you all the way," Bandrumano said, his grin vanishing as he nodded seriously. "I can probably rope Klakshan into this too. Bordra will obviously help – he's always up for something. So, what's the plan?"

"For the moment? Nothing." Turukaishal said, typing on the keypad. "I am sorry to cut this short, but I must contact the Mindbank."

"Understood," Bandrumano said. "I'll round up Bordra and Klakshan, maybe a few buddies of mine as well. I know there are a few dozen Vanguard who are mildly seditious. I can probably turn them to our cause just in case. You're sure about this though? I'm behind you, but I need to know for certain."

"Bandrumano," Turukaishal said, looking up. "When am I ever *uncertain*?"

The Scain's eyes turned yellow again. "Then I'll follow you into anything. Good luck with the Mindbank." The screen went out a second later, showing only a flat black backing. Klara chortled.

"Good timing of your friend," she said. "If things heat up around here, you're going to need all the help you can get."

"How very observant of you, Sherlock," Richard muttered sarcastically. "Please do tell me more."

Before Klaara could respond, the screen lit up again and an old, decrepit figure swam into focus. He looked very much like Turukaishal to the point where, at first glance, the two both looked like Scain. Further examination revealed a difference in the shape of the head, exposing the Mindbank's Scion heritage. A multifaceted crown swam around his head, each segment disconnected from the others and hovering in place by his will alone. Voluminous blue robes, tinged with golden accents, covered his body and made him look even more frail than he already did.

It was his face, though, that seemed so out of place on such an aged body. It wasn't lined with wrinkles due to the passage of time. Instead, it looked hard and leathery – weathered. Worn down by life and strain. His eyes were narrowed, the brow almost permanently furrowed to the point of a perpetual frown. It was the face of a hardened, weary individual.

"Turukaishal," the Mindbank said, his voice echoing spectrally through the imager. It wasn't just a sound – it was a force and a presence as well. All of the occupants of Turukaishal's lab felt his voice seeping into their mind like honey, touching the neurons there. Richard's eyes narrowed while Victoria actively clutched her head in surprise. Turukaishal, long having adjusted to the Scion's mode of speech – called reflection – didn't move. Neither did Klaara, although her eyes watched the screen as the Mindbank continued. *"I hope you have good news for me."*

Turukaishal's eyes almost turned red for a moment, but he controlled them. Unfortunately, his grip on the Data Pad was the outlet. It shattered in his grip, sparking several times before dying for good. He was cut off from his own kind, barring the imager. "Oh I have news for you, your Eminence, but you are not going to like it."

Chapter 41

ERROR: DATA PAD #925410053 NOT FOUND

For the next several minutes, Richard and Victoria watched as Turukaishal stood before the monitor, telling the Mindbank of everything he had witnessed since his arrival on Earth. He spoke of his research and of all the things he had uncovered, although he left the technological prowess (or lack thereof) of the human race up to speculation. He told his leader of the time he'd spent with Richard and Victoria, and of his fight with Klaara. The whole time, the Mindbank's eyes changed slowly to red, his lipless mouth turning downwards in a thinly-veiled scowl. Finally, Turukaishal concluded his speech. "Therefore, based on my findings, the Vahran on this planet are NOT worthy of destruction. I urge you to abort this mission and—"

"Enough of this farce," the Mindbank said, his voice hissing from his slit of a mouth with glacial coldness. Once more, his voice seemed to come from all around them as well as from within their minds. His eyes radiated a coldness that chilled the occupants of Turukaishal's laboratory to the bone despite their flaming red color. *"I sent you there to gather evidence of their evil, not exonerate them with personal anecdotes and circumstantial evidence. You have been fooled, Turukaishal... and you disappoint me."*

"No, Sovakadris," Turukaishal said, using the Mindbank's name for the first time. "You disappoint me." His voice carried equal parts anger, sorrow and disbelief, his eyes shifting between blue and red. Sovakadris glared harshly at him through the imager, and small blue flames crackled near the corners of his eyes. Turukaishal pushed onwards. "Something happened to you – the Sovakadris that trained me wouldn't damn an entire race to extinction. You're holding something back – something that turned you into this. That mission before your inauguration... it was here, wasn't it? I have enough on my platter dealing with Demnechi and his little games – you owe me this much: what happened?"

"Nothing that concerns you, but you are correct." The Mindbank answered, his eyes deepening to one of the most sorrowful blues imaginable before snapping back to red; the transition taking a half a second. *"Something did happen – something so heinous that I will never forget it no matter how many cycles I live. And it is for that reason that I will punish these Vahran – these insects who thrive on the suffering of others – to spare the rest of the Galaxy the pain I have endured. I will pass judgment on them for their sins."*

"Their sins are *nothing*!" Turukaishal hissed, his eyes flashing. "You're going to damn an entire race over a personal grudge. I won't stand for it!"

Sovakadris was silent, regarding Turukaishal with a long, calculating look. Behind him, the Vanguard shifted uneasily in the throne room. Finally, the Mindbank spoke again. *"And what would you do, Turukaishal?"* he asked. *"Would you betray the Scain? Hand us to our enemies to do with as they see fit?"*

"No," Turukaishal said, grinding his teeth together. He knew the next few words out of his mouth were going to change the course of history in one way or another. He had to choose them carefully. "I would never stoop so low as to betray the Scain. If it comes down to it... I'll crush you myself."

His words had the desired effect. Sovakadris sat bolt upright in the throne, his eyes flashing red and orange. *"You dare threaten me?!"* he asked, his eyes glaring daggers at Turukaishal. *"The Mindbank of the Scain?! I'll have you hunted down and executed for treason!"*

"Yeah, Demnechi already tried that," Turukaishal said, waving a hand dismissively. "The Heil I mentioned — it was he who sent her after me."

"I told Demnechi to keep an eye on you and keep you in line if needed," Sovakadris said angrily. *"It seems I was correct to do so. You strayed and were seduced by the lies of the Vahran. If he deemed a Heil was an appropriate countermeasure, so be it."*

"Oh, so now I have *two* of you I'm going to need to mulch, eh?" Klaara asked, striding into the scope of the cameras, one hand on her hip as she cocked her head at the Mindbank. Sovakadris looked at her as if he was going to have a stroke, his eyes positively glowing red. "Y'know," she continued, wagging a finger at him as a cheeky, condescending grin spread over her features. "It's not good business to hire someone and then frame 'em to get out of paying the bill. Just for the next time you try to hire a bounty hunter."

Sovakadris seethed quietly, watching them both. He closed his eyes, breathing deeply through his nostrils before opening them again. This time, they were a deep black again. He turned his gaze to Turukaishal, ignoring the Heil. *"Turukaishal,"* he said, his gaze serious. His voice had lost a lot of its edge as well. *"We do not have to be enemies. You know which side your loyalties have been with for hundreds of years, and you know that, once all is said and done, your loyalties still lie with the Scain. I ask you one more time: join me and aid me in the destruction of the Vahran. If you do not, I will have no choice but to send the Forward Fleet to annihilate you, as well as that ball of dirt you are starting to empathize with. Make your choice, Turukaishal. If you still wish to redeem yourself, draw your weapon and kill the Heil."*

Turukaishal was silent for several moments before shaking his head, drawing his pistol but keeping it leveled at the floor. "You were once my mentor – almost like my father," he said sadly. "You raised me to be who and what I am, but from this moment forward, I walk my own path." He turned his gaze up to the imager. "Just know that, if I had a choice, this would not be that path." He armed the gun, the sound resonating through the room. Klaara jumped back, reaching for her ion sabers in preparation for an assault, but it never came. Instead, Turukaishal aimed the pistol at the imager, his eyes a deep, dark blue. There was a split-second in which Sovakadris' face, his eyes orange with shock, was visible before the high-energy pellet slammed into it.

There was a loud bang as the screen short-circuited, sparks cascading out of the hole as the glass shattered. It fell to the ground, tinkling like thousands of silver bells, before the screen itself detached from its mount and landed on the ground with a deafening slam, striking the workbench on the way down and splitting in half. Turukaishal remained in place, arm still outstretched, aiming the smoking gun at where the screen had been, before slowly lowering his weapon.

"I'd say you just made an enemy..." Klaara said, turning towards the door. "I'm going to go get my ship. I suggest we both get the hell out of here before he sends his lapdogs looking for us."

"I'm leaving, yes," Turukaishal said, turning his head towards her, his eyes still sad and blue, "but not for long. I'm going to the Voyalda Cluster to pick up a few friends. May I borrow your Data Pad for a moment?"

"Sure," she said, waving disinterestedly in the direction of the pad. "Isn't even mine – took it from a Scain that came trying to kill me. What're you planning?"

"Sovakadris knows where Earth is," Turukaishal said, taking the pad from the table and starting to peck at it with his long fingers. "He also knows how weak it is. I"m going to contact a friends – like Bandrumano – and see if they can't help me. I'll spread a few rumors as well, just to keep things nice and stressful on his end, just to buy us some time."

Klaara regarded him coolly for a moment before he handed the pad back to her. "You're really serious about this, aren't you? You're seriously willing to die for... for this?!" she gestured around herself, indicating the world above them. "You're willing to die for the Vahran?"

Before Turukaishal could respond, Victoria spoke. "You would do the same," she said to Klaara. "I know you would. He's not throwing his life away because it's something fun or new, he's standing in front of Earth because he feels it's the right thing to do. And you feel it too."

Klaara tilted her head, her hand going back to her hip as she examined the human before pointing one of her fingers at Richard. "You!" she barked, eliciting a grunt from him as he leaned against one of the workbenches, twirling his cane between his fingers. "You feel the same way?"

Richard looked at her out of the corner of his eye, the cane halting it's motion, before he nodded. "You have implied that you fight because you have to, but not because you want to," he said. "This speaks of someone who is not inherently evil, but who has had to choose a harder road due to circumstance. I believe, like my sister says, that you are honorable enough to choose a harder right over an easier wrong." His lips curled upwards into a sardonic smirk. "Of course, I could be wrong..."

"Poignantly phrased," Klaara muttered, rubbing one finger along her cheek ridges, her head still canted to one side as she watched him. "I've never met a Vahran quite like you, and believe me: this isn't my first time on Earth."

"You aren't likely to," Richard said. "Believe me."

Klaara shook her head. "I repeat myself: It is a pity you were not born a Heil. Someone like you..." she whistled softly before looking back at Turukaishal. "I'm not promising anything, Stretch," she said, "but if my ship's in the same space as yours, I might be able to help you. Maybe. If you ask nicely." She winked at Turukaishal before turning back to the elevators. "*Bonta, ve kerek Turukaishal.*"

With that, the elevator vanished, taking the Heil with it. Turukaishal's eyes watched as it rose out of sight. The moment Klaara was gone, he slumped back against the workbench, suddenly looking very boneless. "Hiin... I'm dead..."

"Turu!" Victoria cried, embracing him around the waist, hugging him tightly. "You were wonderful! You really told that... that..." she nuzzled him, trying vainly to find a word strong enough for Sovakadris.

"Bully?" Richard offered, sighing. "He's holding a grudge and he's going to use everything at his disposal to absolve it, whether right or wrong. He has to be stopped." He turned and nodded at Turukaishal. "You are a brave man... alien. Standing up to an individual in power takes a lot of guts, but it's the only way anything's going to change. It was a long time before I was able to do that, and for the longest time I didn't think I could."

"Up until that moment, neither did I..." Turukaishal muttered.

"Victoria has that effect on people," Richard said, gesturing to his now-blushing sister. "It's a power I wish more people had: she can bring out the good in others. It was because of her that I eventually stepped up to the plate. And I'm willing to bet that she had a large hand in changing your mind and helping you find the strength to stand up to Sovakadris."

"You aren't wrong," Turukaishal said, his eyes pink. "But enough of that: we have to think. Right now, there are three of us. If Bordra helps, he'll bring all of Task Force Kirel – that's five more. Klakshan... Bandrumano... possibly Kridoria..." he trailed off, muttering to himself, his fingers flexing as he counted before curling into a fist and slamming against the side of the workbench. "I can't count on more than twenty to thirty bodies."

"And their forces?" Richard asked, rolling the cane between his palms. "What are we looking at?"

"Sovakadris threatened with the Forward Fleet – that's one of the more powerful fleets in the Scain Armada. One gunship – the *Trident* – and twenty frigates, not counting assembled fighters. That gunship is the main problem, though, as it is worth any fifty frigates with as much firepower as it possesses. It was designed to crack moons, large stations, macrofortress-class carriers and the like."

Both Richard and Victoria were white. "Options?" Richard asked, his brow furrowing.

"I'm going to leave," Turukaishal said, standing up. "I'll regroup with Bordra and Bandrumano, or at least one of them. We know of a few meeting places where "polite society" doesn't go, so we should be relatively safe. I'm going to try heading to our main one. I'll be back though," he said, looking down at Victoria and the tears glistening at the corners of her eyes. "I promise."

"You'd better," she said, crushing him into another hug. "You promised to show me Saturn."

Turukaishal chuckled softly, stroking her hair gently. Saturn was far from the reason behind her sadness, and he felt a crushing weight in his chest at the prospect of leaving them as well. "Take care of yourselves," he said. "I will return as swiftly as possible. Until then, I am allocating you each a pair of weapons. Keep them hidden. Keep them safe. I'll leave this house standing for you as well in case you need it. Here..." he threw Richard his 'debit card' as well. "Stay safe. I need to have a reason to come back."

Richard nodded, slipping the card into his pocket as Turukaishal placed a pair of disposable pistols up on the counter – a smaller variant not designed to connect to a power pack. "Come on Vicky – grab those guns and let's get out of here so he can leave."

"But I don't want him to leave..." she said, releasing him anyway. Turukaishal knelt down, his head almost level with hers as he placed one hand on her shoulder.

"Victoria," he said, keeping his voice calm and even. "I leave you now so that you will have a world to stand on and a future to live for. If I remain, what will happen to this place? This world? I promise you, I will protect this place. Protect you... and Richard... if it takes all I have. But I need you to trust me and believe that I will return to you."

Victoria sniffled. "Alright," she said. "But at least take these with you..." she placed a pair of small presents in his hands, each one small enough for his fingers to curl completely around. Turukaishal nodded, smiling sadly. Christmas. He suddenly didn't want to miss it. He sighed, rising back up to his full height.

"Now go," he said, his voice carrying a commanding tone. "I have much to accomplish. Just remember – give me a reason to come back."

"We will," Richard said, his hand around his sister's shoulders as he guided her to the elevator. "Take care of yourself Turukaishal."

The Scain nodded. "I will...and it's Turu now."

Chapter 42

ERROR: DATA PAD #925410053 NOT FOUND. ERROR PERSISTING. PLEASE REROUTE NUMBER TO BACKUP TERMINAL.

Likharn loomed outside the window as Turu sat at the helm of his ship, his face a mask of grim stoicism. He couldn't believe the mess he had gotten himself into... it was all so surreal. He had just managed to turn his entire species against him and had very little time to act. He'd managed to use one of the other terminals aboard his ship to radio Bandrumano, telling him to meet him on the volcanic planet of Likharn. A small planet at the edge of the Korvus system, Likharn was the perfect place for a defectors' meeting. The system was a trinary star system, the center bogged down by a trio of brown dwarves in a series of elliptical orbits. This all but ensured that there could be no habitable planets – the stillborn stars swung out far enough to crush anything other than one of the gas giants which continued to orbit them, far out of harm's range. Remnants of protoplanets littered the Korvus system as asteroids and meteor swarms, rendering it a hostile and dangerous place.

Likharn, however, was a tiny volcanic world at the edge of the system, orbiting inside the furthest asteroid belt. Due to the tremendous dangers present in the Korvus system, most ships gave the whole barycenter a wide berth. It was fairly simple, however, to slip inside the relatively spacious asteroid field and enter Likharn's orbit undetected – something Turu knew from experience.

The Scain looked down at the object in his hand, turning it over and over in his long fingers and sighing in longing. He'd opened one of the two presents Victoria had got him. A pocket-watch – out of style for a century at least but still a beautiful gift. He'd been so enamored with it he'd let the other gift sit on his dashboard as he twirled the delicate silver chain with his Psionics, watching it dance ethereally before him. On the inside face, someone (and he suspected it was probably her) had installed a single picture – one subtly taken during their time in the library at the precise moment she had hugged him. He felt his eyes pinken slightly at the memory.

According to the watch, it had been three hours since he'd left Earth. A mere 180 minutes. 10,800 seconds. He sighed again, letting his head fall back against his headrest with a dull *thunk*. How was it possible to miss someone this much? He had anticipated that leaving Richard and Victoria behind would be difficult – possibly more so than leaving his friends behind on Chindrus. He knew, or at least before now he'd known – that he'd be able to return to Chindrus and see them again someday. But with Victoria and her brother, especially now, that didn't seem so certain. He'd already gone to the medical bay to see if anything was wrong with him, but other than a slight increase in his brain's delta waves, everything was nominal. He was a perfectly healthy specimen of a Scain.

So why, then, had he just told the Mindbank to shove it?

Before he could ruminate further, his command console beeped at him. His Psionics reached out, drawing the screen in front of him. The flexible base bending to accommodate the motion. One ship had entered the system, heading directly for Likharn at top speed. Scans revealed it to be the *White Streak* – a ship registered to Bandrumano. Turu pushed the console away, revealing the hell-blasted landscape of the planet outside as he opened the shutters to watch his friend's approach.

From his position on a rocky mesa, he could see the surrounding planetscape of the volcanic world. The temperature here rarely dropped below two-hundred degrees on any given day, and the nights were kept warm by the constant eruptions from within the planet. The vulcanism filled the atmosphere with soot and ash, as well as various poisonous vapors. This, compounded with the natural composition of gases including sulfur, carbon monoxide and arsenic, made the world a deadly and hellish place. Even the protites in his lungs wouldn't help him here.

Turu stood up and walked down the bridge towards the main airlock, snatching up a rebreathing mask as he went. This was a Class-II Planet, meaning the high-level hazards here rendered it nigh-impossible to colonize. Technically it was possible, but no one wanted to invest the time or resources. Therefore, Likharn continued to orbit, alone and ignored, at the edge of the Korvus system, its surface boiling and exploding in a hellish dance of self-destruction. The Scain strapped on the mask and the tanks, tightening the straps and opening the airflow. His suit was pressurized and cooled, and he had at least ten hours of breathable atmosphere in the tanks. He stepped into the airlock, hearing it hiss closed. A moment later, he was greeted with a wash of hot, sulfuric air as the outer door opened.

His suit immediately offset the heat, cooling him back down to a comfortable temperature as he stepped out onto the surface of the planet. A buildup of dark, rust-colored clouds in the distance warned of an approaching storm, and Turu had no desire to be caught in it. Likharn's storms brought no water, instead raining down clumps of rock born from airborne ash. He looked skyward, the orange-brown clouds swirling above him as he saw Bandrumano's ship, a Terminator-Class Fighter, descend through the clouds. The sleek craft made a cursory loop overhead before lowering itself onto the mesa several hundred feet away, kicking up a storm of dust and ash in its wake.

The cockpit's roof parted down the middle, the halves sliding to opposite sides as Bandrumano jumped out, landing on the hood before bounding down to the ground and racing over to Turu. He was taller than his friend, but not by much. His face was also rounder, although his cheekbones were far more angular and chiseled. The two sized one another up before Bandrumano touched his forehead to Turu's in greeting. "Good to see you again," he said. "How're you holding up? You look like someone landed a frigate on you."

"I am intact," Turu said as they parted. "I have certainly been better."

Bandrumano clapped Turu on the shoulder. "It shows, you know. Come on – we'd better get inside. My tanks aren't all the way full. I had just returned from Ganovai when you called."

Turu blanched. Ganovai, the homeworld of the Ene'tami, was a Class-V (Garden World) with an atmosphere so poisonous that most races avoided it like the plague. A curious combination of beautiful and deadly, the world was rife with water and flowering plants that could rival those on Chindrus. The atmosphere, however, was a potent, low-pressure concoction of carbon dioxide, sulfuric acid, carbon monoxide and arsenic trihydride. The pressure was so low on Ganovai that parts of its oceans floated in the air as clouds of mist – something which was found on only two other worlds in the Galaxy. "Ganovai?!" Turu said, making a face beneath his mask. "What in Hiin's name were you doing there?"

Bandrumano waved a hand. "*Assistant to the Director of Ene'tami-Scain Relations,*" he said, rolling his eyes and doing an insulting impersonation of Minister Castator. Turu laughed as Bandrumano's eyes flickered yellow. "And to think, as important as that sounds, all I was basically doing was running around to make sure nobody got offended... and doing paperwork. By the way, you ever going to name this thing?" he tapped the hull of Turu's ship.

Turu opened the airlock, gesturing for his friend to enter. "Perhaps," he said. "I just never thought of a good enough name." It was the truth, too. All Scain named their ships, but he'd just left his as *Callsign-242*, which was the standard-issue name it had come with. Eventually, he knew he'd find a name for it and get it registered, but for now it was just easier to call it "the 242".

Bandrumano removed his mask once they were inside, taking deep breaths. "Aaaah, that's the stuff. Glad not to be sucking poison anymore. Ganovai and then Likharn? Yeech... no thanks. Not a second time."

Turu looked at him expectantly and Bandrumano shrugged. "Lemme guess. You want the results? Fine. I got Klakshan and a few of his buddies along for the ride. Bordra is bringing Task Force Kirel, of course, and I got back in touch with a bunch of slackers from the 5th Division who want in on this as well. A group of ten Vanguard are also aboard for this, and Kridoria wants to come along... but sadly, she can't leave the Amara District without arousing suspicion. She did offer, however, to help from the inside if she can."

Turu breathed a sigh of relief. "Head count?"

"Task Force Kirel: six. Fifth Division, twenty-four. Klakshan's old crew: fifteen. Vanguard: ten. Plus Kridoria, myself and you, that brings the total to fifty-eight. I'll put a give-or-take of plus-minus five."

"Sixty," Turu said. "I have two who are willing to fight as well."

"Let me guess," Bandrumano said conspiratorially. "Vahran? Heh, this'll be fun. I can't wait to see how well they actually fight."

Turu nodded. 'Fun' wasn't exactly the word he'd been thinking of. "Tell everyone to begin gathering in the Sol System," he said. "Titan, a moon in orbit around a Class-A world called Saturn, will be our rendezvous. Prep the troops for a harsher atmosphere as well. It's ninety-eight percent nitrogen and an unhealthy mixture of methane and hydrocarbons."

"Unhealthy is right," Bandrumano said, making a note on his Data Pad. "Anything else?"

"I want them prepped and ready to be setting up a mobile command center, installations and ground emplacements. I want the base locked up and fortified as a precaution. Once everything is in position, have Kridoria start tracking the Forward Fleet's motions and relaying them to you. You send them to me. Once that's done, I'll bring the two Vahran out there and we'll discuss tactics. Until then, focus on getting everything set up and keeping it safe and off the radar."

Bandrumano saluted him sharply. "Understood. Anything I should tell Kridoria? She was... ah... worried about you and wants to help as much as she can."

Turu thought for a moment. "I'm going to edit some of my earlier reports – make life a living hell for the Mindbank and his lackeys. I'll need her to get in and swap the files in the data system. She has access, so it shouldn't be too difficult, but tell her to use the standard Vanguard password – D-124-9ZG – to get in the system. It'll keep her from getting caught, I hope."

"Gotcha boss," Bandrumano said as he made the notations in his pad. He paused after a moment and looked up. "You okay? You're quieter than usual, and that's saying a lot."

Turu harrumphed, folding his arms. "It's nothing."

Bandrumano analyzed his friend, crossing his arms. "You look like a spurned lover, you know that? Like you've got someone special on your mind. I know it's not Kridoria – you've never felt the same for her as she has for you – so who is it?"

Turu's eyes turned pink. "It's nothing, Bandrumano!"

"Yeah, and you're defensive too? And embarrassed? Come on, it's me! You can trust me!"

Turu turned away. "To spread it all around the barracks? Yes, I know. Besides, I'm not even sure, to be honest. I have some more research to do..." Could his eyes get any pinker? For Hiin's sake...

Bandrumano chuckled, patting his friend's shoulder. "Interspecies, I take it?" he teased, putting the communicator away. "Perhaps... a Vahran?"

Yes. His eyes *could* definitely get pinker. He could feel it. Bandrumano laughed heartily. "Well I'll be spaced," he said with a huge, wide grin and yellow eyes. "You, the Mindbank's personal favorite, resorting to treason and romancing a Vahran. For shame!" Despite his words, his eyes and expression told Turu exactly how little his friend cared. "Lighten up – it'll do you good."

"From all the chest pains, I highly doubt that..." Turu trailed off, mumbling something incoherent. Bandrumano didn't hear it, and didn't particularly care. He and Turu were old friends, going back further than most could fathom, and he knew that Turu trailed off into grumbling fits when embarrassed or angry. And most of it wasn't fit to be repeated, if he knew Turu.

"Okay, I'm moving out. Want me to stay behind and monitor the Mindbank's troops for a while as well? Might be handy to know where all he's setting up shop." He dropped his helmet back down over his head, the mouthpiece nestling into place.

"Yes," Turu said. "While you're at it, see if you can find a way to destabilize the Scain-Visoth alliance. If those things attack Earth, we are going to have big problems. Or put one of your defectors on it. And relay and and all information to the nodes on the ship – I'll read them there. I kind of smashed my communicator and shot my imager while talking to Sovakadris."

"Tsk tsk... temper temper," Bandrumano chided with a little wave as he stepped into the airlock. "See you later, Turukaishal. Stay safe." The door hissed shut behind him, separating them once more. Turu heard the outer airlock hiss open and turned to head back to the bridge. No sooner had he seated himself than the *White Streak* lifted off, taking off at high speed overhead. It banked sharply to the right, angling sharply upwards and vanishing into the hellish atmosphere.

Turu fired up the ship's engines. It was time to head back to Earth. He'd have to make a refuel run, of course... after so long on Earth, most of the fuel in his tanks had decayed to thirty percent. He called up a list of refueling stations and selected the coordinates for the Camethos Refueling Station in the Broken Verge. It'd keep him off the Mindbank's radars for now. It was a long detour, but would preserve his stealth. He let out a growl as he took off, turning around and flying away from Likharn in the opposite direction.

The Broken Verge lay at the edge of the Galaxy, but he didn't want to crank his ship up to the maximum speed in Dark Space. It might attract more attention than he wanted, so he braced himself for a longer journey: maybe by a day or two.

And all he could think about was that he was going to be missing Christmas with his human friends.

Chapter 43

BEGIN MESSAGE:

LOCATION: Sovereign, Mitragan Province

TIME: 22/29 Local Time

MESSAGE: *Regardless of your attempts to disgrace the name of the Doran Family and of Clan Mitragan, it will not work. We both knew from the beginning that it would be me who succeeded father to the throne, and not you, and your jealousy has finally led you astray. Exactly as I predicted it would. While I cannot say I am happy to know that my sister is going to die, I can say I can sleep considerably easier knowing you aren't out there trying to destroy everything our father stood for. Good bye, sister. May you find honor in the afterlife.*

-Nyylu'Doran kan Mitragan

The harder right over the easier wrong.

Those words echoed in Klaara's mind over and over again. She could see that blasted Vahran, Richard, staring evenly at her as he spoke, as if he was confident beyond a shadow of a doubt in what he was saying. It unnerved her to no extent. Who was this Vahran to presume to speak of her? He hadn't even known her other than a battle in the woods.

She shook her head as she sat in her ship, her boots off and her bare feet propped up on the communications array. Outside, she could see Mars as her ship orbited it. She stretched, her fingers curling into fists as her spine popped. They wouldn't be able to exile her permanently from Clan Mitragan, she was almost convinced of it. Her father wouldn't allow it. Let Nyylu keep her smug letters – Klaara would prove her wrong somehow.

There was a sharp ding on her console and she immediately sat upright. A Scain scout craft had just entered the system, just inside the asteroid belt. She shoved her feet into her boots, the magnetic clasps sealing automatically, but the ship blew past her and headed straight for Earth.

So they weren't here for her. That was good. She sat back down and reached down to remove her boots again before pausing.

Turukaishal wasn't here. If that ship went to Earth, the first place it would start looking was with his Vahran contacts... and she doubted they would be as gentle as he was. All of the Scain probably knew of Richard and Victoria at this point – Demnechi had been feeding her the mission reports Turukaishal had been sending, and she knew they were mentioned in there several times.

So what did she care? Klaara leaned back, kicking her feet up on the dashboard. She had bigger things to worry about than a pair of Vahran... like how she was going to make a living. She'd have to register as a bounty hunter with another empire, but having been given the boot from Clan Mitragan, even temporarily, was going to be a dark mark on her record. And it wouldn't be the first.

She looked out the window at tiny speck in the distance – looking like nothing more than another star – that was Earth. Something unfamiliar gnawed at her stomach and she sighed, palming her face before swinging her boots down off the console and sliding her chair over to the navigation panel.

***

It didn't take her long to track down Richard and Victoria. Most people knew where the man in the greatcoat lived, and were able to point her in that direction. They lived in a smaller housing development between Lakewood and Steilacoom with their backs to a Frisbee golf course. The house, painted a deep green with reddish-brown trim, looked fairly well kept considering its tenants, and not at all unpleasant. Of course, Klaara would always prefer the squarish, magnetite and sandstone buildings of Sovereign, but she couldn't deny the subtle charm of this alien building.

She pounded her fist on the door. "Richard!" she yelled. "Open up!"

A minute or so later, the door cracked open a bit, prevented from opening the whole way by a safety chain. Richard Sinclair stood inside, his sword drawn and his eyes narrowed. "Klaara," he said, analyzing her. "What do you want?"

"You're in trouble," she said. "Let me in and I'll tell you."

He hesitated for a moment, still not trusting her completely. She sighed with exasperation. "Look, I could care less if you want to be pigheaded and get yourself killed, but I don't think your sister wants to die just yet. Does she?"

That did it. The door closed for a moment before reopening, revealing Richard completely. His greatcoat was off, as was his hat, but his sunglasses were present on the top of his head. He sheathed the sword in the cane again. "Come on then. And this better be good."

The interior of their home was just as nice as the outside, albeit a bit dated. Antiques and old books were prominent features, and most of the furniture was older. The color schemes varied slightly, but seemed to focus on royal reds and earth tones.

Richard led her down the hallway and into a sitting room. He leaned against the wall, his eyes narrowed. "Now, what's all this about danger?"

"Scain scouting craft," she said. "It just blew past me in Mars' orbit and headed here. My guess is that they'll be looking for Turukaishal. When they can't find him, they're going to be coming for you — he has your names in his reports. Trust me on that one. I don't know how many heads are in that ship, but you don't want to cross the Scain."

"I know," Richard said, moving into an oak-paneled kitchen and pouring himself a cup of water. "So what can we do?"

Klaara thought about it for a moment. "I'll stay here for a bit, just to see. I don't think they'll try anything during the day, and my ship is currently hidden at the top of the ridge across that main road up there." She waved in the general direction of her craft. "If everything goes sideways, we'll head there and I'll take you with me. We'll go hide somewhere safe until your sister's Prince Charming comes back to save you."

Richard shot her a dark look but said nothing, knocking back the water in a single gulp. "Sounds good. And if they show? I don't think they'll just let us walk up to your ship and escape."

"If they do show, I'll just have to think of something. I'm pretty good at that. Either way, I don't think we should stay here too long. Too easy to track."

Richard looked out the kitchen window. "Agreed. I think your ship is probably the best choice. If we wait a few more hours, it'll be dark. We can sneak out of here and cut through the woods."

"Those woods lead up to the main road?" Klaara asked.

"You have to cut across the Frisbee golf course and then through the parking lot of the mental hospital," Richard said, gesturing with his hand. "From there, we can use the underpass to sneak beneath Steilacoom Boulevard — the main road you keep mentioning. Once on the other side, we have to cross a few dozen yards of open territory and then we're on that hill you hid your ship on."

Klaara nodded, rising from the sofa she'd plopped down on. "Sounds like a plan. Go get your sister and tell her the plan. With your permission, I'll raid your fridge and pack up anything non-perishable so you have something to eat when we reach my ship."

"Forget it," Richard said, heading for the hallway. "Whatever you have, I'll eat. Carrying food is just going to weigh us down. And against Scain, we want to travel light. They're fast enough without us being slower." He paused for a moment, looking back at her. "And one more thing," he said, turning back. "I told you that you'd do the harder right over the easier wrong... and here you are."

Klaara held her tongue as he walked away, lowering her head into her hand. Was she really? Or was she just being as crazy as that idiot Scain? Whatever the answer, she was committed now. She couldn't just back out after offering her ship to the Vahran. She squared her shoulders and stood up, rolling her neck and listening to her vertebrae pop.

Regardless of suspected insanity, she had made the statement to Turukaishal that, if she was in the same system, she'd "look into" helping them. She supposed that was what she was doing now – keeping her word. She smirked, walking to the end of the hallway and peering around the corner. Although the thought of a rematch with Richard later was a thrill she was hoping she got to experience, she pondered as she licked her lips expectantly.

Chapter 44

BEGIN MESSAGE

LOCATION: Sovereign, Mitragan Province

TIME: 02/29 Local Time

MESSAGE: Klaara, I heard about what happened... or at least I think I did. You know how Nyylu is. She claims you betrayed everyone in Clan Mitragan because you hate father. She also says they're going to be trying to kill you, although I know anyone trying to is going to have a hard time of it. You just don't go down easy.

Either way, please tell me that you're all right and, if you get the chance, what happened. In your words. I know Nyylu is our sister, but that doesn't mean I believe her.

-Lyyka'Doran kan Mitragan

Klaara was the first to see them, flitting about in the woods behind the two Vahran's home like wraiths. A pair of Visoth, their wings spread wide, were leaping from tree to tree, holding on with their tentacles. Their five eyes glowed brightly — a series of crimson points of light as bright as any star. She bared her teeth and turned around. "Richard! Heads up! We've got company!"

Richard walked up next to her, squinting out into the night. She indicated the eyes of the two Visoth. One of them was crouched atop the fence ringing their backyard, working at the lock on the fence gate. The other was still out in the woods, firmly attached to a tall pine tree.

The Vahran's hand tensed around his cane sword and he reached for the door lock. Klaara's hand smacked his away. "What are you doing, idiot? They'll kill you!"

"Not before I get at least one of them," he said. "And you can get the other and then get Victoria to safety."

"Uh huh," she said. "And the Scain that are undoubtedly hanging with these things are just going to let us walk away, hm? No dice, Vahran. Besides, you owe me a rematch eventually."

"So what's the plan then?" Richard asked as the back gate swung open. Two Scain moved into the yard, their rifles held up and at the ready. Klaara shook her head, pushing him back away from the door. "Grab your sister and head out the front door. Loop around and cut through the woods. Here's the key to my ship..." she pushed a squarish device into his hand "...if I'm not there five minutes after you arrive, take off without me. And make sure to tell Stretch that he owes me big for this."

"You will die if we leave you behind," Richard said, stepping forward again.

She pushed him back. "Details details. Now go get your sister! GO!"

Klaara opened the back door, closing it behind her and stepping out onto the tiger-wood deck. The sound of her boots on the wood immediately alerted the Scain to her presence, as well as the two Visoth. "What's up."

The two Scain immediately aimed their weapons at her. Her hand moved like lightning, drawing her ion saber as her white hand struck the ground, the ring of glowing light expanding and rising from the ground. The high-energy packets fired from the guns clattered off the shield, pinging in every direction. She grinned, twirling the saber in her hand before lifting the white art field off the ground, curling it over until it became a cone and launching it at the two aliens. They abandoned their plan of shooting at her, instead opting to dive aside as the energy impacted the ground. The explosion threw them apart regardless.

"Sorry folks," Klaara said, running forward with her ion saber at the ready. "If you're planning on killing me, guns aren't the best thing to try."

One of the Scain rolled over, catching her in a Psionic tendril. She snarled, drawing a pair of darts out fo her boot and throwing them in his direction. The first one missed him, but the second struck him squarely in the shoulder. He dropped her with a thud, and she rolled over in time to avoid a spray of gunfire. Instead, she rose up onto her hands, flipping backwards and landing on the deck again.

She surveyed both Scain, watching the Visoth moving in the background. Her face split in a grin as she spun the sword in her fingers, stabbing it into the deck. "C'mon – is that all you've got?"

Klaara grabbed a potted plant, its roots encased in a heavy, terra-cotta base, and threw it straight for the first Scain. She vaulted a chair as he staggered back, having blocked the blow with Psionics but not the force, and rolled beneath another spray of gunfire. She stood up, grabbing both Scain by their throats, and slammed their heads together as hard as she could. Their Psionic fields prevented this from being lethal, but it definitely dazed them.

She turned, punching the one on her left in the stomach, before pivoting on one foot, driving her fist into the other one's head as she kicked the first one in the arm, his gun discharging and punching holes in the garden shed. She struck him with an uppercut, watching as his friend collapsed onto the grass, before smashing his arm hard enough to send his gun flying away. Her fists struck him across the face twice more before she punched him in the chin. His head flew backwards in time to meet her other fist, which bent him double, and the blow would have knocked his head almost all the way to the ground. Her knee swung up in time to catch his face before it got that far, throwing him backwards. She caught his throat and slammed the Scain into the dirt hard enough to dent the grass, smirking as she drove her fist down on his face with all her strength, rupturing his Psionic barriers and bashing in his faceplate.

She dove backwards, grabbing her sword and jumping forward again, aiming for the second Scain, in the process of standing up. The Scain jumped backwards, smashing her arm sideways with his gun before grabbing her wrist. Her eyes widened with surprise as the Scain grabbed her wrist, twisting backwards and kicking her in the back of the knee, dropping her down. He wrenched the sword from her hand and kicked her back onto the ground, lifting it into the air and preparing to bring it down on her head. She grinned up at him. So this was it, then? At least the two Vahran had escaped. She looked up at the Scain, prepared to stare her executioner down, when a blur of motion caught her eye.

Richard leapt off the deck, scooping up a narrow garden rake from the rack next to the steps, and dove straight for the Scain. The rake spun above his head for a moment before he gripped it in both hands, bringing it around like a hammer and stabbing the spikes of the rake through the Scain's barriers. They didn't stop there, continuing through his helmet. Blood sprayed out as the tall alien collapsed sideways, his brain ruptured by the garden tool. Richard landed directly on his falling body, ripping out the rake and turning to face the barely-moving Scain and the two Visoth. "*Blessed be the Lord, my strength, which teacheth my hands to war and my fingers to fight.*" Richard said, his lips pulled back over his teeth as he stood up from the crouch, throwing the bloody rake aside. His sword cane, tucked between his belt loops, was drawn and aimed at the Scain.

Klaara scooped up her fallen ion saber, standing up next to him. "You idiot," she hissed. "You're going to die."

"We're all going to die," Richard said. "But not today. Now either shut up and help me fight these things or stand back and get out of my way."

He stepped forward as the other Scain stood up, wheezing and gasping from his savage beating. Richard regarded him warily, but his eyes never lost their fury. The Scain lifted his arms to fight, but a moment later an ion saber seemed to grow from his chest. Klaara jerked it out, kicking him to the ground. "There's my choice," she said, facing the two Visoth. "Watch out for these things though," she warned. "They can be a bit tricky."

240

"Except for one thing," Richard said. "I'm human."

He threw the sheath of his cane sword at the Visoth on the left before jumping at it. The alien had enough time to smack the sheath aside before Richard had bulled into it, knocking it to the ground and pinning it in place. It trilled madly, its tendrils wrapping around his throat and squeezing, cutting off his air. Richard's sword sheared through two of the tendrils, buying him a moment, before he punched the Visoth in one of its eye stalks, rupturing it and spraying black blood across the ground. It shrieked loud enough to make Richard want to cover his ears, but he couldn't – not with one hand twisted in eye stalks and the other slashing at the constricting tendrils around his throat.

Klaara, on the other hand, had kicked her Visoth sideways away from Richard, mostly to keep them from helping one another, and thrown it against the fence. She punched it hard in the center of the body as it wrapped those foul tendrils around her arm. A hissing emanated from her flesh as it began to burn her, acidic mucus spreading from its appendage. She snarled, pushing past the pain as she drove the ion saber into its body again and again, stabbing through it and the fence behind it. Black blood washed over her arm, burning at her skin as she threw the dying Visoth to the ground, watching it writhe around.

Richard lifted his sword, stabbing it sideways into the Visoth's body. The tendrils were regrowing as he cut them, and he couldn't survive without air forever. The Visoth screeched with pain, releasing his throat for a moment, and Richard kicked it away from him, pulling the sword free and tearing the stab wound larger. Klaara stumbled over, cradling her burned arm, and fell on the Visoth, her saber pointed downwards. Richard pinned the Visoth in place before it could rise, holding it against the ground as the sword penetrated its body. As with him, it tried choking her, but she had already stabbed it. Her burned hand, still wrapped around the saber, lifted the sword into the air again and slammed it down, cutting the Visoth halfway apart. Blood sprayed out as it fell backwards, twitching and writhing in its death throes.

She looked at Richard as they both panted and caught their breaths. "We have to move," she said.

"Now," he agreed, forcing himself upright. "Victoria! Come on! The coast is clear!"

Victoria ran out of the house, holding the two pistols Turu had given them. Richard helped Klaara up, motioning to the back gate. "Come on! We need to go!"

Chapter 45

CHECKING FOR NEW MESSAGES...

...CHECKING...

...CHECKING...

...CHECKING...

...CHECKING...

...CHECKING...

...NO NEW MESSAGES. ENTERING HIBERNATION MODE.

Richard sprinted through the woods, his sword drawn and one of Turu's guns in his off hand. He could hear things moving in the woods around them, and knew that the Scain could Psionically pinpoint them. They had to move. He paused at the top of a hill, looking back. "Come on!"

Klaara came next, clambering up the low hill. Her arms had healed thanks to her White Art, but he could see furrows and scars from the burns even in the dark. She would need medical attention later. Victoria climbed along behind her, the other gun clutched in her fingers. Richard looked around, noting that they were almost a third of the way there. The Frisbee course fell away behind them, and only the mental hospital and the rise opposite Steilacoom Boulevard impeded them now.

It was a dark, cloudy night, which helped mask them from anyone trying to visually see them. Richard's coat had been wrapped around Klaara to darken her, and Victoria was wearing a trench coat that had once belonged to their mother. Above them, the waning moon peeked through the clouds, giving them just enough light to see where they were going.

"You're sure this is the right way?" Klaara asked, her saber still clenched in her fingers, the blade deactivated so as not to draw attention.

Something moved in the trees a few dozen yards away. Richard nodded, motioning to the road. "Right or wrong, it's better than staying here. Come on, let's get moving!"

They raced across the gravel parking lot behind the Western State mental hospital, reaching the road in less than a minute and taking a sharp right. Richard kept his position at the head of the group, his sword cane glinting in the streetlamps they passed beneath. He reached the top of a hill and paused, looking around, before gesturing to them both. "Clear."

The underpass wasn't far, and the group was grateful to finally see it – the same underpass Richard, Victoria and Turu had hidden in during the blizzard. Snow was still piled heavily around it, and Turu's barrier devices had self-destructed. Bits and pieces were scattered here and there. Richard ducked inside, scanning the interior before motioning to Klaara and Victoria.

"We'll rest here for a moment," he said, kneeling down and planting the point of his sword against the ground. "Klaara, the rise is on the other side of this underpass. Can you guide us from there?"

She nodded. "Yeah; I already recognize the road above us. It won't be too much further than this."

"Good. I don't think we can evade them forever, although they'll probably call off the search come daylight. They won't risk being caught out in the open. I hope to be long gone by then."

"And if your buddy Turukaishal comes back?"

"He goes by Turu now," Victoria reminded her, "and I left something for him at the house."

"Good thinking," Richard said. "Everyone ready to move on?"

The three of them sprinted out from beneath the overpass, Klaara leading them. They raced down a dirt road, tall grass swaying on either side of them. They were almost to the hill when the Scain Scout craft flew overhead, a pair of guns extending from the underside.

"*Aelau bakan keviru!*" Klaara cursed, grabbing Richard and Victoria by their collars and throwing them flat on the ground, her black hand slamming into the ground between them. The high-energy blast smashed into a shield of black light, winging off into the night sky. Two more impacts met similar fates before she dropped the shield and ran into the trees on the hill, all but dragging Richard and Victoria with her. "Come on! We're almost there!"

Two Visoth fell from the trees in front of them. Richard pushed past Klaara, jump kicking one of them down the side of an embankment while shooting the other one. He hit the ground, somersaulting and rising again without breaking his pace. Behind and above them, the gunship searched the hill with a powerful light, scanning for their signatures.

"Where'd you park the ship?" Victoria asked as they ducked around a corner, Richard elbowing a Scain in the lower back, the hapless alien having been facing the wrong way. The Scain let out a muffled moan as his spine broke, his body tumbling down the hill.

"Top of this hill – it's cloaked near some ruins."

"The Old Western State? Great!" Richard said, sheathing his sword. "We're almost there. Get going and take Victoria. I'll stay behind and make sure you can get airborne."

"You bet," Klaara said, grinning. "Come on Princess – let's get a move on. Your dearly beloved won't be too happy if you get roasted out here."

Richard checked the ammunition on his gun before starting to back along the pathway, keeping his eyes on the darkest patches. A Visoth peeked around the corner and was immediately shot in the center of its body. It squealed and fell over backwards, thrashing in the pathway before becoming still.

He heard the roar of engines from behind him and chanced a look over his shoulder. Up at the top of the hill, behind several tall trees, he could see the old, graffiti-strewn structure where Klaara would be. Lights illuminated the crumbling concrete and the cold fingers of rebar as they burst from the decaying rock. Richard ran towards the lights, turning and firing over his shoulder as he heard things start moving in the trees.

"Richard, come on!" Victoria yelled, standing in the airlock of the *Gamble* as it hovered amidst the ruins. Richard bounded across the rocks, throwing the gun down as he sprinted straight for his sister. He jumped off a high piece of a fallen wall, landing inside the airlock on his belly before rolling over and looking back outside.

Immediately, gunfire erupted from several places along the treeline, smashing against Klaara's ship. He grabbed Victoria and pulled her down next to him, kicking at the only button he could see. The doors slammed shut, trapping them both inside. There was a moment during which the ship decompressed, and then Klaara entered the airlock, handing them both a pair of patches. "Put these on your chests so you can breathe. And hold on: I'm tracking a few ships incoming."

"Fantastic," Richard said, slamming the patch onto his chest and standing up, racing into the narrow, cramped hallways of the *Gamble*. "Take off! Go!"

"I know!" she yelled back from the bridge, already throwing herself into the navigation seat. "You don't need to tell me how to fly my own ship!"

Richard raced into the bridge, watching as Earth fell away beneath them. For a brief moment, a Scain ship filled their vision before Klaara flew above it, taking off into the night sky, her fingers flying over the keypads. "Get ready, Vahran: this isn't going to be pretty."

"Where do you want me? What can I do?" Richard asked, looking at the terminals.

"Nothing," she said. "Sit tight and hope we don't blow up. The *Gamble* isn't exactly designed for large firefights."

"Oh great," Richard said, grabbing a Heil polyform helmet from one of the racks and putting it on. It sealed to his suit, the internal display winking on. He threw one to Victoria as she entered. Klaara laughed.

"The Scain gave you polyform, huh? Great! That'll save on me trying to put you in it while we're being shot at."

"Would you please focus on getting us out of here?!" Richard yelled as Klaara exited Earth's atmosphere, two of the Scain craft in pursuit.

She was grinning from ear to ear, holding tight to the controls. "Relax kid," she said. "We're in space now: nothing can touch me." The ship entered a steep somersault, flipping upwards and backwards. Richard and Victoria were both thrown against the back wall, the former grunting out a curse. Klaara flipped the ship around, opening fire on the back end of one of the Scain craft. The massive cannon to the left of the bridge let out a loud boom, a streak of light lancing out and stabbing the back of their target.

The Scain craft sputtered, its lights flickering, before a white light engulfed it. A moment later, it was gone completely. Klaara snorted. "Coward... he jumped away."

She keyed in several lines of code. "Pick a star, kid," she said, "we're getting out of here." A huge hologram of the local area expanded outwards, individual points of light winked along the grids.

"Anywhere that's not here!" Richard said, pointing at a star close to him.

Klaara grinned, slamming a lever forward. "Good choice." A moment later, the white light engulfed them as well, propelling them through space faster than light could ever hope to go.

Chapter 46

CHECKING FOR NEW MESSAGES...

...CHECKING...

...CHECKING...

...CHECKING...

...CHECKING...

...CHECKING...

...NO NEW MESSAGES. ENTERING HIBERNATION MODE.

The *Gamble* exploded out of Dark Space with a barely-perceptible boom. Klaara's scanners swept the area, making sure it was clear before moving towards a large gas giant. The screen lit up, identifying it as Veros. The swirling, reddish clouds completely filled the forward window, and Richard couldn't help but stare in openmouthed awe.

"Looks like we lost them," Klaara said. "We'll lay low here, and then—"

Her console bleated at her and she moaned. "Never mind, scratch that. They sent a ship after us. Hold on!"

The *Gamble* swung to the right of the planet, its afterburners blazing as Klaara banked around, turning to face on the single Scain ship. She fired the main gun, sending another lance of light out at their target. The Scain behind the controls barrel-rolled out of the way, the shot barely missing. A hatch below the cockpit opened up, several torpedoes streaming out and hissing their way towards the *Gamble*.

"Awwww..." Klaara moaned as the torpedoes drew close. "Crap."

She flipped the ship into a steep ascent, Richard barely managing to grab hold of one of the seats before he was thrown backwards. He growled loudly. "Stop doing—" anything else was cut off as several loud explosions wracked the hull of the *Gamble*. An emergency light began flashing as Klaara continued to fly straight up, her face set in a mask of determination. Another explosion rocked them, and this time something behind them stopped functioning. The *Gamble* flipped over onto its side, prompting Klaara to start cursing.

"They shot out a thruster," she screeched.

Richard released the chair, dropping downwards and out of the bridge door, his hands scrabbling for purchase along the vertical hallway. He caught a pipe along the roof before landing against the wall. He was off like a shot, opening every door he could find, looking inside. At last, after a few minutes of searching the comparatively tiny ship, he found what he was looking for.

Meanwhile, Klaara was still fighting to gain control of the ship. "I can't turn," she hissed. "Richard, get on the gun. Richard?" she looked around. "Where'd that coward go?!"

Victoria looked around in a panic for her brother, but Klaara waved it aside. "Never mind. Girl, get on the gun. I need you to help me in case he tries to flank me. I can't turn to face him – get on the turret. Now!"

Scrambling along the near-vertical floor of the bridge, Victoria climbed into one of the seats Klaara was waving at. It rotated smoothly down into the floor, the lid sealing shut above her until she emerged in a transparent sphere along the underside of the ship. All around her, space stretched infinitely in every direction, punctuated only by the glow of the star and the looming shape of Veros.

"You'd better shoot him," Klaara said over the speakers. "Just keep the pressure on him!" Something whizzed past Victoria, lilting and bobbing drunkenly. It was a streamlined craft, its four wings looking vaguely familiar to her – like something from a dream. Klaara let out an irate screech. "That little—he took my Rover!!"

The Rover flew straight for the Scain ship, a volley of energy pellets battering the hull before the sleek craft rolled over and shot straight up. The Scain gunship fired after it, two torpedoes chasing it. Victoria took aim with the turret, holding down the triggers as the massive gun began to fire. It wasn't a rapid weapon – rather, it fired dozens of large slugs at once at a slower pace, much like a long-range shotgun.

Klaara was irate. "Richard!! Get your human tail back in here before I feed it to you!!"

"No can do," his voice said, filtered and broken by the static. "You said it yourself: you can't turn. I'm luring him into your line of fire."

Victoria kept up the fire, her heart hammering in her chest. She couldn't believe what she was doing. The gun fired beneath her, booming like a giant's heart as she kept firing round after round towards the enemy ship. Richard kept flying, streaking back towards them. "Klaara! Prime a round! I'm coming right in front of you!"

Klaara said nothing, but the main gun began to warm up. Victoria could feel it moving above her. *"Ready!"* the Heil said. *"Don't die!"*

"I won't," Richard said. A moment later, Victoria saw him fly in front of the *Gamble*, his form silhouetted against the star in the center of the system. Before her brain could realize what she was seeing, the lance of light shot out from Klaara's gun, punching through the hull of the Scain craft on his tail. It split apart, exploding a moment later and throwing shrapnel in every direction. Bits and pieces struck the *Gamble*, and Victoria saw the lights go out. Klaara cursed.

"Damn. Get yourself back aboard the ship, Richard. We're losing power. Life support is stable, but gravity and lights aren't. Better hurry up before you get locked out."

Richard turned the rover around, flying straight for the *Gamble*. *"On my way."*

Victoria felt the turret seat lift back up into the cockpit, and immediately she felt herself lift out of it, floating through the air. Anything that wasn't fastened down – old protite syringes, bullet casings, drink canisters and the like – were already floating around... as well as one angry looking Heil.

Klaara punched a pneumatic hammer aside and drifted down towards the doors. "Looks like I get to fix this thing. I hope your buddy Stretch comes along soon..." she vanished through the door, still mumbling. Her voice rose several octaves as Richard came through one of the airlocks, and Victoria saw Klaara pin her brother up against the wall, all but shouting at him.

She sighed, looking out the main window as the planet Veros rotated lazily in space. She hoped Turu would return soon as well. Things just weren't the same without him here... and she missed him so much.

Chapter 47

ERROR: DATA PAD #925410053 NOT FOUND. ROUTING SYSTEM LOCATED. FILES FORWARDED TO SHIP :242: DATA TERMINAL VIALEIA. RUNNING STARTUP PROTOCOLS.

Turu hated the Broken Verge with a passion. During the formation of the Galaxy, large clumps of debris were spun to the outer edges in three places, becoming the Broken, Shattered and Ruined Verges. In these fields of destroyed planets, brown dwarves, unending asteroid fields and other debris, navigation was difficult if not impossible, and the vast number of gutted, burned-out shipwrecks were a silent monument to the price of failure.

It was only slightly better maintained than the Korvus System – one or two refueling stations and colony worlds existed out here, and that was why he had come. One of the larger space stations out here – Camethos – was fully equipped with a complete refueling station. That, of course, was his target. He needed to get his hands, first and foremost, on some fuel. Secondly, he needed a new tank (or, better yet, two) of coolant for his fusion reactors before they blew up on him. An in-space explosion wasn't on his agenda.

Camethos Station came into view after journeying through the Verge for the better part of an hour. It was an enormous, oblong construction, the central body shaped like a jointed cylinder. Each joint had a long branch growing from either side, making the whole thing look something like a spine and ribcage. The base had a large, zero-gravity platform outside on which one could walk if they had magnetic boots. Long walkways extended from this dock like the teeth of a comb, and Turu flew the *242* close to them.

The walkways shifted, sliding apart to accommodate his ship, as a large metal arm reached up and over the top of his ship, anchoring it in place as he docked. He attached his helmet, extending the gangplank from the airlock to one of the walkways and disembarked, looking around.

Camethos was an Erythian Station, privately owned and managed by the Besodaari Security Corporation. BSC was one of fourteen privatized military groups that, as a whole, acted as the military strength of the Erythian Empire. Turu knew that most privatized armies fell apart, but for the Erythians it had worked. BSC was an old and prestigious company, and his friend Bordra was the commander of Task Force Kirel, which was one of thirty-six task forces managed by BSC. This was the reason he had chosen Camethos Station. If things went foul, he could drop Bordra's name and the Erythian might be called to verify him... in which case he would be in the clear.

An Erythian was waiting for him on the docks, Data Pad in hand. "Nomenclature please?" it said, its gender hidden by the full vacuum suit it was wearing. Turu hesitated, unsure of whether to give his name or his ship's. He decided on both. "Turukaishal, Ship Callsign 242."

"Ship Nomenclature is required," the Erythian said.

Turu groaned in exasperation. "But I just got the ship," he lied. "I haven't had time to think of one."

"You have time now, and there is no time like the present," the Erythian said quickly. "We offer a ship naming service here as well. Choose a name and proceed over to the counter." It gestured toward a low booth on the other side of the docks where a bored-looking female Erythian lounged on the counter. Turu sighed, running his hand over his face. Might as well name it now.

The uninterested female perked up as he approached. "A Scain?" she said hurriedly, her headdress rustling as she stood up straighter. Made from individual tetrahedral plates, it gave her head a streamlined, if not armadillo-like, look. The elenium finish on each of the gave it a glassy, crystalline appearance. "Unusual. This far from the local Triumvirate—"

"I can name my ship here, right?" Turu said, leaning over the counter. He towered over the female by at least five feet. "Captain's Name: Turukaishal. Ship Name: Victoria."

"Victoria?" the Erythian had begun typing as soon as he'd uttered the words 'name my ship'. "Unusual name. Vahran in origin – have you had dealings?"

"No," he lied, glad that the helmet kept his eyes from betraying him. "A friend of mine has, and I liked the name. Can we hurry up? I'm in a hurry." The irony of telling an Erythian to hurry up was not lost on him – they were usually the ones asking others to do so. They spoke and thought at close to the speed of light, and usually in barely-discernible technobabble.

"Confirmed," she said as she handed him a smooth card – his registration certificate. Turu, having brought it with him from the ship, handed her a small disc. This was rolled through a small machine, deducting the five-hundred credit fee from his account. It wasn't like he had to pinch pennies when he was betraying the Scain. He had a huge wad of savings from his backed-up vacation time anyway.

Turu placed his hand on the back of the card, wincing as a needle stabbed him in the palm and took a sample of his blood for genetic confirmation. He slipped the card into one of the chest pockets of his suit. "Where do I refuel?"

"You must first log your entry with the Dock Head," she said, gesturing back to the first Erythian he'd spoken with. "And then you may proceed over to the purchase counter."

Turu growled, stomping back to the Dock Head and giving him the name *Victoria* before sweeping over to a large sign labeled *"FUEL AND SUPPLIES"*.

He purchased a large pair of coolant canisters, giving the order to fill the tanks on his ship as well, and smoothly ducked away from an incoming didactic speech on the importance of proper handling, storage and installation, when the shopkeeper offered. This cost him another 1,200 credits in addition to a 200 credit fee for having them shipped back to the *Victoria* and a 300 credit installation charge. Turu pocketed the credit disc, grunting quietly in agitation. Erythians weren't usually this expensive, but this was the Broken Verge. Way out here, they charged higher prices to compensate for the lack of steady customers. Usually, the only ones through here were bounty hunters or thrill-seekers.

Turu boarded his ship, removing his helmet and inhaling the scent that came with his craft. Now that it had a name, it seemed much more personal. He grinned, his eyes turning golden-yellow. Now he had to head back to Earth. It wouldn't be long before he'd be back and ready to brief the Vahran on the situation. He paused at the Vialeia Terminal, checking for any incoming data from Bandrumano, and saw a single message. He called it up.

Bandrumano's message read the same way the Scain spoke: loose and carefree. The Forward Fleet was only sending a selection of ships against him, including the *Trident*. However, as unfortunate as this was, the massive gunship would be delayed. It was currently at one of the Stardocks around Nihran, undergoing a routine weapons inspection and maintenance. Other than the gunship, Turu could see twenty-two assault carriers, three destroyers and forty-seven individual fighters. This was on the tip of the Fleet's iceberg – maybe he could catch them off guard when they arrived and—

No, the *Trident* would destroy them. It had the second most powerful laser in the Galaxy, next to the Alintean Barghest-class Tactical Cruisers. There was no way he was going to surprise something that could fire nuclear-tipped torpedoes out of its sides and back either. The last thing he wanted to do was get slaughtered because he thought it might be fun to get hit by an O-202. He turned off the terminal, committing the information to memory, and sat down at the helm.

The magnetic arm which had anchored his ship in place up until now retracted smoothly from his ship as the engines fired up, and he felt a momentary swaying motion until his ship's internal computer balanced him out. He pulled out of the station, turning around and holding position just outside of the docks. He oriented the ship using the command console, keying in the coordinates for Sol, and jumped into Dark Space.

He supposed Dark Space was a bit of a misnomer. In reality, it was more lit than not. Whereas in "Light Space" the cosmic void was black, interspersed with the flecks of white which were the stars. Here in Dark Space, the inverse was true. Space itself was a brilliant, blinding white with stars shining black against it. Turu wondered, and not for the first time, how some brilliant individual had concluded that this was "Dark" Space.

He reemerged in the Sol System near Uranus, immediately checking the scanners. There was a hive of activity near Titan, most of it beneath the cloud level, and he smiled at the thought of Bandrumano down there on the ground setting up the emplacements. Klakshan might be there too, but it was always touch-and-go with the Taeski. They never really communicated well. Sometimes, in the middle of a conversation, they'd just up and leave, pursuing some goal only they understood. Klakshan, a lover of the eloquent Scain culture, wasn't usually like that, but if he brought other Taeski along things could be unpredictable.

He passed Jupiter, staring at the roiling red storm in the southern hemisphere. That thing had been going for at least four centuries, and recently it had been joined by a smaller one. Turu looked away: he had things to do. He couldn't just sit here and watch the crimson anticyclonic storms all day.

The *Victoria* soared toward Earth, descending into lunar orbit first to ascertain that he was clear. He could see the International Space Station on his scanners – it would pass between Earth and Luna soon, giving him his window. Turu set his ship down in a crater on the dark side of the moon, waiting.

It took a few hours – Turu checked his pocket-watch periodically, and mostly just so he'd have something to do. He almost wanted to turn around and assist with the preparations on Titan, but he'd have other things to do soon enough. Richard and Victoria would need to be brought up to speed on the situation, properly trained, briefed and outfitted... it was going to take time.

According to Bandrumano's report, the *Trident* wasn't due out of inspection for another ten rotations, Earth Time. There would also be the task of actually amassing the fleet, choosing a Scain to lead it, and then actually moving it through the Galaxy to Earth. Turu wasn't a fool, and neither was Sovakadris. That fleet wasn't going to jump directly into the Sol System – it'd attract far too much attention from the probes hovering in Dark Space. Instead, Sovakadris and the Fleet Commander would try to strike from the western edge of the Galaxy, where the probes were thinnest and the gaps were spacious enough to form a "back door".

Turu fired up the engines as the space station passed, bringing the ship around the moon and entering Earth's atmosphere. Fire danced around his cockpit as he reentered the planet he had come to appreciate, if not outright love. He evened out, pulling a slow loop before descending to the top of a lake.

It was dark, which meant most of the Vahran would be asleep, so he wasn't too worried. The *Victoria* sank slowly to the bottom of the lake, nestling amidst the branches and mud, as he used the *Dirego* to disembark. He'd hide the ship somewhere and contact Richard and Victoria.

Thankfully, the Rover was easy to hide. He parked it in the 'garage' of his old base and checked each floor with his Psionics, hoping to find either Vahran. Unfortunately, they weren't there. He donned his usual disguise and departed, heading for their home in Oakbrook. It didn't take him long to reach the back gate, and when he did, he could already tell something was wrong. There was a putrid stench in the air, like rotten fish and spoiled fruit. He wrinkled his nose and crept up to the back gate, peering inside.

The back yard was a mess. Two Scain and two Visoth corpses were sprawled across the lawn. His eyes widened, his heart beating faster, as he sprinted across the yard and all but tore the back door off the hinges. Inside, he couldn't detect anyone moving. He snarled, looking carefully through each room, hoping to find some trace of his companions. Once he reached the kitchen, he hesitated. There was a single piece of paper on the counter with two words scrawled on it.

The Heil.

So Klaara had been behind this? Turu's teeth ground together as he stormed out of the house, crossing the yard. As he did so, he paused and looked down at one of the Scain. There were numerous holes punched in his helmet, and his ribcage had caved in. The other had a cauterized wound in the center of his chest. Turukaishal knelt down and touched the edges of the gaping hole.

Ion weapons cauterized puncture wounds. This Scain had likely been slain with an ion saber. He looked over at the Visoth — the source of the pungent aroma — and found that one of them had been treated similarly. The other bore numerous puncture and slash marks as well, but from a non-ionized weapon. A blade of some sort. Richard, perhaps?

The Scain growled, touching a tendril of Psionics to each of the four corpses. They disintegrated into powder — there was no sense in leaving them behind for Vahran to find. He swept out of the yard, shedding his disguise as he made his way back to the *Dirego*. If Klaara had harmed either of the humans, she was going to get the beating of a lifetime.

Turu was back aboard the *Dirego*, and subsequently the *Victoria*, within the hour.

Chapter 48

ERROR: DATA PAD #925410053 NOT FOUND. ROUTING SYSTEM LOCATED. FILES FORWARDED TO SHIP :242: DATA TERMINAL METEUSAE. NO CURRENT MESSAGES.

Turu's impulse drives carried him out to the orbit of Mars before he shut them off, coasting around the russet planet. He cast his scanners around, checking the Sol System from one side of the Oort Cloud to the other. It took a few minutes for the pings to return – valuable minutes in which his human friends could be in jeopardy – but ultimately the results came back negative. There were no Heil spacecraft – or indeed, any spacecraft of non-human origin – in the system. He ground his teeth together. That meant she had jumped somewhere with Richard and Victoria.

Heil ships were, thankfully, fairly easy to track... but not if he had nowhere to begin. He loaded up his console, tracking the latest DSC buoys to log jumps in or around the Wastes – the part of the Galaxy in which the Sol System lay. The Scain then filtered out any results he didn't find pertinent – Alintean, Scain, Visoth... he just wanted a Heil ship. It only took him a few seconds to narrow down the choice to two ships.

Both were Model 22 Ark Ships, designed for relatively comfortable living on extended flights – just the sort of ship a bounty huntress would want. The *Gamble* and the *Justice* were both a fair distance away – the former was in orbit around a young, 800 million-year-old star in the neighboring system of Dakina, a mere 10.5 light years away. If his scanners were correct, the ship was in a retrograde orbit around one of the system's planets and therefore was orbiting Dakina in a slow, steady orbit.

The second ship, the *Justice*, had emerged in the Delerue system, probably to visit the only world of any interest: Ganovai. Turu tried to think of any possible reason why Klaara would kidnap a pair of Vahran and drag them all the way to Ganovai. Thinking like a bounty hunter (or at least a sane one, which he was fairly certain she was not), Ganovai was one of the last places she'd want to go. If she was after money, she'd drag them to Besodaari or Raga and sell them to the Erythians or Zyzyt as guinea pigs and genetic samples.

This meant that the *Gamble* was a far likelier target. He immediately plotted a course, vanishing from space with a burst of white light and streaming towards Dakina.

He burst from Dark Space and into orbit around the star, staying a good distance away. His photon shields would only protect him from so much solar radiation. His eyes swept over his viewscreen as the scanners picked up and identified every major object in the system. One of the points of light in the background was scanned and labeled as *"VEROS"* - that was his target. In orbit around that gas giant, he would likely find the *Gamble* and, if he was lucky, her crew. He floored the accelerator, the impulse drives launching him forward.

The Ark came into view soon enough. It was haphazard and oblong, with a boxy crew compartment on one side of the circular bridge and a long-distance firearm on the other. This particular specimen had been heavily customized – the hull plating had been reconstructed numerous times, and the painted word *"GAMBLE"* along the side looked as if a Vahran toddler had done it. Definitely the type of ship he'd expect Klaara to fly.

Turu entered the gas giant's orbit, flying against the rotation to keep up with the *Gamble*. If she didn't show signs of life soon, the decrepit ship would fall into the planet's atmosphere in a matter of days before ultimately being crushed by the pressure. He pinged she ship with his communications array. *"This is the Scain Ship, Callsign 242 "Victoria","* he said. *"Anyone aboard, please respond."*

There were several moments of silence, and he was about to try again when he saw a miniscule figure enter the bridge. Klaara. She walked over and stared out at him, and he heard her voice through his speakers. *"This is Heil Ship "Gamble", I can hear you loud and clear. That you Turukaishal?"* Turu's eyes narrowed. Oh yes. That Heil had better have a good story lined up. The kind that wins awards.

"Gamble, you mind telling me what happened to a pair of Vahran?" he asked, trying to keep his voice neutral. He would shoot her out of orbit if she'd hurt them – launch that scrap heap of a ship into the ominous depths of Veros with her aboard and relish her screams as the gravity crushed her to death.

"Before you go getting all bent out of shape," the Heil spat, *"perhaps you should thank me for saving their lives!"* Her voice was laced with both annoyance and anger, and Turu's eyes lit up momentarily with orange hues. *"They're fine – here on the ship, in fact, so I suggest disarming your guns. I know you're locked on to me. A few Scain and Visoth showed up after you left, probably looking for you. That or they were an advance party from your buddy the Mindbank. I grabbed these two and took off, but they damaged my thrusters and there's something wrong with my power systems. I'm trying to repair them now."*

Turu wanted to cry out of relief, visibly slumping down at his console. The two Vahran were alive and well. His friends. He sighed, all but feeling the worry washing off of him in waves. In its place came a dull sense of weariness that he knew was the byproduct of stress. *"Understood Gamble. Stand by – I'll come aboard and assist with the repairs."* He brought the *Victoria* around to one side of the stranded Heil ship, keying in the autopilot to keep the two craft from drifting together. Without further ceremony, he snapped on his suit, donned his helmet and opened the airlock.

Spacewalks had always made him nervous. There was just so much that could go wrong out in the endless vacuum of space. While drifting in the endless black was strangely comforting, yes, something about realizing how insignificant and tiny you really are starts playing with your mind. Orbiting a B-Class gas giant one and a half times the size of Jupiter was a sure-fire way to spark that insignificant feeling. He attached his safety cord to the outlet on the exterior of the airlock and kicked off, drifting towards the *Gamble*.

Halfway out, Turu drew a small handgun from his waist and fired it at the Ark. A single cable, perhaps an inch thick and propelled by a single jet, extended through the empty void and thudded solidly into the metal outside the *Gamble*'s airlock. It adhered firmly, the nanites bonding quickly with the hull to hold the piton in place. Turu fastened his safety cable to this new line and began to move along them, one hand over the other, until he reached his destination.

He angled himself, his magnetic boots attaching to the outside of the ship, and he sighed with relief. Another spacewalk completed without incident. Once he was sure of his footing, he undid the two cables and allowed them to retract – one into his suit and the other into the gun. He then turned around and pounded twice on the airlock with his fist.

The circular aperture rotated in ninety degrees before sliding open in two neat halves. At least the Heil huntress was going to let him in, although it was in her best interest to do so. Turu stepped in, the airlock closing behind him with a hiss. The small area pressurized before the interior of the cramped little ship opened up to him. Immediately, he felt the lack of gravity. Either Klaara had disengaged it to save power or it had been damaged as well. He deactivated his boots – it would be faster to float – and turned on his radio. *"Klaara, are you there?"*

There was a grunt, followed by a loud thud. "I'm here," she growled. From the strain in her voice, it sounded as if she was pulling something heavy. "You inside?"

"Yes," the Scain said. "Second deck airlock."

"I know. I let you in. Come through the maintenance access tunnel. It's down the hall to your right, on the left hand side. I'm in engineering, trying to get these thrusters back online."

Turu followed the cramped hallway to a circular hatch. Even without gravity, his Psionics proved useful in opening it. The interior was just as tight as to be expected of a Heil ship – he'd been on enough to know – but his slender frame fit neatly inside. He squeezed himself through the tunnel, emerging in the upper hemisphere of a large, oval room. At the far end and below him, the Heil had removed an entire panel from the wall. She was up to her elbows in wires and thermal sinks, drifting spectrally in front of him as she growled and cursed at her ship.

"What happened?" Turu asked as he drifted over to her.

"Stupid, stinking Scain... er, no offense... showed up after you had already gone. I came down to warn your Vahran pals and a group of them showed up in their backyard." She grinned, and Turu suddenly realized that it was that group's corpses he'd found in Richard and Victoria's yard. "Richard and I whipped them, though. No problem. After we dealt with them, we made a beeline for my ship and took off. One of them jumped through Dark Space to trail me, and shot me in the thrusters."

"I humbly thank you for saving them," Turu said, bowing as much as he could in an environment where orientation meant little to nothing.

"Eh, no biggie," Klaara said, waving at him distractedly. "It was good stress relief anyway. I figured you wouldn't want those two unguarded anyway, which was why I offered to stow them away on my ship. Like I said I jumped here – humans call this place Epsilon *Eridani* – and got shot. And no, I'm not giving you a mission statement on it. I know how you military types are. Although I'd recommend you keep an eye on Richard – he's the one who got me the shot I needed."

"What? Richard?" Turu asked in surprise. "How?!"

Klaara laughed, looking over her shoulder. "Y'know—ouch!..." she hissed, drawing back her smoking fingers. "That kid caught me totally off guard. One second he was on the bridge... stupid resistor, get out of the way... and the next I see one of my Rovers flying off. He figured most of it out in the hangar, I assume, 'cause he wasn't having too much of a problem out there. Lured the enemy ship into my line of fire and I blew it to pieces. His docking needs work though – my poor *Lekramia's Spear* is all dinged up down in the hold."

Turu was thunderstruck. Either Richard was one of the smartest humans he'd ever met, or the man had been watching how Turu flew the Rover on their trip into space. The Scain felt a newfound respect for the two Vahran blooming. If Victoria was the nicest, Richard was likely the most clever.

"So that's how you ended up in this fix, huh?" Turu asked, floating perpendicularly to her and gazing into the panel. "Where are the Vahran?"

"Asleep in the crew quarters," she answered, pulling back her singed fingers again. "Richard was tired to begin with – don't ask me how he was able to fly – and Victoria ran herself ragged doting on him when he got back aboard the ship. Once things settled down, they both kind of crashed... and then I found out that we have about ten Earth days until we get sucked down into Veros and killed. Oh joy."

Turu snorted. "We'll be long gone before then."

"I hope so," she said. "Anyway, you picked a good pair of kids... I almost feel bad for having jumped you all."

"Almost?" Turu asked quizzically.

"Well, I *am* a bounty hunter," she reminded him. "A job is a job. Like I said before: I have to eat too, you know. And if the only way to put food in my belly and keep my ship running is to take contracts like the one they put out on you, that's what I have to do. Sorry about that."

Turu nodded. "No, I understand. I just appreciate you not continuing to attack us after the contract... terminated."

"Pfft. No profit there. Maybe after we sack that Demnechi guy I can raid his bank account. That should be fun." She smiled cheekily at him. "I know an excellent hacker on Besodaari."

Turu laughed. "If you want it, take it. I could care less."

She offered Turu her hand. "Then you just engaged my services, Captain Turukaishal."

Turu grasped her wrist, the Heil wrapping her dexterous fingers around his. They stayed like that for a moment before releasing each other. It was a gesture often associate with deals or contracts – similar to a binding handshake. Turu turned and looked into the mess of wires. "Now then. Let's see if I can help with this."

Chapter 49

ERROR: DATA PAD #925410053 NOT FOUND. ROUTING SYSTEM LOCATED. FILES FORWARDED TO SHIP :VICTORIA: DATA TERMINAL METEUSAE. NO CURRENT MESSAGES.

Turu slammed the hatch shut, hiding the wires he'd been working on. The lock mechanism was given a forcible twist using the blue mist of his Psionics, wrenching it around in its housing until it locked shut with a muffled clunk. He'd tried using brute force the first time, but with the gravity out of commission, all he accomplished was spinning weirdly in a circle. This, naturally, amused the Heil on the other side of the room to no end. "That should do it," he said, snapping back the Psionic cloud around the cross-shaped handle. "For the moment, anyway. Your ship is in need of more... involved... maintenance."

The Heil huntress grunted from somewhere above him, prompting him to turn his head towards the ceiling. Klaara had opened another hatch and was firmly embedded to her waist in it. "Yeah, I know." She cursed vehemently as something clanged loudly in the passage. "I think they shorted out som ejunk up here too. Looks like the lights on the forward Decks are out. Did you see any lights on the outside Viewing decks when you came in?"

"No," the Scain responded, drifting up closer to the hatch so he could hear her better. "The exterior was dark."

There was a loud bang, followed by a clearly audible *"Aelau bakan keviru!"* The Heil swung her legs in irritation, growling. "Looks like they may have gone and blitzed my power lines controlling the exterior lights too. If I ever get my hands on them, they'll wish they had never been born... or cloned, or whatever it is you Scain do these days."

Turu ignored her jab, gripping one of the handles near the hatch. "Would you like me to give it a try? I'm taller and thinner – maybe I can reach more of the wiring."

Klaara forced herself out of the shaft, lowering herself slowly until her luminous eyes were visible. "You better not be calling me fat," she said warningly.

"W-what?" Turu stammered, backpedaling away from the Heil as quickly as he could in zero gravity. "No! I'm a Scain – you can fit me almost anywhere."

The bounty huntress laughed. "Yeah, I know. I was just joking. C'mon – if you want to crawl in here, be my guest. I hate doing this crap."

Turu pulled himself over to the opening as Klaara shifted aside. He hoisted himself up through the aperture, looking around at the narrow compartment. It stretched for several yards in either direction, and the main thermal sinks ran over his head. Woven around and between these three large pipes were bundles of wires and, although they had once been bunched neatly into color-coded bundles, they had been pulled apart and spread around the duct. At this point, it looked as if someone had blown up a multicolored bird's nest. Turu ran a hand over his face and sighed.

Most of the wires had been repaired manually – and often shoddily – what looked like dozens of times. Splices, bindings and crude patches could be seen on almost ever cable in sight, and some looked to be held together with bits of string or fabric cut from polyform. "I think," Turu said as he reached for the thermal tongs Klaara had left near the hatch "That I'd have this professionally looked at. I can only do so much."

"Eh, maybe on someone else's coin," Klaara said from beneath him, "but I'm fine playing reactive for now. Ask me again when a fusion cell goes or my main reactor goes offline. Then I'll reconsider."

Turu clamped a pair of wires together with the thermal tongs, the heat melting the solinium together. He looked around for some of the thermal strips used to insulate the wires, and was unsurprised when he found nothing more than an empty box. "Well, at least consider taking a look at the wires running to your Chaos Drive. Right now, it looks like they're ready to break or melt, and probably electrocute you if you stick your head up here again."

"Fun," Klaara said sarcastically. "Can you reach the splits?"

"Yeah," Turu grunted as he pried the thermal pliers apart, using his Psionics to reach for the next wire. "Just finished one of them." He caught the next pair of wires, being careful to avoid the solinium ends, and began drawing them together. "Hiin, you have a few dozen splits up here. It'll be a while."

He heard her kick off the ceiling and dive toward the bottom of the maintenance chamber. "Fine. I'll leave you to it for the moment. I'm going to go scrounge up some food – I'm not exactly a high-class buffet, but if I manage to find something, you want any?"

"Please," Turu said, clamping the next set of wires. Trying to hold the pliers and the wires with his hands was starting to irritate him. Instead, he settled for holding the wires together with his Psionics while he wrapped the self-heating clamp around the exposed ends and pulled the trigger.

The maintenance hatch banged shut as Klaara left, leaving him to his own devices with his upper body embedded in the shaft. He drew another set of wires over with his Psionics, watching them warily as they drifted closer. He'd done a lot of ship repair in his youth, and he assumed it was something like learning to fly a starship. Once it was ingrained in your mind, you could come back to it after fifty cycles and still know what to do. Even so, he'd seen what could happen if an unshielded solinium coupling touched an unshielded Scain. The resulting burns could be fatal, if not at least seriously disfiguring.

Klaara's ship had taken a lot of damage during the fight, but thankfully most of it had been to the internal wiring where it could be fixed. Any hull breaches had already been fixed, most likely while he'd been on his way here, which probably accounted for sixty percent of the repairs. The pressure-resistant plates he had noticed on his way in had been welded down efficiently, and he suspected that Klaara likely partook in more than her fair share of ship repairs.

The hatch below him opened again. "Hey Stretch!" he heard Klaara yell. "I've got some food down here if you're interested."

"On my way," the Scain grunted, pushing himself out of the overhead crawlspace, his body covered in dust and oil. He kicked off the ceiling, drifting down to where the Heil waited for him by the door. She handed him a rag and disappeared back through the conduit that connected the maintenance chamber to the rest of her ship. Turu followed suit a moment later, dragging himself along with his Psionics as he wiped dirt and grime from his face.

I've got a bottle of J'maka too, if you're in the mood for liquor," the Heil said as he reached the commons room, "but other than that I'm a bit short on liquids. I've got a few tanks of hydrogen dioxide and one or two of carbon disulfide... not that I think you're going to drink them, mind you. I've also got a few cases of liquid nitrogen, a tub of dihydrogen monoxide and a can of liquid oxygen. Anything interesting?"

Turu rolled his eyes at most of her list. "If you don't mind, I'll sample the dihydrogen monoxide," he said, pulling himself out of the conduit. Liquid water wasn't an alien substance to the Scain – Velis's surface was forty-nine percent freshwater. Klaara floated through the commons, kicking off a support pillar to reach the various large tanks, stored in an overhead loft. "Why do you keep liquid nitrogen aboard?" Turu asked, watching her.

She grunted as she heaved a rectangular container free from the loft. "Ever see what it does to a Visoth?" she asked, fishing two cans out of the box and pushing it back in. She threw one can down to the Scain, who watched it bounce off the floor before slowing down near him. He twisted the top of the can off, revealing the interior. Built around the interior lip was a simulated "gravity shield" which kept liquids from drifting out. The barrier parted when he brought his mouth near it, allowing him to drink without incident. It tasted heavenly after having his head in a vent for an extended period of time. "They're the main reason I keep it," Klaara continued. "Otherwise, I use it to keep food rations frozen. My freezers run on it."

Turu's eyebrow lifted slightly. Her freezers were remarkably archaic if they still ran on liquid nitrogen. "Visoth are susceptible to liquid nitrogen?" he asked, deciding not to comment lest he irritate her. This was news to him, as the crustaceans had always seemed to persevere through anything thrown at them. They were every bit as resilient as they were aggressive.

"It slows their cells down," she said casually. "Their regenerative abilities stop at that point. Liquid nitrogen in your bullets is the best way to kill the bugs in vast numbers. Of course, that takes a bit of time to prepare, but nothing too bad."

Turu nodded, taking another drink. He'd almost forgotten that the Visoth could regenerate rather quickly. Well, most of their race could. It was one of the more popular implants their race marketed to itself. He wiped his hand across his mouth, clearing the residual water from it. "Ah. Perhaps that information will come in useful if worst comes to worst."

"Which it probably will," Klaara said with a little too much cheer in her voice. She threw her now-empty can into the air, letting it drift away. When the gravity came back on, it would probably fall down and roll under one of the chairs or benches. "Stick with me, Stretch; I've got a billion little tricks of the trade I can teach you."

"I'm sure," Turu said, nodding as he drank from his can. She probably wasn't lying. If she had survived this long as a bounty huntress, she had likely picked up more than a few shortcuts or tricks. "I wanted to ask, by the way, if you'd be helping us fight Sovakadris?"

Klaara snorted as she drifted back down, rummaging through cabinets on the way as she searched for food. "Probably," she said. "I know I'm in until we puree that Demnechi guy. After that, we'll see what happens. I usually like to avoid sticking my neck into open warfare or politics, and this is both. Then again, I'm eager for some payback, and that Richard kid is interesting enough to keep me around, so we'll have to see. Then again, once he's "paid" me, I don't really see a reason to stick around. Ask me again later, eh?"

Turu nodded, taking another drink before tossing his can across the room, watching it sail into a garbage chute. "I suppose you have a point," he said.

"Darn right I have a point," she said, grinning at him. "I'm a bounty hunter, alright? I have to get paid. Playing hero is fine as long as there's something in it for me. Doesn't mean I haven't saved someone's rear for free every once and a while, but I can't afford to do it too regularly. Like I keep saying – a girl's gotta eat."

Turu nodded as she fished out a little tub of nutrient paste, reading the label on it. "Well then, by all means, don't let me keep you."

Klaara snorted. "Yeah," she said, drifting back with a pair of the nutrient tubs. "But we're carnivores, plain and simple. This..." she threw a tub at him "...is hardly what we call food. It's more like food's food. Either way, go ahead and eat up. It's all I've got right now, so I guess we're stuck with it."

Turu nodded, catching the can with his Psionics and bringing it down to his hands. Hopefully the two humans would wake up soon. He wanted to reunite with them soon and confirm that they were unharmed, and perhaps take them to meet the team on Titan... seeing as he still had a promise to show someone Saturn.

Chapter 50

ERROR: DATA PAD #925410053 NOT FOUND. ROUTING SYSTEM LOCATED. FILES FORWARDED TO SHIP :VICTORIA: DATA TERMINAL METEUSAE.

BEGIN MESSAGE

LOCATION: SOL SYSTEM, SOL7, MOON :TITAN:

TIME: 231/381 Local Time

MESSAGE: Geez, could you have picked a worse spot for a base? Methane rivers, dust, ice... and ridiculously long rotation periods. I should kick you in the lower vertebrae for this. Eh. It is not that bad, though. I have definitely seen worse (Translation: Ganovai).

Kridoria just forwarded me the flight paths of the Forward Fleet. Thought you might like to take a look. It seems that Demnechi is going to be leading the charge, as well – he is going to be on board the Trident... how nice and brave of him. Looks like he will be leading the fleet to through Pracean space first before making a slight correction and heading for an arming station in the Iharsh-Daraz domain. After that, he is heading toward the Sigma Veil to negate suspicion. Once he reaches Blemdarch, he is going to wait for a bit, then do a one-eighty and jump straight for Earth.

Hope you are doing well. Base camp is set up and ready to go.

-Bandrumano

Turu braced himself with his Psionics for an unstoppable Zero-G tackle from Victoria. She barreled into him like a train, shrieking in joy as her arms wrapped around his waist. For Hiin's sake, he'd only been gone for the equivalent of a week. He chuckled and embraced her back as Richard skulked into the room, leaning on the doorframe. Who was he kidding? A week? It felt like a lifetime. Oh how he had missed these two.

"I hear you've gotten good at flying Rovers now?" Turu asked Richard, his arms still around Victoria. The man arched an eyebrow, smirking lightly, but said nothing. Turu grinned at him before releasing the woman and standing up. "I also must thank you for my gift," he said, drawing out the pocketwatch she had given him and holding it in front of her.

"Did you see the other one?" she asked, her cheeks turning red and her aura betraying her embarrassment.

"No. I did not want to open it until I had returned," he told her. "I was going to—is there a problem?"

Klaara was snorting into her hand repeatedly, as if trying not to burst into full-fledged laughter. Turu stared at her as if she were insane. She probably was. Klaara finally gave up, leaning on the wall as she laughed. "By Lekramia, I should have seen it coming!"

Turu excused himself from Victoria and marched over to the Heil, his hand gripping her shoulder as he escorted her into a corner. As soon as he was certain they were out of earshot of the two humans, he lowered his head to hers. "Explain. Now."

Klaara was still shaking in silent hysterics. "You and Victoria?"

Turu blinked a few times before her words clicked. "I... no! Um...ah... you see..." he palmed his face as Klaara's laughter increased. "Ugh... that came out brilliantly, didn't it?" he muttered, removing his hand and taking a few deep breaths. "I do not think so," he said at last.

Klaara smirked at him, still chuckling. "Oh really?"

"Yes really," Turu answered.

"Awww. How cute," she said, pushing his chest. "Then watch this..." she leaned around Turu's shoulder. "Hey Victoria!" she called, still grinning like a maniac. "Guess what this genius named his ship?"

Turu felt his eyes flash through a myriad of colors. "What does that have to do—oh..." he cut himself off, palming his face again and waiting for the rebuke. Klaara continued to snicker at him while he thought of all the possible ways to kill her. The Scain walked away from her and sat down on the far side of the room. Was Richard adept at fighting in Zero-G? He hoped not.

"He named it the *Victoria*," Klaara continued gleefully, as if Turu's humiliation was some kind of potent drug to her. "Isn't that touching?"

Victoria's face turned red all the way to the roots of her hair, and her pinkish aura seemed to fill the commons. Richard gave the Scain a baleful stare, more annoyed than outright angry if Turu was reading his aura right, but said nothing. Victoria finally turned to Turu. "Is it true?"

"I... yes..."

She smiled shyly – something Turu found endearing, not to mention he'd missed her smile. She opened her mouth to say something, but Richard intervened, his words biting into the discussion with all the tact and subtlety of his sword. "Do you have a plan yet?" he asked Turu. "I'd rather not see Earth get burned, if that's alright with you."

Turu snapped to attention. "Yes. Well, I have the beginnings of one. Other than the four of us, there are sixty-six able-bodied sentients hiding in the Sol System. We will be regrouping with them just as soon as I have finished repairing this bucket." He gestured around himself, speaking of the *Gamble*.

"Bucket?!" Klaara barked, indignant. Turu smirked, his back to her. Payback for the jab over his ship's name.

"And what are we facing? Odds? Chance of success? Enemy forces and weapons?"

Turu winced. He'd been hoping to avoid this. "I'd rather not calculate the odds," he said. "We're facing the tip of the Forward Fleet, including a Scain Gunship – the *Trident*. I'm not going to sugarcoat anything: our odds are not good."

Richard snorted, folding his arms, but Klaara cut off anything he was about to say. "Hey Stretch. I've got an idea, if you don't mind?" Turu turned around, looking at the Heil curiously. Her eyes were glowing with excitement, as if she could hardly contain herself. Her aura was all over the place.

Turu was willing to grasp at anything to improve their odds. "Go ahead."

"So, a lot of Heil are pissed off about your dad sacking one of the Hierarchs," she said. Turu winced, and Richard frowned slightly at her lack of tact, but both allowed her to continue. "I know a bunch of Heil – Mitragans mostly, and probably the Guilds – that would be eager to hop a bandwagon attacking the Scain. Seeing as I have to go back soon and report in about my "treason", maybe after I'm acquitted I can rally some of them to help us."

"That's not a bad idea," Turu admitted. "How many do you think you could bring?"

"Depends on how mad they actually are," Klaara said with a shrug. "Heck, even if they're calm, I could probably bring at least fifty Heil. Think that'll help?"

"It's better than what we've got," Turu said as he stood up, floating back towards the maintenance chamber. "I'm almost done with repairs, so we should be good to go soon."

A voice spoke behind Turu, once more cutting into the conversation like a razor. The context of the statement surprising even the stalwart Scain. "I'll help."

It was Richard. Turu turned and looked back at the human, his eyes widening slightly. "You'll what?"

Richard nodded over towards Klaara. "I'll go with Klaara. It might help if the Heil can see that there are already two races allied on this front, one of them willing to come along even if there's personal risk involved."

Klaara nodded. "Kid's got a point," she admitted. "I wasn't lying when I said he'd make a good Heil. If he shows up, it'll show that even the Vahran are getting behind this. It'd probably have good results."

Turu looked at Richard. The man's mind was made up – that much he could tell at a glance – but he was having doubts about leaving Victoria. "Richard, if you go, then I will take care of your sister. You know I would never harm her."

"That's what I'm worried about," Richard said, staring down the Scain. It was the first time in Turu's life where he'd felt *small*. Richard's cold gaze seemed to make everything around him seem enormous. "But of anyone to leave her with, you're the best option. I trust you. Don't make me regret it. And make sure to take care of yourself."

Victoria nodded, floating over to Turu. "Don't worry," she said to Richard. The Scain looked down at her – even in Zero-G he ended up being higher than she was – and smiled faintly. If these two were willing to trust him with their well-being, nothing was going to stop him from ensuring their safety. Not Demnechi, not the Forward Fleet, not even the whole Scain fleet.

Klaara interrupted before any of them could say anything. "I'll keep you posted via data terminal if I get the chance," she said. "How much more do you need to do back there?"

"Your stabilizers and anti-gravity thrusters need a bit of fine-tuning," he said. "And if you want, I can take a look at your 8th Dimensional Drive."

"Skip it," she said. "We'll head back to Earth for a minute to switch ships, unless you have spare oxygen tanks for some reason, and then I'll take Richard and split. I'll ride your slipstream the whole way there to save power on my drive. After that... the Mitragan Province calls."

Turu nodded. "Fine. I will head back to the *Victoria* and meet you on Earth – near your departure site?"

"Fine."

Turu kicked back toward the airlock, snagging his helmet from a rack nearby and shoving it over his head. Hopefully, Klaara and Richard would be able to generate a good turnout. With an army of Heil on their side, things would definitely be looking up.

He stepped into the airlock and sealed it. His eyes flashed behind his helmet. Once they engaged the Forward Fleet, there was no turning back. He knew it. But there was no way he was going to let Earth get toasted because the Mindbank held some mystery grudge.

Chapter 51

ERROR: DATA PAD #925410053 NOT FOUND. ROUTING SYSTEM LOCATED. FILES
FORWARDED TO SHIP :VICTORIA: DATA TERMINAL METEUSAE. NO NEW MESSAGES

The *Dirego* hummed down through the clouds, landing smoothly on the ground next to a small lake back on Earth. Turu stuck his head out of the passenger cabin, breathing through the suit's air tanks for the time being. This was a short jaunt, if that. There was no need for him to use up his protites. It was better to save them for longer excursions.

Overhead, the *Gamble* slowly descended from the heavens, hovering above the ground for a moment before one of the ports on the side opened. A figure in a gold-accented suit stood in the opening, silhouetted against the ship's interior lighting for a moment until a luminous path of light stretched from the door to the ground. Victoria walked down the light, illuminated from beneath like some kind of empyrean being, before jogging over to the Dirego. Turukaishal stepped aside to make room for her as she bounded up through the door, quickly seating herself and drawing the X-shaped harness down over her chest. "Ready!" she chirped, smiling at him.

Turu was airborne before the *Gamble* had even closed its doors, soaring back upwards through the atmosphere like a comet. Once in orbit, he docked the *Dirego* inside the *Victoria's* hangar bay, listening to the magnetic locks as they anchored the smaller ship in place, whirring and humming busily. Victoria undid her harness and jumped out of the rover, Turu following behind her a moment later. "So what's the plan?" she asked, turning towards him.

"I promised to show you Saturn, did I not?" Turu said, smiling gently. "And I keep my word."

Victoria leapt around ecstatically, cheering. Turu couldn't help his eyes from turning yellow. She was... well, there wasn't really a word for her. She, like her race, was still an infant. So very new to the cosmos and blind to everything in it, both wondrous and dangerous. Their minds fumbled in ignorance at the very concepts which had led his race to the stars millions of years ago. He felt an almost parental bond with them – that odd urge to protect and shelter these newcomers instead of destroy them. He smiled and shook her head. No – if he had his way, the humans would have a chance. Only a few select members of her species had ever been in orbit, and yet here she was, standing in the shuttle bay of a Scain Class-A Type-II Frigate, preparing to be the first human to take an up-close look at the Jovian planet.

Turu turned and walked toward the elevator. "We'll take the whole ship, not just the *Dirego*," he informed her. "I have business on Titan as well, and I would like to introduce you to some of *my* friends."

Victoria's elation faltered slightly. "Um... they're not going to... uh... try to kill me, are they?" she asked, her voice betraying her hesitation. "I mean... I'm a human and all..."

Turu placed one of his long-fingered hands on her shoulder. "No. Bandrumano and I wouldn't allow it. One or two Erythians might be a bit excitable, but certainly not to the point of harming you. If they do..." he patted his backpack, the rifle and pistol screwed in firmly. "They'll have to deal with me."

The two of them rode the elevator up to the bridge in silence. Turu seated himself behind the familiar controls, sighing contentedly. *This* was where he belonged – seated behind the consoles of his ship. Here, in his cockpit, there were no allegiances. No betrayal or treason. He wasn't a rebel or a traitor. He was a pilot, plain and simple. That's all that mattered. Out there, the differences in race didn't matter either. Alintean. Scain. Iharsh-Daraz. They were pilots. And if necessary, they could become targets in the same way he could become one to them. It all boiled down to the simple philosophy of not getting shot while making sure his opponents did.

Turu pulled away from Earth, gunning the engines and accelerating toward the gas giant. It wasn't as far away, relatively speaking, as some other journeys he'd taken. 800 million miles on average? He shrugged, settling into his seat more comfortably. He allowed the speed on his ship to climb up until he reached the 100k mark and then capped it. At this speed, he'd be there in two hours, give or take, so long as his impulse drive held. Using the 8th Dimensional Drive would cause too many problems, as he was trying to hit a target the size of a proverbial pinhead with his ship at close to ten times the speed of light. He'd just keep overshooting the planet.

"Approximately 133 minutes until arrival, Earth Time," he informed her as he engaged the autopilot and stood up, stretching his shoulders. Once they reached Saturn, the *Victoria* was programmed to scan for a safe orbit and bring them into it, holding them stable until he took control back from the passive CI running the flight protocols. "In the meantime, may I attempt to improve your suit?"

Victoria cocked her head. "Improve?"

"As I explained to Richard, these suits are meant to be shielded," he said. "However, the shielding is usually generated by drawing off about two percent of a Scain's Psionic power and amplifying it. Unfortunately... you aren't Psionic, are you? Therefore, the suit is continually trying to draw off a portion of your Psionic energy... which doesn't exist. While your suit is excellent for moving about in Zero-G environments and on Class-IV and above planets, it will not do in Class-III and below scenarios or combat."

He began to pace as he spoke, his hands twisting in the small of his back. "I was looking through older files, particularly historical ones. I found some old blueprints which may be useful. Turns out the Alinteans tried experimenting with shielding early in their history. They succeeded, and they don't have any Psionics. Now mind you, they only developed the shielding for their spacecraft – the polyform weave they use, coupled with their armor, would be too heavy with a shield capacitor and distributor units, and it would become a liability in some situations..."

Turu took a deep breath, waving a hand distractedly. "Sorry. You're probably not interested in all the minutiae. What I'm trying to say is: perhaps I can build one of the Alintean shield modules and install it in your suit. It'll work, provided I can get it built."

Victoria nodded. "Okay. What do you need?"

"Your chestpiece, for one," Turu said as he waved a hand in the general direction of the cuirass she was wearing. Victoria promptly pulled it off, handing it to the Scain. Turu looked away so she couldn't see his eyes, taking the armor from her. Staring at her while only a thin sheet of polyform separated them was making him extremely nervous. "Thank you," he said. "I will be back momentarily..." He took the cuirass down to his laboratory. Unfortunately for his focus, Victoria decided to follow him and see what he was doing.

It took him almost an hour. Turu worked at the chestpiece until his fingers felt ready to fall off, rewiring most of the inner workings and adding new components where needed. At first, the darn thing wouldn't close completely, so he had to rearrange everything and try again. And again. And again. And the whole time, Victoria stood right next to him, asking him questions about his homeworld. Or his people.

Turu wished he could have asked why she felt it necessary to stand with her chest at eye level as he stooped over his workbench. Every time he turned to grab a tool... If Richard ever found out about this, he was going to *die*.

He finally handed her cuirass back, sighing. "Alright, that should do it," he said, trying to look at the armor instead of at her. Why? Why were the Hiin this cruel? He didn't understand... perhaps delving into the information matrices would be more useful to him... he'd look into it later.

Once Victoria had the cuirass back in place, Turu felt much better about looking at her. It was hardly noticeable that he'd modified her armor – thankfully – barring a few scratches around the bolts that held the pieces together and a single switch on her shoulder. "Alright," he said, rubbing his hands together. "this switch toggles your shield," he explained. "They are designed to cling close to the polyform armor itself, providing you with an additional layer of protection. Most ballistics are repelled, barring incendiary payloads. Energeic rounds, however, are not. Against Scain weaponry, you can take heavy fire for approximately thirty seconds before your shields will fail. Once they do, you have to give them time to reactivate – probably a minute or so."

"A whole minute, huh?" she asked, flicking on the switch. A hum filled the lab, but otherwise there was no visible change. She looked briefly at her hands before turning back to the Scain. "Did it work?"

"Yes," Turu answered, surveying her shields. He could see them – a thin layer of whitish-gold light clinging to her body. "It seems so. Would you like to try out the simulator to test them?"

"Sure!" she said, grinning. "Maybe I can beat Richard!"

Ah, so there *was* a faint streak of sibling rivalry between the Sinclairs. Interesting. Turu smiled, filing the information away for future reference as he motioned to the door. He led her to the Crew Decks and powered up the simulator, drumming his fingers on the controls. He left the homunculus level low – just for starters. He wanted to see how she fought in juxtaposition with her brother.

"Which weapons do you prefer?" he wondered aloud, watching as she took up a stance in the center of the room. The first hologram appeared, and Turu sat bolt upright as Victoria drew the pistol and planted a luminous round straight through its faceless head. The next two ended similarly.

Turu watched, amused and spellbound, as Victoria continued to pop the holograms as rapidly as they appeared. She moved around the chamber, using the simulated rocks and trees for "cover" when the animations began firing back. He watched the kill counter climbing. 154… 155… 156, 157, 158…

When the simulation finally ended, he opened the door and stared at her with eyes of gold. Admiration. "I am shocked," he admitted, pointing to the computer screen he'd been sitting at. "Almost too shocked for words." The leaderboards. Richard's name was sixth on the list – not bad for someone without a shield. "Turukaishal" dominated the other positions. Except for second place. Victoria.

"Wow!" she said, allowing the pistol to retract into the pack. "I knew those lessons would come in handy!"

"Lessons?" Turu asked, perplexed. "What lessons?"

"Richard and Martin took me to a bunch of handgun safety classes, and afterward they started taking me down to the firing range and teaching me how to shoot. I did it to humor them mostly – they're so paranoid sometimes."

"Perhaps rightfully so," Turu muttered quietly, clearing the computer screen. "Either way, I am no longer worried in the least about introducing you to any other sentients in the Galaxy... well, maybe a few..."

Victoria laughed, blushing. "How much further is it?"

"If you look out the window, you will see a familiar sight," Turu hinted as he waved his hand dismissively.

Victoria ran to the window and gasped. Outside, a hazy white-gold sphere hung in the blackness of space. Massive brownish-white rings framed it as they zoomed in from overhead. Turu looked up at the scanners. "Hydrogen, helium, ammonia, methane, hydrogen deuteride and ethane... how fitting of a gas giant."

He piloted the *Victoria* manually, sweeping low and around toward a tiny haze-ball that was tidally locked around the beautiful ringed planet. "Your system," Turu said quietly as he looked at her, "is one of great beauty, and great treasures."

Victoria sighed blissfully. "I know."

Turu looked away. If only she did...

Chapter 52

ERROR: DATA PAD #925410053 NOT FOUND. ROUTING SYSTEM LOCATED. FILES FORWARDED TO SHIP :VICTORIA: DATA TERMINAL METEUSAE. NO NEW MESSAGES

Turu piloted the *Victoria* down through the hazy atmosphere of Saturn's moon, creating contrails in the nitrogen clouds before breaking through the atmospheric layer. Even below the main cloud band, the view was still tinted with brownish-orange dust, which obscured most of his vision. The craft rocked back and forth, buffeted by some of the high-altitude winds, but not enough to be dangerous.

As he descended, Turu saw the shimmering lights of a portable landing strip winking up at him. The strip had been unfolded and bolted to the ground parallel to a large lake of methane and ethane. Turu circled the area, descending slowly through the orange fog, before slowly landing on the strip. The area Bandrumano had chosen was in a basin surrounded by mountains – mere hills in some cases – with a few ponds and lakes of Titan's native liquid. Turu checked his map, correlating it with the data his ship had gleaned from Earth, and translated the names of nearby features. They were in the Xanadu region, west of Shangri-La. The landing site of the Hugyens probe.

The dust his engines had kicked up began to settle as he powered down the ship, leaving him in silence apart from the cracking of the ice beneath his landing skids. He rose, picking up a syringe and injecting his protite mixture, and checked to make sure Victoria's tanks had been filled before handing it to her. "We're here."

"Are you sure about this?" Victoria asked quietly, hesitant to get out of her chair. "What if they don't like me?"

"I'm not worried about that," Turu said, looking back at her. "For one, you're rather difficult to dislike. And if anyone does give you any problems, they will have me to contend with. You have more of a right to be here than anybody else, seeing as it is your planet in danger of being burned."

Victoria swallowed thickly before pressing her tanks to her face, inhaling the protites. She coughed a few times as her body got used to the tiny machines, but stood up a moment later. She picked up her helmet and put it on, locking it in place. It wasn't a necessity, but Turu knew why she was doing it. Sometimes, having the extra layer of the visor made the wearer feel more protected... especially in an unfamiliar territory. Stepping onto the surface of an alien world and into the presence of multiple higher lifeforms was definitely a time someone would want to feel safe.

It struck Turu that, at this moment, Victoria was standing on the same planet as the furthest exploratory probe her people had ever sent. She was so very far from home right now, and looked so out of her element even in the polyform. A quick look at his computers told him all he needed to know. They were over a 1.2 billion miles from Earth. From her home. At that moment, he had a powerful compulsion to reach over and embrace her, just to let her know she wasn't alone out here. But the reality was, she was alone. She was the only human, at least until her brother returned, on Titan.

The outer doors of his ship hissed open, revealing the orange-hued landscape of the Saturnian moon. Wind gusted through the small basin they were in, kicking up the dust and creating small eddies in the air. Far in the distance, outside the depression, he could see one of Titan's cryovolcanos belching water and ammonia from its peak – fluid brought forth from the lower levels of the Moon's strata. It poured down the side, funneling through drainage channels and out of sight. It was truly a spectacular sight to behold.

An Erythian, clad from head to toe in a polyform flight suit, was waiting for them at the bottom of the access ramp. He walked forward, saluting sharply. "Commander Turukaishal. A pleasure to meet you in person. I am Kimbo, Bordra's Vice-Commander. Command Post is this way." He paused for a moment, looking behind Turu and up the ramp as Victoria came into view. "A Vahran? Here?" he questioned.

Turu nodded, slipping back into the Galaxian language out of habit. "Yes. She is under my care, and no one is going to question it further. Are we clear?"

Kimbo saluted stiffly. "Crystal," he said. "This way, please."

Several domed structures were clustered off to one side of the landing strip, and Kimbo led them to the largest one. The others all seemed to be variants of one another: some were tall and had towers reaching up into the orange skies, while others were longer and wider. They had been put together from some kind of corrugated metal which fluttered softly in the wind, and they all shared the same curved architecture and rounded doors. Kimbo shoved his four-fingered hand against a panel next to the door and it slid open soundlessly. He motioned for them to enter before closing it behind them, remaining outside.

Inside, Victoria found herself face-to-face with three aliens. The first as an Erythian like Kimbo, his helmet tucked under his arm and revealing his lean, egg-shaped head. A pair of black, bulbous eyes glittered in their sockets, watching her with a calculating intelligence. His helmet and polyform were both black, the latter adorned with what appeared to be a lilac spiral in place of a visor. Spokes radiated out from the outer loop of the coil, reaching around the sides of the helmet. The way he stood, with his back straight and his other hand behind his back, made him look like he expected trouble from every corner of the room. He also seemed to exude an air of command and control which immediately made her want to stand up straighter as well.

The second alien looked alarmingly like a tall, tan human. He had large, almond-shaped eyes and his skin appeared to be formed from dozens of interlocking scales or plates. He leaned against the wall behind the Erythian, a small flask of amber liquid in one hand and a Data Pad in the other. He looked up and regarded her for a moment through his slitted, serpentine pupils. She met his gaze and couldn't help but shiver, but the exchange was over in a moment. He studied her for that split second as if barely taking note of her species and presence, before returning to his Data Pad. Turu had mentioned this type of alien before: a Taeski.

The third alien was another Scain – the one Turu had spoken with on his imager. Bandrumano. As soon as he realized who had entered the tent, his eyes lit up yellow and his face split into a wide smile. "Turukaishal!" the Erythian said, looking up at him. "Good to see you! How have you been? I hear you were on Earth this whole time! No wonder you never wrote!" he approached and clasped Turu's wrist, the Scain promptly doing the same. The height difference between the two was extraordinary. If Turu was nine feet, the Erythian couldn't have been more than three.

"It's good to see you again, Bordra," Turu said. "You too, Klakshan." He nodded to the Taeski in the corner, who waved his flask in greeting before giving Turu a lopsided half-smile. His teeth were almost normal, save for sharper and longer canines.

"It has been far too long since we were face-to-face, Turukaishal," Klakshan said as he pushed himself off the wall, the flask vanishing into a vest pocket. "If I may inquire, with whom have you come?"

Turu placed a comforting hand on Victoria's shoulder, guiding her forward so the three could see her. "This is Victoria Sinclair," he said.

"Oh? You brought the Vahran after all?" Bandrumano said with a smile, looking up. "Mahnyou Ji'it Tanasmas," he said, bowing slightly to Victoria.

"Uh..." she said, looking at them all in confusion. Turu looked between her and his comrades before smacking himself in the forehead.

He sighed, lowering his hand. "Bandrumano, she can't understand you. There's no translator module in her helmet. It's a custom from the medical bay." He turned and repeated this to Victoria in English, and she nodded.

Bandrumano chuckled, his eyes yellow. "Nice going, Commander. How'd you manage to forget something as important as the translator module? Have you been remembering to zip up your flight suit on the way out of the bathroom as well?"

"Stow it," Turu grumbled, his eyes pink as he marveled at his own stupidity. "If you will all grant me a moment to set the algorithms up, I can have the translator done in a moment or two.

276

Klakshan waved his hand dismissively. "Take your time. The Forward Fleet is not departing tonight, after all."

Mentioning the Fleet sobered everyone in the room. Turu's eyes hardened to black. "But we need all the time we can get nonetheless," he said. "I will return as soon as I can."

Turu and Victoria departed the building, heading back to the ship. Turu was muttering profanities at himself the whole way, still in awe at his folly. Of all the things to forget, it had to be the translator. He opened both airlocks, allowing the Titanian atmosphere to circulate in the ship. It would save them the time of having to switch protites constantly, and they would be here for a while. Not to mention he could recompress before leaving.

Without hesitation, the Scain immediately marched into the Medical Bay and drew out several translators. He cycled through them until he found the Erythian program and opened it up. He had to find out if they still had... he silently cheered to himself. There was a file in the third translator which had been designed to translate English into Galaxian. Fantastic. It would save him the trouble of having to write a whole new program (or fetch Bordra and have him do it). He opened the files and listened to the phonetics. It wasn't perfect, but she could understand what was being said. Not to mention his allies would understand her as well.

"Alright," he said, turning to her. "Please hand me your helmet for a moment." It only took him a few minutes to install the module, grumbling to himself the whole time. He had to open up the back of the helmet and hard-wire it into the integrated systems, as there wasn't a port for old Erythian translators. He flipped the helmet over, looking at it for a moment before handing it back. "Alright. Please put it on."

She slipped it on, locking it in place, and stared at him through the visor. "Vaugot ko aelau Galaxian?" Turu asked.

"No," she answered, shaking her head. Turu nodded, pleased. She had understood him. Now he needed to check the reverse. He shuffled through the drawers for a moment before producing a small cylinder about the size of a can of chewing tobacco. He knelt down, opening her helmet's faceplate without bothering to have her remove it. He slowly screwed the device into place just in front of her lips, running a wire beneath a few metal plates and attaching it to the translator module in the back. He reattached the faceplate, stepping back and giving his work a critical stare. Perfect. The helmet looked as if it had never been opened.

"Vaugot ko aelau Galaxian?" he asked again.

Turu heard two distinct voices. The first was hers, and was quieter as she answered "no". The second was the translation, which analyzed her voice and played it through the speaker on her helmet. In this case, the answer came out "keh". Turu sighed in relief. At least he wasn't going to have to teach her the language manually.

"Alright," he said in Galaxian. "Your translator is working properly. To switch it off and on, use the switch at the base of your helmet. That also shuts off the output, so no one can understand you unless they know English."

She reached up and flicked the small switch. "Say something?" she prompted, running her own test.

"Delgado melmari, meha aelau I jera," he said, feeling his eyes fighting to turn pink at his own words. He hoped the translator was truly off.

She shook her head, turning it back on. "Nope. Couldn't understand it. Okay – let's go back to your friends."

The two of them proceeded to the exit of the *Victoria* in silence, heading toward the same Command Post as before. Turu walked ahead, almost ashamed of himself after what he'd said in Galaxian. How could he have just blurted that?

He pressed the button to open the door, leading Victoria inside and closing it behind her before addressing the group. "Apologies," he said with a slight bow. "That was my oversight. We can proceed now."

Bandrumano wasted no time in picking up where he'd left off. "Mahnyou Ji'it Tanasmas," he said, bowing. Victoria looked panicked for a moment before Turu explained to her.

"Mahnyou Ji'it Tanasmas is a formal greeting with no standardized translation," he explained.

"Ah..." she said, unsure for a moment. "Mahnyou... Ji'it... Tanasmas," she tried, bowing to Bandrumano in return. The phrase didn't sound perfect, but the translators compensated for it. Her problem was hesitating between every word, making sure she had said it right. It sounded halted. Unnatural.

Bandrumano beamed from ear to ear. "Now that that's out of the way, I'm Bandrumano – Scain Rifleman and leader of Kolvaria Team. The tall, scary guy in the corner is Klakshan and the geeky one is Bordra."

'The Geeky One' gave Victoria an exasperated look, as if begging her to never call him by that title. "If Bandrumano is finished, may we proceed? I would like to work on the planning and logistics."

Chapter 53

ERROR: DATA PAD #925410053 NOT FOUND. ROUTING SYSTEM LOCATED. FILES
FORWARD TO SHIP :VICTORIA: DATA TERMINAL EPSIOLON. NO NEW MESSAGES

The table in front of the group hummed to life as Bandrumano waved a Psionic-coated hand. Five triangular segments lowered about an inch into the tabletop before twisting clockwise to reveal a gently curved dome of light. A moment later, a hologram flickered to life and displayed a representation of a planetary system. Bordra walked around the back of the hologram, staring through it. "This is the Blemdarch System: the last stop the fleet will make before it jumps to Earth," he explained. The map rotated to show a top-down view, and circular lines appeared to mark the orbits of the planets. "For the sake of the young Vahran, I will go over the composition of the system."

Victoria sat forward, watching as Bordra reached into the hologram and tapped the nearest planet. The view shifted to show a russet world with a thick brown atmosphere and high mountain ranges running from north to south. "This is Jalia," he said. "A relatively small world of no real interest." He tapped the next planet in a small mini-map in the lower corner of the table. A pockmarked world not unlike Jupiter's moon, Io, flickered into view. Klakshan kicked the table and the image clarified.

"This is Mamant," Klakshan said before Bordra could thank him. "A highly radioactive world which has lost its atmosphere after centuries of decay and solar flare bombardment. Whereas Jalia's magnetosphere can repel a solar flare, more or less, Mamant has been effectively seared. The only activity on the surface now are volcanoes which spew liquid mercury onto the planet's surface, resulting in the reflectivity you see in the hologram."

"Thank you, Klakshan," Bordra said before addressing Victoria. "It is unlikely that our fight will last long enough to become a ground war, but if I am wrong, we will not be landing here. Mamant is—"

"—a highly toxic and radiative death trap which only Iharsh-Daraz and Taeski can tolerate, and the latter only for a short period of time," Klakshan finished.

Bordra shot him an annoyed look, but nodded nonetheless. "Yes. How do you know so much about Mamant?"

"A story for another day," Klakshan said, reaching out and pressing the mini-map before selecting the third world. "Continue, Commander."

An enormous green planet, not unlike Jupiter, filled the screen. Bordra cleared his throat. "Entibaa is the first of the gas giants, and has the largest gravity well. Ships which stray too close will be pulled down inside it and crushed. Entibaa's core is comprised of lead, nickel and uranium, making it extremely dense and active. We will be avoiding it if we can, although if we get the opportunity to drag anyone close enough, I hope we can."

Turu pressed the mini-map and selected the next world – a huge blue gas giant. "If I may handle this one, Commander?" he asked, waiting for Bordra's nod before continuing. "Naisaari is a gas giant with moons which were mined to dust for iskindite, palladium, malkathite and uranium deposits, along with gold and iron. The moons were mined out, leaving only carbon and silicon traces which were then drawn into Naisaari, so none remain. Unfortunately, the nuclear drills which were used have left belts of radiation in the vacuum near Naisaari, which can interfere with machinery and navigation controls."

"So why take a fleet through here?" Victoria asked. "There's nothing here!"

"Exactly!" exclaimed Bordra, pointing one of his fingers at her. "Demnechi isn't an idiot... well, he is... but he's a cunning idiot. If he took a fully armed fleet through an occupied system, everyone would know or suspect something was going on. Therefore, he's using a remote, derelict system which has been isolated from the rest of the Galaxy due to disuse and resource depletion. Nobody goes to Blemdarch anymore. Well, nobody sane. Turukaishal was part of the guard detail watching over the mining operations at Naisaari and a few near Kashelion, which is why he's one of the few who can confirm the radiation zone around the planet."

"Think of it like... ting to sneak out of your home," Klakshan said. "If you attempted to walk out the front door, odds are everyone would know you were leaving. But if you climbed out of a window, you have a better chance. Demnechi isn't so much climbing out a window as he is digging out through a basement, but the logic still stands. If anyone knows he is heading to Blemdarch, which I doubt, they will likely assume he will just jump to one of the far-flung Scain colony worlds, the closest being Horakameston."

"Which, by the way, is where I was born," Turu interjected.

Victoria nodded. "Okay. I get it now... please continue."

Bordra called up the next planet – another gas giant. This one was orange, its cloudy surface ripped apar my numerous red storms in the gas belts. "Kashelion, despite its appearance, is the most stable of the worlds in this system," Bordra said. "There are no obscene gravity wells, or hostile radiation zones, and there has even been Senate chatter about building a station near it. Fat lot of good that does us now, but it's in the plans. We will probably be engaging the enemy near Kashelion for the sole reason that it is large enough to give us cover and has several dozen tiny asteroids orbiting it, as well as six moons, which can give us more cover and a place to force the enemy into a ground fight if we have to."

Turu nodded. "Watch out for Kretus," he said. "That moon is home to a creature we called the *Palithe-Ethraega*, or the Diamond Talon. We encountered it when I was here on security detail, and it managed to tear apart dozens of convoys, but we never actually saw it. It's also attributed to approximately 1,700 Scain and 50 Scion deaths. If we get forced down into a ground conflict, avoid Kretus."

"Noted," Bordra said, already going after the mini-map again and selecting the next world in the system – a hot looking red planet with thick gray clouds and many active volcanoes. "This is Sernomir. Provided we all survive this, which I have no doubts we will, this will be our regrouping point. Damaged ships will also fall back to Sernomir and mask themselves in the heat aura. The volcanoes make it too hot to land, at least for very long, but are an excellent way to mask heat output. The planet glows like a miniature sun in thermal vision, and ships clustered around it are almost invisible."

The next world he called up was miniscule in comparison and looked similar to one of Saturn's moons. "Dosya," Klakshan said idly, "is a ball of frozen rock, ice and methane. Hardly a vacation destination, and likely to be overlooked in the battle due to its tiny size and low surface temperatures." He punctuated his statement with a swig from his flask.

The final planet was Fenyss, which Bordra handled. "Fenyss is the coldest world in the system. The atmosphere snap-freezes if any other planet blocks sunlight to it, and the air is cold enough to jam guns and even lock up afterburners. There are blizzards going at almost all times, some of them with hurricane-force winds. We are going to do our best to avoid Fenyss, especially in the event of ground combat."

The map shifted, and several dozen holograms of Scain ships winked into existence above Naisaari. The hologram flickered again, and Klakshan repeated his solid kick to the underside. It took three this time before the image cleared up. "Based on the angle of approach," Bandrumano said solemnly, "we predict that the Forward Fleet will enter the system here, or very close to it. The smaller ships will likely come first, followed by the *Trident*. We have a chance to blow some of the escort craft out of the sky before they know what's going on, and with the gunship still on the way they will be mostly helpless."

"An admirable plan," Klakshan said, "but there are far more of them than there are us." He rotated the image. "As far as this simulation indicates, we are outnumbered by a minimum of five-to-one. If we were fighting solely on the ground, these odds would not perturb me. In space, however, we are at a severe disadvantage. The vacuum does not take prisoners, and all the foresight in the world will not help us against a veritable wall of incoming fire."

"Klaara'Doran kan Mitragan and Richard Sinclair – the other Vahran – are both en route to secure more troops," Turu interjected. "I expect to hear from them shortly, and I can provide the exact number of troops then."

Bordra drummed his fingers on the table before speaking. "For the moment, let's plan that they don't return at all. I want to know our odds in the event of their failure."

He rotated the map again. "We will enter here; the dark side of Kashelion. Keeping ourselves in the shadows will render us invisible to anything but a high-intensity scan, which won't be on any of the smaller ships." The map, possibly hearing him, produced a series of holograms in the shadow of the orange planet.

Bordra pressed a button, and the two groups of hologram ships moved toward one another. Their side immediately picked off several of the escort craft, only to be annihilated by the lasers from the *Trident* as it emerged from Dark Space. Bordra groaned. "Alright. Redo. We need a way to keep that gunship busy."

"What's our largest ship?" Turu asked.

"That would be my ship," Klakshan said. "The Pinnacle is a Taeski Tactical Frigate: 1,500 macrounits from end to end. I've done personal modification on it, and it is quite robust. Not enough to win in a knock down, drag out fight with the Trident though."

Turu moved one of their ships – the Pinnacle – around the opposite side of Kashelion and into full view of the enemy forces. "The Pinnacle has stronger shields than most of the Scain craft," he explained, "so it can take a few shots. It's also faster than the Trident, isn't it?"

Bordra checked his Data Pad, comparing the two ship models. "Without taking any modifications into account, yes... but not by much. The *Pinnacle* is a Taeski Tactical Frigate, which relies on agility and speed rather than firepower or defense."

"Let me worry about that," Klakshan said. "What are you planning?"

Turu continued. "If we have the Pinnacle draw the Trident's fire for a while, and maybe some attention from the rest of the Fleet, we could hit them in the back. Pinch them."

"But the *Pinnacle* would be as good as lost, wouldn't it?" Victoria asked, looking at the maps. "It's going to have the whole Fleet focused on it."

"And we cannot destroy the *Trident* just by shooting it in the back. Too much armor. It is an SCS-Class Gunship. It can take anything apart from a fusion bomb or a supernova..." he took a long swig of his drink. "Good point though."

Turu sighed, massaging the corners of his forehead. The Trident was a massive problem no matter how he looked at it. One way or another, they had to blow that thing up.

"Could someone get on board and blow up the engines or something?" Victoria asked, looking at the picture of the ship on Bordra's Data Pad. It was huge and blue-gray, with a body silhouette something like a stingray.

"Possible but unlikely," Bandrumano said. "There are twenty entrances to the ship, and most of them are on the upper or middle decks. Getting from these access ports down to the engine room would be a miracle, as you'd have to fight everyone and everything in there every step of the way."

"Detonating the engines would be another miracle," Klakshan added. "Another problem requiring a fusion bomb. You have to somehow crack the casing and overload the core. So how are we going to not only find a fusion bomb, but get it into the ship? The only other entrances are the emergency escape pods, which are sealed until a pod launches."

Turu snapped his fingers before calling up an image of the Trident's inner workings. "Here's a thought," he said. "The energy for the main antimatter cannon is channeled down this pathway. That path leads right into the engine room, where the power is then routed directly from the main reactor. If we could throw a fusion bomb down the mouth of the cannon—"

"Not possible," Bordra cut in. "You would need to have that bomb moving at ridiculous speeds."

"Why?" asked Victoria. "Looks like a straight shot to me."

"The laser is kept closed by five massive lids. These open much like the petals on a flower," Klakshan said in his honeyed voice. His deeper voice made him sound despondent. "These only open when the ship is about to fire. Once they are open, there is a five-second window before the main laser fires. You cannot traverse that distance in three seconds unless you are moving at astronomical speeds."

Turu ran the math in his head, but Bordra beat him to it. "15,000 units per second," he said. "How would you get a fusion bomb moving that fast?"

"Yeah, it's not possib...oh..." Turu said, suddenly growing quiet. He looked away, his eyes following the swirling dust outside one of the windows. "My ship."

"What was that, Turu?" Bandrumano asked, looking at his friend with grayish eyes. Concern. "You alright?"

"My ship," Turu clarified. "The *Victoria*. It has fusion drives larger than most – remember? It's a custom. If I cracked the engine casing on my own ship and wired a bomb into the reactor, it would have the same—if not larger—power of a fusion bomb."

Bordra slammed his fist down on the table, causing the image to flicker. "You are NOT doing a suicide run down the throat of the *Trident*!" he thundered, momentarily seeming much larger than he was. "There has to be an alternative."

"There is," Klakshan said, "but I will broach it only as a last resort. For now, we should assume Turu's plan is the best we have. Tell me, what other complications would arise from his plan?"

"Accelerating Turu's ship to the required speeds," Bandrumano said, wincing. "His engines have a maximum safe speed of 10,000 units per second... 12,000 at maximum before the ship starts tearing itself apart. The plating just isn't meant to hold together under that kind of strain."

Victoria was looking at Turu in shock. The Scain didn't seem remotely worried. In fact, he had suggested the plan as if his own life meant nothing. She wanted to say something. To interject. But her throat seemed to have closed up.

"Multiple slingshot orbits around the various gas giants, making use of Naisaari's radiation zone and Entibaa's gravity well."

The group looked at Bordra, who was sullenly looking at the system map again. "If he started back at Entibaa and spun around it several times while burning his engines at maximum capacity before doing the same at Naisaari and eventually Kashelion would put him at the required speeds. Theoretically, he could achieve speeds up to 20,000 units per second doing this. But there are so many dangers and variables... what if he hits something? A spare piece of wreckage from a nuclear drill? A fragment of a moon? One of Kashelion's major moons? We wouldn't even have a body to bury at those speeds! Not to mention we'd have to figure out how to get the *Trident* lined up with Turukaishal's orbit..."

"That's easy," Klakshan said. "If I fly the *Pinnacle* towards Kashelion, aiming to orbit counterclockwise if Turukaishal is orbiting clockwise, the Trident could be lured into pursuing me. It'd be directly in the line of fire."

"And you would be an easy target for its antimatter cannon," Turu said.

Klakshan shrugged. "At least we can be guaranteed the ship will open the cannon doors for you."

"You could die!" Turu retorted.

"And you *would*!" Klakshan returned. "You are strong, Turukaishal, but I doubt even you could withstand your own ship exploding around you with force comparable to a small star!"

"Really? Oh, how stupid of me, I must have forgotten than I'm not immortal," Turu said dryly. "I'm thinking about it, okay? This is too delicate for an autopilot job, but I'm not exactly planning on going out in a fiery blast by flying it all the way inside. Hiin, I get nervous thinking about piloting a ship with a bomb for an engine in the first place."

"Well, at least I know you've got some sense," Bandrumano said, his face pinched. "You're that committed to this? You're willing to risk blowing yourself to pieces for those Vahran?"

Turu's answer was swift. "No. Not for "those Vahran". For the two I care about, and for the future of their race. If the human race can produce individuals like Richard and Victoria, it can produce more. They, and others like them, deserve a future on their own planet... not a doomed existence like the Arsu. If I have to sacrifice myself for that, so be it."

The room was eerily silent, the three assembled aliens staring at Turu in a mixture of surprise and shock. Bandrumano's eyes flickered with gold. Admiration. He opened his mouth to speak, but Victoria spoke first. "Could you remotely control the ship?"

Turu pondered this for a moment. "It would be possible, but the only kind of remote I have is not that strong. I would still need to be on the *Victoria* to make such precise adjustments."

He sighed. He didn't want to die. He wanted to stay alive to reap the rewards of this battle. But if the only way to victory was to die, then so be it. Vahran deserved the future they could still achieve. And he'd be damned if his selfishness was going to stand in their way. But Victoria's statement had given him an idea. Maybe there was some hope.

And, as an Alintean had once told him: *"So long as life remains, so too does hope. So long as hope remains, an ending has yet to be written."*

Chapter 54

ERROR: DATA PAD #925410053 NOT FOUND. ROUTING SYSTEM LOCATED. FILES FORWARDED TO SHIP :VICTORIA: DATA TERMINAL METEUSAE.

BEGIN MESSAGE

LOCATION: Chindrus, Amara District

TIME: 10/22 Local Time

MESSAGE: Bandrumano has told me about what has happened. I am trying everything I can on this end. The files are switched – hopefully it puts the pressure on the Forward Fleet. They're calling it something else now, by the way. They call it the Cleansing Fleet. It's a smaller detachment, but they are still taking that gunship of theirs.

Turukaishal, after all this is over you will probably never be able to return to Chindrus again without being killed. I... never mind. Good luck out there. Show them why you're one of the best! For what it's worth, I believe in you. In all of you. Tell Bandrumano to be safe – he isn't answering his Data Pad right now.

-Kridoria

Turu crouched in the shuttle bay, his eyes narrowed as he glared at the *Dirego*. He'd ripped most of the metal plating free from beneath the cockpit and allowed the wiring to spill forth across the deck. Much like the *Dirego*, the floor beneath his feet had been torn up in several places as well, cables and wires jutting up through the ground like synthetic roots. He grumbled, leaning forward and continuing his work on the smaller craft.

Bandrumano paused in surprise, standing in the doorway before clearing his throat. "You okay in there?"

Turu grunted something unintelligible from within the Rover's underbelly. Bandrumano waited until the other Scain had removed his head before repeating the question. Turu couldn't meet his eyes. "I am fine."

"It's that Vahran girl, isn't it?" Bandrumano asked, sitting down on a stack of crates in the corner, resting his elbows on his first knees and his chin on his hands. "She means something to you, am I right?"

Turu paused, having returned his head to the interior of the *Dirego*. He slowly removed it and looked back at his friend. His eyes were a hot pink, which elicited a chuckle from Bandrumano. "I figured as much."

"I don't even know what's going on!" Turu finally blurted. He abandoned cannibalizing the *Dirego* and began to pace back and forth in the bay, wringing his hands. "Ever since I met her things have been... awkward. When she smiles, I feel happy. When she's sad I feel the mood in the room plummet. When she's scared I feel..." he waved his arms, his mouth opening and closing as he tried to find the right words. He gave up and lifted a box, his Psionics flaring, and hurled it against the far wall with a frustrated growl. The metal casing blew open along one side, and reactor screws spilled across the floor.

"Hey! Relax!" Bandrumano yelped, jumping off the crates in surprise.

Turu relaxed slightly, taking a deep breath and dropping his arms to his sides. His eyes flickered through a myriad of colors before settling on a moody shade of blue. "Bandrumano, I don't know what's going on anymore..." he admitted. "Everything's just so out of control. Things are hectic enough. If I only knew what was causing these... sensations... maybe I could stop them."

The other Scain shook his head. "Turukaishal, you're one of the most brilliant pilots in the Fleets – maybe even in the Galaxy. This should be easy to do. Here, watch this."

He began to walk back and forth, tapping his chin as he spoke. "If Victoria wanted to go to... Remengard! If she wanted to go to Remengard, what would you do?"

Remengard was a Class-V garden planet, lush and undisturbed. The Senate had written laws for the preservation and care of garden worlds, and Remengard had been one of the first Scain worlds to be approved for the title. Galactic law forbade colonization, but the Senate and the Scain Empire had spent billions of credits to turn it into the equivalent of a public park. Turu blinked in surprise at the question, but answered nonetheless. "I would take her there."

"Okay," Bandrumano continued as he studied the eviscerated corpse of what had once been a Rover. "If she was upset or despondent, what would you do?"

"I would try to comfort her, obviously," Turu said in confusion. What exactly was Bandrumano playing at? This was not just some simple questionnaire, he could sense that much, but he didn't know what hihs friend was aiming for. "Go on."

Bandrumano shook his head. "Turu, your aura is shifting dangerously. I know *exactly* what's plaguing you, but I'm almost afraid to tell you." He looked around slowly, extending his Psionics and checking for anyone else nearby. Just in case, he reached up and flicked off his translator. "Aelau meha es kora," he said in Galaxian.

Turu's eyes turned pink, the Scain recoiling as if struck. "You're full of dung," he said, watching as Bandrumano switched his translator back on, laughing heartily. Hopefully there were no Erythians within earshot who were eavesdropping. "And if you're trying to keep a secret, maybe you should speak in *Scain*," he added.

"What for? The only person I'm trying to keep it from only speaks English."

Turu ground his teeth but said nothing, eventually sighing. He had a sneaky suspicion that it was true. He'd admitted it to her face, although she didn't exactly know it. Yet. The last time he'd tried to keep a secret from her, she'd been conscious enough to remember it. Go figure. His eyes turned pink at the memory.

Bandrumano stared at his friend, curious about the pink eyes and malleable aura. His eyes widened, turning orange. "You didn't... you haven't... not with... wait..." he scratched his head, studying his friend.

"NO!" Turu blurted, waving his hands hastily, his aura tripling in embarrassed intensity. "Nothing like that! She had hypothermia and I was trying nerve stimulation... but humans are different and I grabbed the wrong nerve..." he trailed off into silence. Just when he'd been able to put the memory behind him, or at least compartmentalize it, Bandrumano had to go dig it up again. Providence had a sadistic streak and a vendetta against him.

Bandrumano roared with laughter. "Are you serious!?" he asked, his eyes almost painfully yellow with amusement and mirth. "Oh for the love of the Hiin, Turukaishal, this is why I hang around with you."

Turu stuck his head back in the *Dirego,* trying desperately to find the steering controls. Whoever had designed the Rover needed to be shot... and he'd do it too, if anyone ever invented time travel. He muttered a few curses. Bandrumano and his strange sense of humor were throwing off his concentration.

"Seriously, though," Bandrumano continued. His voice was muffled due to Turu's current position. "I think you should go for it. Kridoria may be the best genetic match to you, but she's not going to fill that gap in your life." His voice, for once, had no traces of amusement or mockery to it. He was completely serious.

Turu crawled back out, reaching for a bolt remover. "What gap?" He was back beneath the *Dirego* before he heard the answer clearly. Bandrumano's voice carried through the metal and wiring, though.

"Everyone needs someone special," his friend said. Turu heard him sit back down. "With us Scain, it's always the same: you get paired with your genetic match, and are bonded for the next few centuries. Usually unhappily, because apparently hating someone means you're genetically compatible or something equally stupid. But every now and again it happens that someone gets lucky and finds a partner they DON'T want to throw from Chindrus to Nihran."

"Your point?" Turu asked as he climbed back out and aimed a kick at the *Dirego*. Stupid thing. He was starting to develop a dislike for Rovers. Unlike starships, where every cable was labeled in easy to understand words like "Power Core, Cable 1", Rovers were labeled wonderful things like "ROV/TH1/A". For the love of the Hiin... still, it looked like he was making progress. He'd just have to finish this project before their attack and he'd be good to go. Maybe.

"My point," Bandrumano continued, "is that it's good that you're turning into one of those cases. You're not going to fall into that trap of just believing that your genetic match is the only one out there. Your heart is stronger than your brain – not smarter," he quickly amended as Turu gave him a sharp glare. "I said *stronger*."

Turu relaxed slightly. "Can you get to the point? I have a lot of work to do."

"Okay, fine you asked for it..." he brought his head next to Turu's. "You. Love. Victoria. You named your ship after her, for the Hiin's sake, and you're willing to blow yourself up for her planet. They just don't make guys like you anymore, you know that? She'd damn lucky. If Kridoria had any sense she'd dump that little position on Chindrus and get over here."

Turu said nothing. It would explain a lot of the sensations... the tightening chest, that yearning when separated from her... his eyes turned pink. "Oh Hiin..." he moaned, allowing his head to lean against the cool metal of the *Dirego*. What was left of it, anyway...

"Yeah, see?" Bandrumano said as he placed a hand on Turu's shoulder. "Do not look so depressed, though. If I were into aliens I might've gone after her myself. Not a bad catch."

Turu laughed mirthlessly. "This one is going to take a long time to process," he said, leaning back. His project with the *Dirego* suddenly seemed miles away, and his head felt as though it had been enclosed in a thick fog. Since when had a simple realization had this much power over him?

"I'll bet," Bandrumano told him as he hopped out of the shuttle bay. "Either way, if you want to chat, I'll be in the Mess Hall – drop by later if you're hungry. They're expecting me over there to supervise the integration of my team, but I told them I wanted to make sure you were okay first. So I do have to get going. Hope to see you soon, Turukaishal." And then he was gone, his footsteps crunching over the thin layer of ice on the dusty ground.

Turu decided that it sounded like a good idea. Food would definitely be a welcome treat. But first he had to clear the cobwebs from his mind. Realizations were all fine and good, but he still had to work—*work,* not pine after—this girl for... he checked the pocketwatch she had given him... six days. After that, he could consider a relationship.

If they both survived.

Chapter 55

ERROR: DATA PAD #925410053 NOT FOUND. ROUTING SYSTEM LOCATED. FILES
FORWARDED TO SHIP :VICTORIA: DATA TERMINAL METEUSAE.

BEGIN MESSAGE

LOCATION: Broken Verge, Refueling Station

TIME: 23/40 Station Time

*MESSAGE: Just left the Mitragan Province. Got a bunch of recruited help too. Factor in 12
Heil Frigates, 10 Heil Lancers, 8 Heil Destroyers, 6 Heil Carriers, 4 Heil Assault Craft and
10 Attack Drones. Not a bad haul, eh? Should improve our chances. Still, it was a bit of a
close call. I don't think the Mitragan Hierarchs were too glad to see me – don't forget I'm
apparently guilty of assisting the murder of their boss. You can thank Richard for most of
this – I was ready to just toss in the flag. I'm en route to your little base, and should be
there soon. Get ready to brief a lot of bloodthirsty Heil, though.*

-Klaara

Turu almost leapt up and danced for joy. Fifty additional ship? Frigates and Destroyers?
This was the best present he could have ever asked for. This was like... he couldn't even
think of an accurate comparison. He quickly forwarded the message to Bordra before
stepping away from Terminal Epsiolon and staring around. His craft was now officially
listed in the resources manifest as the bomb. All he had to do was arm the thing. That,
of course, would wait until right before the mission. If he rigged it wrong and it
detonated here on Titan, the result would probably waste the entire base. Heck, there
was no "probably" involved. This part of the Xanadu region would be reduced to a
smoldering crater.

Victoria poked her head into the cabin. "Hey Turu?" she asked, walking over to him.
"Can I ask you something?"

Turu looked back at her, blinking in mild confusion. "Of course," he said. Something was
wrong with her aura. She looked sad. Despairing. "What's wrong?" he pulled out one of
the seats at the weapons terminal for her.

"Are you really planning on blowing yourself up over this?" she asked him worriedly as
she sat down. "I mean... well..."

Turu smiled gently, reaching out and touching her forearm. "Not anymore," he reassured her. "But please, do not tell anyone else that. I have a plan, though."

Looking around to make sure they weren't overheard (although it was unlikely many of the aliens understood English) Victoria leaned in closer to Turu. "What's the plan?" she asked, taking his bony hand in hers and squeezing gently. Turu felt a tingle shoot up his arm. He forced himself to remain sitting.

"Essentially, to proceed as normal. I am on the manifest as the bomb, and the general plan is to throw the *Victoria* into the *Trident*'s maw. However, during the jump to the Blemdarch System, I am going to relocate to the *Dirego*. I've wired it to the *Victoria* – I can control the ship from the Rover. I'm going to go through the plan as normal, but uncouple at the last possible moment and get clear of the blast radius. I'll then be picked up by Bandrumano and we'll proceed from there."

"I like that plan better," Victoria said, running her thumb over his skin. The electric sensation intensified. Turu turned his hand around and wrapped it around hers, stilling her motion. She looked down at his large hand wrapped around hers and smiled. "I never thought I'd be sitting here," she said as she looked around her before lowering her voice, her gaze returning to his. "I'm scared."

Turu's heart gave a lurch. "Don't tell anyone, but so am I. I'm scared to death. I've seen what the *Trident* is capable of. But you have a choice. You don't have to come along with us. I can have Bordra or Klakshan take you back to Earth, and we can regroup after—"

"No!" she said, shaking her head so vehemently that her expression was hidden by her hair. "Turu, no. I'm not going to just run away!"

"It's not running, it's..." Turu couldn't find any words. His brain, and subsequently his mouth, had decided to stop working. He took a deep breath and forced his body to obey. "Victoria, I want you to be safe," he said, feeling his eyes start shifting towards pink. He was just going to have to get used to it.

Victoria smiled softly at him. "Turu, you're sweet, you know that?" she asked, squeezing his hand. "But that's my planet out there... with my other brother and my friends and everything I've ever known on it. I have to be here. It just wouldn't be right any other way. I have to see first-hand that this plan succeeded."

The Scain now *knew* that his eyes were fast approaching pink, but he found himself uncaring of the fact. He reached out, embracing her with his thin, skeletal arms. He drew her against his chest as he'd often seen Alinteans (and Vahran, for that matter) do. He held her close, unwilling to let her go for a moment until he remembered how to use his arms and slowly released her, coughing self-consciously. "Um... I'm sorry..." he muttered. He knew what Bandrumano had said was likely true, but that didn't mean he was going to start losing control over his body.

Victoria smiled at him, her face radiating happiness, and Turu decided to shelve the problem. Indefinitely. It didn't matter anymore. "Victoria, I want you to listen to me. You, Richard and Klaara are going to be in the *Gamble*. I'll be here, on the *Victoria*. If anything goes wrong, you are to immediately flee, understood? I cannot risk losing you."

"But what about you?" she asked, her eyes widening. "You'll need all the firepower you can get!"

"We do," he acknowledged. "But we will make do with one less ship if it guarantees your safety. Please, just trust me. I promise it will work out."

The way he said it made Victoria believe that it would. Turu looked so confident in their plan, so motivated, that she had a hard time understanding how anything could go wrong. He looked at her with those impossible eyes of his, a small smile playing about the bottom of his narrow face.

"Alright," she said as she stood up. "Anyway, I was also coming to tell you that Borda wants to meet to practice some flight maneuvers. He's gone and set up this elaborate practice ring just beyond the Kuiper Belt."

"Excellent," Turu said as he stood up, swiftly snagging his helmet from next to the pilot's chair. "It's about time we got off this rock! I was starting to feel lightheaded from all the orange."

Victoria laughed, the sound better than any music the Vahran could come up with. He found himself longing for it, strangely. Perhaps he'd still be able to remotely access the Vahran data matrices and get his hands on some.

He followed Victoria outside, literally running into Borda on the way out of the airlock. The Erythian stumbled back, looking at the two briefly before relaxing somewhat. "I was just coming to get you. Bandrumano said I might want to knock first. What did he mean?"

"That Hiin-damned..." Turu seethed, looking around for his friend. "Nothing, Borda. I hear you have a practice run set up for us?"

The Erythian nodded. "Holograms of all the ships, friendly and otherwise, not counting ourselves. I've taken into account the fifty Heil ships you notified me of. They're arriving tomorrow – I contacted this Klaara. Violent specimen, she is." The sentences came out all in one breath, as was typical of an Erythian.

"You're telling me," Turu muttered. He still seemed to be looking for Bandrumano.

"In any case, we should get moving. Please power up your craft. Make sure your protite solution is in working order too – can't have you dropping like a fly in the middle of battle, can we?"

"No, I suppose not," Turu said with a dry smile. He couldn't wait to get into the pilot's seat. There was no need to test out the *Dirego*'s control abilities – he knew firsthand how well those worked. During the pseudo-night Borda and Bandrumano had imposed, he'd taken the *Victoria* on a low-altitude test run. Seeing that escape velocity on Titan was so low he could fly with paper wings, Turu had no trouble in steering via the *Dirego*. It worked like a dream.

"Victoria," he said. "I want you to wait here during the test. Monitor the base along with a few of Bandrumano's security detail."

"I'm not a little kid," she reminded him, pouting inside her helmet. "What if I want to come along?"

"I need to keep a few hands in the base in case Klaara and Richard arrive early," he told her. "They shouldn't be too much longer, and I'd rather Richard saw firsthand that you were intact before he tries to fillet me with his sword, alright?" It was a downright lie, but a convincing one. Thank the Hiin for closed-face helms, or she would have been able to read him like a book.

"Alright," she pouted, turning and walking toward one of the structures. "But you be careful."

"It's a simulation," Turu said in exasperation, "how much trouble can I possibly get into?"

"You could feasibly collide with another ship, an asteroid, or rogue Outer Solar System Object and explode," Borda offered unhelpfully. Turu gave him a glare of disbelief.

"Whose side are you on?" the Scain asked incredulously.

Bordra saluted, attempting to correct himself. "Although with your skill and prowess, Commander, the odds are incredibly slim. All-in-all, you couldn't be safer."

Turu massaged his head in irritation, turning around and striding back into his ship. A practice run would do him some good – he had to get off of Titan and focus his mind somewhere else.

Chapter 56

ERROR: DATA PAD #925410053 NOT FOUND. ROUTING SYSTEM LOCATED. FILES FORWARDED TO SHIP :VICTORIA: DATA TERMINAL METEUSAE. NO NEW MESSAGES

Turu dragged himself back into the encampment on Titan, wanting nothing more than to throw himself into his pod and sleep for the rest of his life. Bordra, the little sadist, had pushed them through nine runs of the simulator. After a close call with an asteroid, he'd also rounded everyone up and moved them over to a nearby star with a few gas giants for better practice. It had been utterly exhausting, and even though he hadn't even come close to the required 15,000 units per second, screaming around a ringed gas giant at 7,000 units per second was still dizzying and a surefire way to make him sick.

The Heil group from Sovereign had arrived, he noted. There were several dozen ships all over the camp, and Turu couldn't look one way or another without seeing the patchwork sapients walking in every direction or tussling on the ground. Bordra quickly formed them into some semblance of order and began a quick headcount. If the lineup was any indicator, it wasn't just Heil that had come along. Included with them were ten Iharsh-Daraz, four Ene'tami, a lone Rhurni and a small group of Zyzyts which were having a difficult time holding still.

Turu was grateful to see the Zyzyt along. They were astounding medics, and he'd heard rumors of people losing sixty percent of their bodies or more and still being treated. Their technology was remarkable, and their understanding of genomes, cloning, medicine, viruses and bacteria could only be rivaled by the ancient and long-dead Ragans. Having the small group present was an immense comfort should anyone be injured.

"Listen up!" Bordra barked, watching as the assembled aliens stood at attention; even the ten foot Iharsh-Daraz. Turu paused, watching momentarily, and had to admit he was impressed. He hadn't seen Bordra personally in years, and it was almost shocking to see how much authority his voice carried. Zyzyts and Erythians had been engaged in an unspoken cold war for the past four billion years. To see them listen to Bordra was nothing shy of miraculous, not to mention a very good sign. Turu continued towards the Mess Hall, listening to his Erythian friend briefing their new troops. After the training that gray psychopath had put him through, he was starving.

Just as he was about to press the button to open the door, it hissed open on its own. He found himself staring into a familiar pair of whitish, luminous eyes. "Klaara'Doran kan

Mitragan," he acknowledged, bowing slightly to her. "I am truly in your debt for bringing so many capable troops. Without you, we—"

"Oh shut up and skip the formalities," she said, pounding his shoulder with a lopsided grin and dragging him inside the mess hall. "I'm no longer 'kan Mitragan' anyway."

"What?" Turu asked, his eyes betraying his shock. "What—how did that happen?"

"Remember my letter?" she asked, releasing his shoulder as the doors closed quietly behind them. "They weren't too pleased to have an accused murderer cropping up on their doorstep." She shrugged it nonchalantly, although her aura betrayed the fact that it bothered her. "I told them I was innocent. Richard tried to corroborate it. They wouldn't listen to him because he was a Vahran, and decided to cop an attitude with him. One thing led to another after that. The short explanation ends with us getting the troops, but I lost my clan affiliation. Not quite in that order, and there was a lot of other crap going on, but you get the general picture."

Turu stared at her in surprise. "You... lost your affiliation?" he knew this happened from time to time with the Heil, but had never known the exact meaning of it.

"The idiots decided to kick me out of the clan. I'm just "Klaara'Doran" for now, until I find something else to tie myself to. Or some—never mind." She looked out the window. "So, how're things going here?"

"Grueling," Turu said as he reached one of the dispensers, fiddling with it as he spoke. "Bordra is putting us through our paces as if the world was ending tomorrow. Don't even say it, by the way." He gave the machine a solid kick. "And it seems someone has drained the food supplies..." he skulked over to another one and this time succeeded in obtaining a tube of flavored nutrient paste out of it. He bit the end off and began to suck the bland, colorless fluid from inside.

"So, when're we actually going to give this jerk the boot?" Klaara asked, hopping up on one of the tables and crossing her legs. "I hope it's soon: he's one big headache and I see a whole ton of medicine around this camp." She grinned at him. "And after all the crap I just had to deal with on Sovereign, I pity whoever gets in my way."

"Good, because you'll be guarding Richard and Victoria with your ship. The two of you will be withdrawing to Sernomir and hiding in the heat haze until the battle ends, for better or worse. And to answer your question, it's in four Earth Days. Ninety-six Earth Hours, if you'd rather have smaller increments."

Klaara opened her mouth to protest, but the door opened and cut her off. "Turu." The Scain turned at the sound of his name and found himself staring across the empty room at Victoria's brother, who looked as intimidating as ever in his hat and coat. "How's it going?"

"Acceptably," he answered, removing the tube from his mouth. That must have been a wonderful sight for the man: a Scain giving him a surprised look with a tube of nutrients hanging out of his teeth. "We are ready to attack in four days. I was just telling Klaara."

The Heil jumped off the table and sashayed over to Richard, throwing a comradely arm around him. "This guy," she said, jerking a thumb at Richard, is the probably the one you want to be thanking for the troops."

Turu looked at Richard in confusion. Richard rolled his eyes. "It was no big deal," he muttered.

"I was ready to give up," Klaara explained to Turu. "Hierarchs wouldn't listen to me and told me I had five days to pack my stuff and get gone. But not only did Richard come along and give me a pep talk, he went on to walk right into the Hierarchs' Tower, pummel three guards and then give those windbags a verbal lashing followed by a physical one."

"You beat up the Hierarchs?" Turu asked in open-mouthed surprise. "No way! Not in a million—"

"I challenged one of them to a Straight Duel, No Arts," Richard said. "He was surprised that I knew how to challenge him, but accepted. Said he was going to put me in my place, and told me we wouldn't use a sword. Instead, he used one of those rocket spears."

Klaara laughed, nodding. "I almost couldn't take the humor," she said. "They knew he had a sword, so they thought that was all he could use. Imagine their surprise when he picked up the spear and put Hierarch Kuurz in his place! I got there in time to witness the aftermath."

"And save my hide from the others," Richard commented. "They decided to jump in and try to pulp my face." He massaged his forearm tenderly.

Turu blinked in shock. They were serious. "And this got you the troops?"

"Kinda sorta," Richard said. "After thrashing a trio of Hierarchs, we were something like celebrities." Richard's face quirked as if he was both amused and disgusted by the idea. "We left the Mitragan Province and went to the Guilds. Had to practically stave them off with sticks..."

Klaara chuckled. "The GuildMaster of Mercenaries dueled him personally, and then tried to hook him up with his daughter."

Richard gave her a baleful glare. "...There weren't enough ships to go around, so we got enough folks to crew them all, plus a few extras, before coming back. I think our total crew turnout just crests 350."

Turu nodded. "Alright... Klaara, I take it you gave Richard a translator?"

"Yep. You bet," she answered smartly.

Turu nodded, "Then I recommend making your way over to see Bordra, if you haven't already," he said. "He will be briefing people on their roles in the upcoming firefight, as well as going over mission parameters. I don't think you want to miss it."

Richard held up his thumb. "I was just over there. I'm with Klakshan aboard the *Pinnacle*. He needs a troop to guard him while he flies that thing, or so they said, so I'm on security with a group of eight Heil and an Iharsh-Daraz."

"I thought you were going to be in the Gamble protecting your sister!" Turu exclaimed. "I'll talk with Bordra, and—"

"I volunteered," Richard said. "Klaara can definitely protect Vicky, and if I'm needed aboard the *Pinnacle*, I'll be there."

"Right," Klaara said. "Because you know how much this guy just loves standing around."

"Either way," Richard said, "I'll take Klaara back over there and find out what she's going to be doing other than protecting Vicky, if anything."

The two of them departed, and Turu watched them leave. They were much more relaxed around one another now, or had reached some kind of mutual understanding. He shrugged it off. They made a good team, if this was the kind of result they could achieve. Plus, they offset each other well. Klaara was wild and uncontrollable, while Richard was calm and calculating, and every bit as good a fighter... if not better.

Turu shook his head, clearing it slightly as he finished the nutrient paste and threw it in a waste receptacle. It landed cleanly within the container, bouncing off the far wall, and Turu smiled with satisfaction.

Now if only he could figure out how resolve this issue with Victoria. He loved her – that was only part of the equation. Did she love him? He didn't know. That was an unknown, and he hated unknowns. Were their species even *compatible*? Hiin above how would he know? Maybe the Terminals did – he'd have to take a cursory peek... out of nothing more than sheer curiosity, of course.

He shook certain images out of his head. Since when had he become such a lecherous... he couldn't think of a negative description that fit him at that moment. He stomped off toward the *Victoria*. He was going to check that Terminal, and he was going to do it *now*. No more unanswered questions. He wanted to be familiar with what was going on in his head, first and foremost. After that, he'd check and see if there were compatibility issues between Scain and Vahran. If there were, he'd drop the whole thing and forget it ever had crossed his mind.

He wanted to pound his head against the hull of his ship. Who was he kidding? After all this, it would be impossible to forget Victoria. Or Richard, Klaara… or anyone else who was involved in this. It just wasn't going to happen. He climbed into the ship and positioned himself at one of the data Terminals. He quickly typed in his authentication code before stretching slightly. It was time for some data mining – and he rather hoped he'd be successful in it.

Turu took a deep breath and relaxed, settling his fingers on the keypad. Time to get to work.

Chapter 57

ERROR: DATA PAD #925410053 NOT FOUND. ROUTING SYSTEM LOCATED. FILES
FORWARDED TO SHIP :VICTORIA: DATA TERMINAL METEUSAE. NO NEW MESSAGES

Turu grumbled in irritation, rising from the console. This was pointless – completely pointless. He'd found mountains of files pertaining to the Scain's reproductive nightmares, as well as their origins in the Zyzyts and Erythians, and how they stemmed from the Ragan's fanatical desire to be genetically perfect. The end result had been sterility, which had resulted in the extinction of the Ragans. A genetically perfect race would never die, and therefore have no need to reproduce. The Ragans got it half right, managing to sterilize their people. They had created the Zyzyt and Erythians in an effort to preserve their genes, but had otherwise been wiped from the face of the Galaxy.

As interesting at it was, though, it didn't help him. There was nothing useful in the terminals. Well, there had been a rather interesting study about hybridization with other compatible species, such as Zyzyts, Erythians or Taeski, but nothing that answered any of his questions about Vahran.

The issue lay with the fact that the Scain had drifted far from nature, at least where reproduction was concerned. While they hadn't reached the same levels of sterility as the Erythians, only one percent of Scain children were born alive. The genetic matching had been instated early in their history, by Mindbank Lucantaia, in an attempt to 'cure' the growing infertility by combining optimal genes. It worked, but it wasn't a solution; just a patch that kept the sterility from growing worse.

Turu massaged his forehead. Maybe Bordra knew something. The Erythians had become proficient geneticists, second only to the Elorskra, in their quest to cure their sterilization. He'd head over to the Commander's tent and see what he could come up with. But as he rose, he realized something. He couldn't talk to Bordra. The Erythian didn't know about his... attachment... to Victoria. Asking him questions about Scain-Vahran relationships would arouse suspicions. No... he'd have to access Bordra's terminal on his own.

He crept quietly out of the *Victoria*, looking up into the darkened sky. Saturn was slowly eclipsing the sun above them, bathing the surface in an ever-darkening night. The cryovolcano in the distance glowed an eerie blue-white, providing a single point of light in the fading dusk, and only added to the majesty of this alien night. The ground rumbled softly each time it belched out another wave of its freezing payload.

300

Like a wraith, Turu slunk across the compound and toward Bordra's tent. The Erythian would probably still be awake, making this stealth mission awkward and tricky. He might have to lure him away, or even lock him in the lavatory or something. He pressed his back to the wall, slowly peering in through the window. The inside was empty – Bordra was absent. Turu quickly slipped inside, keeping his eyes open. He was too nervous to field his Psionics – Bordra would sense it. He'd have to be quick – access the files and get out before the Erythian noticed anything was amiss.

Turu quickly booted up the terminal, loading the files it contained, only to have his jaw drop. What kind of terminal did Bordra keep? There was no sense of stable organization anywhere to be found. All of the files seemed to have their own opinions of where they should be filed. He ground his teeth together and ran a search for *"Interspecies Reproduction"*. No results. He tried again with *"Interspecies Relationships"*.

A slew of information appeared on the screen, listing all viable genetic pairings between different sentient races. Turu began to scroll through them, marveling at some of the connections. Erythians and Elorskra shared sixty-seven percent of their DNA? That fell well within the acceptable limits for hybridization, although it would have to be done in a laboratory. He finally reached the Scain and narrowed his eyes, studying them closely.

Scain were compatible with a few races. The obvious ones were their parent races – the Zyzyt and Erythians, with whom they shared eighty percent of their genes. They shared fifty-six percent of their DNA with Alinteans – too little to be an effective hybrid – but had positive gene matches with Ene'tami and Vahran – sixty-five percent with the former and a staggering eighty-five percent of shared gene material for the latter. That was well within the operational norm. He could hardly believe it. He shook his head, running another search. *"Interspecies Sexuality"*.

He curled his lip as he read through the next document, attempting to keep his distaste to a minimum. Although hardly prudish, Turu really had no inclination to study the types of sexual positions favored by Iharsh-Daraz, or the full list of known sexual fetishes. He shook his head, closing down the files. This was getting awkward. He was about to run another search when the door behind him hissed open.

Bordra walked in, his face buried in his Data Pad. He was so engrossed that he didn't even notice Turu until the Scain tried to inch towards the door. "Turukaishal!" he yelped, almost dropping his pad. "Good grief, I didn't even see you there. What are you doing here?"

"Nothing," Turu lied. "Trying to get a new perspective on some genetics." The excuse was lame, but still close to the truth. He couldn't outright lie, as his eyes would betray him anyway. "Where were you?"

"Lavatories," Bordra said dismissively. "I just can't think well with both bladders full, you know?"

"You take your Data Pad with you to the lavatory?"

Bordra nodded. "Not much time to pause, you know. Plus, as you said, it helps when you need a different perspective." Turu shook his head, trying to clear his head of the thought as Bordra continued. "Anyway, what did you say you were after?" he walked over to the console. "Never mind. I'll just check the backlogs and..." he got very quiet as he typed before muttering quietly. "Interspecies reproduction? Interspecies relationships? Interspecies sexuality?!" He turned and looked back at the Scain. "Why would you be looking at this?"

"It's nothing," Turu said, shuffling towards the door. Bordra hadn't been talking directly to him, though. More to himself.

The Erythian began to pace. "Perhaps you want to help cure the sterility affecting us? No... you wouldn't sneak about if that was the case. You'd ask. That means it's something personal. Embarrassing even. Your searches imply you've had contact with other species. Subjects suggest physical contact. Intimacy, maybe? Hypothesis bolstered by secrecy..." he was thinking out loud as he walked back and forth, tapping his chin with his finger as he spoke to himself. Typical Erythian behavior, from what Turu had observed. They thought so fast that they could build and tear down a hypothesis before most other races could formulate their first.

"Intimacy... physical contact..." he snapped his fingers. "Someone in the camp. Recently arrived with no time to foster a relationship with others? Klaara? Too violent and I suspect in a relationship already. Kridoria? Not here, never mind. Reflex. Only two females I would have suspected considering your history. Topic of intimacy suggest a history with the subject."

He turned and stared Turu in the face. "Victoria."

"W-w-what?" Turu stammered, his brain locking up. He should have known better than to come after Bordra's equipment. Any other Erythian terminal would have been able to provide the same data with a little hacking, even Kimbo's. How stupid was he?

"Your history and familiarity with Victoria encourages coupling and intimacy. It's also cathartic and a good stress relief," Bordra went on, resuming his pacing. Turu blinked, staring at the Erythian as he continued. "Unfortunately, rather weak when juxtaposed with the Heil or Taeski, and yet physically stronger than any of the Ragan sub-breeds. Curious."

Turu's wits finally returned and he snapped. "Stress relief?" he asked incredulously. "You think this is about *stress relief?!*" he hissed, his eyes flashing to red for a moment. "Come here and let me show you something about stress relief! I care more about her than anyone I've ever met and you're chalking it up to *catharsis?*"

Bordra never flinched, but did stop pacing. "Apologies, Turukaishal. I never meant to imply that you don't care about her. I was just stating facts. Intercourse is good stress relief. I never suggested it was the only reason."

"Oh..." Turu said, feeling slightly sheepish. "Sorry."

"No apology needed," the Erythian said with a wave of his hand. "Your response is normal to a perceived slight. Your heart rate is elevated as well – paranoia and stress, most likely – meaning you're more likely to have an increased chance of reacting passionately." Bordra walked over to the terminal and began to type. "In any case, files do exist about this topic. I'll forward them to Terminal METEUSAE. Also, one more thing..."

"What?" Turu asked, scratching the side of his head out of nervousness and relief.

"Please be careful. You seem happy with her. Bandrumano and I were discussing it earlier, although I didn't realize she meant *this* much to you. She is fragile, though, and only slightly less so than you. Damaging her would damage your mental state... possibly beyond repair. So please – take care of her. For your sake as well as her own."

"I will, Bordra," Turu said, nodding. "Believe me, I will."

"Of that I have no doubt," Bordra said, turning around again, rubbing his palms together. "Now then, anything else I can help you with?"

Turu shook his head. "No, thank you. Other than keeping this a secret, that is."

"Doctor-patient confidentiality, Turukaishal. I never speak of things like this unless your health comes into question," the Erythian reassured him. And then his gray face split into a mischievous smile. "In addition to the files I sent you, I have a few pamphlets if you'd like. Positions favored by humans. Erogenous zones. Tender points. I also have ointments that, while untested, could feasibly intensify her feelings, and-"

"You know, Borda, I do have a rifle," Turu reminded him. He was now convinced that his eyes were never going to change back from pink. Ever. They were going to be permanently stuck this color, and he was going to have to walk around in public with his helmet on.

"Yes, well, wouldn't recommend using that during intercourse. Result could be... messy, not to mention that Victoria would likely not appreciate it." Bordra grinned and winked at him.

Turu did his best not to laugh, but his now-yellow eyes betrayed him. "Thanks Borda," he said as he turned to go. "I appreciate it."

"Any time, Turukaishal," the Erythian said with a small, and yet oddly warm, smile. "Just remember that I consider you my friend."

"And you're mine," Turu said. "Just promise me you're going to survive this upcoming fight."

"I will if you will," Borda said, his face returning to its usual serious mask. "And above all – make sure you come back for Victoria. She cares deeply for you, and I have known Vahran to do strange things when they are deprived of the one they love indefinitely."

Turu nodded wordlessly, leaving the structure and heading back out into the orange night. Borda watched him go before smirking and moving over to his terminal.

He'd almost made it back to his terminal when Turu heard Terminal METEUSAE chime. Borda's file should have arrived earlier, so it was something else. He jogged through the airlock and sat down, opening the most recent messages.

The first was Borda's files that he'd sent. Those would be read in a moment. The other was also from Borda. The subject message was *"Thought this might be helpful."* Curious, the Scain glanced at the attachment. *A Theoretical Guide to Pleasing an Interspecies Lover*. Turu grit his teeth. "That Hiin-damned..." he laughed, moving to delete the file. And then he paused. "Might not hurt to take a look, though..."

Chapter 58

ERROR: DATA PAD #925410053 NOT FOUND. ROUTING SYSTEM LOCATED. FILES FORWARDED TO SHIP :VICTORIA: DATA TERMINAL METEUSAE. NO NEW MESSAGES

Turu leaned back against the wall, watching the various Heil ships flying in and among their prior group as they danced and wheeled in the thick atmosphere above him. Practice. Bordra had predicted that there was a possibility of Demnechi's troops dragging them down into atmospheric combat, either in the gas giants or some of the minor terrestrial worlds. They had to be ready in case it happened, so the hard little taskmaster had pushed them through three grueling runs. Turu had finally decided to sit down and tell Bordra to proceed without him. He'd already proven his competency behind the controls, and didn't need to shoot around and blow up holograms.

His palms itched. He wanted live combat. He wanted to punish Demnechi, Sovakadris... anyone else who was a part of this. They had betrayed his trust. They had betrayed him. They knew he would follow the Mindbank's orders without question, and because of it he had almost been the messenger of the Earth's destruction. He set his jaw, staring off across the icy landscape. They were not going to destroy Earth. Period. Demnechi was the first target – Kridoria had contacted Bandrumano a little while ago saying that their opponent had boarded the *Trident* and had assumed the role of Commander. She'd asked to speak to him as well, but he'd declined.

Klakshan sat down next to him, leaning back against the same wall as the Scain and uncapping his flask. Flying the *Pinnacle* was only feasible in space, as the larger ship could easily break free from Titan's gravity by accident. As a result, his ship had been replaced with a hologram, leaving him to wander around the camp. He watched the overhead ships with detached interest for a while longer before speaking. "Turukaishal, my old friend, you seem to have something weighing on your mind. Would you care to share it with me?"

Turu looked at him askance. Klakshan didn't gossip, nor was he ever unnecessarily unkind. He was a bit sharp, and sometimes almost mystic or arcane, but definitely trustworthy and one of his oldest friends. The Scain sighed and looked back up at the ships above him. "Just thinking about the upcoming battle," he confessed. "I don't want this to be my noble last stand and then have it mean nothing."

"What do you mean?" Klakshan asked, one of his arms twisting unnaturally as he pocketed his flask. His reptilian body flexed back into position, aided by dozens of cartilaginous vertebrae in his arm – something which never failed to make Turu shiver.

Klakshan's entire body was flexible and soft, braced with layers of muscle. Having descended from the serpentine Okulaurum, it was almost impossible to break anything in his body apart from his skull, and he could flex in unnatural ways. He usually maintained the appearance of a standard biped, but relaxed and flexed himself in the presence of those he trusted, Turu included. He turned his head towards the Scain without moving his shoulders. "Please, explain."

"If I charge in there and die," Turu said, "what have I accomplished? The Fleet will just continue onwards to Earth, possibly chuckling at my demise."

Klakshan retrieved his flask with the same fluid motion and took a swig before responding. "Our existences are all futile, Turukaishal. We are born into this life and stagger from one place to the other, never understanding our purpose. By the time we find a niche in which we fit, it is time for us to die. Our lives are ultimately meaningless. However, it is our actions which redeem us from this bleak fate. You are standing for what is right. For what you believe in. And these," he gestured above him, "are soldiers willing to fight and die for that same belief, no matter what. The strength of something like that cannot be merely ground underfoot."

He took another long drink from the flask, and Turu was half-tempted to ask what was in it... but knew better. The last time he'd asked, he'd regretted it immediately. Taeski were impervious to poisons or toxins, meaning they could consume substances which would kill him – something Klakshan had proven long ago by drinking mercury. Turu had sworn from that day on never to drink anything the Taeski offered him. "No matter what happens out there," Klakshan continued, "you will have made a statement. Even if you die, your beliefs and convictions are not something Demnechi, or even the Mindbank, can take away. Maybe they will destroy Earth. Maybe the Vahran will go extinct. But someone else will rise to challenge the Scain. And when they find out that another martyred himself, it will spur them on to victory. But I do not think you are going to die."

He waited until Turu was looking at him before he continued. "Our existences are futile. What we do with them is not."

Turu said nothing, looking back to the ships above him. "What about Victoria?" he asked. "If I fail, like you said, her homeworld is gone. Up in flames... and without even deserving it."

Klakshan said nothing for a while, sipping at his drink. "You obviously care a great deal for that woman," he said quietly, "so I will tell you something. She likes you. A lot. Even I can sense it. But dying for her is not the way to impress a woman. If you truly love her, you will find a way to *live* for her. It is a common belief among the Taeski, and one I urge you to take to heart. Dying for someone does no more than deprive them of the one they love, and leaves them defenseless the next time they are in danger. If you truly love her, you will fight and live!"

306

"Then I will live," Turu said, forcing himself off the wall and standing up, towering over Klakshan's seated form as he stretched. "Demnechi will not brush me aside so easily. I will find a way to stop him if I have to board his ship and kill everyone inside with my bare hands."

Klakshan nodded. "I have no doubt of your conviction, Turukaishal," he said as he took another drink and offered the flask to Turu, who quickly declined. The Taeski chuckled and withdrew the drink, finishing the last few drops.

Turu walked off, meandering through the camp. He finally found his way back to the *Victoria*, hoping to find its namesake somewhere nearby. He hadn't seen her in a while, and wanted to check up on her. So much had happened, and so quickly. Her aural signature was present, so he began to follow it until he ultimately located her – fast asleep on one of the thermally heated cots in the Medical Bay.

The Scain sat down across from her, looking at her sleeping form. She was so small. So fragile. He had a powerful urge to pick her up in his arms and wrap his body protectively around her. To keep her safe from the universe and everyone in it. He sighed quietly, shaking his head. He knew he had fallen, and fallen hard, for this girl. He was also aware of the fact that this was one plunge he was unable to rescue himself from. But at that moment, as he watched her chest rise and fall with each gentle breath, he didn't feel the need to save himself. He was more concerned with saving her.

He gently reached out and brushed a stray lock of hair out of her face. She shifted slightly in her sleep, but did not awaken. Turu was mildly glad for this. He would have looked so... he didn't even know what to call it... if she had awoken and found him hovering around her resting place like some kind of specter. He shook his head, standing up. It was best to leave her in peace.

The past few weeks had taxed her, and probably Richard, more than either of them had ever thought possible. Contact with an alien lifeform, an impending threat to their homeworld, going into space... it was a miracle neither of them were gibbering madly. As Turu turned to leave, pushing one of his hands down on the cot without thinking, he felt her hand shoot out and seize his wrist. He froze, slowly turning and looking down at her. He expected her to be awake. Possibly angry or confused by his presence.

Instead, Victoria was still asleep – exhausted beyond words. She curled against his hand, sighing gently. Turu stood there, feeling incredibly awkward. Now what? If he tried to wrest his hand away it might wake her up, which would be bad, or at least lead to awkwardness. But he couldn't just stand here until she woke up, could he? She would awake to find him standing there, trapped in her slumbering embrace... and end up in the same scenario as if he woke her up now. Turu gently tried to ease her hand off of his. The more he tried, though, the tighter she grasped. The Scain sighed in exasperation. He wasn't sure what to think or do.

Turu heard the airlock open and his heart rate tripled. He couldn't be caught like this! He forced his aura down; praying whoever had come in wasn't perceptive enough to notice it. Or that they wouldn't come nosing around in the crew quarters. He closed his eyes, trying to listen.

"Turukaishal? You here?" Turu relaxed slightly, but kept his aura subdued. It was Bandrumano. For a Scain, his friend's aural reading abilities were virtually zero. If it had been Richard, he would have died on the spot. The last thing he needed was an accomplished fighter finding an alien looming over his sleeping sister. He heard Bandrumano above him, on the bridge, before hearing him mutter something indistinct.

"Please, just go away..." Turu begged, hoping his friend wasn't in the mood for a search-and-find game. He heard the other Scain kick something – probably a Terminal – out of aggravation before stomping back to the airlock.

"If you're here, you might want to get out here. Bordra has something to discuss with you! He says its 'personal'!" the airlock doors hissed closed, and Turu let out a long, shuddering breath. He slowly tried to pry Victoria's fingers loose again before almost slapping himself. An idea struck him, and he gently reached down with his other hand and ran his fingertip along the side of her face. Victoria twitched slightly at the sensation of his thin fingertip, but didn't awake.

Frowning slightly, Turu repeated the procedure a few more times. Eventually, he got his desired response. Victoria rolled over, wiping at her face for a moment in an attempt to brush away whatever was irritating her. As she relaxed slightly to brush at the spot he'd been worrying, he snapped his hand out of her grip and slunk out of the Medical Bay feeling very relieved. He quickly rode the elevator up to the bridge and opened the airlock, forcing his eyes to return to their normal color.

Bandrumano was on his way back in and jumped in surprise. "Where the heck were you?" he asked, staring suspiciously at his friend. "I called for you and everything. What gives?"

"I was slightly caught up in something," Turu answered. "My apologies. What did you need?"

"Bordra has something 'private' for you," Bandrumano said, placing emphasis on the word *private*. "Probably something for you to give to that Vahran girl, hm?" he winked suggestively. Turu resisted the urge to trip his friend, instead settling for a baleful stare.

He followed Bandrumano through the compound until they reached Bordra's structure. He opened the door, watching as his friend jogged away, waiting until he was well out of earshot before speaking. "Bordra? You wanted to see me?"

"Yes," the Erythian said as he mulled over his Data Pad. "Forgot to mention something the other night. You might want to take this." He handed Turu a thin vial of clear liquid. Turu looked questioningly at the Erythian until he continued. "I forgot about possible biological vectors," Borda said sheepishly. "Amateur mistake. Possibility of sexually transmitted diseases. Cross-species, it could be potentially deadly."

Turu looked into the vial. "And this is...?"

"ISB-064. Powerful immunizer. Take it prior to any... activity. Prevents the spread of contaminants from or to you. ISB-064 only works for sexual vectors."

"Meaning...?"

"It won't protect you from other diseases," Borda said. "You will be protected from any intercourse-related biological issues, but others – such as botulism – are not part of that serum's function."

Turu nodded, pocketing the vial. "I see. Well, I appreciate your help again."

Borda bowed. "Anytime. Wouldn't want you keeling over from a fungal infection. You are my friend, remember?"

Turu smiled sadly, turning and leaving the facility. "Yeah. I remember." In three days, he might lose some of his friends. Borda, Klakshan... Bandrumano... it was possible some of them would not return. He looked at the sky, hidden behind the russet clouds, and frowned.

Chapter 59

ERROR: DATA PAD #925410053 NOT FOUND. ROUTING SYSTEM LOCATED. FILES FORWARDED TO SHIP :VICTORIA: DATA TERMINAL METEUSAE. NO NEW MESSAGES

The remaining days passed with relative speed, and Turu seemed to find some kind of comfort in the routine that he fell into. He primarily drifted between practicing space maneuvers with Bordra and sleeping in his pod for short bursts to renew his energy, but still managed find time for other, less necessary activities. He paced back and forth on the bridge, waiting for Bordra to give him the signal to leave – the signal that meant they were going to finally engage the enemy. He wanted to get flying and sack Demnechi – to put their plan into action and see if it worked or not. Just sitting around like this drove him crazy; it always did before a mission. He wanted to get out there and get it done.

Victoria and Richard distanced themselves from the group somewhat, preferring to remain by themselves instead of including the other aliens, Turu and Klaara notwithstanding. Richard preferred to spend his time in the command post, staring at the holograms of their last simulated battle. It was as if he was testing himself: trying to analyze their strategy for some unknowable reason. Perhaps he was trying to prove himself. Perhaps he was discerning their competency as strategists. Turu would never know. The world's worth of knowledge hidden behind that man's stormy gray eyes would be forever locked away from him, this much he knew.

Turu awoke one morning, finally, to the sound of the camp being disassembled. He looked out of the Victoria, unsure of whether or not he was dreaming. Everything suddenly seemed surreal, but there it was: the Erythians were slowly collapsing the makeshift encampment, packing all of the parts back aboard Bordra's frigate, the *Contagion*. Each building was reduced down to several segments before being stacked into elongated crates for transport and storage.

Turu stretched, walking through his ship until he came to one of the airlocks. He stuck his head out, finding the closest Erythian. "Are we getting ready to leave already?" he asked.

Kimbo turned and saluted. "Yes Commander. The remainder of the camp is still waking up. Might I suggest attending Commander Bordra's closing speech at the Mess Hall before we close it down?"

Turu nodded and made his way over to the aforementioned building, entering quietly and standing in the back. It looked as though the proceedings had just begun, which was a relief as it meant he wasn't too terribly late. He felt like a heel for sleeping just a tad longer than he should have, but he'd worried himself into a fitful sleep last night with thoughts of the upcoming battle.

"I will not lie to you," Bordra said as he paced back and forth in front of the assembled aliens, "the odds are not in our favor. I can guarantee that some of you will not be here to share in our victory. I respect all of you too much to lie to you and tell you that this will be an easy victory. It won't. But regardless of what we face out there, remember what you are fighting for and why."

He paused, turning to face the group, his hands behind his back and his head held proudly aloft. "Think back to before your race reached the stars," he said. "What if the Scain had descended upon you, instead of these Vahran? Many of you do not know the kind of terror which comes with being besieged by a race with technology far surpassing your own. A war with no means of victory. But these Vahran are going to feel that terror. That hopelessness. Or they will if we do not succeed."

He brought his fist into his palm. "Where is the honor in what the Scain are doing right now? The glory that they so often speak of? There is none! You there—" he gestured to a Heil in the front row "—your species fights for glory. For honor. For conquest! And yet even you know that this is no war. This isn't even a skirmish. It will be a slaughter, plain and simple. There is nothing to gain from this, and it is *wrong*. We, the few brave souls in this room, are all that stand between the Vahran and their destruction."

There was a murmur of assent from the assembled troops as Bordra went on. "Many of you know the Vahran by rumor. Those rumors are wrong. Regardless of origin, the Vahran are defenseless. Helpless. Now is our chance to prove that we are evolved. That we are the higher lifeforms by protecting them at their weakest."

Turu saw Victoria and Richard sitting near the front of the group, watching Bordra as he spoke, and both of them were nodding. For a moment, Turu thought that Bordra was going to bring one or both of them up to speak, but instead he handed the floor off to Bandrumano. Turu bit his lip slightly. His friend hated public speaking with a passion. As relaxed as he could be, the Scain walked up to the front of the group and took a deep breath.

"The Mindbank is a Scion," he said. "His reach extends far and wide, and his Psionic powers are unmatched. Currently, he is undefeated and unopposed. Once we go through Demnechi, we will be going after the Mindbank. Demnechi is not the root of the problem: Sovakadris is. His little Councilor is just an obstacle to overcome – a stepping stone on the path to victory."

Bordra continued, his voice picking up where Bandrumano's left off. "Scions are powerful. Deadly. They have ten times the power of a normal Scain, and are usually only used as soldiers, diplomats, translators or courtesans. They hold extreme power among the Scain Empire, serving as the leaders of the Vanguard forces and holding positions within the society."

"We know the Mindbank can defend himself," Bandrumano said, pressing his hands together. "He disappeared almost seventy years ago, and spent fifty-five days as the captive of another species. He managed to not only survive, but to break free of their confines and avenge himself upon his captors. This is a being that is far more powerful than Demnechi. His councilor defends him unnecessarily. It is time we break this worthless shield and continue onward to preventing this cataclysm from ever reaching fruition."

Their army roared in agreement, applauding and waving weapons in the air. Turu clapped his hands as well, although he felt none of the same enthusiasm. He was taking a pair of innocent Vahran into the middle of an uneven firefight. He bit his tongues, frowning.

"Turu," Bordra called out, motioning him over as their group began to break apart. "Come here for a moment."

The Scain picked his way through the group, easily towering over the other aliens by at least two feet. He came over and stood by the Erythian, looking down at him. Bordra wasted no time in explaining. "Klakshan and Richard have volunteered to jump first and check the surrounding area," he said. "They will then hide in the shadow of Kashelion, where their heat emissions will be masked, and wait for us to arrive."

Turu looked over at Richard and saw the Vahran gave him a brief nod. Bordra continued, stifling Richard before he could begin speaking. "Victoria will be riding with you until we reach Blemdarch, at her request. Upon arrival, you are to make contact with the *Gamble* and transfer her into Klaara's care. You will be jumping in approximately one tenth of a standard rotation period before their fleet arrives. This will give you time."

More than enough time, actually. Turu nodded wordlessly, his throat constricting. At least Victoria wouldn't be on board with him during his suicidal charge. He couldn't live with himself if he got her killed. "Understood," he said as Victoria came to stand by his side.

"Turu, I recommend you start working on that fusion core of yours as well," Bordra said as he walked off.

Richard looked at them both before Extending his hand to Turu. "Good luck," he said, shaking the Scain's hand. "I hope to see you when this fight is over."

Turu bowed graciously. "As do I," he said. "And you be careful, alright?"

"Gotcha," Richard said as he turned and moved over to where Klakshan was sitting. Turu and Victoria headed back to the Scain's frigate, climbing aboard and sealing the airlock. Turu dragged himself into the laboratory and opened a small hatch labeled "Maintenance".

The engine was a massive spherical beast, connected to both ceiling and floor inside another spherical chamber. Turu climbed up along one side of it until he reached a section ear the top and slowly opened one of the various metal sheets that held the fusion core shut.

Within the gleaming metal orb lay a miniature sun, probably ten feet in diameter. Various ports collected and converted the energy it gave off, cycling it through the ship. Turu pried the piece of metal open further and jumped back down, heading over to a small box he'd placed there the night before.

He opened it, looking at the payload within. A REBR2 Tactical Nuclear Device. He tucked it under his arm and ascended the sphere again. With the care and delicacy of a surgeon, Turu affixed the REBR2 to the inside of the fusion tank, just below where he had pried it open, using a gooey resin to hold it in place. Once he had finished, he reached down and twisted a small crank on the surface of the device. A tiny red light flashed multiple times as the crank went around before turning blue. The device was now armed and ready for remote activation.

Turu pushed the metal plating back together and welded them shut. When that device was triggered, it would destabilize the magnetic containment field surrounding the miniature sun. The small star was only held together by the field, and would rapidly expand through local space at just over the speed of sound. Anything caught in its path would be destroyed. Setting off an explosion of this size would completely annihilate the *Trident*'s engine core.

Without the core, the primary systems aboard the *Trident* would destabilize and fail. Life support, gravity and lighting would fail first, followed by the seals on the airlock doors and residual power. Backup cells could hold the *Trident* steady for a while, but power loss wasn't the only danger. In addition, the *Trident*'s own fusion reactors would betray it without the engine core to provide energy to their shields, triggering a secondary fusion explosion. The blast would snowball as it engulfed each of the *Trident*'s five engines, hopefully either gutting or outright killing the larger ship.

Or that was the plan anyway.

Turu climbed out of the Maintenance chamber, closing the hatch behind him, and looked around. There was nothing here worth saving. This ship, the *Victoria*, was a pale comparison to its namesake. If he had to choose between the two, Turu knew which one he'd go for. He left the laboratory and entered the armory, picking up any and all weapons he would need. With practiced ease, the Scain attached a scoped rifle, pistol, and anti-air cannon to a large backpack and slipped it on. The remainder of his weapons had been distributed among troops as needed. Any other valuable pieces of technology were safe with Bordra aboard the *Contagion*. Or as safe as could be, anyway.

If worst came to worst, Bordra was expecting some boarding craft. They would need all the firepower and small arms they could get. The last thing Turu wanted was to be boarded and find himself strapped for weapons. Of course, he'd be moving fast and light. At the speeds he'd have to reach, boarding him was next to impossible. He still wanted to be careful.

Sighing, and wishing he didn't have to be a part of this mess, Turu ascended the lift to the bridge. The problem was, there was no one better suited to flying the *Victoria* than he was. It was a heavily customized ship, with lots of work being done by his father's team on Sillothel. He'd heard rumors of gifted individuals who could fly Scain ships, namely a few Alinteans, but no one here at the camp.

And that left only one person to do the job: him. He was the only one who knew how to handle the ship like a professional; the only one who could perform the complex maneuvers required for this mission. And most certainly the only one he would allow to do it. In reality, he knew he wouldn't allow someone else to bear his burden. This was his task, and he would complete it.

But it didn't mean he had to like it.

Chapter 60

ERROR: DATA PAD #925410053 NOT FOUND. ROUTING SYSTEM LOCATED. FILES FORWARDED TO SHIP :VICTORIA: DATA TERMINAL METEUSAE. NO NEW MESSAGES

Richard walked up the gangplank towards the yawning opening in the side of the *Pinnacle*. He couldn't help but be awestruck by the sheer size Klakshan's vessel possessed. It was easily a quarter of a mile long, and several hundred feet at its widest. It didn't look aerodynamic in the slightest, the body kinking upwards and downwards in odd places, and forking near the rear. Antennae and dishes littered the top, seemingly stuck in place with no sense of order. The exterior needed a new coat of paint, but the several massive glyphs had been painted along the front, and Richard could only assume it was the ship's name or serial number. He couldn't read the letters.

He stepped into a wide five-sided hallway. Above him, set in the crease of two of the angles, were long diodes which emitted a pale blue light. He hefted his cane and set off along the hallway, following the directions Klakshan had given him earlier. Just before the door sealed, he looked out across the surface of Titan. The *Victoria* lifted into the air a short distance away, carrying Turu and Victoria along with it. In an oddly sentimental moment, Richard wondered if he was ever going to see the tall alien again.

He followed the hallway towards the bow of the ship, avoiding the first three turnoffs and taking the fourth. This led him into an elevator which, without any required input, began to whisk him upwards. He leaned on the wall, watching as he passed the first two floors before stopping at the third. The elevator slowly rotated to his left, revealing an opening through which he walked, following another pentagonal hallway.

Klakshan was waiting for him on the bridge, already working with some of the Heil he had taken with him and sorting them into redundancy seats around the bridge. Outside, the dusty wind savagely battered the window as other ships lifted off, hurling dust and dirt against their ship. Klakshan turned as Richard entered, nodding. "Welcome aboard my humble craft, Master Sinclair," he said with a slight bow. "Your volunteered assistance is greatly appreciated. I understand you are quite the warrior."

"Nothing special, just human," Richard said as he tapped his cane against the metal floor. "I just do what I have to. What about you? Turu tells me you're not exactly a person to trifle with either."

"I do what I must," Klakshan said with a quirk of his lips. "However, during the upcoming firefight, I will be defenseless as I fly the ship. I need you, along with a small contingent of Heil, to repel boarders should we have any."

"Sounds fun," Richard said, starting to unbutton his vest and shirt, revealing the polyform armor beneath it. "Where do you want me to stand? Near the door?"

Klakshan steepled his fingers, nodding. "I think that would be wise..." he whipped around suddenly, coming face to face with a group of large Heil, each one taller and broader than himself. Richard's eyes flicked over them, counting seven in total. They looked like trouble. "Can I help you?" Klakshan asked them coolly.

"Maybe," the Heil answered. "I thought I was going to take orders from him," he pointed at Richard, "not you. What's going on?"

Klakshan cocked his head. "I am captain of this ship," he said. "Master Sinclair takes orders from me, and therefore you do as well."

"But he's the one we followed, not you!" the Heil protested. "How do I know you're strong enough to lead us? He's the one that beat the Hierarchs. He's the one—"

"He's the one telling you to listen to Klakshan," Richard said, removing the last of his outerwear, revealing the black polyform in its entirety. "And unless you want me to flatten you like I did Kuurz, you'll listen."

Klakshan held up a hand in Richard's direction. "Although that is appreciated, I do not require your assistance." He turned back to the Heil. "Which of you is the leader of this group?"

The Heil in the front pointed one of his thumbs at himself. "That's me: Draak'Velan. Why?"

Klakshan pressed his fingers together again. "So tell me, Master Velan... if I defeat you in combat, will I have proven my strength to you? Will that appease your desire for bloodlust?"

The Heil snorted. "As if you could," he said, his nose rising haughtily into the air.

The Taeski's lips quirked and he looked back at Richard. "Would you be willing to ensure his six associates do not disturb us?" he asked.

"With pleasure," Richard said, moving forward. "Hey! You guys!" he waved at the other Heil. "Why don't you come here and enjoy the show?"

The other six moved over and stood next to Richard, folding their arms and watching Klakshan. It suddenly dawned on Richard that all of them were taller than he was by a minimum of three inches. He hoped he wasn't going to have to fight them all.

Klakshan bowed to the Heil. "Are you ready? This is your one and only warning."

The Heil snorted. "Whenever you are, 'captain'."

The fight was over before it began. The Heil threw a punch towards the side of Klakshan's head to open the bout, and never got further. Klakshan blocked it with his wrist, his hand snapping up with lightning fast reflexes. Before Draak had a chance to react, Klakshan's arm twisted as if it lacked bones entirely, slithering around the Heil's forearm before squeezing like a boa constrictor. The sound of cracking bones filled the bridge, and Draak let out a pained yell. Klakshan's grip tightened further until Richard was certain he was going to rip the unfortunate Heil's hand off, but he released him a moment later.

Draak's arm was visibly compressed from his wrist halfway to his elbow, and his hand hung limply at the end of his arm. Klakshan shook out his arm, pressing his fingertips together as the Heil fell back to the ground. "You may go now, Draak. You may require the use of protites in addition to your White Art to heal your arm."

One of the six Heil near Richard snarled and took a step toward Klakshan, reaching for his ion saber as he went. Richard's arm reached out and grabbed the offender by the shoulder, spinning him around. Before the Heil could react, Richard had punched him squarely across the jaw. "Back down!" he snarled as the Heil stumbled away, clutching his jaw. The other five, rather than rushing Klakshan, immediately moved over to their fallen leader, speaking hurriedly in their native tongue. Two of them went down on one knee, their white hands touching the ground as they began to heal Draak. One, probably an assistant leader of their little group, jerked his thumb towards Klakshan, waving his other hand as if asking what Draak had been thinking.

Klakshan, in the meantime, had moved over to a stack of crates in the corner of the bridge, seating himself languorously on top and drawing out a Data Pad as if the actions of the Heil were no more than a trifle to him. Richard was about to move over to him when a female Heil with an elaborate ion axe slung over her shoulder walked up to the Taeski and began speaking to him in low tones. She was soon joined by two more, both wielding spears. Klakshan looked helplessly at Richard, who merely shrugged. He knew how it worked from spending time with Klaara. Do something impressive enough and you ran the risk of ending up with a fan club.

The human chuckled as Klakshan finally rose, shooing the females back to their posts with mild agitation stamped on his features. Serving on the Taeski's ship was going to be interesting, to say the least. He cracked his neck before moving to stand near the door when he felt a hand fall on his shoulder.

Instinct warned him to duck more than anything else, and he dropped his body low to the ground as a fist swung past where his temple had been a moment before. His palms hit the ground as his legs whipped backwards, catching the offender in the shins and sweeping his legs out from beneath him. The Heil fell to the deck with a curse as Richard rose again, turning and looking down at him. "Nice try," he said to the Heil he'd punched, "but I didn't beat Kuurz by accident. Now get back to your post before I make you regret it."

The Heil grumbled, but grudgingly marched back to his position. Richard walked over to the door and picked up his belongings, shoving them over with the crates in the corner before picking up the ion saber Klaara had given him. He fired it up for a moment, making sure it was working, before donning his helmet. He paused for a moment before slipping his greatcoat on over the polyform – he wore it too much and just felt naked without it, even in the polyform. He admired himself in the glass as the ship began to fire up the engines – it wasn't a bad look.

Properly attired, he took up position by the door, his eyes surveying nearby weapon locations. A rack of guns was mounted on either side of the door, and he had his ion saber... not to mention all of the Heil in the room were armed as well. "Ready when you are, captain," he said to Klakshan.

"Understood," Klakshan said as he inserted his hands into a pair of sockets on a central dais. Violet light engulfed his arms to the elbows and a thick band of light encircled his face. "Make certain to hold that position no matter what. If I am injured, none of you can fly this ship. We will be a stationary target for the *Trident*."

"Got it," Richard said, the sentiment echoed by several Heil. Richard leaned on the saber and waited. It wouldn't be long now before they were in battle. He cracked his shoulders, waiting next to the door: the silent sentinel.

Chapter 61

ERROR: DATA PAD #925410053 NOT FOUND. ROUTING SYSTEM LOCATED. FILES FORWARDED TO SHIP :VICTORIA: DATA TERMINAL METEUSAE. NO NEW MESSAGES

Turu sat at the helm of the *Victoria*, his fingers wrapped around the controls as he stared out into the brightness of Dark Space. The ghostly half-images of planets and stars whizzed past him, and he couldn't help but think about the upcoming battle. This could very well be one of his last hours alive, and he was wasting it staring at nothingness.

Somewhere else on board, Victoria was exploring all the little nooks and crannies of his ship, saying goodbye to it in her own way. Turu had already come to terms with losing the craft. It wasn't easy, but it was the only way—the only *plan*—they had. He sighed, massaging his forehead with one hand. He was about to rise and look for Victoria when he heard the door behind him open.

It was Victoria. Not only was she the only person on the ship, but her aura was unmistakable. At the moment, though, her aura was scattered and jagged. She was worried, and over a great many things. The colors and textures of her aura were shifting and diaphanous, never remaining in any one configuration for very long. Before she could even utter a sound, he had flipped the ship to autopilot and turned his chair to face her.

Victoria hesitated as he turned around, unsure. Turu smiled gently, beckoning her closer. "Come," he said. "Something is troubling you. What is it?"

"I—I—Yeah..." she sighed, nodding. "It's just... why? Why do we have to do this? Why do so many people have to fight and die? Why do you have to do this?"

Turu sighed softly as she approached. "The only answer I have for you is that fate is a cruel and capricious mistress," he said at length. "Why do any of us ever have to fight? In a perfect universe, we wouldn't have to. But moments like this define the boundary between war and peace, hate and love, good and evil. If there was no conflict, we would have nothing to juxtapose peace against, and it would mean nothing. That doesn't mean we have to like it though."

She nodded, leaning on the wall next to the pilot's chair. "I just... I don't want you to die, Turu!" she said at last, looking helplessly at him.

"Oh trust me," Turu said, "I don't want to die either. I'm young for a Scain. By your calendar, I've still got at least six hundred years before I'm an old man. I don't want to just throw that away. But..."

"But?" she asked.

"But you can't tell me that my one life means more than the seven billion on Earth, and the trillions that are yet to be conceived and born in future generations. Your planet deserves a future," he said, sighing. "And if I have to die for that future, so be it."

Victoria stamped her foot. "But why YOU?" she asked, pointing at him. "You could die, Turu, and all for a race that isn't even aware that this is happening! They'll never know it was you who saved them!"

Turu reached out and took her hand, clasping it between both of his. "Victoria, you and I are members of different species... different cultures and worlds... but there will always be the concept of right and wrong, and variables like race or awareness should not affect that differentiation. Right is right, wrong is wrong. And before you ask 'why me', I'm the only one who can fly the ship."

She sighed, nodding and biting her lip. "I just... I couldn't live with myself if something happened to you..."

"But if I don't try," Turu said gently, "you won't be living at all. And *I* can't live with myself if that happened. So please, try to understand."

She nodded, taking a deep breath and looking up at him. "Okay... okay. I'll try." She blinked several times as if trying not to cry. "For what it's worth, even if I hate you being in danger... thank you."

Turu smiled, drawing her off the wall with a Psionic tendril, pulling her body against his chest as he rose from the chair to meet her. She felt so small and fragile against him, and he instinctively wrapped his arms around her. She melted into him, burrowing her face into his chest. "Turu..." she whispered. "...I..." her voice cracked and fell silent.

The Scain backed up a little bit, tipping her chin up with one finger. "What is it, Victoria? What troubles you?"

She pushed him away, chewing her lip gently before speaking. "Turu, I love you," she said, her face flushing. "I know you probably don't feel the same way, and I know it's crazy or stupid or whatever because you're a Scain and I'm a human and all that, but I do..."

Victoria continued to ramble even as Turu's brain flatlined. Had she just told him she loved him? Even though he'd longed to hear the words, right or wrong, he'd still been unprepared. "Victoria," he said, trying to get his brain back online.

"...and I know you're some super space-man alien and we're just apes running around on Earth, but I really do love you with all my heart, even if you don't feel the same way..."

"*Victoria!*" Turu said a little more forcefully, watching her jump slightly and trail off into silence. He reached out and drew her close to him, sitting down in the chair so that their eyes were level. "Victoria, you know I care about you, right?"

She nodded, swallowing thickly. "Yeah... you wouldn't be doing this if you didn't care about me or Richard or anyone back on Earth..."

"I'm not talking about any member of the human race other than you," Turu said pressing one of his fingers against her chest. "I care for you more than I care to say."

"W-what do you mean?" she asked, trepidation coloring her aura.

Turu's eyes were pink. "Do you remember when I spoke to you in Galaxian? Back while we were testing the translator?" he asked.

"Yeah," she said, "I was so frustrated because you never told me what you'd said."

"Delgado melmari, meha aelau I jera," Turu repeated, his eyes silver. "Literally translated, it means '*Forever mine, love you I do*'... or, more syntactically correct, "Forever mine, I love you"."

Her eyes widened, her breathing falling short. Her aura fractured around her, and Turu recognized the same mental flatline which had plagued him a moment before. He rested one of his hands on her shoulder. "Victoria, I love you. It's a shame that I only have the courage to tell you now, when I'm about to go off to war, but I'm glad I can tell you at all."

She nodded. "Then Turu... can you do me a favor? Just one?"

"Anything," he said, meaning it completely at that moment.

Victoria swallowed nervously. "Kiss me... just once... just in case."

Turu's brain flatlined again before his body reacted on autopilot. His hand reached up, cupping her head lovingly. His fingers brushed against the nape of her neck, eliciting a flurry of goosebumps from her flesh. He drew her forward until she was standing between his knees. With a final deep breath, he pressed his thin, lipless mouth against hers.

It was an unusual sensation – something he'd never experienced before, as Scain only kissed their mates. Her lips were soft and full against his mouth, and her breath tasted sweet and fresh. Her hands rose up, cupping his cheeks even as her tongue brushed over his mouth. He instinctively parted his lips, feeling her tongue slip inside. She gasped, drawing back a moment later and looking at him. "You have two tongues!?"

He nodded and blushed. "Is that a problem?" he asked, suddenly self-conscious.

"Not at all," she said, grinning impishly, "but now I know how you tied that cherry stem together." Her lips were back on his before he could react, her tongue probing both of his. He twisted them around hers, pushing it back into her mouth as he kissed her passionately. She let out a moan which set his skin to vibrating, his whole body shivering as they finally broke apart.

She looked up at him, her cheeks flushed, and smiled. "Mmm... imagine that... my first kiss is with an alien."

Turu caressed her cheeks. "No regrets, then?"

"None whatsoever," she said, smiling. She searched his eyes. "Turu... where do we go from here?"

"I don't know," Turu said. "Scain don't generally court others. We are assigned mates. But at this exact moment, I can't do anything. Not until all this is over. But once it is... if you're still willing... I'd like to try if you would."

She squeezed his hand. "I'll wait for you," she said. "I want to know what it's like to be in a relationship with you."

"I'm sure you say that to all the suicidal alien commanders you meet," Turu said, chuckling slightly as he pressed a kiss to her forehead.

Victoria laughed, smiling up at him, her cheeks still slightly pink. "So, what's my suicidal alien going to do after all this is over?"

Turu sat back in the chair, releasing her for the first time as he steepled his fingers. "I probably won't be able to go back to Chindrus," he said, "but that doesn't bother me. If they weren't ready to stand up to Sovakadris when seven billion lives mattered, nobody there is my friend. I was thinking about going back to Earth and hiding out there... live like a human and learn more about them."

"Haven't had enough of Richard and myself yet?" she teased.

Turu laughed, waving a hand. "You two are the ones I like. I'll never get tired of you, although Richard's constant threats are a bit unnerving. But what about you? What will you do when all this is over?"

Victoria shook her head. "Knowing what's out here now, I don't think I could ever just return to Earth and pretend nothing happened. I want to see more."

"Maybe I can take you," Turu said, "provided I can secure a ship before returning to Earth. I know of a beautiful little spot on Variaeg where you and I could go."

She smiled, nodding. "I'd like that."

The *Victoria* exited Dark Space with a subsonic boom, pulsing the vacuum around them. Turu looked out the window as Blemdarch's blue-white light filled the cockpit, the dwarf planet of Mamant orbiting slowly beneath them. "Would you like to take a walk with me?" he asked. "Join me in the observation deck... just the two of us? You can get a spectacular view of the system from there."

She blushed and smiled, nodding. "I'd like that... a lot."

Turu took her hand in his and led her down the length of the bridge towards the elevator. He smiled, feeling her small hand in his, and brushed one of his thumbs across the back of her hand, feeling her shiver. The two of them stepped into the elevator, watching the doors close. Victoria turned and, just before the doors blocked out the light of Blemdarch, pulled Turu's head down for another kiss. Turu smiled against her lips, his hands moving to her hips as the doors closed, leaving the two alone with one another.

Chapter 62

ERROR: DATA PAD #925410053 NOT FOUND. ROUTING SYSTEM LOCATED. FILES FORWARDED TO SHIP :VICTORIA: DATA TERMINAL METEUSAE. NO NEW MESSAGES

Turu stared out of his cockpit, his face set in a stoic mask. This was it: do or die time. Below him, orbiting Kashelion at a slightly lower angle, was the *Gamble*. Victoria was already on her way down, being guided along by the safety line... and soon, even that too would be severed and he would be alone. Left with nothing more than the eerie silence of space inside a ship which could very well be his tomb. At the prospect of being separated from Victoria, the Scain felt a deep, cavernous sensation creep into his chest.

"This is the Gamble," Klaara's voice said over the intercom. *"Victoria is on board and secured."*

"Copy that, *Gamble*," Turu said automatically. He could almost feel the thick cable retracting into his ship as the sensation of isolation grew. He'd never been bothered by being alone on his ship before, and had often enjoyed the solitude and the quiet. But that was so long ago... back before he met Victoria... in what felt like another lifetime. Back before he'd known what it felt like to care for someone. He chewed on his lip before responding. "Fall back and take up orbit around Sernomir."

He sat back and drummed his fingers on the console as Klaara responded. *"Acknowledged,* Victoria. *Good luck out there. You better come back in one piece: you still owe me a rematch."*

Turu didn't respond, staring out of his window at the millions of glittering stars. He wanted to do something—anything—just to alleviate the tension of waiting. Within moments, Demnechi's fleet would come bursting into the system, locking on to the only visible ship: the *Pinnacle*. Shortly after that, Bordra would lead the first half of their troops through, emerging above Blemdarch itself and striking the fleet in the rear, igniting the battle in earnest.

It didn't take long. His scanner bleated at him as the first wave of ships burst from Dark Space directly above Naisaari's radiation zone — just as Bordra had predicted. Before the ships could even re-orient themselves to face the *Pinnacle*, Turu's radar picked up Bordra's squadron coming into view. Several of the enemy ships blinked out as the formation scattered, looping back around and aiming for the traitors under Bordra's command. Another group took off after the *Pinnacle*, firing at it from afar as Klakshan steered it towards Kashelion.

Less than a minute later, an enormous red stain appeared on the sensor array. The *Trident* had arrived. That was Turu's signal; he gunned the engines, roaring into an accelerated orbit around Entibaa, remaining at the furthest reaches of the deadly planet's gravity well. He checked the gauges – 4,500 units per second. He wasn't even close to fast enough. He needed more power.

Outside, Turu caught alternating snatches of vision as he whipped around the gas giant. He could see Blemdarch, burning bright and blue-white against the inky backdrop of space, and then it was gone as suddenly as it had appeared. In its place, he could see the fight opening in earnest. Shots were being fired back and forth across the empty void of space, energy bolts from the Scain ships bursting across shields like deadly lightshows. Spears of light from the Heil craft slammed against the Scain's barriers, sending reverberations through space that managed to rattle the plating of the *Victoria*.

Turu checked his gauges again. 5,100. He set the ship to autopilot for a moment, maintaining synchronous orbit above Entibaa, and pulled himself out of the pilots chair. He paused just long enough to grab his weapons pack and put it on before racing down to the Shuttle Bay.

Down in the lowest portion of his ship, directly beneath the fusion drive and the engines, the vibrations of his ship's increasing speed were amplified. Every explosion from outside seemed to rattle through his body, shaking his thin skeleton to the core. He didn't hesitate, racing over to the *Dirego* and throwing himself inside, transferring control of the primary systems to the Rover. The inside of the cockpit's glass viewscreen changed, showing him the same view he'd seen up in the cockpit. Blemdarch. Battle. Blemdarch. Battle. The same two scenes repeated over and over, the alternation continuing as he sped around the gas giant.

With a few keystrokes, Turu pulled away from orbit. The engines protested the action, creaking and groaning above him. They were never meant to exceed 12,000 units per second at maximum, and he had to push them past that: as high as 15,000 at a minimum, to clear the *Trident's* laser.

He saw Klakshan's ship, the *Pinnacle*, bank hard to the right as it brought the massive Scain gunship into its sights. Klakshan wasted no time, firing several rounds to get the ship's attention. Subsonic reverberations echoed through the *Victoria* as the Taeski frigate's rounds impacted the gunship, cratering the metal plating along one of the wings. It wasn't enough to bring the ship down – not by a long shot – but it was enough to draw its attention well away from whatever Turu might be doing. Turu steadied his flight path as he streaked across the empty expanse between worlds, aiming for Naisaari. He felt his ship tug slightly as he entered the gravity well, and guided his ship into it. The radiation sensors warned him of the hazard zone, and he silenced them. It didn't matter anyway. He wasn't going to be here for long, and he wasn't actually inside the field.

Turu watched the battle outside with detached fascination, as if in a dream. His speed was still climbing – 8,300 units per second now. He was relying strictly on the hologram images to determine his position and to figure out what was going on outside. Relying on his eyes at this speed was impossible. He watched as a pair of Heil Frigates ganged up on a squadron of Scain Fighters, tearing them to pieces with repeated fire from their piercer units. Rubble spun past him, disappearing into Naisaari's swirling mists. The explosions rattled his ship like a toy, echoing throughout local space.

And high above the battle, Turu could see the *Trident*. It was massive, its wingspan easily the size of a city. The wings spread wide out to either side, the body flat and tapered. The silhouette was intimidating – like a carnivorous stingray waiting for its prey. Turu watched in awe as the five metal flaps on the front, each one as long as his ship, slowly folded back to reveal the yawning emptiness of the antimatter cannon.

For a moment, nothing happened. And then light began to spiral slowly inwards, spinning into that dark maw like water into a drain, coiling over itself again and again until it had coalesced into a brilliant sphere of pure white luminescence. A star in its own right, the light dancing across the polished surface of the *Trident*. The ship banked sharply, trying to keep the *Pinnacle* within its sights. And then without warning, the cannon fired.

The blinding ray of light streaked out from the barrel and shot across the void toward Klakshan's ship, a deafening explosion marking its launch. It missed the frigate, but not by much and likely due to Klakshan's acrobatic flying, and slammed into one of Kashelion's moons, Roisor. The small, rocky moon exploded as if it were made from wood, chunks of shrapnel flying in every direction before slowly falling into orbit around the gas giant. The shards which fell furthest in vanished into the orange, swirling depths. The laser continued onwards, piercing the upper clouds of the gas giant and emerging from the other side.

The *Victoria* passed directly beneath the laser as it faded away, leaving shimmering remnants in its wake. The rubble of Roisor continued to slowly orbit Kashelion, some pieces drifting down into the clouds and vanishing forever.

Turu's scanner lit up, announcing dozens of additional ships. The remainder of their fleet – Bordra's backup unit led by Bandrumano – entered the fray. Fire poured into the ships from behind, blasting several dozen out of the fray before the enemy even realized they were under fire from the rear. The *Pinnacle* continued to hold the gunship's attention amidst the chaos, but numerous escort craft turned around to engage the newcomers.

Turu launched himself out of orbit again, this time streaming toward Kashelion and praying that he didn't strike any of Roisor's fragments. This would be his last relay before he launched himself down the throat of the beast. From space, he may have looked like a silver streak dashing between planets. A two-hundred thousand ton missile streaking across the bleak expanse at 10,000 units per second. He hit the gravity well again, remaining outside the range of the moon fragments, and began his spiral around the third and final gas giant in the system.

The *Trident* hesitated for a moment, as if Demnechi or his crew suspected something was amiss. Klakshan, from within the *Pinnacle*, took this opportunity to launch several B-232 Stinger missiles from the sides of his ship, directing them back at the gunship. They burst across the bow, the explosions lighting up the blue-black material, but did very little damage other than shearing off a few automatic turrets.

Turu stabilized his orbit around Kashelion, watching the massive ship turn its attentions back to the *Pinnacle*. This was it – his final relay. He just had to hold out until his ship gained the extra 5,000 units per second he needed.

Chapter 63

ERROR: DATA PAD #925410053 NOT FOUND. ROUTING SYSTEM LOCATED. FILES FORWARDED TO SHIP :VICTORIA: DATA TERMINAL METEUSAE. NO NEW MESSAGES

Richard bounced off the floor as Klakshan rolled the *Pinnacle* partway to one side, the human grabbing at the floor as he slid sideways. Another shot from the *Trident* screamed past, this time coming close enough to shear off a communications array. Klakshan remained rooted in place, his legs apart as he righted his ship and increased the power. Richard scrambled upright, using his ion saber like a crutch, and ran back over to the door.

The Heil who would aid him in the event of a breach were picking themselves up from the ground, shaking their heads or massaging bumps and bruises. "Everyone okay?" Richard called, waiting for the nods and mutters from the security team before turning to Klakshan. "Any boarding craft incoming? I thought we'd have seen some by now!"

"We have," the Taeski replied. "I've just been able to shoot them down thus far. You're in luck, though: a contingent managed to get through my defenses while I was evading the *Trident*. Get down to the lower hall and keep them busy – they are locked on to the forward portion of Deck 1." He paused for a moment. "All hands, brace for impact."

Richard was thrown into the door, his polyform helmet smacking against the metal before he landed on his back, shaking his head to clear the stars from his vision. A Heil paused to grip his shoulder, helping him to his feet. "Good grief," Richard yelled. "What was that?"

"The boarding party has attached itself to the ship, resulting in atmosphere loss in Decks 1, 2 and 3," Klakshan said. "They are cutting through the hull. Grab whatever firepower you need and get down there. It's an attempt to take the weapons batteries offline. If they succeed, we're defenseless."

Richard slammed his hand against the panel, opening the doors into the main hall. He paused long enough to scoop up a Scain weapons pack from one of the lockers along the wall before racing out of the bridge, five Heil hot on his heels. "Klakshan," he said into the helmet's communications network. "How do I get down to Deck 1?"

"Manual access port – that's the fastest way," Klakshan said, the entire ship tilting to one side. Richard caught a pipe along the wall to keep from being hurled off his feet.

"Get back to the elevator and open the control box inside. Pull the blue lever. Just be careful – with the breach, the shaft may have lost pressure."

"Understood," Richard said as the ship tilted towards normal again. As soon as his feet touched the deck he was off, running back to the elevator. The Heil gathered their footing and chased after him, their weapons already drawn.

As Klakshan had predicted, the minute Richard opened the shaft there was a minor explosion. The hatch was sucked inwards, dragging Richard with it. For a moment, the hinges seemed to hold, but even they buckled under the force of the vacuum. The doorway broke free, and Richard was slammed into the opposite wall. "Damn it!" he cursed, clutching at a fuse box to keep himself from being sucked down into the shaft. "Don't you have artificial gravity or something?!"

Klakshan's voice was laced with sarcasm. *"I could always turn it on, but then we won't have as much power in the thrusters. If you'd like to make us an easy target for the Trident, that's the fastest way."*

"Okay okay, geez..." Richard grumbled, letting go of the fuse box. He was dragged down the shaft until he hit the bottom, breaking his fall every few feet by grabbing a pipe or unmarked box along the walls. The Heil descended behind him, doing the same thing. "How do we stop the decompression?"

"Worry about the boarders," Klakshan told him. *"We'll deal with the decompression later."*

"Well, there's no more hatch to keep it at bay," Richard told the Taeski. "At this rate, you'll lose the atmosphere on the upper decks as well, unless you can seal this shaft."

"One moment... once you are outside the shaft, seal the maintenance hatch the same way you opened the one above. The seal is pressurized – it will keep the vacuum at bay."

"Good stuff. Thanks Captain," Richard said, pushing the heavy door open. His helmet's readings immediately alerted him to the lack of an atmosphere. He ignored the little blip and stepped out into the corridor. The minute the Heil had followed him, he sealed the hatch as instructed.

"I'm reading atmosphere loss for Decks 4 through 9 have ceased," Klakshan told him. *"Well done."*

Richard snorted, pulling a Scain rifle from the weapons pack. "It's hitting a button. Even I can do that."

The hallway was eerily quiet without an atmosphere for sound to move through. Not only that, but once the pressure seal kicked in, Richard found himself floating in zero-gravity. He growled, preferring to have his feet firmly planted on the ground, but kicked off the wall nonetheless. "Which way to their breach?"

"You're close," Klakshan told him. *"Go to the end of the hallway and turn right. They'll be coming through the left wall. You should be able to see where."*

Richard nodded despite the fact that he couldn't be seen. He flicked the safety on the rifle, making sure it was off, before beginning to pull himself along the hallway floor as fast as he could. The one advantage he immediately noticed, apart from moving faster, was that if Klakshan tilted the ship left or right, he wasn't going to be thrown against either of the walls.

No sooner had he rounded the corner than he saw the site of the breach. Five massive spikes had been driven through the hull, each one tipped with gleaming silver barbs. At the center, Richard could see a glowing beam of light as the Scain on the other side worked on cutting through the wall. He growled a curse, launching himself down the hallway, turning back to the Heil. "Try cutting those barbs," he ordered. "I'll deal with any interruptions."

The opening that had been carved was already large enough to fit the barrel of a gun through, and Richard took advantage of this, sticking his rifle into the aperture and firing several shots. He heard several surprised shouts from the craft on the other side, but wasn't going to put his eye to the hole to confirm it. Instead, he reached back to his backpack and grabbed one of the Scain grenades attached to the side. Priming it, he stuffed it through the hole and followed it with the barrel of the gun, opening fire again.

There was a loud explosion from the other side of the wall, followed by yells and shouts and screams of pain, as the grenade exploded. Any Psionic shielding in the pod was destabilized for a moment, rendering his rifle highly effective against the occupants as he blindly angled it back and forth.

One of the Heil behind him cursed. "Can't cut this," he growled. "It's iskindite. Not even our sabers can get through it."

"Fine then," Richard said. "I've softened them up. What say we finish the job?"

Chapter 64

ERROR: DATA PAD #925410053 NOT FOUND. ROUTING SYSTEM LOCATED. FILES
FORWARDED TO SHIP :VICTORIA: DATA TERMINAL METEUSAE. NO NEW MESSAGES

Turu was surprised at how well they were doing. Of their 69 ships, they still had 57.
Enemy forces had been whittled down to 177 from the original count of 252. The
counters on the side of his scanner helped boost his mood. He checked his speed.
12,000 units per second. He had to go faster – much faster. He dumped as much energy
as he could into the thrusters, hearing them creak and groan in protest as they passed
their safety limit.

Turu's heart was pumping at probably seven times its normal speed. He felt the plates
of the outer hull shifting slightly, although not enough to cause a hull breach quite yet.
He looked at the ceiling, and it dawned on him that the Shuttle Bay rested directly
beneath the Maintenance Chamber. If the bomb in his engine detonated prematurely,
he was going to be one of the first things to go.

One of the control units on the far side of the room suddenly popped and fizzled, smoke
and fire roaring from the terminal and filling the chamber. Turu checked his speed
again: 13,400. Not fast enough. His ship was coming apart, already having passed its
terminal velocity, but he needed more. He checked the hologram window again. The
Trident was in a good position – if it turned and faced the planet he could take the shot
now, but he didn't have enough speed.

As his speed climbed past 14,000 units per second, several of the overhead plates began
to drop from the ceiling. One bounced from the *Dirego,* landing on the ground nearby
with a deafening crash. The lights in the bay shifted from blue to red, pulsing on and off
as they sought to alert him to the danger. Without the plating overhead, wires dropped
from the overhead compartments like vines, the thermal lining melting away and
exposing copper centers which sparked and glowed. The ship's systsems began to fall
offline, starting with the least pertinent. Exterior lighting failed first, followed by the
primary cannon, secondary piercer units, tertiary turrets and non-emergency interior
lighting.

The shuttle bay was shaking itself apart, and Turu was afraid to look at the small chart
showing his ship's overall condition. He knew it was bad, and he didn't need the details:
it was proof enough that his Shuttle Bay was on fire. He checked the power conduit
chart. All of the emergency systems were still online – protocol required that non-

essential systems were cut first, hence the guns and lights. Turu cast his eyes over to the speed meter. 15,000. On the nose at the moment, but he saw it slowly continue to climb.

There was a terrible wrenching of metal, followed by a crash overhead. Turu forced himself to look at the outline of his ship and choked. The tail of his craft – a one-hundred foot stabilizing fin – had just ripped free of the structural body of the *Victoria*. It was gone, sucked away into the slipstream behind his accelerating craft.

"*Pinnacle,* this is *Victoria,* do you copy?" he yelled into the communicator, his heart feeling like one consistent thrum. He checked all of his systems. "I am at required velocity and ready for immediate assault."

The *Pinnacle* was silent for several seconds, and Turu checked his scanner. Had the ship finally been shot down? Finally, after what felt like an eternity of being trapped in the burning remnants of his hyper-accelerated ship, Turu heard Klakshan's voice through the static. "Copy that *Victoria*. Beginning approach of Kashelion."

Chapter 65

ERROR: DATA PAD #925410053 NOT FOUND. ROUTING SYSTEM LOCATED. FILES FORWARDED TO SHIP :VICTORIA: DATA TERMINAL METEUSAE.WARNING. DATA TERMINAL METEUSAE OFFLINE. SYSTEMS OVERLOADED. MALFUNCTION. RECOMMEND REROUTING DATA TO ADDITIONAL TERMINAL. MESSAGES WILL BE STORED REMOTELY. ATTEMPTING TO LOCATE ADDITIONAL TERMINAL. NO HOST. NO HOST. NO HOST. NO HOST. NO...

Richard crouched to the left of the glow, the Scain having resumed their task of cutting through the wall. The minute the opening was wide enough to see what he was doing, he was going to open fire and take his chances. He had to finish this – and quickly. If another boarding group got through Klakshan's perimeter, and he suspected it was only a matter of time, he couldn't afford to be tied up here.

The Scain were no longer using a device to cut through the metal. Instead, a thin beam of blue Psionic light had been projected into the hallway, hot enough to burn the far wall. Richard, crouched at least a foot and a half from the beam, could feel the heat as if he had his face in an oven. He clenched his fingers tighter around the rifle, lifting it closer to his cheek, nodding at the Heil.

The beam had now made it halfway across the radius of the prongs coming through the wall, and had burned a long groove four inches across into the plating. Richard was rather surprised to find out that the wall wasn't as thick as he assumed. For some reason, he'd been expecting this frigate to have big, thick walls. Instead, the metal was less than six inches thick. Whatever material they were made from was remarkably strong.

At last, the beam shut down and the Scain began forcing the metal open. Richard lifted his hand, readying the signal, as a Scain recklessly pushed his hand through the opening. "Now!" he yelled, watching as one of the Heil brought his ion saber down, severing the Scain's arm at the elbow. Without his suit pressurized, his body decompressed inside the boarding craft. Richard wasted no time, moving into position and aiming through the slot.

His grenade had done more damage than he'd estimated, killing at least four of the Scain on the other side of the wall. Three were left, one of them covered in blood from his recently-slain ally. Globules of blue-black Scain blood drifted within the chamber, and Richard could see the stains on the traumatized Scain slowly coalescing into spheres and drifting off his red polyform suit.

He opened fire, breaking the face mask on one Scain and watching his body go over backwards, convulsing as he decompressed in the vacuum. The other two lifted their rifles, preparing to fire. One of Richard's Heil jammed an ion spear through the gap, impaling the first Scain even as he began firing. The rounds passed cleanly through the crevasse in the wall, killing the spearman instantly. Richard snarled, firing a round through the other Scain's face before he had a chance to do any more damage.

One of the Heil touched his left hand to the ground, his White Art spilling into the craft through the crack. A moment later he rose, shaking his head. "No survivors," he said. "The pod is empty of life."

"Good," Richard said, rising as well. "Let's get back to the bridge."

"The sooner the better," Klakshan informed him. *"I've got another boarding craft on approach. It's headed for the observation deck. I'm sealing it and venting the atmosphere now to slow them down, but I can't hold them off without compromising the ship."*

"On the way, Captain. What's the status of the *Victoria*?"

"Turukaishal has reached the required speeds," Klakshan said. *"His ship won't last long at those speeds, and it sounds like it's already coming apart. Thermal scans indicate that it's hemorrhaging atmosphere, and it's currently going through a limited power cycle, shutting down everything but life-support and emergency lighting."*

"And Turu?"

"Alive, if just barely so. He'll be fine. He's been in worse than this. Not by much, but he has."

Richard was already en route back to the maintenance shaft. "Is there a way you can seal this hatch behind me? Remotely?"

"I can attempt to," the Taeski said. *"Give me the signal."*

The hatch came into view a moment later, and Richard grabbed the side and almost tore the face plate off. He jerked the blue lever into position, feeling the familiar rush of decompression, and dragged himself back inside the shaft, waving the Heil through. "Go ahead!"

"Done," Klakshan said, the door banging shut behind Richard. He heard it seal tightly, which was a relief until the atmosphere equalized, dropping him on his chest. He pushed himself upright, immediately locating a series of indentations in the wall which could pass for a ladder. "It worked. On my way!"

"Don't you ever slow down?" one of the Heil asked as Richard threw himself against the ladder, grabbing each pocket firmly and dragging himself up. It was much harder when wearing the heavy polyform armor, but he didn't pause for a moment.

Richard snorted, grabbing a pipe for a moment. "I'll rest when I'm dead," he said. "But right now, there are dozens of ships risking themselves for MY planet. I'm not going to do any less than they are. Now come on!" He started upwards again, pulling his armored body upwards, grunting. "This would be so much easier with servos."

"Servos are expensive," one of the Heil grunted, climbing up behind him. "While you're wishing, why don't you just fly up?"

"I wish," Richard said, half-laughing as he reached the first landing. He dragged himself up and located the next ladder on the opposite wall. The shaft wasn't very wide – perhaps eight feet at most – so Richard braced himself and leaped across, grabbing one of the indents. He hung there for a moment, scrabbling to get his footing, until he felt something push on his feet. Surprised, he looked down to see a platform of white light beneath him. One of the Heil had pressed her hand to the wall. "Thanks!" he called, wasting as little time as possible in ascending the ladder.

By the time he reached the top of the shaft, he felt the boarding craft slam into the ship like a bomb. Everything shook, knocking him to his knees. One of the Heil windmilled his arms, letting out a yell as he pitched backwards. Richard launched himself over the edge, grabbing the edge of the door as he caught the Heil by his belt. "Grab my arm!" he grunted. The Heil did as instructed, hanging above certain death until two of the other Heil used their White Arts to bring him back against the ladder. Richard helped him up over the final hurdle, turning back to the bridge. "Klakshan, what's the status of the boarding craft?"

"Already in the ship," Klakshan said. *"I've got visual on them with the security array, but they're destroying the cameras as they approach. Fall back to the bridge: we'll hold them here."*

"How many are there?" Richard asked as he began running, his booted feet thudding against the metal of the deck.

"Six – three riflemen, a sniper and two with shotguns."

"Copy that," Richard said, rounding the corner towards the bridge. "Open the doors."

They opened with a hiss as Richard and the remaining Heil entered. He turned, switching out the rifle on his backpack for a shotgun and drawing his ion saber. "Can you seal the doors?"

"Already done," Klakshan said without breaking his focus. "The *Trident* is right behind us. We are entering our final dive towards Kashelion."

Richard nodded, hearing motion outside the door. "Good. Then let's hope Turu can end this quickly."

"And if not," Klakshan said pleasantly, "it has been a pleasure knowing all of you."

"Oh shut up," Richard growled, "and focus on flying that ship. Sir."

A thin blue line of light began to cut the bridge doors open. All of the Heil in the room drew weapons, preparing to go on the offensive if necessary. Richard stowed the ion saber, bringing the shotgun to bear. If it was a fight these Scain wanted, it was a fight they were going to get.

"What are they using to cut through the door?" Klakshan asked. "Blue light or yellow?"

"Blue," one of the Heil called back.

"Psionics," Klakshan stated. "Good. That will make this easy."

Richard scoffed, rolling his eyes. "Easy. Right. Because fighting nine-foot psychics is just a cakewalk." He primed the shotgun, the blue light already halfway down the door. Unlike with the hull, the beam wasn't penetrating the door completely. Flickering through every now and again, but otherwise melting the door from the outside.

The first lock disengaged as the Psionic light burned through it, and the blue light winked out. There was a moment of rest before it started again, this time at the bottom of the door moving upwards; aiming to cut the second lock. Klakshan shifted his stance, entering a steep dive as the *Trident* fired its laser. There was a tremendous boom, and the entire ship was thrown forward. Richard slid across the floor, coming to rest against the back of Klakshan's legs. "What the hell was that?!"

"We've been hit," Klakshan said. "They took my port thruster off with that shot. Our speed is steady for now, but my next maneuver will drop it permanently. Turukaishal had better finish this quickly."

Richard scrambled back to the door just as the second lock disengaged. The heavy doors swung open, revealing all six of the Scain standing in the doorway. In the same moment, Klakshan tore his right hand free of the control dais, drawing a large pistol from his hip and firing blind at the door. Richard actually saw the Taeski's arm flex and compress from the force of the recoil, but his aim was true. The round flew across the bridge and struck the leading Scain in the face, tearing his head apart like a melon. Dark blue blood splattered back across his companions as he fell to the ground, his shotgun clattering to the deck.

The shock on the faces of the Scain was all the window Richard needed. He lunged forward, his own shotgun firing twice, and took out two of the riflemen. A Heil threw a spear from behind him, impaling the other shotgunner as he lifted his weapon and took aim at Richard. The other rifleman turned to run, but a Heil leapt on him from behind, burying an ion saber through his back. The sniper, at the end of the hall, fired his weapon and blew the Heil in half.

Richard snarled angrily as the sniper took aim at him. He threw himself flat, hearing the shot sail overhead, and threw his ion saber like a discus down the hallway. It struck the barrel of the sniper rifle, knocking it out of alignment for a moment. Richard raced forward, closing the distance as fast as he could. The sniper brought the rifle up again, aiming for his head, but Richard was faster. He pulled the trigger on the shotgun, watching the high-energy pellets fly down the hallway. Although not within killing range, the shots still knocked the Scain backwards. Another shot finished him.

Klakshan turned slightly as Richard re-entered the bridge. "I have been shot," he said, referring to the large hole in his left thigh. He was supporting himself on his other leg, his teeth set with pain. "My focus is broken. If Turukaishal does not end this soon, we are not going to escape."

"Turu will do it," Richard said. "Just focus on keeping us alive for now."

Chapter 66

ERROR: DATA PAD #925410053 NOT FOUND. ROUTING SYSTEM LOCATED. FILES FORWARDED TO SHIP :VICTORIA: DATA TERMINAL METEUSAE.WARNING. DATA TERMINAL METEUSAE HAS SUFFERED EXTREME DAMAGE. SYSTEMS OVERLOADED. MALFUNCTION. RECOMMEND REROUTING DATA TO ADDITIONAL TERMINAL. MESSAGES WILL BE STORED REMOTELY. ATTEMPTING TO LOCATE ADDITIONAL TERMINAL. NO HOST. NO HOST. NO HOST. NO HOST. NO...

Turu could feel more and more of his ship coming apart in the cacophony around him. Things were crashing around on the upper floor, rendering his radio virtually worthless. Turu made sure his mask and his tanks were locked in place before he opened the rear bay door. With a loud whoosh, the ramp lowered itself out into the void beyond, revealing the inky blackness of space. The fires around him were immediately extinguished as the atmosphere was vented into space, the flames withering without a viable source of fuel. Sparks continued to rain from severed wires, dancing across the deck. The *Dirego* slid backwards, coming to a stop thanks to the two thick cables connecting it to the far wall – the cables which allowed Turu to control the *Victoria*. He punched the radio button, the vacuum around him having quieted the noise from above. *"Pinnacle, what is your status?"*

"Approaching Kashelion at 1,200 units per second," Klakshan said, his voice no longer sounding smooth and honeyed. It sounded pained and stressed, likely due to the fact that there was a city-sized gunship breathing down his neck. That was enough to rattle even the most stalwart of Taeski. *"We have a straight shot lined up with your orbit. The* Trident *is right behind us."*

Turu nodded. "Copy that. Give the signal when the laser ports begin to open!"

"Understood," Klakshan said. *"Provided we can evade the next shot. The* Trident *has damaged our port-side engine. Our next maneuver will cost us our current speed. If you do not succeed, we are dead in space."*

"Sure. No pressure," Turu said to himself, flicking several switches on the dashboard.

"You alright in there, Turukaishal?" Klakshan asked. *"It sounds like everything is coming apart."*

Several of the command terminals long the far wall, which up until now had been straining at their moorings, tore free of the loosening deck plates. They flew out into the starry expanse behind him before being whipped away by his slipstream. Turu followed their motion with his eyes, gazing into the infinite vastness of space. To one side, its details blurred by his speed, Kashelion rotated solemnly like the eye of a God – uncaring and unwavering. "That... is an accurate diagnosis," Turu said dryly.

He spun faster and faster around Kashelion, awaiting that one signal that would end all of this. His cue was in Klakshan's hands now, and he prayed the Taeski would give the order soon. He could hardly see at his current speed, and his hologram screen was beginning to short-circuit, marring the images with lines of static. All around him, he could hear the subsonic explosions of the ongoing battle, the concussive force tearing through the weakening infrastructure of the *Victoria* like physical blows.

"Victoria," Klakshan said. *"Prepare to escape orbit.* Trident *incoming from vertical ascension 63.3, planet degree 128.5 – one-hundred and fifty thousand units and closing fast."*

Turu began to feverishly key in the flight path, the *Dirego*'s controls sparking. His gauntlets protected him from any burns he would have suffered, thankfully, but the sparks weren't a good sign. He swore, looking outside. One of the long cables connecting the ship to the *Victoria* had been damaged by a fallen ceiling plate. His navigational controls were shaky at best.

His radar had some notches around the outside that represented five degrees apiece. If he estimated it, he might have a few brief seconds to correct his course for a perfect shot. He marked the line between degree "125" and "130" before checking the controls for ascension. They still worked, which was a miracle he didn't plan on taking for granted. He keyed in the 63.3 – something he thankfully didn't have to worry about doing manually, and prepared himself.

"Escaping orbit in five..." he said automatically, "four... three..."

He checked his damaged hologram screen. One more lap after this and he'd be launched at the *Trident* like a bullet. He made sure that the remote detonator for the REBR2 nuke was attached to his suit before he gripped the controls firmly in his hands, almost tight enough to crack the casings on the joysticks, running through the math in his head.

"Ninety thousand units and closing," Klakshan said. *"Laser doors opening!"*

Turu gunned the engines, the meter briefly spiking up to 15,500 units per second as he tore away from the planet's gravitational pull. Four seconds. He had four seconds before he was inside the mouth of the *Trident*. He aimed the center of his hologram screen at the yawning mouth of the giant ship, hurtling through the void of space like a silver streak – indistinguishable in form or function. He might have been a missile. He might have been a ship. His shape didn't matter, and at this speed nothing could identify him.

Bits and pieces of his outer hull flaked off under the stress, whipping back into the interstellar medium. Behind him, he'd formed a tail like a comet, pulling debris behind him as he raced forward. Three seconds to go. Turu made some minor course corrections, aligning himself with the hideous aperture on the front of the gunship. He could almost see Demnechi's smug face on the bridge, thinking this battle was already won — a victory for the Scain Empire's unjust agenda.

"Well won't you be surprised," Turu growled, hunching over the controls. He kicked the door of the Rover open, preparing to escape the *Victoria*. Two seconds. He was perfectly aligned. The laser's hatches were wide open, and he could see the beginnings of the light spiraling in as the cannon prepared to fire at the *Pinnacle*.

Turu leaned out the door, his pistol in hand, and fired at the cables holding the *Dirego* in place. They snapped with a burst of sparks and static, dividing the Rover from its parent ship. The *Dirego* was on its own once more and, with one second before impact, the ship tumbled out of the back of the *Victoria's* shuttle bay. It bounced and swirled through the maelstrom of debris sucked behind its parent as Turu kicked the Rover's engines into full swing, retreating towards Kashelion as fast as he could. Behind him, there was a brief blip before the *Victoria* vanished down the gunship's maw, disappearing forever into the darkness.

The laser's firing sequence sputtered for a moment and winked out, interrupted by the object which had come hurtling into the engine core. The *Trident* seemed to falter in space for a moment before the damaged console in front of Turu blinked to life. He answered it, watching as a static-rent image of a sharp Scain face appeared, its eyes yellow. Demnechi.

The Councilor was sitting on the bridge, his fingers pressed together as he guided several meditation orbs around his head, looking like a miniature cosmic system. He was adorned in his formal, malkathite-lined robes, the designs mirroring the vines and leaves found on Chindrus. He smiled when he saw that his call had been answered. *"Turukaishal,"* he said, spreading his hands a few inches apart in greeting. *"It's been a while."*

"Go die in a fire," Turu said flatly, still flying his Rover as far as he could from the *Trident*. He had no wish to be caught in the blast that was going to finish this smug bastard. He was going to sit there on his precious ship as it exploded like a case of grenades around him. "You're a dead man walking," he added.

Demnechi laughed, a reedy sound which grated on Turu's nerves... more than usual anyway. *"My tech crew noticed a ship... the Callsign-242—come crashing into the engine core,"* he said casually. *"If you were aiming to damage the core with brute force, you failed. The shielding is far too strong — I thought even you would have known that..."* he gave Turu a falsely-apologetic smile: one which meant absolutely nothing. *"So now the question is, what were you hoping to accomplish by throwing your ship at me? Martyrdom? A last defiant act before I tear this band of rebels apart?"*

Turu smirked at him as soon as the Rover was outside of the blast radius. He kept the engines burning, just to be sure, as he leaned back in the pilot's seat, holding up the detonator – a thin, black object with an orange button on the top. "Hey Councilor," Turu said mockingly, twirling the detonator between his fingers. "On Earth, I learned of this wonderful little holiday called Christmas."

Demnechi's face shifted for a moment, betraying his confusion. *"What?"*

Turu found immense satisfaction in knowing he'd momentarily derailed Demnechi. "You see, it's the one time of year they make a point to be as nice to one another as possible, even going so far as to buy expensive and lavish gifts for each other. For family, for friends, and sometimes even for people they don't even know. Did you know that?"

Demnechi's eyes turned blood red, his temper finally getting the better of him. "Do not toy with me, Turukaishal! What is that?"

"Well, I didn't think it would be right if you missed out on the festivities," Turu said, smiling and shrugging. "So I decided to get you a present. That ship in your engine core, nestled right up against your oh-so-powerful shielding?" he held the detonator to the screen, letting Demnechi get a good long look at it. "That's the *Victoria*. A Celestial-Class Frigate with a quad-core fusion drive as a power source."

Demnechi's eyes turned orange with shock as he realized what he was looking at. Turu leaned in as close as he could to the camera, wanting his face to be the last thing Demnechi saw. "And it's got your present on board. Merry Christmas, Demnechi!" He brought his thumb down on the button, triggering the REBR2 within the *Victoria's* engine.

An internal explosion shook the *Trident* from stem to stern, both of the wings wobbling slightly, the metal flexing from the unnatural motion. The exterior lights flickered several times before a second explosion rippled through the gunship. This one tore its way out of the underside of the ship, spraying debris into space. The exterior lighting flared from the energy overflow before they began to go dark, each light exploding in a shower of glass and sparks. Demnechi was hurled against his console, his eyes blood red, curses foaming from his mouth.

Another explosion silenced the rest of his cursing, this one blooming along the wings of the *Trident,* tearing enormous chunks of metal and decking free and throwing it randomly into the void. Another explosion gutted the *Trident's* spine, blasting searing pieces of hull plating into space like a volcano as the reactor's overflow reached the upper weapons deck. Missiles exploded in their housings, adding to the damage the ship was sustaining. More and more explosions burned across the hull, adding to the fearful majesty of the dying ship. Turu sat impassively in the *Dirego*, watching with narrowed eyes as the gunship writhed in its death throes. One of the massive wings tore completely free, spinning sideways as it fell into Kashelion's atmosphere and vanished forever.

A hand clawed its way up onto the bridge control terminal, dragging the seething face of Councilor Demnechi with it. Turu was mildly surprised to find the communications still operational, but turned his hardened, black-eyed gaze to the screen regardless. "Turukaishal..." Demnechi hissed, trying to pull himself up further. The repeated blasts had probably knocked him around enough to break several bones. His face was a mask of bluish blood, the source being a wide cut above his eyes. "I swear... by the Mindbank... you will—"

An enormous explosion ripped the front of the *Trident* to shreds. The communicator winked out, showing nothing but static as the bridge disintegrated under the force. Turu leaned back in his chair, continuing to watch the carnage. It was over – Demnechi was dead. And then, in an unprecedented feat of destruction, the *Trident* bent itself in half before unleashing a colossal explosion, the light burning like a second sun. The blast expanded through space, the concussive force far outstripping the blast radius of the *Trident*, and slammed into the *Dirego* like a missile, spinning the Rover end over end through space.

Turu fought with his controls, seeking to right the little craft before it was hurled into Kashelion. It flipped sideways, and he gunned the engines as he zoomed beneath a cross-section of the upper decks. All around him, Demnechi's remaining ships were scattering. Bordra and Bandrumano's squadrons had doubled back, weaving through the debris to pick off survivors. The *Pinnacle*, one of its thrusters missing entirely, was limping into orbit around Kashelion to recover.

The *Dirego* evened out in time to slam head-on into a large chunk of metal – one of the wedges which had comprised the hatch to the antimatter cannon. Turu fell roughly to one side, his body coming into contact with the door of the Rover. He heard the bones in his right arm crack and splinter under the force and couldn't help but cry out. His leg, pinned between his body and the door, twisted at an unnatural angle as well. He didn't hear it splinter so much as he heard several loud pops. Worse still, weakened by the vibrations in the *Victoria* and the concussive wave, the door of the Rover broke open and Turu spilled out into space.

Thinking quickly, Turu managed to use his Psionics to grab the lip of the doorway, dangling in the vacuum like a pennant. He slowly dragged himself back into his ship, wincing and groaning at any motion of the right side of his body. Once inside, he slumped across the seats, cradling his arm against his body, waiting until his breathing returned to normal.

As soon as he could, Turu reached up and deployed a distress signal. One of the other ships would come around and pick him up, and he could start assessing the damages to their army and plan for phase two. He laughed weakly in his helmet. He had survived. He'd returned from a suicide mission. His laughter increased in volume as he lay in the remains of the *Dirego*, a wide grin on his face.

He half-wished he could be present to see the look on Mindbank Sovakadris' face when he heard about this.

Chapter 67

Mindbank Sovakadris, the esteemed leader of the Scain Empire, dragged his weathered body up from his chair and floated on a Psionic cloud over to one of the windows. His elegant robes fluttered about him as if caught in a gentle breeze, the blue material masking all but his head. Ornate malkathite designs were woven down the front and around the collar and wrists, and the precious metal glimmered in the light of the setting sun.

Beyond the transparent window, the planet Chindrus stretched away from his tower to meet the horizon. Down below him, the lights twinkling to life as the light of Mordakrelai faded away behind the Kevordala mountains, lay the Amara District: the capital of his empire and the crown jewel of the Scain. The white iskindite spires reached for the sky, ringed with glass and metal balconies and decorated with flowing vines and multicolored flowers. Trees grew in the city squares and along the sides of the roads, and narrow channels ran alongside the streets, filled with softly bubbling water and lit from beneath with warm, golden lights. From up here, at the top of the Mindbank's Tower, Sovakadris could see the citizens of the Amara District closing down their shops and making their way to their homes for the night. The spherical dwellings of his people floated serenely in the residential districts around the edge of the district, just within the walls.

Far in the distance, hundreds of miles away at the base of the Kevoradala Mountains, Sovakadris could see the blinking lights of the Eccemeria District – the future of his people and the survival of the Scain. Even now, they toiled day in and day out on two fronts. They sought to not only uphold the genetic matching which had been instated by Mindbank Chesadaya, but also to research possible cures for their sterility. The Mindbank stared out at those tiny lights, his black eyes incomprehensible.

A figure in red polyform armor entered the room. Sovakadris didn't turn to address the newcomer, but instead spoke directly into their mind. *"What is it?"*

The Scain spoke quietly. "A message from the Blemdarch System," he answered.

"Bring it to me," Sovakadris intoned, turning partway to face the newcomer.

The Scain walked across the room, kneeling before presenting the Mindbank with the Data Pad in his hands. "It appears that the *Trident* was destroyed in battle. The remaining ships have either been destroyed or fled. That treacherous scum Turukaishal is more dangerous than—"

An arm, made purely from blue-white Psionics, lashed out from within the billowing blue robes. At the end, four clawed talons raked across the Scain's face, knocking him to the ground with a scream. His right eye had been ruptured, and clear vitreous mixed with his bluish blood as he lay on the floor.

"Turukaishal was the most competent, honorable and trusted member of the Vanguard," Sovakadris said coldly. *"And despite his defection, he is to be addressed respectfully. You would be so fortunate as to be even a tenth of what he is, even now. Get out of my sight before I take more than just your eye."*

The Scain, still gasping and sobbing in pain, crawled over to the door on three of his limbs, the fourth clutching his ruined face. Sovakadris waited until the doors had shut behind him before looking down at the Data Pad.

A summary of the attack on Blemdarch was contained within, terminating with information about the loss of the *Trident*. The information had been recorded from the on-board computers and the security footage of several ships including the *Trident* itself. Sovakadris watched the screen as it played back the events of the battle, culminating in the explosion of the gunship.

"I underestimated you, Turukaishal," he said quietly to no one in particular before throwing the Data Pad over onto his desk, turning to face the window once more. *"It will not happen again."*

He sent a Psionic command through the tower, waiting for a few moments until the door opened again. A Zyzyt drifted in, perched in a black, organic chair. Several luxite screens were suspended in the air in front of him, and he was running his fingers across the keypad in his lap. "You called, your eminence?"

"Indeed," Sovakadris said. *"Make sure all public information about me is sealed, and dispatch an alert to all law enforcement bodies to investigate searches pertaining to my whereabouts. Also, book me a flight to Teraneus. I do believe my ship is ready for departure."*

"The *Pillar of Creation?*" the diminutive green alien asked. "Yes it is. The final report came in yesterday. I sent it up to your terminal."

"Thank you, Rodega, but I haven't had time to check it. If it is ready, then please have them ready it for me. As soon as we get to Teraneus, we will be boarding it."

"Yes sir," Rodega answered, typing feverishly into the keypad. "Anything else."

Sovakadris waved him away without a word, and the Zyzyt turned his chair back to the door, zipping away without another word. He was used to being dismissed like this, and it didn't bother him anymore; not after ten years on the job.

Sovakadris resumed staring out the window, watching the sunset. Rhoditrand was visible in the darkening sky, the moon casting a glow down on the valley in which his District sat. He stared up at it, as he so often did, and watched it grow steadily brighter and brighter, the craters becoming more and more visible.

If he looked hard enough, he swore that sometimes he could still see her as she lay in his arms, the gaping hole through her chest. He could see himself, young and naïve and concerned, holding her body in his lap as her heart became her enemy, pumping the last of her blood out of her body as she gave a final, shuddering breath before growing still and cold in his arms.

Sovakadris shifted slightly and his robes parted, revealing his folded arms. His right was a normal Scain arm, thin and withered with age. His left, however, was a black mechanical device which was firmly anchored to his shoulder. Spherical joints in the shoulder, elbow and wrist gave this prosthetic an unparalleled range of motion, while the ring-shaped palm and four clawed fingers allowed him to use it as well as his flesh-and-blood arm. His bicep and forearm were comprised of two curved bars each, with enough space between them to fit his other hand.

He held it up in front of him, watching the fading sunlight play over the metal and revealing a hint of violet accents in it. Diodes in the arm glowed softly with a muted inner light. As he flexed the fingers, he could hear the primitively constructed metal joints clicking with the motion. Back then, back when he'd known her and first received this prosthetic, he'd hated it. Until he'd mastered transferring his Psionics into it, the arm had been no more than a dead weight at his side. It lacked servos or wiring of any kind, and was operated purely by his own natural abilities.

Now, in an ultimate twist of irony, the arm was a bittersweet link to the past that he tried so hard to forget sometimes. He balled the metal fingers into a fist and pressed his forehead against them as he memories drifted unbidden into his mind. The pain, the rage, the guilt... seeing her sprawled on the hallway floor, bleeding out as her own species refused to even acknowledge her existence. It was almost too much to bear. He slammed the metal hand into the window, the claws raking down the glass and leaving furrows in it... furrows which quickly repaired themselves until he was staring at his reflection again. His eyes were as blue as the ocean and contorted with the pain of his memories.

He had been lucky. A survivor.

She hadn't.

Sovakadris turned his blue eyes to the sky, feeling them turn red as the anger and sorrow mingled together, forming a potent mixture. They would pay, he promised himself. They would *all* pay. He, the Mindbank of the Scain Empire, would see to it personally. But this upstart Turukaishal was threatening him now. *Him!* Despite the deep and grudging respect he held for the younger Scain, Sovakadris knew deep down in his heart that this could go no further.

The Mindbank dragged himself back to his chair, seating himself in it. Sometimes, the pain was a good thing. It washed over him in waves and reminded him that he was still alive. Still capable of exacting his revenge on the ones who had taken the light out of his life. He sighed, drawing the skeletal black arm within the folds of his robe again. He wasn't going to falter now. He had waited so long to see justice served... so long it felt like a whole other lifetime.

As he sat there, staring out at the horizon of Chindrus, Sovakadris felt the tears running down his face. They followed the lines and grooves in his aging, weathered face, and he pressed his flesh hand into his eyes, trying to stifle the tears which burned on his skin. None of the other Scain or Scion could even hope to understand. They had never lost as he had, and they never would if he could protect them. He waited, sobbing quietly in his spacious, empty throne room, until the tears had passed. He leaned back in his chair, running the tips of his fingertips along the bags beneath his eyes.

He turned and allowed his chair to carry him to the door of his quarters, seat moving on Psionics alone. He had a meeting with a visiting Alintean liaison soon – he couldn't appear before her looking like a heartsick lover, bawling over a love that had long since died. Then again, an Alintean would probably understand better than any member of his own species... a fact which left the aging Mindbank feeling isolated and alone, even among his own people.

And as he floated down the corridors, mentally trying to prepare himself for the meeting, all Sovakadris could feel in his chest was a deep and hollow sadness. A void comparable to the one lurking just beyond the atmosphere.

Chapter 68

Klakshan leaned against the control board for a moment before drawing away, the wreckage of the *Trident* filling the windows. "It is done," he said, turning back to Richard. "Signal the *Gamble* – I am sure you wish to be reunited with your sister."

Richard nodded, wiping sweat off his face. "Yeah... yeah, that's a good idea," he said, his heart rate still feeling like a constant buzz. They were alive. *Alive* after facing impossible odds. He walked over to the communications array, sitting down with a sigh. "I can't believe we made it."

Klakshan released himself from the master control, turning and looking at Richard as the human worked at the array. "Then why did you volunteer?"

"Not just this ship," Richard corrected. "Any of us. This should have been a death sentence."

"Then I repeat: why come along?"

Richard removed his helmet, wiping at his forehead before setting it down. "That list is growing as we speak. Even if I didn't sign up, I'd still be trapped on Earth if the Scain attack. Secondly, that's my planet they're threatening to burn. If I'm not along to fight for Earth, what kind of message does that send?"

Klakshan nodded. "A valid point," he agreed. "But coming out here is dangerous. What does dying prove?"

Richard pressed the button on the dashboard, bringing up a camera feed of the interior of the *Gamble*. "*Gamble,* this is the *Pinnacle*. Fight's over, you can come on in. We're in orbit above Kashelion – come join us."

"*All right!*" Klaara exclaimed, her face splitting into a wide grin. "*You beat 'em? I knew you would! I'll be on the way in a minute. Turu with you?*"

"No," Richard said. "His Rover got clear of the blast, but we have to wait until he activates a beacon."

"*Yeah yeah. I can't wait to get my hands on him. That plan was brilliant!*"

Klakshan nodded. "Indeed it was," he added. "I wish to congratulate him as well. He has performed admirably."

Richard leaned back in the chair, massaging the bridge of his nose as Klaara severed the link before looking up at Klakshan. "So now what?"

The Taeski knelt down, examining the bullet hole in his leg. It wasn't bad, from what Richard could see. The energy pellet had pierced his leg just above the knee, cauterizing the wound as it went. A few cracks in the burnt scales bled lightly, but otherwise Klakshan was unharmed. "I suppose," he said at length, "that is up to Turukaishal."

He rose, calling up a semi-transparent screen which rose from the top of the master control. A silhouette of the *Pinnacle* was displayed on it, with certain areas flashing. "Hmmm... it seems they not only damaged a thruster," he said quietly, "but they tore it off entirely. How very unkind." He turned back to Richard, lowering the screen again. "If this is enough of a warning to the Scain not to trifle with your world, then this may have been our final battle. However, I have lived among the Scain for most of my life. Mindbank Sovakadris is a stubborn and determined individual. Once he has set his mind to a task, it is virtually impossible to dissuade him. I do not think he has ever actually abandoned a course of action. I suspect, therefore, that Turukaishal will attempt to engage him."

"So what's this Mindbank guy like? Sounds like a pigheaded idiot."

The *Gamble* flew past the window, slowly turning around to link up with their starboard airlock. Klakshan shrugged slightly. "He is not a villain, if that is your question. Mindbank Sovakadris has spent the last seventy years protecting the Scain Empire and her people, repelling attacks from the Sov-Nikan and even guiding us through a conflict with the Anu'bai. Even as we speak, his forces are holding the parasite at bay near the outer limits of the Voldarsaska barycenter. I do not know why he is doing this. I do not know what he has against you. But I do know that somewhere inside him is still the good person whose reign I grew up during."

Richard cocked his head as Klakshan continued. "Mindbank Sovakadris was merely a politician back when I came to Chindrus. Within a short time, following Mindbank Tyrundul's death, he was elected as the new Mindbank and took over the Scain Empire. During his political years, he was an idealist and somewhat naïve. I do not know what has become of him now, or why."

"People change," Richard said as he got up, heading to the door. "It happens, even to us 'Vahran'. I know that very well. In any case, I'm going to meet Victoria at the—"

A Scain Fighter, one wing badly damaged, flew past the window, looping around and aiming straight for the *Pinnacle*. Richard took one look at it and bolted, racing through the hallways. Klakshan turned, seeing the ship inbound, and threw himself to the deck. "Get down!" he yelled, sealing his polyform helmet as the ship opened fire. Energeic rounds slammed into the front window, blasting it apart. The bridge's atmosphere decompressed, sucking anything not nailed down out into the vacuum. Klakshan grabbed hold of the deck plating, anchoring himself in place even as two Heil were whisked past him and out into the endless void.

Richard, in the meantime, heard the bridge decompress behind him. He didn't stop, racing through the pentagonal corridors towards the starboard airlock. He'd seen it on the outer hull when boarding on Titan, so he knew it couldn't be far. He sealed his polyform helmet just in case, rounding the final corner. Victoria was already in the hallway, and turned to see him racing towards her. "Vicky!" he yelled. "Seal your helmet!"

She did so without hesitation. "What's going on?"

"Scain Fighter," he explained. "Get deeper into the ship – I don't know if it's going to come around for another pass. Klaara!"

"Yeah yeah, I heard you," the Heil answered from inside the *Gamble.* "I just have to grab—"

Richard watched in horror as the interior of the Heil's ship seemed to slide sideways, the pressure seals around the airlock hissing and breaking. Several explosions from the front of the *Gamble* signaled the return of the Scain Fighter. Klaara pressurized her helmet, lunging for the door, but was belted sideways by a flying pressure tank. The smaller ship spun away from the *Pinnacle*, listing crazily. Richard closed his eyes, taking a deep breath, and sprinted towards the opening amidst the decompression.

"Richard!" Victoria screamed as he leapt out into space, lunging for the *Gamble* before it was too far away. He didn't answer, flying across the few dozen meters separating the two ships, and grabbed hold of the outer hull.

"Klaara!" he yelled into his helmet. "Klaara, answer me!"

The radio was silent, and Richard feared for the worst. He crawled along the outer hull like a spider, grabbing the airlock and swinging himself inside. He sealed the door from the inside, feeling the artificial gravity kick in as he looked around for the Heil, his boots making muffled thuds on the ground.

Klaara was pinned beneath a heap of material on the far side of the room, one of her arms being the only thing visible. Richard bounded across the room, arriving at the rubble in time for another volley from the enemy ship to spatter across the hull. He braced himself against the pile, grabbing an oxygen tank and heaving it to the far side of the room. The cabin flipped upside down, shuffling the debris across the floor and partially freeing Klaara's upper body. "Klaara!" Richard yelled, grabbing her by the back of her polyform. "Come on! Talk to me!"

She stirred slightly, looking around. "Wha—?"

"We're under fire!" Richard said, shoving part of a prefabricated bench off her legs. "I need you to get the *Gamble* moving. Now!"

Klaara pushed at the bench, helping Richard move it off her. "Missed one?" she asked, shaking her head, still partially dazed.

"Looks that way," Richard grumbled, freeing her right foot and shoving her free of the pile. "Scain Fighter – slightly damaged. Damn guns still work, now *come on!*"

Klaara staggered to her feet, racing forward towards the cockpit, Richard hot on her heels. She opened the doors, feeling the whoosh as the atmosphere decompressed. There was a hull breach on the bridge. She grabbed the door to keep from being sucked out, bracing her heels against the floor tiles. She kicked off, flying through the vacuum, and grabbed the pilot's chair from behind. "Richard!" she yelled back at him. "Get to cover! This is gonna be messy!"

Richard nodded, kicking the door shut behind him, hearing it seal. The atmosphere within the crew compartment was gone, and the artificial gravity was weakening. They were losing power. He sprinted across the room, bounding in the lowering gravity, and followed the hallway downwards. He had an idea, albeit a suicidal one, and it was the best he could come up with on short notice.

Klakshan, in the meantime, had managed to evacuate the remaining Heil from the bridge, sealing the doors behind him. "*Contagion*, this is *Pinnacle*, are you there?" he shouted into his communicator.

"*I'm here, Klakshan! What's wrong?*" Bordra's voice asked, sounding concerned. And rightly so – Taeski didn't usually shout.

"Scain Fighter – just blew the bridge to pieces," the Taeski hissed. "We've got Victoria on board, but her brother launched himself out into space after the *Gamble*. They're drifting out there somewhere, and Victoria says it doesn't look like they have power!"

"*Understood. We're on our way. Any injuries?*"

"Bumps and scrapes, mostly," Klakshan said, looking around at the surviving Heil, including those trickling up from other decks. "A few fatalities during the battle and two more on the bridge. I can't get back into the bridge to operate the cannons without compromising the atmosphere in the whole ship – and not everyone has polyform!"

"*I'm deploying an Erythian Lancer-II,*" Bordra told him. "*Hold tight.*"

"I'm trying. The Fighter keeps making passes at us. I'm missing one engine already, and it took out the bridge and has been hammering at my communications arrays. I've got redundancies, but I don't know how long I have until I find them."

Bordra swore. *"Maintain radio silence. Don't give him anything to look for. My team is on their way."*

Chapter 69

Klaara gripped the controls in one hand, flicking switches across the dashboard with the other. Her reactor was hemorrhaging fuel into space, and she was losing power to her primary systems. She shut off the gravity in the ship, rerouting the power into her main engine. The thrusters spun up, firing halfheartedly as she took off through space, the *Gamble* flying upside-down in relation to the *Pinnacle*. The belly of her ship scraped along the underside of the Fighter as it flew by, sparks flying as the impact almost jolted Klaara from her seat.

Richard felt the ship lurch, the lack of gravity ablating the impact to a certain degree. He still slammed against the doors to the Rover Bay hard enough to daze himself, and had to shake his head several times to clear the fog from his vision. He tasted the coppery tang of blood in his mouth, and realized that he'd probably bitten his lip or tongue, even if he couldn't feel the injury. He forced the doors open, praying the Klaara had kept things in working order inside.

Her Rover hung eerily in the hangar, drifting at an angle in the zero-gravity environment. Cabling and support wires which would have kept it suspended against the ceiling now twisted around the room like the tentacles of a giant squid, and some had broken during the bombardment. Fuel had spilled out, and now floated around the room in amber globules as big as his head. He kicked off the wall, pushing one of the thicker wires aside as he made for the Rover, hoping it was spaceworthy.

The fuel line leading into the ship wasn't severed, and it didn't take him long to twist the manual release valve and force it off. The tank on the Rover itself had a secondary lid which took a little more work. The large, three-pronged handle required quite a bit of force to turn, and it was difficult to achieve the required levels without gravity. Richard ultimately had to brace himself against the hull and twist as hard as he could before it locked into place.

He drifted upwards, jerking the support wires out of the hull sockets as he went. The tension in some of them resulted in whip-like motions as they were freed, some almost striking him in the head and chest as they snapped past him with incredible force.

The door to the Rover didn't require a password to open. It looked like it may have once needed one, but the panel next to the door had been broken open; wires spilled out and dangled down the side. Richard suddenly suspected the Rover might have been stolen, and he began to have suspicions about the *Gamble* as well.

Klaara, in the meantime, had managed to pull away from the *Pinnacle* to give herself some mobility room. It wasn't going to last long, though. Her reactor was already down to seventy percent capacity. There was a massive fuel leak, probably along her starboard hull. That area had given her trouble before, and it would be just her luck to have the seals break open now of all times. She set her jaw, turning the ship over in a tight barrel roll to avoid a subsonic attack from the fighter before plunging downwards and to the side. Whoever her enemy pilot was, he was an admirable one. He flew well, and remained right on her tail.

Richard threw himself into the driver's seat of the Rover, slamming the door. There was no time to worry about whether or not it was stolen. He just needed it to get out of the bay doors. He threw a large lever to his right, drawing on his knowledge of Turu's rover and hoping the two were similar. The interior lit up brightly, the interior of the windshield lighting up with the integrated display. He looked down at the dashboard, looking for anything that looked like a weapon. Klaara had shot at them in the blizzard – this thing had guns. He needed them now.

He pressed one of the buttons at random, hearing the rear engines fire up. "Oh no..." he said, looking straight ahead at the unyielding bay doors. "Oh no no no no no no...!"

The Rover launched itself forward and slammed into the doors at full speed. Rather than bouncing off, as Richard had expected, the Rover kept going. It blasted the doors out of their tracks, sending the metal flying into space. The Rover Bay decompressed, sucking out a fair amount of the resources Klaara had kept inside. Richard grabbed the controls and aimed the Rover to the side, looping back around. He needed to find the weapons on this thing, and fast. That Fighter was going to notice him soon.

Klaara saw the blip on her dashboard as the atmosphere was sucked out of her starboard bay and swore. A moment later, she saw her precious Rover – the *Angry Princess* – fly past the cracks in her windshield. Only one person could be behind that, and she immediately pinged it with the short-range radio. "Richard, what the *hell* do you think you're doing?!"

"Giving you a break," Richard told her. *"Make some repairs if you can – I'll keep him busy."*

Richard hung up the radio before Klaara could argue, swooping towards Kashelion and watching the Fighter bank hard to one side before coming after him. "That's right," he said quietly. "Let's see you follow this."

The ruins of Roisor were still in orbit around the great orange gas giant, and Richard flew straight towards them. The fighter launched a volley at his back, and his instrument panel lit up like a Christmas tree, warning him of the incoming shots. He aimed the nose of the ship downwards, watching some of the pulses tear overhead. One struck him in the tail, but only damaged the cosmetic plating. He spun sideways, looping around a fragment of moon larger than a city block. The Scain Fighter, a much larger ship, rolled sideways to evade the fragment and continued its pursuit.

Richard looped back around, aiming for the *Pinnacle*. If Klakshan was still holding the bridge, maybe he could shoot this annoyance down. He pulled the nose upwards, flying straight up before twisting around and flying downwards at an angle. The Scain Fighter remained in pursuit, firing constantly as if hoping to strike more than a glancing blow.

"Richard! I've got a gun online!" Klaara yelled. *"Get him to come this way!"*

Richard had no idea which way "this way" was, but a tiny icon appeared on the display. He took a chance, spinning like a drill bit before angling sideways towards it. The wings of his Rover spun like the blades of a windmill as he corkscrewed for a moment, leveling out upside-down in relation to the Fighter. He saw the *Gamble* open fire as a bright spear of light streaked out, missing the Fighter by what seemed to be inches.

Another point of light followed the first, and this time succeeded in shearing off the wing of the Fighter, striking it in the weakened part Richard had noticed earlier. The Scain ship spiraled crazily to one side, spinning in what seemed like every direction at once. Richard pumped a fist, grinning madly, only to see it right itself for one critical moment. In that time, it fired a gleaming proton missile directly at the *Gamble*.

He saw it streak away from the dying craft and immediately grabbed the radio. "Klaara! Get off the bridge! Now! Incoming missile!" He yelled, hoping she heard him as the Fighter exploded behind him, showering the area in debris and scrap metal.

"What? Awww, crap!" she swore, and he could hear her moving around. Richard punched the engine of the Rover to maximum as he raced the missile back to the *Gamble*. He wasn't going to catch it – no way in hell – especially not without knowing how to fire this ship's guns. He couldn't even try shooting it down.

The missile struck the bridge with a burst of whitish-blue light. Glass shards and debris fountained out of the *Gamble*, and Richard bit his lip and prayed as he brought the Rover around at high speed. He didn't know where the brakes were, so he had to wing this and hope for the best. He aimed himself at the Rover bay doors and flew forward, kicking open the door and bailing out as he entered. The ship collided with the far wall, bending almost completely in half before drifting sideways. He slammed into the far wall, his vision going white for a split second and more blood filling his mouth. As soon as he could move again, Richard forced the doors back into the main hall and made for the bridge. He didn't have go all the way there, though, to find the fate of his partner.

Klaara was face down in the crew quarters, the doors to the bridge having sealed automatically to keep the atmosphere from venting. She drifted lifelessly in the middle of the chamber, her reddish blood congealing in the air. Bits and pieces of metal and shrapnel had embedded themselves in the back of her head and neck, and blood continued to stream from the wounds.

Richard's heart almost stopped as he launched himself over to her, his hands fumbling about her neck as he felt for a pulse. It was strong, but not steady. Irregular. She moaned and croaked something unintelligible about "damn Scain", and Richard gave her hand a squeeze. "Hang in there," he ordered her. "Do you have an S.O.S. Beacon?"

"...corner..." she rasped, and he followed her gaze to several pill-shaped objects. One of them was pure white, adorned with an unusual symbol. Back on Sovereign, he'd been treated by a medic who wore all white. He hoped the same colors held true. He pulled a T-shaped bar out and downwards, hearing the beacon activate, before kicking over by Klaara.

"Just hold on," he said, moving back over to her. "Someone will find us soon."

Klaara barely nodded, her eyes unfocused. Richard took her hand in his and squeezed it. "I'm not going anywhere," he told her. "Just relax... and don't you dare die."

Chapter 70

Turu could dimly hear voices around him. His head pounded and swam, his heartbeat echoing in his skull with a slow, dull rhythm which let him know he was still alive. Not that he needed the drumbeats in his head to tell him that when every inch of his body hurt as if he'd fallen off the Mindbank's Tower. Even his fight with Klaara hadn't done this much to him. He parted his lips – causing more pain with even such a trivial action, and moaned involuntarily. *"Where am I...?"* he wondered, trying to cast his Psionics around. It amplified his headache to intolerable levels so he quickly shut it down.

He knew he was on a bed, or perhaps some other flat surface with cool thermal padding. He could hear the distant thrum of an engine somewhere above and behind him, so he guessed he was on a ship. He could also hear the steady stream of beeps coming from near his head, which he assumed to be some kind of heart or EKG monitor. A medical ship, then? That was unusual. The manifest of available craft he'd looked over on Titan hadn't listed a medical ship. He finally gave up trying to deduce his location and forced his eyes open.

Several dozen Zyzyt bustled around, checking the readouts on the heart monitor near his head and speaking in short, quick bursts to one another in their native tongue. Some were standing against the far wall at what appeared to be a mobile gene bank, holding vials of blue-black blood aloft and sifting through data streaming across consoles. He ground his teeth and tried to sit up, looking around in confusion. The motion caused his heart rate to increase which, in turn, alerted the green aliens to his motion. "You need to lie down!" one of them barked, almost jumping over to Turu's bedside and placing a diminutive hand on his shoulder, trying to push him back down. "You've suffered severe trauma to your nervous and Psionic systems, and your bones haven't fully regrown yet."

"Regrown?!" Turu asked incredulously, blinking at the Zyzyt. "What—how long have I been here? What happened? Where the Hiin am I? Where's Victoria?!"

One of the other Zyzyts walked over, and by the rank and insignia on his chest Turu was able to identify him as a senior lab technician. "Commander Bordra hailed our ship and requested aid," he said. "We picked up your distress beacon upon entering the system and picked you up. You were adrift in the wreckage of a Rover: Callsign 242 *"Victoria"* main ship registration. The *Dirego*, I presume? Either way, most of the bones in your right arm and ribcage had been badly damaged. That's what we're working on right now. We've managed to regrow them and implant them in your torso, but they are still going to be prone to breakage. What did you do to them?"

"I slammed into a door," Turu muttered, pressing a hand to his forehead. "Now where's Victoria?"

"The ship? I'm afraid it was listed as destroyed. The registry expired at—"

"Not the blasted ship you idiot! The girl! A Vahran with long brown hair!" Turu's heart monitor had risen to an almost continuous shriek. "I swear to the Hin—"

Two Zyzyts grabbed his shoulders, their tiny size belying their true strength, and attempted to hold him still as the senior technician addressed him. "Victoria, as in the Vahran girl, is safe. She has been temporarily placed in the protective care of her brother Richard, as has the Heil bounty huntress, Klaara," he said. "Both her brother and the Heil sustained injuries during the fight, but are healing well."

Turu relaxed slightly, his eyes returning to a more subdued, irritated crimson. "I want to leave. *Now.*"

"Your right leg was *powder*," the technician reminded him sternly. "It will be a while before you can walk again."

"It wasn't a request," Turu said, his eyes narrowing. "I'll use a booster and supplement with my Psionics."

A dome was moved over him, attached to a long, hinged arm. It projected heat across his body, monitoring his internal functions. He gripped it with his aching hands and forced it away in irritation, sitting up and gripping his swimming head. "Which room is she in?"

The nearest Zyzyt, one of the minor-grade techies, waved his hands in agitation. "Y-you can't just get up and—"

Turu seized the little alien with his Psionics, dragging him close. They stared at each other, the Zyzyt's black eyes less than an inch from Turu's red. It didn't last long before the smaller alien caved. "Rooms Shasia Six and Seven," he gulped nervously. Turu dropped the alien on his rear, forcing himself to his feet. He stood shakily, feeling his leg threatening to give out. The rest of the Zyzyts hovered nearby, as if waiting for him to fall flat on his face. He looked around, his eyes scanning the cabinets. Zyzyt medical facilities were usually stocked with just about everything he could need.

With a brief extension of his Psionics, he brought a Booster winging his way from a wall cabinet. He stabbed it harshly into a vein, injecting the solution into his system. A few seconds later, his sight blazing and revealing the neural pathways of the assembled Zyzyts, he wreathed his damaged leg in Psionics and staggered out the door.

He was definitely on a ship – the hallways were almost completely circular, save for a flatter portion near the bottom, and lined on either side with lights. Doorways stood off to the left and right, each one labeled in Galaxian. He checked his own door before closing it: Shasia One. At least he wasn't far. Generally, the first four rooms on any hospital ship were reserved for intensive surgery. He'd been in one of them, which gave him a clue as to how bad he'd been when he had been picked up. Still, at least it wasn't far to Shasia Five and Six.

He dragged himself down the hallway, his hand supporting him along the whitish metal, until he reached a door labeled "Shasia Four". He was about to pass it when he saw a familiar black hat moving back and forth inside. He shoved the door open and looked inside.

Richard was pacing back and forth agitatedly, dressed in his usual garb. His sunglasses were in his hand instead of on his face, and his steely eyes bored holes in the floor. He looked up as Turu entered, his mouth open as if to shout, and then relaxed when he saw who it was. "Turu!" he said, stopping his pacing. "Thank *God*. I thought you were another of those little green eggheads. They've been coming in every few minutes and trying to run tests on me."

Turu chuckled and shrugged. "Good to see you in one piece," he said. "I was just planning on checking on you and Victoria."

"Yeah," Richard said, folding his arms. "You gave her quite a scare. For a while, nobody could find you because you'd already been picked up. These green guys—"

"Zyzyts," Turu corrected him. "Ancient cousins of the Erythians."

"Whatever," Richard said, briefly rolling his eyes. "These 'Zyzyts' picked up your distress beacon and took you aboard at Bordra's request, although we didn't know it at the time. They then picked us up from the *Pinnacle* – we were banged up quite a bit during the fight. When Victoria saw you being wheeled around, almost dead, she fainted on the spot. She's across the hall in Shasia Five. I suggest you go see her before I kill you for worrying her like that."

Turu flinched slightly. Richard probably meant it too. "Right away," he said, not bothering to mention that he'd been hoping to run into her first. Richard was liable to get the wrong impression and beat him to a pulp. "Glad to see you're doing well." He closed the door behind him, hearing Richard resume his pacing. He looked back in time to see Richard don the sunglasses, masking his gaze. He briefly wondered what had the man so worried before he resumed his graceless walk over to Shasia Five.

Victoria lay on a similar bed to the one he'd woken up in, and looked half asleep. Her face was pinched and drawn with what looked to be worry or concern. Turu stepped inside and quietly closed the door in case she was actually resting. He walked up to her bedside, looking down at her.

She turned slightly and looked up at him, her eyes suddenly brightening as she sat partway up. "Turu!"

"Ssshhh," he said, taking one of her hands in his as she reached for his face. "It's alright. I'm here."

She stretched up, embracing him with her other arm and planting a soft kiss on his cheek. "I thought you'd died!" she said sternly as she leaned back, searching his face with her eyes. "Those green guys wouldn't tell me anything!"

"They're Zyzyts," he told her, as he had Richard. "Their entire race is dedicated to medicine. They could probably revive the dead if you gave them enough time. I was in good, if not slightly pushy, hands. As you are." His hand involuntarily went to her face as he ran his thin fingers through her hair before cupping her cheek. She leaned into his hand, reveling in his touch. Turu smiled. "Richard terrified me when he told me that you'd fainted."

Victoria blushed, but smiled knowingly. "You think I was worried? You should have seen him when they brought Klaara aboard. He was shouting and carrying on like you wouldn't believe, and wouldn't let go of her hand. I think he likes her more than he lets on."

Now *that* would be something. Richard and Klaara? Turu almost threw the idea aside before pausing. He and Victoria were from different worlds, weren't they? Why not? There wasn't anything really stopping the two, and he certainly wasn't going to get involved. They were intimidating enough when they weren't mad ad him, and he had no desire to incur their wrath.

He almost grinned until his brain caught up with the extent of Victoria's sentence. "Klaara was injured?"

"After you nuked the *Trident*," Victoria said, "Klaara brought the *Gamble* over to the *Pinnacle* to drop me off with Richard. A leftover ship decided to attack, and Richard ended up jumping out into space to save her. But the ship fired on them and she ended up hurt. The *Gamble* is being repaired down on the lower decks, but Klaara isn't well enough to fly it. The Zyzyts won't let her go."

Turu sighed. "What's wrong with her?"

"Something about her "White Art" - whatever that is," Victoria said, looking up at him and awaiting an explanation.

"The Arts are the Heil's inherent ability. Their black hand is offensive while their white hand is defensive. By placing either on the ground, they can activate a field of effect with themselves as the center. With the Black Art, they can manipulate objects, people, even mass, gravity, weight and energy. With their White Art, they can heal themselves, heal others, erect shields, or even perform actions similar to my Psionics."

Victoria turned crimson, and couldn't meet his eyes. "I hope it's not *exactly* like your Psionics," she said, finally looking back to him with a coy smile on her lips. Turu's eyes immediately turned pink.

"Er, no... not *exactly* like—are you trying to seduce me?" he asked, blinking in confusion. Vicoria laughed, a sound Turu was so very glad to hear. He reveled in the sound for a moment as she explained.

"No, I was just teasing you," she admitted. "Do you *want* me to seduce you?"

Now Turu was convinced that Providence enjoyed toying with him. He felt a wicked plan form in his mind, and decided there was no harm in acting on it. He leaned in close, putting his mouth right next to her ear. His hairlike fingers touched briefly at the back of her head as if threatening to sink into her skin and stimulate her nerves while his other hand alighted on her thigh. "Perhaps," he breathed. "But not here."

He backed off, carefully concealing his eye color. Victoria's face was bright red and gooseflesh stood out on her arms and neck. Turu smiled down at her, his eyes cryptic, but inwardly he couldn't help but smirk at finally getting one up on her. Mission complete.

Chapter 71

After completing his objective to make Victoria blush, Turu stepped back out in the hallway and made for Shasia Six to see Klaara. Turu knocked hesitantly – Heil were known to get very touchy inside hospitals or medic ships, as most were used to patching themselves up with their White Art, not the more "invasive" methods used by other races. Turu had no desire to run afoul of the bounty huntress. He waited outside until he heard a gruff "What do you want" before pushing open the door and sticking his head inside.

"Oh, Turukaishal," she said, simmering down a bit when she saw who her visitor was .She waved one of her hands at him, beckoning him to come inside. "What can I do for you? I'm afraid the list is rather limited at the moment..." she gestured to her body in the hospital bed.

"I was just popping in to see how you were doing," Turu told her, stepping inside and closing the door. "Victoria informed me that you had suffered an injury during the battle. How are you?"

For one moment, Klaara's face looked frightened and lost, and she couldn't meet Turu's gaze. She finally took a deep breath and spoke. "My White Art..." she said at length. "I caught a whole bunch of shrapnel in my neck and back when they torpedoed the bridge. One piece ended up in my head. I was paralyzed from the neck down. Couldn't move. Richard ended up keeping the *Gamble* steady while the Zyzyts brought me aboard. I couldn't even speak, and Richard couldn't speak for me because he doesn't know Heil physiology. If not for Bordra, we'd have been cooked. When I woke up a few hours ago, the Zyzyts told me they'd have to perform surgery on the lobe in my brain that controls the White Art... it was bleeding badly and was in danger of damaging the rest of my brain, so they took it out. I—I..." she trailed off, looking down at her hands.

Turu pulled over a small cushion which floated at waist height and sat down on it. The pad descended slightly beneath his weight before balancing out and lifting his weight up to the edge of her bed. "Klaara?" he asked quietly. The bounty huntress was usually brash and harsh. This was a side of her that worried Turu immensely.

"I can't use my White Art anymore," she confessed at last. "The lobe was almost fully severed to begin with. Even if they'd tried fixing it, they said there was too great a risk that a partial activation of my Art would restart the bleeding, and that a full hemorrhage could be fatal. If I try to use it, it'll either fail or kill me. One of the two. They said there was like a point-oh-five percent chance that I could use it, but I'm not banking on those odds." Turu didn't argue. He wasn't about to gamble with 0.05 percent either... not after narrowly escaping death in his most recent battle.

Hesitantly, he reached out and squeezed her shoulder. "If it makes you feel any better, the only way I'm able to stand up without falling on my face is with a Booster..." it sounded lame compared to her injury, and he felt like a heel, but it seemed to cheer her up a bit.

Klaara snorted, a smile tugging at the corner of his mouth. "Well, good to know that the all-powerful Scain can still take a few bumps and bruises along with the rest of us," she said. "And speaking of bumps and bruises, you should've seen Richard when they brought me in here. He almost started killing Zyzyts."

Turu cocked his head in curiosity, and Klaara continued. "They rushed me in here, talking as fast as they could and rushing around that he couldn't get any answers. They just kind of pushed him around like he wasn't there, or walked between his legs, or pushed his coat away like a curtain. He couldn't get a straight answer out of any of them, so he finally drew his sword and cornered the first one he saw. That got him shouted at for attempting to breach the doctor-patient confidentiality, and he was then confined to quarters until after my surgery."

The Scain's eyes turned yellow. The idea of Richard threatening the almost-harmless Zyzyts was almost a reason for him to laugh. Klaara gave him a half-annoyed look, as if begging him not to encourage Richard further. She finally gave up and grinned at him, fighting not to laugh. "He's gonna hate me, you know... he'd finally found a decent partner. Hell, so had I. Now I can't heal myself and he's going to have to be all kinds of extra careful."

Turu squeezed her shoulder again. "Richard won't hate you," he said with a small smile. "If anything, he'll probably—wait, *partner?!*"

"Yeah," she said with a shrug. "We kind of became training partners, rivals, whatever you want to call it. After he pulled me out of that slump on Sovereign..." she trailed off, as if she didn't want to go further, before shaking her head. "Suffice to say, we get along fairly well now. We both learned quite a bit on that little jaunt."

"Well, that's good to hear," the Scain said as he smiled at her. Richard could do with a partner, and he would do with fewer problems if they were traveling together. Plus, if Richard and Klaara kept each other reasonably well balanced, he and Victoria could—

"You look like you're scheming something," Klaara said suspiciously. "What, thinking of your 'LifeMate' in the other room?"

Turu's eyes turned a color of pink he'd never known they could reach. "W-what?! She's not my—"

"Sure she is. You just don't know it yet. Anyway, what's next? Demnechi's gone, but we still gotta go further up the chain and squish the big guy, Sovakadris, right?"

Turu nodded. "Yes, but it's not quite so easy as just 'squishing' him," he said. "Sovakadris is a Scion – an exceptionally powerful breed of Scain. He has abilities the rest of us, myself included, can never develop and he has no compunctions about using them. Ablities I wish I could master: telepathy, dematerialization, phasing, levitation... I think he can even teleport. That and he has a Psionic reserve equal to a hundred normal Scain."

Klaara leaned back onto the bed. "How in the name of Aruned do we beat something like that?" she asked, her eyes narrowing angrily. "He sounds invincible."

"He isn't," Turu assured her. "He was almost killed a while back. I don't know what happened – it was all very hush-hush – but I know that ever since he's been changed... twisted and weathered, broken and hardened. His aura feels as hard as steel and as cold as ice."

"Yeah. Joy. Wonderful. Last thing I need on my agenda – getting squashed by a Psionic superbeing. You just *know* that was on my bucket list."

Turu sighed. "Yeah, and it just so happened to be on mine too. What a coincidence," he muttered dryly. "Anyway, it doesn't matter at the moment. We don't even know where he is. I'll bet he fled Chindrus after the *Trident* was sacked. He knows I'm going to set my eyes on him next. If I know him, he's headed to either Domagard, Holvestam or Cressadon – he has safe houses in all three systems."

"So what do you want to do then? Split up and check each system individually as soon as we're patched up? Not a good idea if you ask me. He'll have his fleets scouring the Galaxy for you in earnest now. You jut blew up his baby."

"He can get over it," Richard said from the doorway, startling Turu. "Blasted Zyzyts finally let me out. How are you?" he asked, directing his query to Klaara.

Klaara looked at Turu and swallowed before answering. "I can't use my White Art without risking my own life... not at all, in fact. That blast and the shrapnel did more damage than it seemed."

Richard looked at the ground for several seconds, one hand pinching the bridge of his nose, before he turned his gaze back to her. "That isn't what I asked," he said. "I asked you how YOU were doing."

Klaara seemed surprised by his question. She looked at Turu. "Can we have a moment?" she asked. The Scain nodded, rising from his seat as Richard walked over. "I am going to go request medical files on you all from the captain. Do I have the authority to act as your Commander?"

"Yeah, go ahead," Klaara said. Turu nodded to her in thanks and left, hearing Richard sit down on the little seat next to her bed as he closed the door. He sighed. Perhaps

Victoria had been right – perhaps there was something going on between those two. He grinned. Now *that* would be a couple he would pay credits to see.

He marched down the hallway, looking for an elevator. He found one at the very end where his room had been, near Shasia One, and ascended to the bridge deck. Most Zyzyt starships were built along certain guidelines. Medical Bays and Quarters were usually in the center of a ship. Crews ended up clustered there, more often than not, and therefore it should be in a protected area. The bridge was always on either the top level or the bottom, depending on make and model.

Turu stared imposingly at the two Zyzyts guarding the bridge. He didn't want to provoke them – merely dissuade them from trying anything with their guns. Zyzyt usually used nonlethal weapons: their penchant for medicine generally bred them to be nonviolent, but that didn't mean their guns were pleasant. These two were carrying the stun-gun equivalent of shotguns. Close-quarters, random spray, CQC-style weapons. "I need to see your captain," he said brusquely.

"Under what circumstances?" the guard on the let asked.

"I need to request an authorization code to access the medical files for my crew," Turu said. "Please, just let me by."

The two Zyzyts shrugged and opened the door. Apparently they decided that a Scain limping along on his Psionics alone wasn't much of a threat. Turu hated admitting that they were right. Turu dragged himself onto the bridge, wishing nothing more than to crawl in bed and sleep, and up to the captain's dais.

"What are you doing out of your bed?" the captain spluttered, looking at Turu in alarm. "Wait… Turukaishal?!"

Turu squinted at the Zyzyt before hesitating. "Aninay?"

The Zyzyt broke into a wide smile, revealing rounded purple teeth. "You remember me! It's so good to see you again!"

Turu was relieved. Aninay had been a close friend of his way back before Limkalan, during his Academy days. The two had gone separate ways, each joining their respective fleets after graduating, and had been able to send sporadic messages every now and then. They'd been trying to coordinate a meeting for years. "I just wish it was under better circumstances," Turu admitted. "Listen, I need the medical records for my crew. Can you do me that favor?"

"Yup. No problem at all," Aninay said as he turned and began typing on one of the consoles. "Geez – I knew we'd picked up a Scain, but I never thought it was you. And two Vahran. AND a Heil mercenary. What the heck are you doing out here? This is in the middle of the Blemdarch System!"

"Sit down, Aninay. It's going to be a long story," Turu said as he drew up a seat, leaning forward towards his old friend and beginning his narrative.

Chapter 72

Aninay sat in stunned silence, his eyes wide as Turu finished his tale, the lanky Scain sitting back in his chair. He shook his head, massaging his eyes before speaking. "You... you betrayed the Mindbank?" he asked finally, "And to top it all off, you just killed one of his Councilors and blew up a seventy trillion credit Scain gunship, and just to make a statement?"

"Well when you put it like that, it does sound a bit excessive," Turu admitted as he massaged one of his temples with his spindly fingers. "But it was either that or the Earth was going to get charred... what else could I do?"

The Zyzyt captain shook his head again, pressing his fingertips together. "Well, I won't lie... I'm impressed. You always struck me as Sovakadris' little pet. You reported directly to him, took missions straight from his mouth... I hate admitting it, but—"

"Look, I know how it must have looked, alright?" Turu grumbled peevishly. "But that was my job. Well, at least until he assigned me to a post on Earth to analyze and eventually assist in the destruction of the Vahran. That's when things changed, Aninay! The Vahran aren't devils!" he sighed, looking imploringly at his friend. "Look, do you think I would have brought two of them with me if I thought they'd betray me?"

"No," Aninay said, "I suppose not. Besides, I hear that one of them seems to have an intrinsic ability with ships."

"That'd be Richard," Turu said. "He saw me fly my Rover and picked up the nuances rather quickly. Klaara was able to guide him through a trial-by-fire operation of the *Gamble*. He also held his own in a fight against a Heil bounty hunter who was trying to kill me." He thought it wise to omit the fact that said bounty hunter was now traveling with him.

Aninay looked impressed, but it was always difficult to tell with Zyzyts. Their faces didn't move much. "Well then, what about the other one? The female?"

Turu looked away. "She's Richard's sister," he said, "and—"

The Zyzyt sighed, leaning over and patting Turu's knee. "Turu, listen to me... I know it's rich for me to talk of matters like this, but hear me out. If you love the girl, let her go. For her sake."

The Scain looked back, aghast at his friend's words. His eyes tilted between blue and red. "What? Why!?"

"You're a Scain, she's a Vahran. You're also a traitor to your own people, for better or for worse, and you're putting her in harm's way by bringing her along. Even if you do love her, what happens if Sovakadris succeeds? If you die, what will that do to her? To her mind? Believe me, Turu... I hate saying it like this, but you have to distance yourself from her. And even if you succeed, what kind of life would you two have together? You'd be forcing her to live a friendless existence, on the run from your own people, suffering through endless protite injections, biosuits—"

Aninay sighed, rubbing his eyes. "I feel like the worst kind of friend for offering this advice," he admitted. "Maybe I'm way off. Maybe you two have some deeper connection that I'm not including in my projections. Maybe that cliched expression the Vahran have come up with—love conquers all—has something to it. Maybe you'll both live long and happy lives, surrounded by many happy, hybrid children. Bu those are all maybes. Variables. Do you really want to risk her happiness—her *life*—on an unstable variable?"

Turu stared down at the floor. He hated the fact that Aninay could be right. He wasn't a Vahran, and she wasn't a Scain. Even the Elorskra, for all their genetic prowess, couldn't change that. He felt a tear leaking from his eye and brushed it away with his Psionics before Aninay could see it. Damn the Zyzyts and their logic.

"I don't blame you for defying the Mindbank," Aninay said. "I'd have done the same in your situation. But to take a Vahran as your consort is just..." he sighed. "...why would you martyr yourself by being with—"

"I am *not* martyring myself," Turu said firmly, fighting to keep his voice from shaking. "Every time I'm near her, I feel... just..." he fought with his brain, trying to produce the word he was looking for. "Euphoric? Blissful? Content? Complete? I don't even know," he sighed. "All of the above, maybe?" He looked up, his eyes searching his Zyzyt friend's face.

Aninay rose, handing Turu an access card. "This'll get you all the data you need on all the ships and their occupants we picked up," he said. "It'll also give you medical updates on all of them, as well as painkillers and medications any of them need. I'm headed for the Blind Crevasse Refueling Station. If you want, we can let you out there. It'll give you time to go over the data."

Turu accepted the card, bowing his head in thanks. "Aninay," he said solemnly, "I will give what you have said some thought, but I cannot promise to follow your advice."

The Zyzyt smiled wistfully. "Love is a powerful emotion, and one I wish races like mine or Bordra's could spend time developing. I have seen both the greatest happiness and the deepest sorrow, both peace and war, arise from that one simple word. In the right hands, it is a tool of creation and life. In the wrong hands, it is a weapon stronger than anything the Iharsh-Daraz could conceive. Even stronger than the Progenitors."

Turu found that he couldn't meet the Zyzyt's eyes. He knew the sensations he'd experienced with Victoria. He'd felt the possessiveness even before he'd become aware of their origins. He'd felt the protective instinct. He'd felt emotions growing between the two, and had done nothing to stop them... not that he regretted his inaction.

Aninay watched his friend for a moment. "I will tell my crew to get your ships spaceworthy as soon as they can so you won't be stranded here for longer than is necessary. I give you my word as your old friend that I will not betray you to the Mindbank should he or his guards ask. But I cannot risk my crew helping you overtly. If I find anything, I'll let you know. But I hope you know I can't just go charging off with you on a whirlwind adventure like the old days. I have a crew now, as well as several consorts. Two of them are pregnant, and the children are stable. I have a life to lead on my own now... please understand."

"Of course, Aninay!" Turu said, nodding. "I couldn't ask you to leave all this behind. My congratulations to you for the two pregnancies. I know how rare they are for all of us. I hope the children grow up to be a tenth of what their father is."

Aninay waved at Turu, his cheeks darkening. "You honor me with your words, but they are not needed. I just hope they grow up healthy and happy. That's enough for me."

Turu rose, nodding. "I agree. That is the least one can hope for. However, as nice as it has been talking with you, I have to get back to my duties. My crew is still down in the Shasia sector awaiting my return."

"Of course, Turukaishal," Aninay said, smiling thinly at his friend. "I wish you the best of luck, and I hope you come out of this alive. If you do... you're going to have to track me down and tell me how you did it."

Turu made for the door, nodding. "It's a promise," he said as he re-entered the lift. "Stay safe until then."

"Easier for me than you, I suspect," Aninay said as he returned to his seat, hearing the doors hiss shut behind him.

Turu returned to the Shasia Sector and re-entered Victoria's room. He approached her bed and knelt down, taking her hand. "As soon as you're able to walk," he told her, "we are leaving. Aninay, the captain, is an old friend of mine. He can't help us officially, but he won't betray us either.

Victoria smiled at him. "I'm good. The Zyzyts said I can go whenever the ship is ready. Where are we going next?"

"First, I am going to have a talk with our crews. After that, it's off to Nihran: ancient homeworld of the Alinteans. Sovakadris often visits there as a diplomatic liaison. I'm going to see if he's in that area. If not, then I know someone who can tell us. Either way,

I can try accessing a terminal there to see if his ship docked recently, and maybe even get a flight plan or itinerary. I'm sick of this game, and I want it over once and for all. Once he's gone, the assault on Earth will collapse. The Visoth will no longer be tied to our race, and the rest of the treaty will dissolve."

Victoria squeezed his hand affectionately, her eyes looking up at his. "Thank you."

Seeing those eyes looking up at his, so wide and trusting and thankful, he knew Aninay was wrong. He wasn't going to leave her – not in a million years. He leaned forward and placed a chaste kiss on her forehead. "You're welcome, little Victoria," he whispered.

Chapter 73

Turu watched as the last of his makeshift army trickled into the room – Bordra, with his hand around his chief technician, Arerra – before leaning forward onto the table in the war room. Aninay had attended out of curiosity, and was leaning against the far wall, watching him intently, waiting for him to speak. The Scain cleared his throat, the sound echoing around the room, before speaking.

"First of all," he said, "I wish to tell you all how proud I am of you all for your actions against Demnechi and his fleet. You accomplished great things out there; things any one of you has the right to be proud of. You successfully engaged the Scain Empire's assault fleet and won – not an easy task. I know it came with a cost – some of those who fought alongside you didn't make it. Maybe you knew some of them, maybe not. Nonetheless, their sacrifices will be remembered."

There was a murmur in the crowd as he pushed himself off the table, walking back and forth at the front of the room. "But now the question looms: what next? What do we do now that we have defeated Demnechi and his fleet?"

He stopped and drew out his Psionics in force, creating a three-dimensional image in the center of the room. Some of the assembled being drew away from it as it began to twist and form into a distinct shape. A moment later, a glowing representation of Mindbank Sovakadris joined them in the room. Turu kept his arm outstretched as he spoke. "This is Sovakadris!" he told them. "He is the one who organized the assault on Earth in the first place. It was he who created the treaty between the Heil and the Scain with this goal in mind. This is your target."

He closed his fist, the image shattering like glass before being drawn back into his body. "Mindbank Sovakadris is a powerful foe, far greater than any you will have faced in the past. He is the leader of my entire race, and is not there by accident. His Psionics have virtually no limit, and he has abilities which scare even me. But we cannot falter, not now! Now is when we have to strike."

Turu folded his arms across his chest. "What compounds this is that our enemy knows we are coming. He knows that the fight will not end so long as he wishes it to continue, which is why we will come after him. He knows we will either attempt to kill him or force him to call off the assault. He also knows that he will never call it off, which means only one alternative: death. And he will not go easily."

He pointed out at the group, which was staring up at him. "But despite these odds, he is still mortal. He *can* still be killed. He was grievously injured once before, an injury which cost him his arm. Sovakadris is not a God, he is a madman. And as much as it pains me to say this, the Galaxy will be a better place once he is gone."

The Scain walked back up to the center of the stage at the front of the war room. "Sovakadris is gone. We won't find him on Chindrus. He is fleeing even as we speak, proving that even he fears for his safety. But fleets cannot track down a single man, even aboard a ship like his. Therefore, I am going to go forth and find his flagship. Once I have, I will call all of you. In the meantime, I have tasks for all of you – tasks which are far less dangerous. I promise."

"Bordra and Task Force Kirel, I need you to analyze Scain communications traffic – try to find anything pertaining to Sovakadris or his location. Anything you find, send it to me so I can put this quest to an end. Aninay, if you or your team find anything, I would appreciate it as well, but I know you cannot officially help me. Do not data-mine any channels... but if you find anything, I would appreciate you sending it my way."

Aninay and Bordra both nodded in unison before Aninay leaned over and whispered something to his gray counterpart. Bordra recoiled for a moment, the age-old distrust for his cousin species guiding his reactions, before he settled in to listen. Turu took note, but did not comment. He turned back to the group. "To the Heil groups here, I urge you to stand by and await my orders. I know waiting is difficult for such a noble and battle-hardened race, but I implore you to please do so."

"We will do so," one of the Heil answered. "We will wait for your word and, when you call for us, we will be ready. Until then, we will be training."

"Thank you," Turu said before turning to Klaara. "And to you, Klaara, I ask the use of your ship. Mine was used as an improvised bomb, and I have no means of transport."

"You and the Vahran are more than welcome," Klaara said from the back row. "Just don't get any bright ideas about blowing up my baby. You'll have bigger problems than the Mindbank."

Turu chuckled and nodded. "I would not dream of it, Klaara. We will leave as soon as you are ready – our destination is the ancient homeworld of the Alinteans: Nihran."

She nodded. "Yep. Ready when you are."

Turu pressed his palms together and addressed the group. "You all have your orders," he said. "You are dismissed. Good luck, and I look forward to seeing you all on the field of battle when we locate the Mindbank."

As the Heil cheered, celebrating the conclusion of his speech, Turu looked to the back row at Klaara and nodded. She nodded in return, giving him a thin smile. On either side of her, Richard and Victoria gave him a thumbs-up. He returned the gesture awkwardly before turning away from them. This was it: he was going to find Sovakadris and put an end to this madness once and for all.

***

Mindbank Sovakadris sat in the throne room of the *Pillar of Creation*, trees growing out of the floor and enveloping him in their arms. The leaves afforded shade and cool comfort from the harsh glare of the whitish start outside. Birds flapped through the treetops, tweeting merrily to one another. The Scion looked down at the Zyzyt floating at his side. *"Rodega,"* he said, his voice echoing inside the diminutive alien's mind. *"Have you completed your appointed tasks?"*

Rodega nodded quickly, his fingers never ceasing to peck at the luminous keyboard. "Indeed, your Excellency," he said. "The trap is set."

Sovakadris nodded, steepling his fingers. *"Excellent work,"* he said. *"As soon as the bait is taken, tell the pilot to take the* **Pillar of Creation** *and do what needs to be done. And make sure there are no survivors. I do not want any mistakes."*

"As you wish," Rodega said without batting an eye. "Your trap is guaranteed to lure him in, and I am certain with the *Pillar of Creation*'s firepower, Turukaishal will be permanently removed from the equation."

"As much as it pains me, yes," Sovakadris said. *"It is such a pity, and such a waste of a good soldier... and a good friend. But he cannot jeopardize the mission."* He sighed, his eyes a deep, melancholy blue. *"Afterward, I want you to sweep the area. Find his corpse. Make sure it is given a proper burial... perhaps on Velis. He was born there – it would be a fitting location."*

"Sir, are you sure that is wise? Expending government funds for the burial of a traitor could damage your public view."

"I am not concerned with that, but if it helps you sleep at night, use my personal account. Turukaishal was like a son to me and, defector or not, he will be treated with respect even after death. He will be given a proper burial, and that is the end of it."

"As you wish, sir," Rodega said with a curt nod of his head, making a memorandum.

"Thank you. You may go now," the Mindbank said, pressing his fingertips together and watching as Rodega sped away, his chair floating over the flagstones leading up to the throne. As soon as he had descended the stairs and vanished from sight, the elderly Scion looked upwards.

Rising behind his throne was a statue, its hands clasped together in what might have been prayer. He rested his head back on the throne, closing his eyes before reaching out with his Psionics and tracing the outline of the statue's face. *"Soon,"* he whispered to no one in particular. ***"Soon we will have our revenge... my Selene."***

Above him, the impassive stone face of a human woman did not respond.

To Be Continued...

Glossary of Names and Terms

Names

Alaniel *(Ah-Lawn-Ee-El) – An Alintean Flight Officer*

Aninay *(Ann-I-Neigh) – A Zyzyt medic and old friend of Turukaishal's.*

Aquon *(Awk-You-On) - A young cabinet minister under Sovakadris.*

Arerra *(Ah-Rare-Ah) – Bordra's second-in-command*

Aruned *(Are-Rue-Ned) – A God of the Heil*

Bandrumano *(Bon-Dru-Mono) – Turukaishal's oldest and closest friend*

Bordra *(Bor-Dra) – An Erythian Task Force Commander and friend of Turukaishal*

Castator *(Cast-Ah-Tor) – The Scain Minister of Foreign Affairs*

Chemleki *(Chem-Leck-Ee) – Chief Geneticist of Eccemeria Laboratories*

Demnechi *(Dem-Neck-ee) – A Scain Politician and antagonist to Turukaishal*

Draak'Velan *(Drock-Vell-On) – A Heil aboard Klakshan's ship*

Eumarth *(You-Marth) – One of the sons of Aruned*

Ferthoroyia *(Furth-O-Roy-A) – Turukaishal's father*

Holengard *(Hole-In-Guard) – One of the sons of Aruned*

Juurak'Metel *(Jew-Rock-Met-El) – A Heil in charge of the Laqian Shipyards on Sillothel*

Kevilkamas *(Keh-Ville-Caw-Mas) – Turukaishal's uncle and Ferthoroyia's brother*

Kimbo *(Kim-Bo) – A member of Bordra's Task Force*

Klaara'Doran *(Klar-Ah' Dor-Ahnn) – A Heil Bounty Huntress sent to kill Turukaishal*

Klakshan *(Clock-Shaun) – An old friend of Turukaishal's – a Taeski blacksmith*

Kridoria *(Kree-Dor-Ia) – Turukaishal's betrothed*

Melokridai *(Mell-ock-red-eye) – An old friend of Turukaishal and Bandrumano*

Neromaniel *(Narrow-Man-Iel) – The Vice-Commandant of the Scain Vanguard*

Omyuris *(Omm-Your-Iss) – An Alintean Dignitary*

Rodega *(Row-Dega) – Sovakadris' personal attendant*

Sovakadris *(So-Va-Kaw-Dris) – The Mindbank; a Scion and leader of the Scain Empire*

Turukaishal *(Too-Roo-Ky-Shell) – A Scain soldier and the primary protagonist.*

Veeil'Mikran *(Vee-Ill Mick-Ron) – A Hierarch assassinated by Turukaishal's father*

Vinyaiah *(Vin-yai-yah) – The Commandant of the Scain Vanguard*

Vyiira *(Vie-Year-Ah) – The GuildMistress of Diplomats*

Yiimir *(Why-Mere) – The GuildMaster of Mercenaries*

Races

Alintean *(Ah-Lin-Tee-En)* – *An ancient and noble race from across the Galaxy*

Anu'bai *(Ah-New-Bye)* – *A vicious, merciless parasite which scours the Galaxy*

Arsu *(Are-Sue)* – *H30-based liquid lifeforms*

Elorskra *(El-Or-Skraw)* - *Dinosaurian lifeforms which specialize in genetic augmentation*

Ene'tami *(A-Net-Ah-me)* – *Aerial aliens who drift on air currents with gas bladders*

Erythian *(Irith-Ian)* – *Intelligent, genetically-minded dwarf aliens*

Heil *(Hail)* – *Battle-hardened and battle-loving aliens with energeic powers*

Iharsh-Daraz *(Ee-Harsh-Da-Rawz)* – *Massive insect-based aliens*

Progenitor *(Pro-Gen-It-Or)* – *Ancient synthetic machines with a vendetta against organic life*

Rhurni *(Rue-Er-Knee)* – *Old, reclusive aliens from the edge of the Galaxy.*

Scain *(Sain)* – *Tall, psychic aliens*

Scion *(Sigh-On)* – *A sub-species of the Scain with even more Psionic power*

Sov-Nikan *(Sov-Nick-An)* – *Tripedal plant-like aliens and long-time rivals of the Scain*

Taeski *(Tay-Ski)* – *Reptilian aliens with the ability to predict other beings' motions*

Vahran *(Vaw-Ron)* – *The Galactic name for "human"*

Visoth *(Viz-Oth)* – *Pentagonally-symmetrical aliens from an aquatic world*

Zyzyt *(Zizz-It)* – *Relatives of the Erythians specializing in medicine.*

Stars

Blemdarch *(Blem-Dark) – A whitish-blue star where Turukaishal battled Demnechi's fleet*

Dakina *(Dah-Keen-Ah) - A star close to Earth where Klaara took Richard and Victoria*

Delerue *(Della-Roo) – A distant star system with Ganovai as its only point of interest*

Horakameston *(Hora-Kam-Eh-ston) – Turukaishal's birthplace and a Scain colony*

Korvus *(Della-Roo) – A trinary star system considered hazardous by most*

Mordakrelai *(More-Dock-Rely) – The Scain home system*

Oritseal Amiliurnus *(Or-It-Seal Ah-Milli-Ern-Us) – The Galactic name for our Sun*

Planets

Alpidra *(Al-Pyd-Ra) – A gas giant in the Horakameston system. Turukaishal was born on one of its moons.*

Belphan *(Bell-Fan) – A Scain colony world housing many military strategy points*

Chindrus *(Chin-Drus) – The Scain homeworld*

Dayislia *(Dayis-Lia) – A far-flung fringe world under the control of the Sov-Nikan*

Dosya *(Doh-See-Yah) – A planet in the Blemdarch system*

Edomai *(Eddo-Mye) – A Scain colony world*

Entibaa *(Ent-ee-Bah) – A gas giant in the Blemdarch system.*

Fenyss *(Fenis) – A small, frozen world in the Blemdarch system*

Ganovai *(Gan-Oh-Vye) – The Ene'tami homeworld*

Gelmore *(Ghel-More) – A fledgling Scain colony world*

Jalia *(Jah-Lia) – A planet in the Blemdarch system*

Kashelion *(Caw-Shell-Ion) – A large gas giant in the Blemdarch system*

Likharn *(Lick-Harn) – The only known world in the Korvus system*

Limkalan *(Lim-Kaw-Lawn) – A distant, frozen ice world*

Mamant *(Mah-Mahnt) – A planet in the Blemdarch system*

Mer *(Mer) – The Visoth homeworld*

Naisaari *(Nye-Sorry) – A gas giant in the Blemdarch system*

Nihran *(Near-On) – The Alintean homeworld*

Raga *(Rah-Gah) – The Zyzyt homeworld*

Sernomir *(Sir-No-Mere) – A small, volcanic planet in the Blemdarch system*

Sillothel *(Sill-O-Thell) – A Heil colony world under the control of Clan Laqian*

Sovereign *(Sawv-Ren) – The Heil homeworld*

Teraneus *(Ter-Anus) – A gas giant in the Horakameston system*

Veros *(Vare-Os) – A gas giant in the Dakina system*

Virathanca *(Veer-Ah-Thon-Kah) – A Scain colony world*

Moons

Anicum *(An-I-Cum) – One of Chindrus' moons*

Byzacis *(Bi-Zack-Iss) – One of Chindrus' moons*

Chalis *(Chal-iss) – A sub-moon orbiting Velis*

Kretus *(Kree-Tus) – A moon of Kashelion*

Rhoditrand *(Road-I-Trand) – One of Chindrus' moons*

Roisor *(Roy-Sir) – A moon of Kashelion; destroyed by Demnechi*

Velis *(Vel-Iss) – A moon of Alpidra and Turukaishal's birthplace.*

Places

Amara *(Ah-Mara) – The Amara District; capital of the Scain Empire*

Camethos *(Kah-Meeth-Os) – An Erythian refueling station*

Denuval *(Den-Oo-Vall) – Another district on Chindrus*

Eccemeria *(Ecka-Meria) – The Scain genetics district*

Iso'ysial *(Eeso-Why-Seal) – An ocean on Dayislia*

Kevordala *(Kev-Or-Dala) – A range of mountains near the Amara District*

Kinbara *(Kin-Bara) – One of the regions on Sillothel*

Koratar *(Cora-Tar) – A frozen district near Chindrus' north pole.*

Mengaia *(Men-Jye-Ah) – A cavernous city on Nihran where most weapons are made.*

Mis-Niguac *(Mis-Ni-Gwack) – An island in the Iso'ysial ocean.*

Seygahn *(Say-Gan) – A nebula near the Erythian Empire*

Heil Clans

Laqian *(La-Key-On) – A clan of shipbuilders and pilots*

Mitragan *(Mih-Trag-in) – A clan of mercenaries and thugs*

Other

Aelau bakan keviru *(Ae-Lau Back-On Kev-Er-Oo) – A curse in Galaxian*

Barghest *(Barg-Hest) – A type of Alintean ship*

Diathua *(Dye-Ath-You-Ah) – The Scain number for zero*

Dirego *(Dir-Eggo) – Turukaishal's Rover*

Elenium *(El-Ee-nee-Um) – A rare element with a glassy appearance*

Energeic *(Ener-Jay-Ick) – Of or pertaining to energy; a term coined by the Scain and Scion*

Galaxian *(Gah-Lax-Ian) – A standardized language spoken by many races*

Gaphet *(Gafet) – Lightly furred carnivorous insects found on many planets*

Hiin *(Heen) – Elder Spirits; part of the Scain belief system*

Kirel *(Kirr-El) – The Erythian and Zyzyt equivalent of "A"*

Malkathite *(Malk-Ah-Thight) – A rare metal prized for ornamentation and decoration*

Meteusae *(Meh-Too-Say) – The Scain number for five*

Palithe-Ethraega *(Pah-Leeth Eth-Ray-Gah) – Literally "Diamond Talon"*

Psionic *(Sigh-On-Ick) – Energy powers inherent to the Scain and Scion*

Shasia *(Shaw-Seeya) – The Erythian and Zyzyt equivalent of "PH"*

ABOUT THE AUTHOR

Philip Alexander Troy was born in New Orleans, Louisiana on March 12, 1988, the firstborn son of Guy Kent Troy Jr. and Ingrid Maria Troy. As a young child, he was taken to Worms, Germany as part of a military family, where he attended kindergarten. He returned to the United States in time to attend Shining Mountain Elementary school in Spanaway, Washington as well as a Montessori School nearby. His family, still active duty military, later moved to Hampton, Virginia, where he finished his Elementary-level education.

Two years later, he returned to Washington State with his family to settle down permanently in Lakewood. Before finishing his education at Pioneer Middle School he was diagnosed with Aspergers Syndrome. As a direct result, he was forced to endure the misguided attempts of school faculty throughout his term in High School as they attempted to "help" him – something he adamantly maintains he did not need.

Upon his graduation in 2006, he attended a year and a half of studies at Pierce College's Fort Steilacoom campus before departing in favor of independent study. Between 2006 and 2009, he immersed himself in studying astronomy, evolution, genetics and many other avenues of learning. On January 24, 2010, he began writing *Twice-Shadowed Saint* and completed the first draft on March 25, 2010. He eventually sat down on October 2, 2011 to finalize his draft and prepare it for publication. After making the decision to split the novel into two parts, the first part was officially completed on May 6, 2013.

Philip has also written over sixty short stories and has plans for over twenty novels taking place within the same universe as *Twice-Shadowed Saint*. He plans to continue writing, with his next step being *"Twice-Shadowed Saint Part II: The Savior"*. In addition to this, he has also announced plans for a deluxe edition of *"Twice-Shadowed Saint Part I: The Soldier"* which will include bonus content and illustrations.

www.ingramcontent.com/pod-product-compliance
Lightning Source LLC
Chambersburg PA
CBHW020933020726
47495CB00002B/475